Dow

C000149814

By the same author in this series

Chaffinch's
Joseph and His Brethren

Down in the Valley

H. W. FREEMAN

Old Pond Publishing

First published 1930
First paperback edition, 2005

Copyright © H. W. Freeman, 1930
Copyright © Estate of H. W. Freeman, 2005

The moral rights of the author in this publication have been asserted

All rights reserved. No parts of this publication may be
reproduced, stored in a retrieval system, or transmitted, in any
form or by any means digital, electronic, mechanical,
photocopying, recording or otherwise, without prior permission
of Old Pond Publishing.

ISBN 1-903366-92-5

Published by
Old Pond Publishing
Dencora Business Centre
36 White House Road
Ipswich IP1 5LT
United Kingdom

www.oldpond.com

Cover painting: 'Kersey, Suffolk' by Leonard Squirrell
reproduced by courtesy of the Ipswich Borough Council
Museums and Galleries.

Cover design by Liz Whatling
Typesetting by Galleon Typesetting
Printed and bound in Great Britain by Biddles Ltd, King's Lynn

To
F. J. PREWETT

Publisher's dedication

To
ASTRID MASSEY
1928–2005
friend of Betty and 'Jack' Freeman

I

IT was a month since Mrs. Mulliver had died. The thought suddenly invading his mind, Everard Mulliver dropped his book and let it slide off his knee on to the smooth turf below his chair. A month had passed since that important event, and here he was, still lazing in his garden and drowsily, though not without considerable enjoyment, ambling through the pages of Cowper's *Task*. It was not what he had intended doing – so far as he had intended anything definite when, the evening after his mother's funeral, he had solemnly told himself that he could now do as he liked. After that instinctive, almost involuntary, recognition of what was indeed a plain fact, old habits and a natural indolence had taken possession of him again and he had fallen back upon the poetry and gardening which had been almost the sole distractions of his previous life.

It was, strangely enough, his incipient sleepiness over *The Task* which roused his mind to action; he wondered if he was really enjoying it. He was certainly appreciating it – if only it would not make him so sleepy. His mother had been dead a month: he woke up and remembered that he had once been discontented. Gardening and poetry were pleasant things – Cowper had been fond of them too – and his own garden was, in its reposeful way, very beautiful. He had had a free hand with it, and this sunken arbour where he was now sitting, floored with specially procured moorland turf

1

and positively embowered with tall, dreamy lavender clumps, was the inner sanctuary of a whole mosaic of traditional, sweet-smelling herbs which he had designed for himself – he had studied his Elizabethans to good effect; and this did something to mitigate the ugliness of the prosperous red-brick, late-Victorian villa in which he lived. It was difficult to blaspheme gardening in such a spot, or poetry for that matter: what had Cowper said of The Pleasures of Retirement? But he himself was not yet retired. Gardening and poetry he could well promise for his old age, what better? But he was not yet old, God forbid! Just turned thirty-three!

He sat up in his chair to look into the matter. Of course he was discontented, if only he would not be too lazy to remember it. To think what he had put up with in those thirty-three years! Not gross material suffering or oppression, but just subtle and persistent frustration of the spirit, negation of his own true character: and yet it could in no way be helped. He remembered the early years in that pretentious villa on the outskirts of Bury St. Edmunds, when the little boy, burning to run wild, had time and again broken bounds to cook potatoes in the neighbouring fields with rough little village boys; only to be searched for, recaptured, punished, imprisoned again and admonished to be a little gentleman. Then, later on, the sturdy and still rebellious boy of sixteen, unwillingly enduring his hewing into formal shape at a small public school, had begged to be allowed to go to an agricultural college and train as a farmer; the country blood in him strove hard. But Albert Mulliver, his father, was not going to countenance any such nonsense. He himself could just remember his early days in a remote village wide of Halesworth where his father, Amos, had kept the post

2

office and general shop. Amos Mulliver had then moved to Bury and taken a small grocery business on the edge of the town. He had prospered and bought a larger business in the centre, which Albert soon after inherited. Albert was a good businessman, and in twenty years he had built up a flourishing county trade which brought him in an income such as Amos had never dreamed of. Right from the beginning Albert was determined to rise in the world, and even while his prospects appeared still modest, if not precarious, he made a beginning by setting his cap at the daughter of an impoverished architect and winning her. It was quite certain that Ada Mulliver did not love her husband: but as her parents could do nothing for her and she herself, besides being plain, had been brought up to do nothing for herself, she could not refuse him. However, emotions aside, she could not complain. Albert, only too pleased to have married a lady, was considerate, almost indulgent to her, and his social aspirations coincided completely with her conception of life as it should be lived. It was she who prompted him to build the pretentious villa in the new residential quarter at the edge of the town and to send their son to a minor public school.

Thus there was no question of Everard's being allowed to revert to the barbarism which both his parents sincerely considered the rustic life to be. There was, indeed, a short clash of wills in the household before the boy's resistance quite collapsed, but finally he subsided into the vocation planned for him, which was to enter his father's business, learn all that was to be known about groceries and carry on the family tradition. His leanings towards agriculture, having had no support in his nurture or surroundings, soon became

3

obliterated, and he, as well as his parents, came at length (when he thought of the matter at all) to regard them as nothing more than a passing whim. On the other hand, the instinctive unwillingness with which he had entered his father's business left its mark upon him. He was a passably good businessman, and if not so shrewd as his father, at least capable of succeeding him; but however diligently he served his father, there was a secret flavour of unconcern, almost mockery, in his attitude to it. Not that on social grounds he despised it at all: but simply, his heart was not in it. However, having inherited a streak of indolence from his mother and finding life at least comfortable, he let himself drift in the channel which his elders had carved for him, dabbling half-heartedly in the petty social diversions of their suburban circle.

Then, in his twenty-first year, came the War. He enlisted, took a commission and tasted a new kind of freedom. After four years in the trenches (he was wounded three times) he returned to England at the Armistice, like so many other young men, disillusioned and discontented, with no other purpose in view but to waste no more of his life providing the county families with prime butter, bacon, cheese and sultanas. But it fell out otherwise. His father had died suddenly during the War and the business had been carried on in his absence by the manager and a few faithful old hands: it was hardly possible to leave them in the lurch. Moreover, there was his mother to support, and in the state to which she had now become used – it was clear that she expected nothing less. Perhaps, if he had been firm, he could have overborne her, sold the business and gone his own way, whatever that was. But at the time not knowing, he decided to return temporarily to his former channel until he found out. Since then his own natural capacity for drifting and his mother's influence had kept him there.

Mrs. Mulliver had become in her latter years a tiresome, selfish old woman, and without making any severe demands on life itself she was very exacting to those with whom she lived, in particular to Everard. When he was not in the office, she always had to have him within reach. When she had got him there, she made little enough use of him; but he had to be there. He could not help her to read the gimcrack romances on which she spent most of her days, nor add much lustre to her frigid tea-parties and social evenings; but a single afternoon's neglect of her for a round of golf or a motor-drive in the country brought such a stream of injured reproaches upon his head that he seldom had the courage, or rather energy, to indulge in them. The result was that he mostly stayed at home, where his father's origins naturally turned him to gardening and some aberrant, beauty-loving trait, transmitted through (not from) his mother, to poetry – mainly reflective poetry, that he read slowly and savoured deliberately like good wine. His reading brought him few thrills, but an even, soothing content which in the circumstances was perhaps more fitting; and for that he pursued it, with a wistful, subdued earnestness that was determined to extract from it the last drop of satisfaction. It was indeed worth while probing *The Prelude*, *The Task* and *The Seasons* to their depths or distilling out the metaphysical essence of Donne and Blake; if only because there was nothing else in life besides, although he was never quite unaware that there should have been – nothing, that is, besides gardening, and he gardened in the same way; no professional gardener could do more with the moss rose, the globe artichoke or the quince than he.

A woman might have changed all this, but none of the women he found in his mother's circle. Had they attempted to meet him on his own mental ground, or again, had they approached him in vigorous animal honesty, he might have paid some heed to them; but having a social game to play, they could not *afford* to be either serious or wanton. Everard had actually been engaged to one of them for six months, more to please his mother than for anything else. He was rather relieved when she gave him up, as she did in spite of his eligibility, having found another man equally eligible and more congenial and empty-headed, less of a prig, as she put it – the phrase came to Everard's ears. 'The bitch!' he had muttered and gone back philosophically to his asparagus beds, pondering with regret on the War and newly discovered riotous desires, all in pickle now: it hardly seemed credible.

His mother had been to blame for all this. Easy enough on the surface for a strong man to kick over the traces and live as he wanted: but Mrs. Mulliver had reared the horse and herself seen to the fitting of the harness from the very beginning. Short of putting her out of the way, Everard was powerless to change a thing, and he had endured until the end, doing his best by her, rather dutifully for the human being than affectionately for the mother in her. But now she was gone and he did not feel very sorry for it; he was not even shocked at not feeling sorry. He was free, free to do what he liked: innumerable capacities for evil revealed themselves in him. After thirty years of systematic thwarting he deserved a fling. He sat up still straighter in his chair and the quiet smell of the lavender about him seemed to cloy in his nostrils. His cap should go right over the mill; it was high time. How many years since he had last been drunk? On Armistice night, was it? That would be a good beginning: beer, pints of beer, expanding mirthfulness, divine, idiotic vapourings, gradual detachment from the tedium of consciousness leading to the final oblivion of drunken stupor. He knew all about it, not excepted the crapulous gloom of the ensuing morning: but it was all worth it if only for the change, for the brief absence from one's ordinary senses. That night he would be indubitably drunk – preferably among strangers.

II

HALF an hour later Everard set off in his car with all
the grimness of a man who is leaving the whole of
his past life behind him. But as he drew out into the
country, his grimness departed and a lightheartedness
took its place, the lightheartedness of a boy who knows
that he is going to do as he likes and there is no one to
stop him. It was good, too, to be out in the limpid
summer air and see things – trees, grass, hedges –
growing. He did not take much notice of them, but
they were background; and he was getting an appetite
for his drink.

He drove as the road led him, through Stowmarket
and Hadleigh, until he found himself on the bank of the
Stour at Dedham, and then turned at random up the
valley, a real, unmistakable valley, near two miles wide
and rising to sensible heights on either side of the lazy,
winding river that it cradled in a haze of grey-
shimmering willows and fluttering, purple-plumed
reeds; a real river valley, doing nothing by halves.
Mossy Tudor gables, half-hidden, peered out at him
from crowding elm branches; the cow lowed yearn-
ingly after its calf; here was the dim shadow of a
deserted byre in a tussocky, trampled pasture; there
wheat-ears, already tinged with yellow, rippled volup-
tuously in the breeze with delicate rustle; little neck-
laces of white cloud glided overhead. The landscape of
the Stour that day was as placid and winsome as when

Constable first painted it. But Everard's mind ran upon beer, the bitterness of beer and the way it rolls coolly over the tongue, stinging it: six o'clock seemed a long way off. So he ran on, through one drowsy little river-town after another, Stoke-by-Nayland, Nayland, Bures and last of all, Sudbury, where he left the river and bent his course in the direction of Bury again: it would be as well not to be too far from home, whatever happened when the time came, the time when he was drunk.

But the main road tired him − it seemed a sign of servitude − and he turned out of it with sheer aimless perversity into a tangle of by-roads belonging to a new landscape of little hills and gentle valleys. The roads, to a motorist soul, were execrable; the flints marshalled themselves with military stiffness in line and column to bite and punch the tyres with almost animate ferocity. But Everard had transcended the motorist soul. He rather welcomed the jolts and lurches with which every other yard of the road greeted him and the vicious grate of stones beneath his wheels, finding something invigorating in the mere struggle with matter; the earth must be striven with before it smiles. On he went as the roads commanded, swerving, circling, dipping, rising, his sight only skimming the pattern of fields, hedges and woodland that unrolled before and beside him, his thoughts still fixed upon the true consummation of the day's need. Then something caught his eye and held it fast. It was a grey church tower, tall, square and solid, with great stepped buttresses climbing up its corners and a battlemented parapet at the top. It was on the crest of a hill and dominated the landscape, so over-whelming the body of its church as to make it almost invisible. No house near it was to be seen; it might have

9

sprung out of the earth or dropped from the sky, serving no human congregation, but accepting the silent worship of the spaces around it. Everard was fascinated. Like a child pursuing the rainbow, he felt that he must reach it and touch it with his hands to see if it was real or not; but like the rainbow it was elusive and for a long time it seemed to come no nearer for all his speeding. Then the road began to ascend, the land on his right dropped away and a valley began to form, streaked with a long file of slender, feathery willows that betrayed a stream; beyond, a slope ran up to a ridge, a long ridge, that began to show as a link with the church tower which at last was beginning to near. Everard saw that he would have to cross that valley before he reached the tower; the next turning to the right therefore; he watched for it.

The road turned suddenly, ascending still more sharply, some chimney-pots appeared across the valley – there was something real between him and the church, the valley was not a mere obstinate mirage after all. Then tall trees shut out church, valley and all, a cottage reared up at the side of the road; he was at the head of a village street.

He stopped and gazed in wonder. There below him, in all its length and deep slenderness, stretched the valley and, strung across it like a chain hanging from the churchyard steps, the village street, which, but for one little compact offshoot of houses to the right, was the village. It was a vista of white walls, earth-russet tiles and clinging thatch, of overhanging gables and soaring chimneys, winding a little, serpent-like, down to a ford at the valley bottom and up again to the solemn, presiding church tower. From top to bottom there was no conformity between house and house; but the harmony which they created was inescapably manifest, clothing the valley with the naturalness of a perfectly fitting garment. It was as if a whole street from some staid Tudor burg – mayhap from Lavenham itself, that old, dead wool town a few miles away – had been bodily transported there to make a village, complete and self-contained, without encumbrance of outskirts.

The more Everard gazed at it and the more he lingered upon its details, the more its astonishing completeness held him; it was a harmonious entity, a work of art. Only by a deliberate effort could he withdraw his eyes from the contemplation of it to move his car in to the side of the road, where he proposed to leave it. For it was clear that go down he must and, walking its length, become part of it himself, at least, for a few moments: and it was equally clear that he could not take his car down with him; such a thing had no right in the presence of such a work of art. His car had never occasioned him such a thought before – there was no sentimental nonsense about him where machinery was concerned – yet it came to him with a sudden instinctiveness to behave like this: he was conscious of this himself for a moment as he stepped down on to the road, and he wondered what it meant. Then he began to descend the slope and the spell took him once more. Even in this intimate closeness to its details he did not become any the more aware of them than he had been at his first gaze. The timbered Elizabethan gables, the thatched roofs and whitewashed lath-and-plaster walls, the few plainly modest Victorian cottages of mellowed red brick, all melted softly into the whole – chaste and dignified, and yet without sophistication: it was not conscious of being a work of art; it was a village and gave every sign of being a village. There were orchards and vegetable gardens, tools leaning up against outhouse walls, a few old men and children peering and housewives pouring out tea behind open cottage doorways.

Almost in the very cup of the valley stood an ancient timbered inn, huddled upon itself and bearing the sign of *The Olive Leaf*, and across the ford at the beginning of the upward slope a faded red-brick farmhouse, long and straggling, with a great clustered chimney-stack; at the top of the slope Rose Cottage and Woodbine Cottage jostled gables, the one lovingly overhanging its garden, the other staggering superciliously back from it. It all seemed too sublimely Arcadian to be true: and yet it was true, Everard could see. Last of all the church. A steep flight of ragged stone steps led up to the church-yard where it stood, a grey, battlemented pile with graceful pinnacled porches and airy perpendicular win-dows, looking a little humble at the foot of its great, dwarfing tower, which was proportioned rather to the glory of God than the size of its congregation. From the churchyard steps Everard once more encompassed the village with his eye; it still remained whole.

He walked slowly down again to the ford, past a cottage that proclaimed itself to be Lindmer Post Office – so the place had a name and was not a dream, in spite of its noiseless street, empty of faces. He re-crossed the ford by the little footbridge, walked up to the inn and passed through the door, without willing it, almost without knowing it. He was in the bar-parlour now, looking across the counter at the casks on their wooden cradles and the rows of blue china mugs. The inn-keeper's brisk 'Good evening' brought him to his senses again; there was real life in the place after all. He ordered beer, and burying his lips in the froth let it roll coolly over his tongue, stinging it; this was his first drink since mid-day and there was something kindly in the blunt feel of the coarse china mug – as if it gave support. He fetched a contented sigh and looked around him.

The innkeeper stood half-invisible in the shadow by his casks, obviously taking stock of Everard out of the corner of his eye and at the same time listening to the conversation of two men who were sitting at the end of the bar. There was no one else in the room, it being yet little after six o'clock. One of these two was a short, perky little man, with a prominent paunch and a waxed black moustache. He cocked his head from this side to that and looked the other up and down with an air of assurance, rather like a vulgar, over-fed robin eyeing a worm. The other was an ageing man with grizzled beard and whiskers, tall and curved in the back; his features were gaunt and weather-beaten, but he seemed obviously the nobler person of the two. By his manner, the little man was apparently trying to convince him of something.

'I tell you,' he was saying, rapping his fingers on the edge of his glass for emphasis, 'a tumble-down cottage like that ain't no manner of use to me.'

'But that'll bear doing up,' said the old man. 'That's owd, but the walls are good; some new thatch and a little plaster'd work wonders.'

'That's as may be,' retorted the perky little man, 'but it won't make a garage. I want somethink as'll look like a garage, nice strong red or yellow brick and slate roof and all. Besides, I've been used to living in a decent house.'

'Well,' said the old man, shrugging his shoulders, 'that ain't for me to persuade you. You're buying the place.'

'Yes,' replied the little man, 'I've been on this earth some years. There ain't much you can learn me. Well now, Mr. Runacres, I'll be seeing you on Monday and we'll get that all fixed up. Ten o'clock at the lawyer's, eh?'

'That's it,' the old man assented, with what seemed rather a bad grace.

The little man drained his glass of bitter and strutted out splay-footed with a nod to the innkeeper. A moment after, the intermittent spurting of a refractory motor-bicycle engine set up outside the window; it became regular and then died rapidly away as the machine raced off up the hill.

'A real nasty little man, that, Mr. Chinery,' said the old man, still gazing after him out of the open window.

'You're right, Henry,' replied the innkeeper, shaking his head, 'but we shall have to make the best of him when he's a neighbour.'

'What's that?' Everard brought his mug down on the counter with a thump. The other two started and stared suspiciously at him.

'I said we should have to make the best of him,' repeated the innkeeper after a pause, 'seeing as he's a-going to be our neighbour.'

'What, is he going to build his red-brick garage here, in this village?' Everard demanded hotly.

'Yes, that's it,' the old man answered dolefully.

'Yes,' put in the innkeeper, 'and two petrol pumps besides, and next door to my house. I don't say it 'on't bring me trade; but I don't like it, somehow. That'll spoil our village. We're all one street like, as we are, and that'll sorterly cut us in two.'

Everard gasped at the unholiness of such an act. A red petrol pump, a yellow petrol pump, a pink garage; the outer harmony and the inner peace ravished, murdered, defiled: his indignation swelled.

14

'And does he live in the village too?' he said, pointing to the old man.

'What, Henry Runacres?' said the innkeeper. 'He do, sir.'

'Well, how can you sell your cottage to such a man?' demanded Everard, turning to him.

'Ah well, sir,' he replied, with a frightened, pleading look, 'I can't help myself, I can't. I want the money bad and that's the truth. That's my son, you see. He was working for a baker in Lavenham, a Mr. Cheers, I dare say you know him, sir. Well, he was doing well till he got sorterly familiar with his master's daughter and they runned away together. Well, that'd have been all right enough, ondly he helped hisself out of the till as well – sort of journey-money like, for his honeymoon. I don't blame him, sir – we're only young but once – but I want to keep him out of prison; and the ondly thing I've got left is that there cotterage, ain't it, Mr. Chinery?'

'That's the truth,' replied the innkeeper. 'Henry's a rat-catcher, sir, and he've only got the old-age pension over and above what he get a-catching of rats; and you do a good deal to keep your own flesh and blood out of gaol.'

'And no mistake,' Runacres nodded in confirmation.

'Look here,' said Everard suddenly, clapping his hand on the old man's shoulder. 'How much are you selling it for?'

'Well,' replied Runacres, shifting uneasily under Everard's firm grip, 'that's an owd place and the thatch is rather pore and the wall's wore through in one place and that wholly want doing up, but there's a nice bit of garden and thirty rod of orchard. I'm asking him a hundred and forty pound for it.'

'Has he paid you yet?' said Everard.

'Not what you might call paid me,' replied the old man, 'but he've promised to give me the cash on Monday when he get the deeds. He want that wonderful bad. He's a retired plumber, he is.'

'I'll give you a hundred and fifty for it,' said Everard shortly.

'What!' The old man gaped at him.

'There you are, Henry,' said the innkeeper. 'I call that handsome.'

'Yes, Mr. Chinery,' said the old man with a suspicious sideways glance at Everard, 'but how do I know he mean what he say?'

'You can have fifty pounds down,' said Everard, releasing his shoulder and taking out his cheque-book.

The old man caught his breath and stared while Everard wrote the cheque.

'I hope I've got your name right, Mr. Runacres,' he said, thrusting the cheque into his hand. 'I'll get my solicitor to work on it on Monday and you can have the rest as soon as the deeds are handed over.'

Henry Runacres dangled the cheque between limp finger and thumb.

'Well I'm damned!' he exclaimed.

'Is that all right ?' said Everard.

'Becourse that is, Henry,' said the innkeeper. 'I'm your witness. Do you stick to it, man. He's a gentleman, he is.'

'Well, I suppose that's all right,' grumbled Runacres, 'but what do you want to do with it, sir?'

'I don't know yet,' said Everard, 'but I shan't pull it down, anyhow. It's empty, isn't it?'

'That is,' replied the old man. 'That only want doing up.'

'Good,' said Everard. 'Well, that's settled. Let's have

16

a drink on it. Three pints of bitter, Mr. Chinery – you'll drink with us, won't you.'

'Becourse I will,' replied the innkeeper. 'Proud to, I'm sure.'

He bent down to his casks and drew three mugs of beer.

'Well, here's confusion to the Sudbury plumber,' said Everard, raising his mug.

'Ay, that's it,' growled Runacres, 'and your good health, sir.'

They all three took a steady swig and put down their mugs; but Everard picked his up again and drained it.

'I must be off now,' he said. 'You'll hear from me soon about the cottage; only don't say how you came to sell it, will you? Goodnight.'

'No, sir, that we 'on't. Goodnight, sir.'

Everard walked out of the inn and paused for a moment on the threshold to sniff the growth-scented evening air and run his eye this way and that up the long village street, gracious and cloistrally quiet. He smiled with satisfaction, feeling that he had done something to preserve its spirit. Then, with hardly a glance at the rather dilapidated empty cottage next to the inn which he proposed to make his property, he plodded back up the hill to his car.

He drove back to Bury in the same hazy and abstracted frame of mind, thinking of nothing in particular, yet full of placid contentment. It was only when he reached his house and found all the servants out as, in anticipation of his debauch, he had given them leave to be, that he perceived he had forgotten to get drunk: but, being already not a little intoxicated with Lindmer itself, he was not disturbed by his broken resolution.

III

THE following Monday morning Everard Mulliver was seated in his cosy office far away at the top of his big grocer's shop, with a tiny cup containing a thimbleful of choice Indian tea in his hand, preparing to taste it; there was a row of samples on little square papers before him on his desk. Being occupied with the loftier matters of general supervision and commercial speculation, he did not have so much direct contact now with the raw material of his trade, although he still made a practice of spending at least half an hour a day in the shop, standing like a presiding deity in some commanding position whence he could observe both his staff and his customers; it was good for both, especially for the customers. It was obvious to them that he was no ordinary grocer; he was not only well-dressed, but tall and, in a solemn way, distinguished-looking, and that alone in the eyes of the quality was not without its effect on the groceries. It was convenient, too, to be able to discuss the flavour of last month's Stilton or the required cut of next week's gammon on almost friendly terms with such a man; he could be very helpful. So, in their amiable way, the quality had patronized Everard Mulliver when he presided in the shop – until the last few years or so, when he in his turn had begun to patronize them, and in order to obtain his oracular responses on spaghetti and Indian chutney they had to approach him as an equal on the general topics of their own and his circle, bringing in the groceries as an apparent after-thought. But if this was the limit of his activities in the shop itself, there was one province on the practical side of his business which he kept in his own hands: he prided himself on his taste in tea and coffee, and he did all the blending in the establishment himself, for both connoisseurs and coarse, debased palates alike. It was one of the finer points of the trade, and the leisureliness and sensory subtlety of the operation attracted him. On this particular morning he was setting out to devise a special blend that would counteract the peculiar hardness of the Bury water; it might prove a profitable line, and for their own sake he was looking forward to the morning's experiments.

He had just raised the diminutive cup to his lips when the telephone bell rang. He put down the cup and took the receiver. It was Mrs. Graynorr speaking; would he care to make one of a tennis party on Thursday afternoon – dance afterwards? Everard paused and stared at the little heaps of tea. He wondered if he did care. There would be Mrs. Graynorr's three daughters and cider cup and the usual young men. He kept Mrs. Graynorr waiting quite a long time while he wondered – so much so that she called 'hullo' three times, to assure herself of his attention, before he answered her, playing for time, that he would ring her up, if he might, later on in the day.

He turned to his teacup again. The tea was cold and he had to throw it away and make some more. He was actually rolling this brew on his palate when the telephone bell rang again. He hastily swallowed the tea and took up the receiver. Mrs. Barnulph was giving a flannel dance on Friday week. He pondered that for a moment and then gave the same answer as he had done to Mrs. Graynorr.

He started on another sample now, feeling a strange satisfaction, without knowing why, that he had not yet committed himself to these invitations. Three more came during the course of the morning, one for a theatre party and two for dinner, to all of which he returned similarly and successively more impatient answers. Indeed the last time he almost shouted, 'Please ring me up again; I'm tasting tea!' and jammed the receiver down with violence.

But instead of turning to his tea again, he lay back in his chair and laughed. Why was Bury society so attentive this morning? Perhaps since his mother's death he had become more eligible, and having as if by tacit understanding given him a month's grace to mourn her, the mothers of daughters (curious that they all were) had all sprung to the attack simultaneously. He laughed again. He was not unused to such invitations (though never before in such a clutter), but they had never before seemed so unimportant; it was as if he had suddenly passed into some other world remote from these people. He laughed once more. It was strange that the mere purchase of a tumble-down cottage in a country village should have so downright an effect. But that was the cause, certainly enough, and Everard knew it. Ever since Saturday his mind had been running on the place, now overtly when he rehearsed to himself all the attractive possibilities of the situation, now in an indefinite, half-conscious manner, forming a sort of pleasurable undercurrent to his other thoughts and acts, among other things to this morning's tea-tasting. In buying this cottage he was acquiring a personal share in Lindmer, in something he liked, that was the important thing; and with that share a responsibility, pleasant, but a responsibility. Obviously the cottage must be done up, and then? – well, he could sell it again, let it – or live in it himself. He had considered all three courses, vaguely, delicately, saving them up for future voluptuous contemplation. Actually he was contemplating them all the time, under his thoughts as it were, especially the last. Those telephone calls, jarring with this state of mind and alien to it, made him impatient; he wanted to be left alone with his secret, like a man communing stealthily with his familiar spirit. Besides (it was coming to the surface at last), he had something far better to do now than accept such invitations, something that was going to occupy more and more of his time. He was going to live in that cottage, as he might have known all along if he had but taken the trouble to bring himself to a decision: so far he had preferred to enjoy his little web of ideas as a nebulous whole. But now his course became evident, he knew at once that he was going to live in that cottage and that reminded him that he had not yet bought it. What if the old man used his cheque as a lever to extort a still higher price from the Sudbury plumber? It was not safe to wait any longer.

He did no more tea-tasting that day, but after a brief call on his own lawyer, he dashed off to Lindmer in his car. The old rat-catcher had remained faithful to his (second) agreement, but the plumber was already back at the inn making a fine to-do about the appointment that Runacres should have kept in Sudbury that morning, and inveighing furiously against the gent from Bury who had so lightly stepped in to steal the bread out of a poor man's mouth, as he put it. On Everard's arrival there was a short, sharp passage between them, beginning with a heated argument and ending with a vigorous burst of mutual vituperation,

21

which Everard, having given as good as he got, cut short by taking Runacres' arm and shepherding him out of the room to the top of the hill, where, scrupulous as yesterday, he had left his car. By the end of the day the process of conveyancing the property was well on the way; a Lavenham builder had been engaged to repair the house inside and out, and the Lindmer thatcher was to start work on the roof next morning. After that Everard settled down to his tea-tasting again.

It was not until mid-September that the cottage was ready for habitation. Everard paid several visits during the summer to see what progress the general refurbishment was making, to measure the rooms and make arrangements for furnishing them. He was becoming more used to Lindmer now, his first amazed worship of it having given place to a workmanlike interest in the practical problems of setting up house there, not unmixed, however, with a good deal of quiet affection. His friends in Bury, hearing that he had acquired 'a weekend cottage in the country', which he made an excuse for evading the increasing flow of invitations, were secretly much tickled by the idea, especially as he refused to disclose its whereabouts, and bombarded him with enthusiastic suggestions for furnishing it in period and out of period from the Bury antique shops. This problem of furnishing had indeed perplexed him somewhat. He certainly did not want to produce an interior like a bristling archeological museum, and yet new furniture in such a place would be like new wine in old bottles; a house that had been long lived in required furniture that had been long lived with. One day, while returning from a visit to inspect the new thatch, he happened upon a village where one of the inns was changing hands, and arrived just as the sale of furniture and effects was beginning. Two mahogany Pembroke tables, a set of straight-backed walnut chairs, all well-worn and mellow, a square, almost dateless oak dresser, two low, round armchairs, rather like crinolines, a square settle for a cosy corner and several other un-assuming Victorian pieces were just what he wanted, and he snapped them up at once, together with a whole battery of plain china-ware and kitchen utensils, and a wooden brewing tackle thrown in. The engaged couples of the vicinity, who had come in the hope of picking up a useful piece or two on the cheap against their wedding days, were quite annoyed at the vora-cious insistence of the intruder. But Everard was too excited at his luck in finding exactly what he wanted to pay any heed to their sour looks, and he went away completely oblivious of his temporary unpopularity.

The cottage itself, within its modest proportions, was built after the pattern of the village church, with tower, nave and chancel; that is to say, it consisted of three sections placed end to end and descending one from the other like a short flight of enormous steps. The loftiest section, that corresponding to the church tower, was surmounted by an ample thatched gable facing the village street and contained downstairs the sitting room and upstairs the chief bedroom, both of them spacious square rooms with windows in all three outer walls. The nave of the cottage, thoroughly dwarfed by its tower like its model on the hill-crest, provided another bedroom, far less pretentious than its neighbour and lighted only by two tiny dormer windows nestling in the thatch, and a corresponding room on the ground floor which was the kitchen. The chancel was a very diminutive excrescence from this section, not rising to the height of a second storey, and contained the scullery.

Everard's public house furniture went into the cottage as if it had been designed on purpose and gave him a very comfortable parlour and an efficient kitchen. As for the upper storey, it was obvious that the room beneath the gable was at present sufficient for his needs, and he furnished it severely with his old army camp-bed and a plain deal washstand and chest-of-drawers that he had picked up at another local sale; the other little room could well remain empty for the time being; it might come in handy later on for storing the apples from that thirty rod of orchard which stretched away in the direction of the stream behind the grassy, weed-tangled plot of ground which had once been the garden. For the last two months both garden and orchard had been continually in his thoughts; he knew exactly what he was going to do with them.

At last all the workmen were gone – the mason, the painter, the carpenter, the thatcher – and the shabbily picturesque ruin had become quite a model of smart-ness with its sleek new thatch, its dazzling whitewashed walls, its dark-brown door and window frames. Within doors it was no less spick and span. The brick floors downstairs and the oak boards upstairs had been scrubbed, the walls and woodwork glistened with new paint and paper, the furniture was all in position and, most important of all, a woman, a Mrs. Quainton, wife of the village horse-doctor, who lived next door with a tuft of horsehair under his eaves as a sign of his profes-sion, had been engaged to clean and cook for him whenever he was there, and generally to give an eye to the cottage during his absence. She had been recom-mended by Mrs. Chinery, the innkeeper's wife, as a very worthy woman and capable housewife, who wanted and deserved to earn a little pocket money, and Everard, satisfied with her clean, respectable appearance, gladly accepted her without further inquiry.

It was a lovely, luminous, early autumn afternoon when Everard at last settled in for his solitary housewarming. Not wishing to be encumbered with his car, he had taken a bus out the greater part of the way from Bury and done the remaining two miles to Lindmer on foot. The whole of the broad river valley along which his road at first led him was suffused with warm, mellow light; through the pure, tranquil air the distant slopes became sublimed into essence of soft, lustrous colour; fresh-broken ploughland patterned against pale stubble and still, green copses. An occasional farmhouse, a sprinkling of new corn-ricks, a few rows of surviving barley-shocks or newly carted manure heaps, diversified the pattern, but the all-pervading spirit was sweet, soft light. The massive church tower of the village, his own village, suddenly came into sight and led him up to the top of the ridge which separated the broad, shallow valley from the deep, narrow valley where, at his feet, Lindmer lay. There was light here, too, but in contrast with the black shadows and sharp outlines of an enclosed space more individual, more intimate, more lovable than the hazier beauties of its more capacious neighbour.

He walked down the village street, feeling a little excited in the role of householder, come at last to claim his own, and a little self-conscious because the village people knew all about it and head after head came to the cottage windows and peered at him from behind the curtains as he passed. He opened the gate of his little front garden, unlocked the front door and threw his bag down on the kitchen floor. It was wise of Mrs. Quainton not to be there to meet him; he wanted to have the place to himself for this first quiet, private converse with it. He went through all the rooms, one by one, looking carefully at all the furniture, here and there rearranging a chair or table, feeling the curtains and looking at the views from the windows, opening the kitchen cupboards to see what stores Mrs. Quainton had laid in; she had forgotten nothing, admirable woman. Having examined the whole house down to the minutest corner, he went outside and looked over the two small wooden outhouses and the bright, well-cared-for garden tools which he had himself brought out from Bury. Then out into the garden again to tap the hard ground with his toe and try to estimate the number of weekends he would need to make it look anything like ship-shape, to point out to himself for the sixth time the position of his prospective strawberry bed and celery trench. From the garden he trailed into the orchard where, with his feet hidden in the long, tangled grass and his eyes fixed admiringly on the ripe-hued, laden branches, he became too much absorbed in the ecstasy of mere proprietorship to attempt calculating what he should do with all that fruit. Picking up a wind-fallen russet, he began to munch, and that commonplace animal activity brought him to earth again, bearing it home to him that it was time to come down from the pinnacles of contemplation and get to work. He straightway fetched a spade, and throwing off his coat began to dig solidly and quietly like an old hand. He soon had his fingers in the cool moist earth – nice rich, black stuff, he noted – pulling out the weeds; he liked the rough, clinging feel, the pungent, damp smell of it. A robin hopped down by his spade and began watching for worms. 'Where there's a man, there's a robin,' he laughed, reminding himself of the Suffolk proverb, and then gave an eye to the line of his trench; these villagers probably thought he did not know how to use a spade; he would show them.

Two hours later, when his loins were beginning to sting a little with the digging, someone called him from the back door – the scullery door, to be precise, the front door opening into the kitchen. It was Mrs. Quainton asking him if he was ready for tea. He inwardly blessed the woman for her sense of timeliness, and after a few professional glances of appraisal at the new black stain he had raised in the greensward of his garden, he picked up his coat and walked up to the house. Mrs. Quainton was in the kitchen making the tea.

'I've laid the table in the parlour, sir,' she said. 'I've made you some toast; but I haven't lighted your fire; you can put a match to it if you feel cold.'

Excellent woman, he told himself; she took thought without asking or being asked. He thanked her, and having washed his hands at the sink in the scullery, went into the parlour, thinking more of the domestic qualities of his housekeeper than of her person, which he had not observed very closely. That she was fairly tall, wore a clean pink apron and talked without any suspicion of dialect, he had noticed, but he was far too much occupied with his own agreeable new sensations to trouble about forming any more definite impression of her.

Tea was a pleasant, comfortable affair. He was sufficiently fatigued to be glad to sit down, sufficiently hungry to relish well-made toast and a spicy dough-cake that might be of Mrs. Quainton's making – he must ask her that. It did not matter that he was alone or had left the books he had brought with him still locked up in his bag in the kitchen. There were so many things in the room that he could not yet weary of looking at – the cosy settle in its corner by the fireplace with its prim little blackleaded hob-grate, the chairs and tables, the solid china-ware, the three old woolwork pictures on the walls, exhibiting Christ and the woman of Samaria, an elongated, rather philosophic peacock and a very grand nosegay of highly coloured but nameless flowers, together with, over the mantel-shelf, a chaste black and white engraving of Lindmer church which he had discovered on an old bookstall in Bury. From one to another his eyes moved round the room and round again, drinking in their virtues with lingering satisfaction. Then, when he had exhausted these things, from the chair where he sat, he had a view out of each of the three casement windows; one of these was admittedly poor entertainment, being nothing more than the end wall of the adjacent inn – though even there he could count six black, rough-hewn timbers, – but the remaining two prospects, of his garden and the village street, were full of matter for the eye. So, with increasing comfort and content, Everard thought and gazed and ate and drank, till finally he discovered that the teapot was empty, and being still afflicted with an inordinate thirst, got up from the table with the teapot in his hand to get some more hot water. By habit rather than design he opened the kitchen door almost noiselessly, so that Mrs. Quainton did not hear him come in. She was standing at the sink, holding a handkerchief to her eyes; a queer little sound – a sort of faint, complaining whimper – made itself heard from behind her shoulders, which twitched significantly; she was unquestionably crying. Everard hesitated, embarrassed, on the threshold; perhaps it would be more discreet to withdraw; or had he done something inconsiderate which had pained her?

'Mrs. Quainton,' he said quietly.

She faced round with a start, and perceiving him, mopped her red eyes hurriedly with her handkerchief; then, regaining control of herself with the help of a couple of valiant sniffs, she smiled wanly at him.

'I am sorry, Mr. Mulliver,' she faltered in a weak, husky voice, 'that you've caught me crying like this. But the fact is that, that – I was getting some salad ready for your supper tonight and the onions always make me cry. I simply can't stop.' She picked up a small brown shallot from the sink for evidence.

Everard laughed.

'Oh, I see,' he said in a relieved tone. 'I thought perhaps something was the matter. But I can perfectly well do without onions, Mrs. Quainton, if they make you cry like that.'

She laughed, a strange, hollow laugh, and Everard found himself thinking that she must be far older than he had imagined the first time he saw her – nearer fifty than forty.

'But did you want something, sir?' she added, in a more natural voice.

'Well, if there's a drop more hot water—,' said Everard, holding up the teapot.

'Of course.' She took the pot from him.

'I'm very thirsty today,' he said, while she filled the pot, feeling that his presence needed a little more explanation, and at the same time reminding himself that he must get in a stock of good China tea at the cottage; it would not do to go on corroding his gullet with this crude, strong stuff.

Mrs. Quainton handed him the pot with a quiet, composed smile and he retired to the parlour thanking her.

Back in his chair again, pouring himself another cup of tea, he pondered over the incident. Mrs. Quainton really had been crying; shallots drew no tears until the skin was off them, and even then they never produced such whimpering or made the shoulders quiver like that: and yet, how swiftly she had regained her balance and was smiling at him, as calmly as if nothing whatever had happened. But that could not explain away the reality of her tears, her red eyelids and the queer, burnt look in her surprised black eyes when she rallied them to meet his own. He had a clear enough impression of her face now, deep-orbited and high-cheekboned, with long, clear-cut, faintly curving nose, wide, low forehead and small, pointed chin; her cheeks, pale and a little sunken, stood out sharply against her smooth black hair, which was drawn close around her head and parted in the middle; her thin, pale lips lifted slightly at the corners, which softened their otherwise straight outline. It was, in all, a sensitive, dignified face, but, as he saw her, an essentially, if mysteriously, old face, as if its pronounced, rather bleak contours had been precisely constructed for the framing of sorrow and the devouring, tragic look that he had caught on her features in that moment's space. For some time, as he continued to drink his tea, his mind dwelt upon her; it was a little disturbing, to say the least, to find his sedate, middle-aged housekeeper crying over the sink in the equable atmosphere of this precious retreat of his – on his first day too, in the midst of all the new paint and

30

chattels. But he could conjecture nothing useful or probable about her and supposed that she had her griefs like other people; anyhow, she had recovered quickly enough and had not bothered him with them.

Tea over, he went out into the garden again and dug until darkness was falling. The sheeny black patch of dug earth was very satisfying to the eye as he contemplated it from the tool-shed, cleaning his spade – a neat, thorough piece of work, well broken up, and not a weed showing. Mrs. Quainton was in the kitchen again when he came in, preparing his supper, though he had not observed her comings and goings from the house next door where also she had her being. There was no sign of tears on her face now, she greeted him cheerfully and remarked, to his satisfaction, that he was getting on well with the garden. They had quite an agreeable flying conversation while she laid the table, about the lettuce and winter cabbage he proposed to put in. She talked very sensibly he thought, and seemed all the better for her cry; and when he had finished the cold supper she had set before him, he felt he had done very well in engaging her. She smiled quite brightly when she came in to clear the table and he praised her damson tart.

'Yes, I'm quite proud of my pastry,' she said, with a little twitch of her mouth. 'I'm glad you like it.'

'I think the house is a credit to you,' he added, 'I'm delighted with it.'

She smiled, colouring a little, and to Everard's surprise, when she smiled, it seemed as if some of the years dropped from her face. She thanked him, and having asked him what time he wanted his hot water and breakfast in the morning, discreetly retired for the night. Everard congratulated himself once more on his good fortune, and lighting his pipe, settled down in an armchair to re-read *The Pleasures of Retirement*. Gardening and poetry still – there was not much change in his occupations; but there was a great difference in the setting.

IV

THE little throng of church-goers was straggling slowly down the hill after morning service and Everard among them, apart, but not unhappy. This was his fourth weekend in Lindmer and he had felt a sudden hankering to go to church. It was years since he had done such a thing; religion was one of the conventions which Mrs. Mulliver had not insisted upon. Nor were the inhabitants of Lindmer a notably Sabbath-keeping community, as the number of idlers outside *The Olive Leaf* at the bottom of the valley testified. Still, it was one of their common activities and it would be friendly to share in it, although he hardly knew any of them yet; and, moreover, he wanted to see the inside of the church. He was glad now that he had gone; for just to be there and let his eyes wander over the ancient stone and timber work with his thoughts trickling slowly after, was pleasant enough. With the virtue of Gothic it was full of light which streamed in pure, quivering shafts through the chaste perpendicular windows, and that, in spite of its modest proportions, gave the church an appearance of spaciousness. There was solid black timber in the roof of the nave and some pretty stone mouldings on the walls of the long side-chapel, together with a group of bright-coloured armorial blazons; and beside his own pew stood a battered but massive square font. Everard could not help thinking of the masons and carpenters who had built it all and how proud they must have been when it was finished, how proud the priest when he sang his first mass in the new church and how proud his congregation when they heard him. The collects, the psalms and the lessons fitted well in such a place with their stately, embalmed beauty of word and cadence, and it quite stirred him to hear the Bible read aloud again. The sermon might have spoilt the harmony if he had listened to it, but he was quite happy looking at his neighbours' heads and wondering what thoughts they hid in them. The young man in front of him, to judge by his glances, seemed preoccupied with a girl in the opposite pew, across the aisle, and she seemed preoccupied with her hat, which she was continually fingering and readjusting; the little boy in front of her turned round every three or four minutes to stare at Everard; and the remainder of the congregation with their eyes stolidly fixed on their own bellies might well be thinking of their Sunday dinners. After these not very profound conclusions he sleepily let the shafts of light carry his own thoughts out of the window to the valley below and all that was in it, and there they stayed until the rector with a resounding 'And now to God, the Father' brought them back to church.

The little knot of idlers outside *The Olive Leaf,* having gloated their fill over the descending file of church-goers as if they felt that they themselves, ceremony notwithstanding, had had the best of the morning, retired in twos and threes to the inn, and when Everard passed the door, there was only one man left standing outside. He was an ugly fellow of about thirty, cross-eyed, red-nosed and unshaven, in patched and ragged clothes worthy of a tramp. He stepped forward as Everard came past, and accosted him.

'May I ax you an important question, sir?' he said in a hoarse, throaty voice.

'You may,' said Everard, stopping.

'I wanted to know, sir,' said the man, ineffectually clearing his throat, 'if you could tell me where to get a nice bit of dinner. I've been living rough all the summer and I've walked sixteen mile this morning, and I tell you, sir, I'm hungry and tired; that's the truth, I am, sir.'

'Are you tramping for work?' said Everard.

'That's it, sir,' replied the other eagerly, 'and glad I should be if so be as I could find work. I'm that tired of being idle. But you'll excuse me saying it, sir, but that have been a long way and I'm real hungry. I must have something to eat, but I ain't got the wherewithal, sir. I thought 'haps you could tell me what to do, sir.'

'Oh, did you?' said Everard, rather tickled at the man's thirst for information and studious avoidance of a direct request. 'You a Suffolk man?' He had already scented the dialect.

'Yes, sir, I am,' replied the man. 'Indeed, sir, I was born in this here village and my owd parents live in a cotterage at the top of the hill.'

'Well,' said Everard, quickly picking him up, 'why not go and ask them for a meal?'

The man, feeling that he had committed an indiscretion, shuffled his feet and hesitated.

'Ah, sir,' he stammered, 'they're that pore and I'm wholly ashamed to beg of 'em. I like to keep my self — hic — respect. They ain't seed me for sixteen year and I shouldn't like to come back like this arter all them years. Now would you, sir?

'But I'm starving,' he added desperately. 'I wish — hic — you could tell me what to do, sir.'

Just then a trap splashed through the ford and ambled past them.

'Hullo, Tom,' said the driver, with a jerk of his whip.

The unshaven one nodded.

'They seem to know you well,' Everard grinned, 'after sixteen years.'

'That they do,' said the man, with a serious look. 'I'm wholly surprised.'

'You've kept your boots remarkably clean,' said Everard, looking down at his freshly greased boots, 'after all those miles, haven't you?'

'I'm wholly careful of my appearance, sir,' he replied, with such an emphatic nod that he brought on quite a fit of hiccoughs.

'Sixteen miles and sixteen years,' Everard laughed. 'That makes a mile a year. Suppose we go in and have a drink.'

'I'm wholly thirsty, sir,' replied the starving man eagerly.

The bar was fairly full when Everard entered, followed by his disreputable companion. Every one stared and not a few grinned behind their sleeves.

'Two glasses of bitter, Mr. Chinery,' said Everard.

There was a wired wooden target for dart-throwing on the other side of the room, and while the innkeeper was drawing the beer, Everard strode over and pulled out the darts.

'Now then, old friend,' he said, 'let's have a game; loser pay the drinks. What d' you say to a hundred up?'

There was a titter in the bar. Everard's squint-eyed friend stuttered a moment.

'As you like, sir,' he managed to say at last. 'I like – hic – a bit of sport.'

'Come on then,' said Everard, putting down his beer.

'I'll keep the score,' shouted old Runacres, who was among the company.

Everard was not an expert dart-thrower, but at least he could hit the target, whereas his opponent, who was now becoming a little unsteady on his legs, could seldom register a hit more than once in three times. The onlookers roared with laughter and egged him on with cries of 'Come on, Tom!' He was evidently well known there.

'All right,' he hiccoughed, 'do you leave me alone. I know what I'm a-doing of.'

It took Everard ten minutes to carry his two matches twice round the scoring board, and amid cheers and laughter Runacres declared him the winner.

'Well, you pay then, Tom,' said Everard, laughing himself.

Tom made a drunken grimace and rummaged in his pockets.

'I suppose I do,' he said, pulling out half-a-crown and planking it down on the counter.

'I thought you said you hadn't enough to keep you from starving,' cried Everard triumphantly.

There was another burst of laughter, even louder than before, and a tall, broad-shouldered man with flowing brown moustache and bright blue eyes stepped forward; Everard remembered having seen him in the blacksmith's shop. He wagged his finger in Tom's disconcerted face.

'Now, Tom Cobbin,' he cried, 'that's time you stood me that quart you bet me fifteen minutes ago. You've lost your bet.'

'What bet?' asked Everard.

'Why, sir,' exclaimed the blacksmith, 'when he seed

you a-coming out of church just now, he say he was ready to lay a quart of bitter—'

'Mild,' expostulated Tom.

'No, bitter, wasn't that, Henry?' said the blacksmith, appealing to old Runacres.

'Yes, bitter that was, Jack,' said Runacres.

'Well, sir,' continued the blacksmith, 'as I say, we seed you a-coming down the hill and Tom, he laid a quart of bitter he'd get the price of a quart out of you if we'd leave him alone. So we cleared off indoors and left him to try his luck; but fare to me that was you got the free drink out of him and sarve him right.'

'He'd had a glass or two too many,' said Everard, taking out his pipe, 'to pull it over properly. And when he said he was very particular about his appearance, I knew there was something wrong.'

Another roar of laughter greeted this remark.

'He meant his boots,' Everard added drily.

'Ay,' nodded Runacres, 'whatever he do, he'd never mend his face.'

Poor Tom stood by the counter, squinting uncomfortably at the floor down his inflamed, squat nose.

'Still he've allus looked like that,' added the blacksmith mercilessly, 'right from a babby; and then, of all things, he go and work for a knacker and that don't improve it. I know one day they'll skin him and boil him down by mistake for one of these here gorillas.'

Everard, feeling a little sorry for Tom Cobbin, tapped him kindly on the shoulder.

'Cheer up, Tom,' he said. 'I can't offer to have another drink with you 'cause you've had too much already.'

'By the way, Mr. Mulliver,' put in the innkeeper, 'what tale was that he now tried to spring on you?'

'Why, Mr. Chinery,' replied Everard with a wink, 'I don't think I ought to tell you in front of Tom.'

Tom took the hint and sidled out of the room on rather uncertain feet. At the door he turned round for a last sally, as though feeling that his departure needed some justification.

'I must go and see my pore owd parents,' he said, and slouched off up the street, followed by a howl of laughter.

Most of the company were sitting round a table at one end of the room where a brisk fire was crackling; there had come a bout of sharp, frosty weather in the end of September. They made room for Everard at the corner nearest the fire, and sitting down among them, he related Tom Cobbin's pathetic cock-and-bull story to them.

'Poor Tom,' said Runacres, while they were still chuckling over it, 'he allus do take it so hard when he's beat. It don't matter whether that's a quoit match or a horse race, he must win; and he mostly lose. Jack Tooke here'll bear me out.'

The blacksmith nodded.

'Still,' said Everard, 'I mustn't forget he very nearly beat me by sheer politeness – he never asked me for anything – until he tripped himself up. Which reminds me, Mr. Tooke, your pot's empty and Tom and I owe you a quart. Mr. Chinery, a quart for Mr. Tooke.'

'Thank you kindly,' replied the blacksmith, 'that's handsome of you, Mr. Mulliver, but I'll share that with Henry Runacres. Make that two pints, Mr. Chinery. Don't want to drink too much afore dinner; do, that sp'il it.'

'Talking of quoit matches,' said Everard rather

39

irrelevantly, as they puffed quietly at their pipes, 'have you got a quoit club here?'

'Ay, that we have,' replied Tooke, 'and here's our seckertary on my left, Jim Farrow. I expect you know him already; he's the shoemaker, he is.'

Jim Farrow was a little man with a pale triangular face which seemed nearly all moustache. He started as the blacksmith brought a brawny red hand down with a slap on his back, and the moustache lifted deliberately like a trap-door to release a thin, piping, almost falsetto voice, such as is not uncommon in the Eastern Counties.

'Yes, Mr. Mulliver, I'm seckertary,' it said. 'I don't know if you play quoits yourself.'

'Well,' replied Everard, 'I know the difference between a ringer and a lady, but that's about all.'

'Oh, Mr. Mulliver'd soon pick that up,' put in the blacksmith, 'wouldn't you, sir? That's only knack like. Why, Jim Farrow here's a reg'lar devil with the quoit, though you wouldn't think so to look at him, would you?'

'Yes, that's the truth,' piped the little secretary of the quoit club, lifting the trap-door in his face again, quite undisturbed by the blacksmith's one-sided compliment. 'If you'd like to join, Mr. Mulliver, you'd be wholly welcome. The subscription ain't ondly a shilling and we have some rattling good matches of a Saturday arternoon. I remember the last time we played 'em over at Hintlesham, I could not keep my arm off Jack's neck when he driv me home, and I did try my best. You'll bear me out in that, 'on't you, Jack?'

'Ay, you were wholly soused that night,' growled the blacksmith. 'You see, Mr. Mulliver, he'd ricked his back winning the match and the liquor went to his hid;

but we can promise you some good sport.'

'I'd be very glad,' said Everard, 'a bit later on, though. I shall want all my Saturday afternoons just now for the garden; there's a lot of breaking up to do.'

'Oh, that's all right,' said Farrow. 'Matches don't begin till Easter and you'll be done by then, fare to me.'

'And a wholly fine job you're making of that and no mistake,' said a short, squat man in a deep voice from the other end of the table. 'That's as good a piece of digging as I could have done myself, as the saying is.'

'And you ought to know, Nesley,' said Jim Farrow. 'He's the rector's gardener,' he added to Everard in a confidential whisper. 'His name's Onesimus Honeyball, but we call him Nesley.'

'I'm proud to hear you say so, Mr. Honeyball,' said Everard. 'But I expect you can see I shall want all my time for it. Shall have to put off quoits for a bit.'

'Still, Mr. Mulliver, what about a bit of ferreting of a Sunday morning?' suggested Runacres, lifting his head with a dignified, aristocratic air, worlds above rat-catching, ''cause you don't go to church every Sunday, I doubt.'

Everard laughed.

'I don't know about that,' he said, unscrewing the stem of his pipe. 'But if I don't go to church, I could well put the time in pruning some of my trees and there's still the bullace left to pick – that is, if it'll give no offence on Sunday.'

'Give offence?' drawled Jack Tooke contemptuously. 'Don't you worry about that, Mr. Mulliver. Why, Jim Farrow allus ring his pigs of a Sunday 'cause he say you can't hear 'em squeal so bad when the bells are going.'

The door opened and two or three men came in.

Everard took a feather from his pocket and went over to the fireplace to clean the stem of his pipe.

'Where d' you go a-ferreting?' he asked casually, with his back to the company.

'Oh, several places,' replied Runacres. 'As good as any's up on Farmer Kindred's land by the copse, towards Lindmer Tye. Yes, and there's a pretty gal live up that way too,' he added with a sly wink.

'You 'on't catch her with a ferret, Henry,' guffawed Tooke.

'No, she want a nice young man like Mr. Mulliver,' said Runacres, 'but, begging your pardon, sir, there is good sport to be had up there.'

'Do you mean with the ferrets?' queried Everard, screwing up his pipe and backing to his seat again without looking round.

There was thunderous laughter at this, but all at once it vanished into an abrupt, hollow silence, as of a shot singing-bird. Everard lowered himself into his seat and leaped up with a start; there was someone sitting in it. A short, square-shouldered man it was, of immensely powerful build, with pale, watery, slightly bloodshot eyes, a crushed-looking nose and a cruel, straight, thin-lipped mouth; but for two grizzled side-whiskers he was clean-shaven. He wore a suit of coarse green whipcord with trousers heavily stitched at the bottom, horse-dealer fashion, and a black bowler hat. Everard swung round and faced him.

'That's Mr. Mulliver's seat,' said the blacksmith.

'Well, he wasn't sitting in it when I came in,' replied the newcomer, fixing his cold, watery eyes on the blacksmith in a cold, watery stare; he had slipped in at the last moment, just as Everard left the fireplace.

'Still you might have guessed,' Tooke persisted.

'That ain't my business,' replied the other. 'That chair was empty when I came in, and I'm a-going to sit in it.'

'Don't you bother, Jack,' said Everard familiarly. 'It doesn't matter. I'd as soon stand by the fire. Where's my drink?'

He made to pick up a glass from the table, but the newcomer grabbed his wrist.

'What the hell are you doing?' he growled. 'Can't you leave other people's drinks alone?'

Everard glared angrily at him for a moment and the fishy, evil stare that met his eyes froze his anger into a sick loathing, as of something sub-human. He relinquished his hold of the glass and the man let go his hand.

'Well, what do you expect,' he burst out hotly, 'if you sneak into other people's seats behind their backs? Why don't you put your bloody drink where there's no mistake about it?'

There was a murmur of approval round the table; he had hit back well, they thought.

'Gentlemen,' interposed the innkeeper, 'this house have allus had a good name.'

Everard, picking up his glass, went over to the end of the mantel-shelf and leant against it. The newcomer said nothing, and having looked Everard up and down a few times, dropped his eyes to his feet and began to sip his beer, warming his feet the while against the fire and spitting frequently on the floor. The conversation was completely hushed and no one had the courage to revive it. Everard stared sullenly at the fireplace; the others glanced sideways over their mugs at one another and at the intruder at the end of the table, who, however, took no notice of anyone and went on drinking his beer and warming his feet. When five minutes had passed in this strained silence, he suddenly drained

43

his glass and without a word stumped noisily out of the room. The others looked after him till the door banged behind him; for a moment no one spoke.

'Well!' ejaculated Tooke with a gasp.

'Who's that bloody swine?' hissed Everard between his teeth.

'Bloody swine, that's just what he is,' answered Runacres. 'That, Mr. Mulliver, is Steve Quainton.'

'What, the horse-doctor?' asked Everard with a startled look.

'The horse-doctor,' Runacres repeated.

'The one who lives next door to me?' said Everard. 'The one as live next door to you,' replied Runacres solemnly.

'And husband of my Mrs. Quainton?' persisted Everard incredulously.

'Mrs. Quainton's husband, that do for you,' came the answer.

'He's allus like that, the bastard,' said Jack Tooke, having recovered from his astonishment, 'though I've never seed him quite so uncivil as that. A surly swine he is, as 'd sarve anybody a dirty trick; he spet and drink and smoke and never a word for anybody and no thought neither, except ondly for his own bloody self. He's a rare fine neighbour for you to have, Mr. Mulliver.'

'I've never seen him before,' said Everard.

'No, you wouldn't,' replied the blacksmith. 'He go away early and he come back late and thank God we don't see much of him, the bastard. Shooting hosses and castrating pigs, that's all he's fit for.'

'There's a nice husband to be married to,' boomed Nesley Honeyball suddenly. 'I'm reg'lar sorry for Mrs. Quainton.'

44

'Ah,' exclaimed Jim Farrow, excitedly pulling up the trap-door from his mouth to give his speech freer issue, 'the rum 'un is, she don't fare to mind. I never seed a more cheerful woman in my life. She's allus a-smiling and I don't know how she do it. That's a fair rum 'un, that is.'

'Yes, you're right,' said Everard, nodding thoughtfully. 'She is one of the cheerfullest women I've ever met and she is always smiling.'

'Well, 'haps he's different at home or 'haps she like that sort,' said Honeyball sententiously. 'There's no knowing what some folk like, as the saying is.'

'That's right,' agreed Jack Tooke. 'You don't know whether to be sorry for her or not.'

'Still, I must say,' put in Mr. Chinery in a sepulchral voice from across the counter, 'I think Mr. Mulliver have showed great forbearance, considering the provocation, and my house have allus had a good name. I feel grateful to you, sir.'

'H'm!' Jack Tooke grunted. 'I don't know. I've been blacksmithing now these thirty year and I reckon I've got some meat on my bones, but if there's one bloke in this village I shouldn't be in a hurry to take on, that's Steve Quainton. I once seed him haul a young Suffolk bull out of its stall by the hind leg. That was proper frightened and wouldn't budge a finger till he got to work on it. He've got arms like my anvil and his chest is wonderful deep, though he is short. I'd stand up to him if it came to that, but I tell you, I ain't wrapped up in it, not by a long way.'

'Well, that's as may be,' said Nesley Honeyball, rising from his chair, 'but fare to me my Sunday dinner'll be getting cold. I can already smell Mrs. Chinery dishing up behind there.'

'Ay, that's the truth,' said Runacres. 'That smell of roast pork make my mouth right water, that do.'

'You're right,' said Jack Tooke.

They all rose to their feet, and having sucked the dregs out of their mugs shuffled slowly out into the street, where they all said 'farewell' and raised a finger to Everard before they scattered up one hill or the other to their respective dinners. Everard turned thoughtfully in at his garden gate.

V

THAT afternoon Everard, having digested Mrs. Quainton's ribs of beef and apple dumplings, set out to pick his bullace. His previous Sundays he had spent in picking the apples and pears and the greater part of the earlier sorts had already been sold in Bury; for although the old orchard had been neglected now for many years and badly needed the pruning knife, it still bore far more fruit than he could hope to consume by himself in a twelvemonth. The later-ripening pippins and russets and the big, hard, keeping pears were stored on wooden trays in the little spare bedroom, which could hardly have been better furnished than with those fine long rows of every mellow colour from dull russet to flushed vermilion, and exhaled sweet odours of juiciness, rich as the colours themselves and penetrating to every corner of the house. And now the time for the bullace had come; the frost had caught them and they clung like strings of big golden grapes to the dark branches of the two twisted and wizened old trees that bore them. It was a niggling job picking them, and at first Everard thought of shaking them from the branches and gathering them up off the ground; but the grass was long and they would have bruised too; it was better to take the ladder to it and pick them. It was not unpleasant either, standing there on the ladder and raking handful after handful of the little golden balls into basket after basket slung up on the branch before

47

him; nor was the work so pressing that he could not afford now and again to stop his picking and, leaning his head back on a crook in the branches, gaze up through the twigs at the little smears of wispy cloud in the blue sky above him. Several times he lay thus, thinking hot, bitter thoughts about Steve Quainton, wondering why he had chosen to plant down his sour, blighting presence in such a peaceful spot, and whether he would ever have the courage to fight such a man. He wondered, too, how Mrs. Quainton could live with him and, presumably, like him; because it would be very difficult to dislike him without showing it, and Mrs. Quainton, as they had said at the inn, was always cheerful and sunnily smiling. It was true that often, when she was smiling, she did look old and there had been that first day when he found her crying; he could almost, but never quite, believe her story of the shallots. Then a piece of twig and a few shreds of pale-grey lichen, sailing down from the topmost branches, fell into his eyes and, made him squirm round to rub them, an abrupt end to his reflections. But that did not stop him, after another bout of picking, from lying back in another place and pondering again on the virtues of this housekeeper of his, who, besides being so clean and respectable, could talk quite sensibly about other things than housework and was so pleasant with it all; she was like a piece of good luck that went with the cottage, so different from all the women he had imagined as his housekeeper, with some differences, too, that he could not quite understand, a little mysterious.

The glimpse of a starling perched high up in the branches of the other tree, that was already picked, carried Everard's thoughts away from Mrs. Quainton again. The bird sat there all alone, a little huddled among the branches, preening his feathers and gossiping to himself in a soft, confidential twitter; and all the time he watched Everard out of one wise, malicious eye as though, if the truth were known, he were privately cursing him and his fruit-picking. Everard laughed quietly to himself as he caught the watchful gleam in the bird's eye.

'Ah, old friend,' he muttered, 'the orchard's empty now, isn't it?'

His lips had not properly closed on the last word when a heavy bullace, snapping its stalk from a twig above, fell and hit him full on the mouth; it bounced on to his shoulder and rolled slowly down his coat till he caught it in his hand. He held it up to the light between finger and thumb and looked at it; it was bursting – transparent – amber-ripe. But instead of eating it, pricked by an impulse that was more truly friendly than anything else, he took a shy from his half-recumbent posture at the starling on the adjacent tree. It was a bad shot and went wide, but the starling took offence and flew off to a distant pear tree from which he eyed Everard reproachfully, cursing out loud now.

'Sorry, old man,' said Everard, who had not really meant to frighten him. 'Don't run away. Waste of a good bullace that.'

He looked down at all the full baskets by the foot of his ladder and the big enamel bath already half-full. He could easily spare a bullace to shy at a cheeky starling; only, it struck him, what was to be done with all these pecks, all these stone of bullace? It was useless trying to sell them. Good enough fruit, and yet people were strangely indifferent to them; in the country, as often as not, they were left to rot on the trees. If he ate bullace tart and bullace pie for a week, he would hardly empty the smallest of the baskets; and then they would begin to go bad. Nothing remained but to give them away, but to whom? Mrs. Quainton had no orchard to her little garden, where, he remembered, he had never seen anyone at work; perhaps she would be glad of them. There she was, disappearing through his back door to get the tea ready. He bent to his picking again, to finish the tree before she called him.

In spite of his efforts, however, he was still on the ladder when she came to the back door to tell him tea was ready, and ten minutes after that, when she came right out into the orchard and stood by the tree trunk looking up at him.

'Don't you wait for me, Mrs. Quainton,' he called, pausing to mount a rung higher. 'Leave the kettle on the fire and I'll make the tea myself. I've one more bough to clear.'

'I'm in no hurry, Mr. Mulliver,' she answered. 'I'll carry some of these baskets in for you.'

'Thank you,' said Everard, 'but mind you don't hurt yourself; they're heavy, and don't touch the bath whatever you do.'

'All right,' she said. There was a tinkle in her voice, as if she were half-laughing at him.

Everard went on picking furiously for another five minutes, until he had stripped the last handful from the bough. Mrs. Quainton was just carrying the last basket in when he came down from the ladder, and hoisting the loaded bath on to his shoulder with his empty gathering-basket on top, he followed her into the house.

'There, what a fine lot!' she said, pointing to the array of baskets on the kitchen floor, as Everard crossed the threshold and slid his own burden down beside them.

'You shouldn't have carried all those baskets in,' said

Everard, 'but thank you all the same. They're too heavy for you.'

'If you can carry that bath, Mr. Mulliver,' she replied, just a little archly, 'I can carry the baskets. But what are you going to do with all that fruit?'

Everard scratched his head and looked at her.

'I want to give 'em to you,' he said.

'Oh Mr. Mulliver!' The blood rushed to her cheeks and she lowered her eyes. He watched her for a moment, but she did not raise them.

'Well, you'll have them, won't you?' he said.

There was a hiss and a rattle, and the kettle began to boil over. Turning her back on him without a word, she rushed over to the stove and started making the tea. Everard still watched her.

'You'll have them, won't you?' he repeated.

Busy with the kettle, she feigned not to hear him, though it was obvious that she could. He thought he saw her hastily brush her hand across her eyes, and fearing that perhaps he had offended her in some way, turned and walked quietly into the parlour without saying any more. From there he went up by the little cupboard staircase and washed in his bedroom instead of using the scullery sink as he generally did after his work. He came down still wondering at her strange behaviour; perhaps, being different from the ordinary village people, she had some scruple of pride about receiving gifts, though it was no uncommon custom among country people both to give and to receive them. He had been down fully ten minutes and was beginning to feel rather alarmed about her when at last she came in with the teapot. He looked up at her anxiously. Her cheeks were still a little flushed, but she was smiling.

'Oh, Mr. Mulliver!' she exclaimed, as she put the teapot down, 'you must forgive my rudeness. It was so kind of you to offer me those bullace.'

'But won't you have them, Mrs. Quainton?' he said.

'Do you really mean to give me all those, Mr. Mulliver,' she said, 'and leave none for yourself?'

'Well,' he replied with a smile, 'you might give me just a pie of them next time I come down, but I'd like you to have the rest, really.'

'Oh thank you, thank you ever so much,' she said, 'but you must pardon the way I behaved just now. It was so kind of you and—' she hesitated, looking away from him, 'I'm somehow not used to that sort of thing and – and it took me aback a little, you see.'

'Of course I see,' said Everard with a reassuring smile. 'That's all right, Mrs. Quainton.'

To tell the truth, he could not see at all, and what puzzled him even more was a strange, youthful brightness which gleamed in her dark eyes and irradiated her whole face, as if an imprisoned maiden were struggling to escape from the matronly features; he could see that she must once have been rather handsome.

'I'm so glad you don't mind,' she said, 'and if you really don't want the bullace, I shall be very glad to have them. I'll make a pie and some little tarts; and then I'll try to get a few late blackberries to mix in and make some jam. Then you can have a pot whenever you like.'

'Thank you very much,' said Everard. 'I was afraid perhaps you didn't like them. And it is silly, I think, how people in the country'll spend hours pricking their fingers to get blackberries and let their bullace rot on the trees in their gardens. They're just as good.'

'Yes, they are,' she replied readily, as though her

tongue had been loosened and she were glad to talk. 'I think that's a really nice little orchard of yours. I expect you've seen that one on the other side of the street, that belongs to Mr. Farrow. It's much bigger, but I like yours best.'

'Well,' said Everard, 'I think the same. Of course, his are all young, fresh trees, properly planted out, and he'll get far more fruit than I ever shall, but I do like my crooked old trees with their overhanging branches and rough bark and streaks of lichen; and I'm sure I shall never turn up that tangly grass in between now, to plant bush-fruit as I thought of doing.'

'No, it would be a pity,' she replied. 'In the spring-time it's full of primroses and violets and oxlips – lady's fingers we call them; and then, if you planted a few daffodils in the grass—'

'No, I don't see myself digging that up,' said Everard.

'And then,' she went on, 'you ought to see your orchard when the blossom's all out. It's all so much higher up than Mr. Farrow's 'cause the trees are taller – just like a floating white cloud; and when you prune it, it'll look even lovelier – especially those two Gennetons.'

'Ah,' said Everard appreciatively, 'that's the best apple of the year. They call them "June Eating" in the town.'

'Yes,' she said, 'so sweet and juicy and such lovely red stripes; they always come about middle of harvest.'

'There's a Quarrendon too,' he added, 'and a Golden Nob, though I haven't tasted any of them. Old Runacres had most of the early fruit.'

'Ah, what we call Quarantines,' she laughed. Everard lifted the teapot to pour himself a cup of tea. 'Oh dear!' she cried, 'here I am, talking and talking away to you and your tea all spoiling. And I don't expect you want to talk at all. I'm so sorry, Mr. Mulliver, but my tongue carried me away.'

'Don't stop, Mrs. Quainton,' said Everard, 'so long as you don't mind my eating.'

'No, I must run away,' she said, a little reluctantly. 'I've got a pork cheese for your supper and I want to see if it's set properly.'

Everard was glad to talk to her about the orchard; she was worth listening to; but before he could detain her further, she was gone. He did not stop thinking about her, however, as he went on with his tea. This was the second time she had behaved rather strangely and this time she had not regained control of herself so quickly as before. He could not make her out: it seemed odd that a bushel or two of bullace should upset a woman of such natural good sense and cheerfulness – though with a husband like Steve Quainton it was not at all improbable that she should be unused to kindness as she had said; and then, that young, maidenly look of hers, he wished he could fathom it, because, besides being curious about it, he admitted to himself that he quite liked her.

After tea he went upstairs to arrange a few still unsorted pears and found enough work besides, picking over the rest of the fruit for sleepiness or over-ripeness, to keep him busy till supper-time. He found the pork cheese on the table along with the other cold food, but Mrs. Quainton had already gone back to her own house and Everard was sorry, because he wanted to go on talking to her about his orchard, and now he would have to wait till she came in to clear.

Supper over, he sat down by the fire with his pipe and was about to open a volume of Crabbe when he

54

heard voices outside his window that he recognized; there was no mistaking the shrill pipe of the shoemaker or the deep rumble of Nesley Honeyball. They passed on down the street, the inn door banged and all was silent again. Everard poised his Crabbe on the tips of his fingers and looked at it waveringly. His chair was comfortable and there was a good fire in his little grate: but it was only a step to *The Olive Leaf*. He threw down his book and slipped out of his door in the path of the two voices. It looked as if gardening alone were going to survive.

VI

THE next two months wore away quickly enough for Everard, or rather, his weekends at Lindmer, because the intervening spaces in Bury dragged intolerably, and as time went on he was more and more tempted to abridge them, first by filching Saturday morning from the week's work and in the end by leaving his office at mid-day on Friday, not to return until the following Monday afternoon: four days a week of his paternal master's eye was ample for an old-established and smoothly running concern like Mulliver and Son's, as it was still called. Meantime the more pretentious suburban garden, once so trim, was beginning to show the lack of that affection which will humanize even the untidiest garden, for it was now left to the ministrations of a jobbing man who came in on odd days during the week. The servants, whose work was now considerably reduced by Everard's absences, ought not to have grumbled, but in secret they did grumble, being old-fashioned servants who felt that a man ought to be completely bound up with his house, especially if he had been born and bred in it. Nobody came to tea now, and there were no dinner parties, as a good part of Everard's evenings had to be devoted to making up arrears of clerical work, too important to be escaped, even if he had wanted to entertain at all, which he did not. The servants very definitely regretted Mrs. Mulliver, far more, indeed, than Everard. Members of his mother's old circle and his own more familiar customers laughed at him when he said his hands were too hard and rough now for bridge-parties and dances, and complained that he was growing into a recluse: young ladies were not so particular nowadays, mothers of daughters told him, they even liked a little elemental coarseness in a man. But it was no use now, he had slipped through their fingers.

The cottage garden, however, was shaping well, but the work had not been light; it was not all so easy to dig as the first few rod he had broken. There were some patches that had been trampled to the hardness of rock and had lost all goodness for growing anything worthier than the twitch and bell-bind which overran the place. Everard was determined to be rid of this incubus from the start, and week after week he scraped away in the black soil, sifting and uprooting, until there was hardly a grain that had not passed through his fingers. By the end of November, however, all was dug, weeded and manured; there were several rows of thriving winter cabbage and lettuce, a few hearts of endive blanching and a whole company of globe artichokes, the most ornamental things in the garden, and likely to remain so until the little parterre of grass and flowers that he had promised himself was properly laid out. The sight of all this work accomplished, although there was so much else yet to do, filled him with a comfortable feeling of satisfaction, and there was behind that a remote, deep under-pleasure which he did not examine and only knew as a sense of heightened well-being: at least, that the life suited him was clear enough.

In such a frame of mind Everard stood in his orchard surveying his own handiwork one fine soft morning, the last Sunday of November, and wondering how soon he might begin the pruning of his fruit trees, when he heard someone knocking at his back door and strolled slowly up the garden. It was Henry Runacres. He was carrying a gun in his hand, and a square wooden box slung over his shoulder by a leathern strap.

''Morning, Mr. Mulliver,' he said. 'Jack Tooke and Jim Farrow are now going along o' me up to Farmer Kindred's at the Tye to do a bit of ferreting and we didn't know if 'haps you'd come. We'd be wholly glad. I've got my eye on one or two good holes.'

'It's very kind of you, Henry,' said Everard, 'but you know, I was thinking of getting to work on my apple trees; they want a whole lot of cutting out.'

'Oh, you can leave that there place of yourn alone for one morning, Mr. Mulliver,' protested the old man. 'You've sure done enough to desarve a holiday. The ground's all dug; them trees can wait.'

'Well, p'raps you're right,' said Everard, smiling, 'and I will come along with you; it's such a fine morning.'

'That's right, sir,' said Jack Tooke, who with Jim Farrow behind him had edged his way round to the back door. 'Shame to stay slaving away like that. We'll show him some sport, 'on't we, Jim?'

'That we will and no mistake,' said Jim, and all four men moved off out of the garden into the village street.

Everard had no great love for the sport of ferreting, but it was good to be out in the air on such a soft, sunny morning, rare for November; and he liked being with the three men, having already drunk many pints and played several friendly games of darts and shove-ha'penny in their company.

They took a path which led them out along the stream at the bottom of the valley with its line of slender, feathery willow trees. After about half a mile they turned aside from the stream and climbed up a rough cartway in the direction of a farmhouse that lay half-way up the slope, a large rambling old place of dark, time-worn red brick and, like the rickety old barn beside it, badly in need of repair.

'That's old Bob Kindred's place,' said Jack Tooke, as they passed it. 'He know we come up here now and again and he's glad to have the rabbits kept down.'

'The place for us,' said Runacres, pointing to a small thatched cottage some three hundred yards further up the hill, 'is on the edge of that there covert, behind the cotterage. There's allus a wonderful lot of rabbits there.'

They took a short cut across a field of springing corn and came to a stop in a dry ditch on the edge of the covert, a short way from the end of the cottage garden.

'There,' said Runacres, 'that's a good thing they've cut that hedge down; we can see what we're about. This burrow's as good as any. Do you hold my gun, Jack, and give 'em hell when they bolt. Come along, Bet.'

He took the ferret out of the box, a handsome, sinuous little animal with a thick cream-coloured coat and long bushy tail; its pursed little eyes shone like lamps of coral.

'That's a nice-looking little bitch,' said Jim Farrow, as he watched Runacres tie a string round her neck, 'and she fare to handle wonderful kind. I don't like these here savage ferrets that tear you to bits.'

'Ay, she is kind,' said Runacres, pausing to hold her up and scratch the top of her head, 'and she work wonderful well – unless the rabbit don't bolt, and then she set and suck and suck, once she get her teeth into it; you can't get her away.'

59

'Well, I reckon they ought to bolt all right here,' said Jim, 'this is a wholly big burrow.'

'Ay, that is,' said Runacres, bending down and slipping the ferret into a hole. 'Now do you look out, Jack.'

The blacksmith took up his stand on the lip of the ditch, holding his gun ready, with Everard at his side. Jim remained in the ditch a little way from Runacres, leaning up against a tree-stump and puffing at his pipe. Runacres began paying out line as the ferret disappeared.

'Ah, she've stopped,' said Runacres, putting his ear to the hole, 'but I can't hear nothing. Do you put your ear to the bank, Jim.'

Farrow obeyed. 'I can't hear nothing neither, Henry,' he said.

'She's off!' cried Runacres excitedly, paying out line again. ''Struth! she's going wonderful. Look out, Jack, something'll be out in a minute.'

He went on paying out line as fast as it would go, while Jack Tooke stood on the opposite bank in a tense attitude, his eyes glazed and staring and his finger on the trigger. All at once Jim Farrow uttered a piercing shriek and leaped high in the air with two feet of cream-coloured ferret dangling from the seat of his trousers. He came down with a thud and rolled over on his side.

'Get up, you bloody fool!' roared Runacres, rushing over to him. 'Do, you'll crush my ferret.'

'That's all right, Henry,' quavered Farrow, clutching desperately at the slender white body behind him. 'I wish I had squashed the little bitch.'

Runacres seized the ferret by the throat and gradually eased her teeth out of Farrow's trousers. He carefully examined her muzzle.

'That haven't drawn much blood,' he said. He

stroked her ears soothingly. 'That's all right, Bet, poor little Bet.'

'Poor little Bet be damned!' piped Farrow, gingerly fingering his trousers. 'What about my buttock, and that's my best pair of pants.'

'Well, what the hell did you want to go and set right on the rabbit-hole?' retorted Runacres in an aggrieved tone. 'There's Jack up there a-waiting for the rabbits with the gun and you a-stopping 'em from coming out.'

'There wasn't no rabbit in that hole, Henry,' replied the shoemaker ruefully, still rubbing the sore place. 'Do, I shouldn't have a hole in my best Sunday pants.'

'What's the damage, Jim?' gasped Everard, with a hand over his mouth in a vain attempt to choke his laughter.

Farrow put a trembling hand inside his trousers and felt the wound.

'Ah, that's only grazed the skin on my left buttock,' he said with a sigh of relief. 'I had a hole through my right in the War. Lucky she got a good big mouthful of pants first; do, I should have had another to match.'

Jack Tooke and Everard could hold out no longer and dissolved in convulsions of laughter.

'Oh Jim, Jim,' guffawed the blacksmith, 'you fared just as if you'd lost the tail of your shirt when you jumped up; I never seed such a thing in my life.'

'Well,' replied the little man querulously, from behind his trap-door of moustache, 'I reckon you'd have done the same; and Henry say she set and suck and suck, once she get a hold. I thought you said she was kind, Henry.'

Everard and the blacksmith went off into another burst of laughter.

61

'Yes, kind to the right sort of folks,' growled Runacres, who was still caressing his ferret. 'I reckon you must smell strong of rabbit.'

'Ugly little bitch!' muttered Farrow.

'You just now said she was nice-looking,' panted Jack Tooke, quite weak with merriment, 'but don't you mind, Jim; do you rub in a drop of turps.'

'He'll be all right when he's had a drink,' added Everard.

'Well, that burrow's no good,' said Runacres, as if the shoemaker were responsible for it. 'We'd best move on a bit further, and lookye here, Jim Farrow, I 'on't have you in this ditch along o' me no more.'

'Don't you worry, Henry,' said Farrow, still tenderly soothing his hams, 'I ain't a-coming near that animal agin.'

They all moved on up the ditch and tried several more burrows, but luck was against them and not a single rabbit bolted, although the ferret killed one in the hole and they had great difficulty in hauling her out. Finally they turned back along the ditch until they came to the hedge of the cottage garden, where they stopped.

'Now I'll lay my gun there's a rabbit here,' growled Runacres. 'Do you keep your eyes open, Jack.'

'They 'on't escape me, Henry,' replied Tooke doughtily.

''Haps there've been poachers here,' ventured Farrow.

'Well, I reckon they didn't snare 'em in their pants,' growled Runacres sarcastically, as he put the ferret in the hole. 'She's going fine, I heard her squeal. Look out, Jack, look out . . . there you are!'

A rabbit bolted from a hole five yards away and

headed straight for a small gap in the cottage garden hedge, which ran at right-angles to the ditch. The blacksmith took careful aim and fired just as the rabbit was disappearing through the gap.

'What did you wait so long for?' said Runacres, looking up reproachfully.

'I wanted a good aim to make sure of him,' replied the blacksmith. 'Don't you fret, Henry, I got him all right; I seed him flip his hind leg.'

Runacres walked up to the gap and parted the bushes on both sides.

'No sign of him,' he said. 'You missed him, Jack – at that range!'

'I tell you I didn't!' shouted the blacksmith, 'I swear I seed his hind leg flip with the shock and surprise of it; he've crawled away and hid hisself among the cabbage.'

'Well, we can't get in and see,' said Runacres sullenly, ' 'cause they've got barbed wire in the gap.'

'Well, let's go round to the door,' said the blacksmith, 'and ax owd Mother Gathercole to let us go and see. That's there in the cabbage, you mark my words.'

Runacres hauled the ferret up again, and when he had shut her up in the box, they all moved on. As they came level with the cottage, they were startled to find a tall young woman waiting behind the garden gate, with a great sheaf of lustrous, dark-gold hair over her shoulder which she was combing; there was a cold gleam in her eye.

'What do you mean by shooting in our garden?' she demanded haughtily.

'We weren't a-shooting in your garden, miss,' explained Tooke rather haltingly.

'You were,' she snapped, still combing her hair.

'No, miss,' protested Tooke. 'I shot a rabbit in the

ditch and that slipped through your hedge to die. We were going to ax you to let us look among the cabbage.'

'Well, you won't find it,' replied the maiden coldly, "'cause I saw it bolt through our back hedge into the copse and you've blown our best head of winter broccolo to smithereens.'

'Oh!' exclaimed the blacksmith, clutching his chin in dismay, 'I haven't got no broccolo in my garden.'

'Nor me in mine,' added the shoemaker.

'Nor me neither,' echoed the rat-catcher. Everard suddenly bethought himself of his neglected garden in Bury.

'I've got some,' he said, 'but they won't be ready for a full month.'

'Ah, that's the thing of it,' cried Tooke, 'if you'd be so good, Mr. Mulliver, and I'll pay up.'

'If you don't mind waiting, miss,' said Everard. She looked hard at him.

'That was a wholly big head,' she said doubtfully. 'I've never seen such a big head in my life.'

'Well, I warrant I'll beat it,' said Everard, laughing. 'It's a special seed I got hold of last spring; only you must tell the truth if it beats yours.'

'Yes, I'll tell the truth,' she replied coldly.

'All right, then,' said Everard, 'that'll be some time after Christmas.'

'Don't you forget,' said the girl suspiciously, tugging the comb out of her sheaf of hair.

'He 'on't forget,' said Tooke and Runacres, both together, 'he's a gentleman, he is.'

'And don't you come shooting in our garden again,' she added sharply. 'That's wholly dangerous. Keep right away. That might hit me another time.'

'All right, miss,' said Runacres, 'I'll keep an eye on

him next time; he's allus a bit jim when he get a gun in his hands. 'Morning to you, miss.'

They moved away from the gate in a body, Everard quite naturally doffing his cap, a town custom which none of his companions, with corresponding naturalness, observed. The girl stopped her combing for a moment and stared curiously at him; then, the corner of her mouth twitching into the faintest of smiles, she turned and went into the house.

'There's a cool filly for you,' said Jack Tooke, as soon as they were out of earshot. 'See how she laid down the law and went on a-combing her hair all the time.'

'That fair took my breath away,' gasped Farrow.

'That wouldn't have happened,' grumbled Runacres, 'if only you'd learn to shoot proper, Jack; and here we are with the rabbit lost, and Mr. Mulliver have got to fetch you that broccolo.'

'Well, I'll pay for it, anyhow,' said Tooke, on the defensive and a little surly.

'No, you won't,' put in Everard. 'I've got plenty in Bury, more than I know what to do with. But who's that girl?'

'That's Ruthie Gathercole, that is,' replied Runacres.

'Who's she?'

'Well, her father,' continued Runacres, 'used to rent the farm next to Bob Kindred's, but ten year ago he died, and his wife, she sold up and came to live in that there cotterage with Ruthie; she've got a bit of money, she have, not a wonderful lot, though – enough to keep going like.'

'What does she do?' said Everard.

'What, Ruthie?' said Tooke, who had now quite recovered his temper. 'Why, she toil not neither do she spin, in a manner of speaking. I suppose she help owd

Mother Gathercole in the house, but there ain't much to do, that stand to reason.'

'They keep an owd pony and trap,' added Farrow, from whose mind this new subject of conversation had ousted all thought of his buttock, 'and you often see her driving about in the lanes, summertime mostly.'

'She knows her way about, I should think,' said Everard.

'She do that,' replied Runacres, 'and she've got a precious sharp tongue; and she don't think too little of herself neither.'

'No, I don't care for her somehows,' said Runacres. 'Not my idea of a woman.'

'Got a sweetheart?' asked Everard.

'No, not as I know on,' replied Jack Tooke. 'Chance for you, Mr. Mulliver.'

'Not at my age,' grinned Everard. 'I've got all my work cut out to grow a broccoli big enough to satisfy her.'

'And you didn't see hern afore Jack blew that to bits,' said Runacres, 'so you 'on't know if yourn is bigger.'

'Well, I'll grow one bigger than she's ever seen,' said Everard, laughing. 'I don't reckon she'll beat it.'

'Well, I'd like some of that seed,' said Farrow, and the conversation then deserted Ruthie Gathercole for the cultivation of vegetables, which they continued to discuss until they were back in the village again, in front of Everard's gate.

'Well, farewell, Mr. Mulliver,' said Runacres. 'We haven't given you much sport, I'm afraid.'

'Still,' replied Everard, with a sly wink, 'the entertainment more than made up for that. Farewell.'

'Till tonight,' added Jack Tooke, his mind on *The Olive Leaf.*

'What good chaps they are!' said Everard to himself, pulling one of the low, round armchairs up to the parlour fire; then, his thoughts harking away to the cottage on the valley-side, he found himself building up again more slowly the momentary picture which Ruthie Gathercole had left in his mind. That sheaf of dark-tawny hair, pouring down over her shoulder, not curly nor yet straight, but thick and exuberant like a wreath of traveller's-joy in the hedge; no wonder she had not followed the fashion and had left it uncut; she combed it affectionately, as if she were caressing a live creature. The outline of her face, as far as he could recall it, was full and squarish, her eyes dark, perhaps dark grey; certainly her expression had been hard and cold, as befitted a woman standing up for the safety of her vegetables. She was tall and full-bosomed, too, a ripe country maiden, with a strain of Flora or Pomona in her bearing. But after her hair, what he best remembered was her neck; it was in keeping with the rest of her, strong and pillar-like, but on the swell of her throat the skin shone milky-white, with an almost liquid softness which to touch would be like stroking a violet petal.

At this point Everard pulled himself up with a little laugh of self-mockery: it was as well that he lived in the village and not in the vale. And now that he thought of it, it seemed strange that in all those years that he had lived as his mother dictated, thwarting all his other natural instincts, he had seldom or never looked at a woman in this light, although he might have been expected to turn that way for consolation, as men had done in war-time; whereas now, with those other instincts finding every day fuller satisfaction, he had caught himself groping out in a new direction: but after all, it was, perhaps, just the quickened vitality of his new life which quickened his need of a woman. Of course, there was Mrs. Quainton in the house: but she was older than himself and his feeling for her was far other. He was almost fond of her, they were such good friends, though he knew very little more about her than at first, except that she had once had a little boy who was now dead – for she was quite unforthcoming about herself and he did not press her on the subject; nor did they talk of her husband, who was seldom to be seen. But their general relations in the house were now quite easy; she talked to him on other topics and she seemed to have lost her queer terror of his kindnesses and even exchanged little gifts of garden stuff with him in country fashion; which reminded Everard that Christmas was approaching and it would be a pleasure to him to buy her a present; he must keep his eyes open when he returned to Bury. There was also that head of broccoli to be selected and marked down for Ruthie Gathercole; far simpler, indeed, to buy one from a greengrocer's in town and send it to her by post. But she had, as it were, challenged him to go one better than hers, and if the truth were known, he was not at all averse from another visit to Ruthie Gathercole. He was still smiling at himself when Mrs. Quainton tapped and came in with the joint.

VII

DECEMBER drew on and Christmas came steadily nearer, though rather too steadily to please Everard, who had promised himself a whole week's holiday at Lindmer. There were still plenty of things to do and he was eager to finish the winter pruning so as to be able to get on with the hedges; so eager, indeed, that half-way through the day before Christmas Eve he fled away from Bury, leaving Mulliver and Son's in all the pother of the Christmas shopping to take care of themselves. There was something of a gale blowing that afternoon, but in spite of Mrs. Quainton's remonstrances he stayed out in the bitter wind and stinging rain, hanging on to the top of his ladder and snipping away at his apple trees. Next day he went on with the same work in the same weather; it was not sursing that he complained of feeling tired when Mrs. Quainton brought his tea in. For answer she walked over and laid her hand on his forehead.

'Yes, I thought so,' she said. 'It's feverish you are.'

She packed him off early to bed that night with a hot-water bottle and a stiff tot of hot rum and lemon. When he woke up next morning, she was standing at his bedside with the breakfast tray in her hands.

'Well, how do you feel?' she said.

'My mouth's rather dry,' he replied sleepily, 'but I feel nice and warm and comfortable, as if I'd been drunk. I wasn't, was I?'

'No,' she said, laughing and feeling his forehead.

'I didn't give you all that rum. You may get up today, but you mustn't go out, mind.'

'Oh, Mrs. Quainton!' he complained.

'You mustn't,' she repeated.

'Oh well,' he said with a smile of resignation, 'if you insist, I suppose I mustn't. But look here, Mrs. Quainton, if I stay in, I think you ought to come in and talk to me to keep me company; because, of course, it's Christmas Day, I'd quite forgotten.'

'Why, so it is,' she exclaimed. 'A merry Christmas, Mr. Mulliver!'

'Thank you,' he said, turning over and pointing across the room. 'That reminds me; you might fetch that brown-paper parcel, on the drawers.'

She put her tray down on the dressing-table and picked up the parcel he had pointed out.

'You open it,' he added.

She obeyed, producing from the outer wrappings something twisted up in tissue paper, which proved to be a string of painted china beads.

'They're for you,' said Everard, looking anxiously at her; he hoped she was not going to cry.

'For me?' she cried, opening her eyes wide. 'They are so pretty. You are kind, Mr. Mulliver. And I forgot all about you.'

A real brightness came into her cheeks and her eyes shone. Everard was content.

'Well, come and amuse me this afternoon instead,' he laughed. 'You will, won't you, Mrs. Quainton?'

'Well, yes,' she faltered, 'that is, I'll see. P'r'aps my husband'll be going out. You'll be wanting your breakfast now. They are lovely. Thank you, Mr. Mulliver.'

She went downstairs, still admiring the beads.

Everard lay late that morning, and when he came downstairs, read desultorily among the few contemplative poets he had installed in his parlour, yawning a good deal over them; he seemed to have lost the habit these last two months. However, he was not sorry to be indoors; it was still raining and blowing hard.

At one o'clock came his Christmas dinner, succulent slices of goose and a quite perfect plum pudding on which he complimented Mrs. Quainton; in addition he opened a half-bottle of claret which he had brought down in honour of the day, but it was difficult to be festive all alone. Mrs. Quainton had been quite bright and talkative, but she had said nothing about coming in later on, even when she cleared the table. He sat on for some time after dinner, idly turning over the leaves of an unread volume of Crabbe and staring out of the window, wishing Mrs. Quainton would come in; he must talk to someone. There was a grind of wheels from next door and Steve Quainton's high dogcart went lurching down to the ford. Everard followed his massive back with a grim eye until it disappeared from view: where could the ugly brute be going on an afternoon like this? Surely no pigs to castrate on Christmas Day.

Five minutes later Mrs. Quainton came in; she had put on her best dark-blue dress and her new beads for the occasion.

'My husband's just gone off to Sudbury,' she said a little breathlessly, as she sat down in the chair which Everard set for her. 'So I can come in after all.'

'Those beads look quite nice on,' he said, 'at least, to me. I was a bit afraid when I bought them.'

She coloured a little.

71

'Yes, don't they?' she said. 'You couldn't have chosen better, Mr. Mulliver.'

Then for a few minutes they were awkwardly silent, just because, for the first time, she was there expressly to talk; if she had had a tray in her hand, laying the table, the words would have come easily enough. Everard coughed once or twice, but it was no use talking about his cold; it would lead nowhere.

At last, for the sake of saying something: 'What exactly are you going to do with that bit of ground you said was to be a flower garden, Mr. Mulliver?' she asked.

'You mean that bit near the house?' he replied. 'Well, I haven't yet thought out the design properly, but I'm going to have a place where I can really take my ease in the summertime. I shall have some nice comfortable grass and little beds with box edging.'

'And what'll you plant in them?'

'Oh, everything that smells sweet – lots of lavender, and big clumsy roses and night-scented stock for the evening and things to draw the bees – thyme and marjoram – I love the sound of bees – and, of course, hollyhocks and evening primroses; but I must have a garden that smells nice, and then I can go to sleep in the middle of it all – when I'm tired of watching the apples grow.'

'That does sound nice,' she said, smiling, 'and you will want to sleep if you work all the winter at it the way you've been going on. But won't there be anything else?'

'Oh yes,' he replied, grinning. 'Of course, I'd forgotten. I'm going to have a great wide strip of marigolds right across the bottom of it – one solid strip of flaming orange. I've always longed to try that.'

'What, common cottage marigolds?' she said, a little surprised.

'Why, yes,' he said, 'don't you think they're lovely? And then, Mrs. Quainton, I shall ask you to make me marigold puddings.'

'Marigold puddings!' she repeated incredulously. 'You're laughing at me, Mr. Mulliver. Is it something like pigeon's milk?'

'I'm quite serious, I assure you,' said Everard, still grinning widely, 'even though I don't look it. Nobody ever will believe in them until they've tasted, and then they say no more.'

'Well, how do you make them?' she inquired.

'The foundation, of course,' said Everard in his best culinary manner, 'is eggs, milk and breadcrumbs, baked in a tin, like any other pudding.'

'Some puddings,' she corrected.

'I yield there,' he replied. 'Like some puddings, and then you just mix in marigolds, the petals – as many as you like.'

'And what happens?' she said, making a wry face. 'They smell so strong.'

'The marigolds disappear in the cooking,' he replied, 'and the pudding turns a lovely rich yellow and tastes, not like the smell of marigolds, but something infinitely more delicate and elusive.'

'I don't fancy it, somehow,' she said, slowly shaking her head.

'I don't mind your saying that in the least,' said Everard. 'It always happens that way. When you've tasted, you'll say no more about it, but just go on eating.'

'Shall I?' she looked quizzically at him. 'I never thought I should have to make such unchristian things when I offered to keep house for you.'

'That's nothing to what you'll have to do,' said Everard, wagging his finger at her, 'when I've got all my herbs planted. You make very nice salads as it is; but then I'll show you how to make even better.'

'How, Mr. Mulliver? I'm always ready to learn.'

'Why, mainly by putting more things in.' Everard was warming to this, his pet subject; it was the first time he had discussed it with her. 'Young leaves of primrose, violet, hollyhock; sorrel, peeled borage-stalks and, let's see, rampion, burnet and purslane.' He burst out laughing at the end of the enumeration.

'I believe you're using wicked words, Mr. Mulliver,' she said, 'or else you're laughing at me.'

'I'm perfectly serious,' he rejoined. 'And then I've forgotten the seasoning; just a leaf or two, chopped up fine, of thyme, marjoram, sage, hyssop, fennel and tansy – only the tiniest scrap of that or it'll stink everything out – and marigold.'

'No, don't forget the marigold,' she mocked. 'Where ever did you get all these new-fangled notions from, Mr. Mulliver?'

'They're not new-fangled, Mrs. Quainton,' he protested. 'They're as old as the hills; and the people who used them were your ancestors, though why all you country folk have forgotten them, I can't think. It's strange, too, Mrs. Quainton, how it was all the nastiest recipes that lasted longest, all the remedies, I mean – up till the last generation, anyhow. My father, who was born near Halesworth, could remember being dosed with yarrow tea for measles, and I expect you can too.'

'No, I can't,' said Mrs. Quainton. 'How old is your father?' she added more gravely.

'Well, he'd be sixty-four now,' replied Everard, 'if he were alive.'

'How old do you think I am?' she asked in a low voice, with a queer little pout.

Everard looked at her and then at the hearthrug, trying to calculate. That time he had found her weeping at the sink she had looked almost fifty; at other times, when she was pleased, as she had been this morning, there was a maiden of twenty in her eyes; at the moment her face bore a pensive, elderly cast. It was no use trying to strike an average between the two extremes; then he remembered Steve Quainton.

'Well, you're not more than forty,' he said, trying to be generous.

She shook her head, a little sadly.

'I was thirty-four yesterday,' she said.

'Why, one year older than I am,' he cried, amazed; and then, dismayed at his mistake, 'I was badly out, Mrs. Quainton. I'm so sorry. It's true that—'

She stopped his flow of apologies with a gesture of her hand.

'No,' she said in a low voice. 'I know I look more than my age, and no wonder. I've had a lot of trouble.'

As she spoke, she certainly did look much more than her years. Everard thought once more of Steve Quainton.

'Your husband must be a good deal older than you,' he ventured.

A stunned, frozen look came into her face, as if the thought hurt her.

'Yes,' she said significantly, 'he is – twenty-four years.'

Everard dropped his eyes a moment and then raised them again.

'Did you, did you—' he hesitated, 'marry him of your own will?'

There was a distinct pause before she opened her lips, looking quietly into his eyes.

'Do you think so?' she murmured.

Everard, knowing the man, nodded understandingly.

'I was married at eighteen,' she said, and sighed. Everard shuddered. Then leaning her elbow on her knee and her head on her hand, she went on, looking into the fire. 'My father was Congregational minister at Long Melford; he was very kind to me and gave me quite a good education; so was mother too. As soon as I was old enough, I intended to train as a nurse; but when I was only seventeen, my father died quite suddenly and mother and I were left alone in the world. She had a little, from what father had saved, but it was not a quarter enough to live on, so I had to give up all idea of being a nurse and go to work in a stationer's shop to keep both of us, as mother was too old to work. We went to live in a tiny two-room cottage and I know she suffered a lot, poor thing, because she thought it was such a comedown. Well, we'd been living in this way about eight months, when Stephen, that's my husband, began paying attention to me. I must tell you something about him first. He was a sort of dealer in horses and cattle at Long Melford and he'd been in quite a big way of doing: but when he first began to cast eyes on me, he'd run through almost the whole of his money, though not many knew of it; he was always drinking and betting and – and – worse than that, as I learnt afterwards. He'd already had one wife – she had a weak heart and he drove her into the churchyard after ten years – and his two sons were already grown-up with homes of their own – they hated him. Well, he was forty-two at the time, and I was eighteen, and though p'r'aps I shouldn't say it, I was a pretty girl

76

in those days, though I know you can't see that now. Well, I suppose he must have thought something like this. "Here am I, almost ruined; the people in the town think I'm a bad lot and my children hate me and won't have anything to do with me. But I'm only forty-two; they think I'm down and out, but I'll show them what I can do; I'll carry off a girl of eighteen, one of the prettiest in the town, and make a slave of her too; that'll teach 'em to despise me; it's more than they'll do at forty-two." I think that's what he must have felt, to make him want to marry me, because he was always going about with other women in Long Melford and everywhere else. He just wanted to show off, and p'r'aps he wanted someone to look after him in his old age. Yes, I think that's what it was.'

She paused to rest her voice.

'But didn't you stand up for yourself?' asked Everard.

'I did my best,' she replied, 'but I couldn't help myself. Wait a minute, where was I? Oh yes, I said he started paying attention to me. Well, that's not really quite right, because all the attention was paid to my mother. He didn't love me, of course; he just wanted my body and he knew I couldn't bear the sight of him; besides, he couldn't have made love to anybody if he'd tried, such a lout as he was. No, he got hold of mother and said he wanted to marry me, made out he was well off and she'd be happy and comfortable for the rest of her days. Well, the long and the short of it was, he managed to take her in and she said to me, "Laura, Mr. Quainton wants to marry you and I think you'd be very wise to accept him; he's ever such a nice man." "But, mother," I said, "I don't love him, and besides, he's old enough to be my father." "Well, he'll be all the more able to love and cherish you," she said, "and he'll be able to give you a really good position in the world and you'll come one day to love him." "But he doesn't love me, mother," I said. "Pshut! child," she said, "you know nothing about such matters, you're only a chit. Besides, I think you might think a little of me now I'm getting old. He's promised me a comfortable home along with both of you." "Oh, mother," I said — I began to cry, I remember, "you know I'd work myself to the bone for you; you shan't ever want while I'm alive." "Yes, Laura," she said, "but you know I've never been used to living in this style: neither have you, and I think you owe something to your mother."

'Well, that was how it started. She encouraged Stephen and he was always about the house so that I couldn't get away from him. I remember the first time he told me he wanted to marry me; I shivered and turned away, and then he tried to kiss me, and I pushed him aside and ran out of the room. Then, all the time mother went on at me and grumbled about the food and the cold, and said the neighbours looked down on her — her father had been quite a well-to-do builder in Haverhill. And so it went on. She'd quite set her heart on the marriage and in the end, after three months, for her sake, I married him.'

She paused again, still looking at the fire. Everard kept silent. She flashed a glance up at him to see if he was still listening, and finding his eyes hanging steadfastly upon her own, cleared her throat and continued.

'I think at the last I half-believed what mother said about the advantages of marrying — the comforts and position; but that didn't blind me to the other side of it. I could guess what it would be like: it was even worse than I had expected.'

Her lips twisted into a grimace of loathing and she

shuddered involuntarily at the memory.

'I think you've seen him close,' she went on, looking up at Everard, who nodded. 'I nearly always say "him"; it's so hard to bring myself to say "Stephen" or "my husband." Well, you know what he's like, and you can imagine it'd be bad enough for, for a refined girl to have to live in the same house and sit at the same table with a man like that, with that cruel face, those horrible, cold, watery eyes and dirty, yellow teeth, a man who talks in that rough, coarse voice, always stinking of whisky and spitting all over the kitchen floor – that would be punishment enough. But to have to sleep with him and give yourself—' she broke off suddenly and looked up at Everard with scared eyes. 'Oh what dreadful things I'm saying!' she whispered. 'Why do I tell you all this?'

'Go on,' said Everard in a sick, husky voice, without taking his eyes from her.

She swallowed hard and went on.

'Let me see. Yes, we went to Clacton for our honeymoon, yes honeymoon,' she repeated the word with a hollow, sardonic laugh. 'It came out afterwards that he'd borrowed the money to do it. I could never tell all I went through that week, in mind and body; he did what he liked with me. It was like, like – oh, what am I saying – being savaged by a boar in the hogyard – I knew all hell couldn't be worse than that horrible, horrible week.' She shuddered again. 'I came back feeling as if I'd been trodden down in a swamp, with my lungs full of mire, and I've felt half-stifled ever since. Then after a time, I suppose,' she shrugged her shoulders, 'you get numb to it. When we came back from Clacton, we moved from Long Melford to Clare, further up the river – the Stour – where he was setting up business again, and it was then I began to find out that he was almost penniless. He never told us outright, and I'm sure mother never thought it was anything more than just "temporary difficulties", as he put it, but he borrowed nearly all of her little store of money to tide him over. He was always careful to be civil to me in front of mother; but I never had a kind word from him, he was always out of the house all day and most of the evening, drinking and betting his money, mother's money, away. And then at night – I had to endure him, till he got tired of me, no longer a new toy for him, and he went after other women; the neighbours used to tell me about it. I did everything to keep all this from mother, because I was afraid she'd never forgive herself if she knew the truth, and I think I managed it. We certainly lived in a bigger house at Clare than our little cottage in Melford, and although we weren't really so comfortable, mother always seemed to think she was much better off there. I think it was the position which counted most for her. And anyhow, she died before he had got through all her money and the worst came; not long before, though. I think perhaps it was best she died when she did. We'd been married four years, and I remember the morning before the funeral, I was in the bedroom putting a last touch to the coffin before they screwed it down. He came in and found me crying. "Why isn't dinner ready?" he asked. That's the sort of man he is. Well, after that things went from bad to worse. He gave up the dealing and had to take any work he could get for other dealers and auctioneers and vets, and I had to make do with what little money he brought back. Then, to make things worse, I had a baby boy and he was always grumbling at me as if it were my fault. He no longer had any call to be civil to me, you see, now mother was dead, and he made no secret about going with other women; he used to laugh about it in the house and say he'd have me when he wanted me, which he did. He never hit me or laid hands on me, even when he was drunk, but there are far worse ways of murdering a woman than that; and he knew I was bound to him and couldn't help myself; just his slave to cook his food, wash his clothes and – warm his bed for him. How I brought that child up I don't know – we were living in rooms at the time; he never did a hand's turn for me, I had to plan everything myself. The boy was a nice little chap and I was very fond of him – he was the only thing I had to console me. And then, when he was five years old, he died too. I know I was heart-broken at the time, but I sometimes feel it was better after all that he did die; it was such a terrible life for him. And he, he – my husband I mean – never even went to the funeral though I was really glad he didn't.

'Well, after that things improved. He'd been working with a vet for a bit and he'd always had to do with horses, so he set up on his own as a horse-doctor. We left Clare and went to Nayland for a year, but there was too much competition there and we came here, four years ago it is, because there's more work to be had in the country. And here we are. He's out all day at work and comes home late at nights when he's had enough beer and cards and I'm his slave; I keep his house, he takes all the money you give me for my work here, and he used to read all my letters when I had any. I never go out; I just stay at home and work. Now do you wonder if I look six years older than my age?' There was almost a note of challenge in her voice as she ceased and looked up at him.

Everard took a deep breath and nodded slowly, still gazing solemnly at her.

'The marvel to me is,' he said at length, 'that you can stay so bright and cheerful with it all; I should never have guessed all that ghastliness behind; I don't know how you do it.'

'Ah,' she replied, 'I used to do that for mother's sake, so that she shouldn't know; and then I did it for the boy's sake – I didn't want him to grow up sad. And after that it became a sort of habit. I don't want people to see and I don't think there's anybody who knows the whole story – except, now, you.'

'Yes, yes, I see,' said Everard slowly, and then, unable to help himself, shuddered violently. 'Do you, do you still have to put up with him at night?' he asked haltingly; the idea of it made his mouth taste foul.

'Yes,' she replied, 'when he thinks he will; though not so often now, he's getting on, you see. After all these years I've learnt to bear it, but I've never got used to it, and every time it happens it makes me feel older and look older than ever. That was why you found me crying that afternoon when you first came into the cottage.'

'Ah,' Everard breathed, 'I thought there was something.'

'Yes, and I guessed you thought so,' she replied, with a wry little smile. 'It was that, and seeing you come into your new cottage with everything fresh and smart and looking so happy; it reminded me of the day when I first went into my first – his – house, such a different day that was.' She stopped and noticed that he was staring hard into the fire. 'There!' she cried, thinking he was tired of her story, 'how I have run on talking, and you asked me to come in to keep you amused. I am sorry.'

'Don't say that,' replied Everard, sitting up in his chair and facing her. 'I was trying to collect my wits. Your story has dazed me, rather; it's, it's terrible.'

She coloured a little. 'You know, I never thought I could tell anybody such dreadful things – and I've told you everything; but I somehow thought I could, I thought you'd understand, because you've been so kind to me. Do you know, it's so long since anybody was kind to me – more than sixteen years, I think, ever since my father's death – that I could hardly believe it when you spoke nicely to me and gave me things. It was so strange that it hurt me. That was why I behaved in that silly way over the bullace. You must have thought me terribly rude.'

Everard smiled at her.

'No,' he said, 'I only wondered, and now I understand. But I wonder now how you stood it all.'

'So do I sometimes,' she replied, 'but I suppose I shall go on like it now till I die; it won't be long, I expect.'

'That would be a pity,' said Everard.

'What do you mean?'

'Why, after you've stuck it so long, you deserve something better. You've never lived, Mrs. Quainton, and you've a right to live, and at your age you've a duty to yourself to live.'

'Yes, but how can I?' she half-wailed. 'What is there for me?'

'Why,' he replied, 'get a divorce, run away from your husband, both.'

She gaped at him as if astonished.

'But, Mr. Mulliver,' she faltered, 'what would people say, and my father, if he were alive?'

Everard bent forward in his chair.

'Listen, Mrs. Quainton,' he said earnestly. 'You must

forget the clergyman's daughter and remember you're a woman. You shouldn't stay another moment with such a man. You should have left him years ago.'

'But what to do?' she said desperately, holding out her hands.

'Why, to work for your living,' he answered, 'and be free.'

'He'd never let me,' she said, shaking her head. 'Besides, he could half-kill me if he wanted to.'

'He wouldn't dare,' said Everard. 'Besides, you've never tried.'

'But what should I do out in the world?' she said. 'I don't know my way about, and a woman all alone, everybody sets on her. Besides, I don't want to starve; I know what poverty is well enough.'

'You wouldn't starve, Mrs. Quainton,' he said gently, 'though you might have to struggle; but then, it would be worth it.'

'Oh, I couldn't, I couldn't,' she moaned. 'I'm so afraid of that man.'

'No, you aren't really,' he coaxed. 'You're a brave woman, Mrs. Quainton, but you want to be just a bit braver. It's wicked to waste a life like that.'

'Oh, Mr. Mulliver,' she cried, 'don't say that after all I've suffered. I thought you sympathized.'

She began to cry softly into her handkerchief. Everard saw his mistake; she was in no mood for heroic courses.

'So I do,' he said more gently, 'and more than I can tell you, Mrs. Quainton. I'm sorry if I spoke sharply; I wanted to help you, but I had to speak my mind. Still, if you don't want to run away, I think you might demand to be treated better at home. Why shouldn't you have all the money you earn here? He does nothing for it.'

'No, no, I couldn't do it,' she said tearfully, still busy with her handkerchief.

They were both silent for a minute or two; it distressed him to see her crying like that.

'I hope, Mrs. Quainton,' he said, a little diffidently, 'I hope whenever you're in trouble you'll come and tell me – and if you ever want any help.'

She nodded and wiped her eyes.

'Yes, I will,' she said, in a rather weak, ragged voice. 'It's done me such a lot of good just telling you all this. You are so kind, I can tell you things; only I oughtn't to burden you with all my troubles, Mr. Mulliver, I'm such a silly woman.'

'No, don't think that,' he said, 'I want to hear them.'

'Thank you,' she said; then, looking at the clock, 'Why, it's nearly four o'clock. I must go and get tea ready, and what will the neighbours be saying?'

She got up from her chair, and with a little smile back at Everard from the door, hastened out of the room.

Everard sank back in his chair with a troubled sigh; her story had hurt him and still hung like a weight upon his brain. He could picture Laura Quainton now as a young thing – she was not so far from the maiden in her features as he had imagined – slim and graceful of body, her fresh, white cheeks just tinged with colour, her black eyes sparkling, her teeth even whiter than they were now, her whole face, from the low, broad forehead to the fine, tapering chin, vivacious and full of character. To imagine such a gentle creature in the brutish embrace of Steve Quainton – with his yellow teeth, his watery eyes and stinking breath, and for ever spitting on the kitchen floor, a sort of human sacrifice – it made him feel sick, and yet his mind would come

85

back to it. The wonder was that she still knew how to be kind and gracious, and had not been shattered into hopeless, misanthropic gloom. That needed a high courage, but even while he admired her for it, he wondered why it had never entered her mind to rebel; the very suggestion of rebellion made her shrink back on her sorrow as if all she wanted were consolation, and what room was there for that in the midst of all this undisguisable wretchedness? Perhaps she had lived so long with her sorrow that she could not conceive herself without it, perhaps secretly she was a little fond of it, so that in part it was its own consolation. But that seemed cruel, and he could only suppose that the quality of her courage was to endure rather than be brave, actively brave. If somehow he could help her to acquire the other kind of courage and free her from this abomination, a piece of common humanity – he knew with a sudden clearness that he would give his right hand to do it.

Then Mrs. Quainton came in with the tea, rather silent and looking her oldest, it seemed to him; he vowed himself to the task.

VIII

EVERARD dropped his flasher in the grass, pulled off a coarse leather gauntlet and mopped his damp forehead with a handkerchief. It was the last morning of his Christmas holiday, not the last day, because after lunch he was pledged to go back to Bury, straight to his office, to pick up once more the wearisome threads of the provision trade and ascertain the result of his Christmas campaign. It was really his duty to be back that same morning, but he could not bring himself to leave the last two rod of his orchard hedge untrimmed. It looked ridiculously abandoned, standing there all by itself; the business could well spare another half-day and, to be just, he really owed himself another whole day, to make up for the time his cold had wasted; and, more compelling than anything, he liked hedge-cutting, better than digging, weeding, planting, fruit-picking even. The hedge had not been disturbed for seven years or more and towered above him, a rampant, indiscriminate tangle of thorn, briar and bramble, elm and dogwood, with here and there a patch of oak or hazel. Everard had decided to buckhead it, which was not merely to lop off projecting side-growths and over-hanging branches, but to fell all its extravagance breast-high, and a hedge does not submit to such treatment without a stout resistance. The blackthorn branches bounced back in his face when he struck them, the bramble coils, clinging unseen, wreathed themselves round his legs, the dog-rose thorns found

87

their way through his pigskin gauntlets; even a tough elm switch at times could leave a burning weal on the cheek. But Everard rejoiced in the tussle, hacking and slashing, tearing and slicing, with the heavy, cleaver-like hook for the saplings and thick stuff, and the slenderer, curved flasher for the thin, wiry twigs, knowing that however many bruises and scratches he carried away, he was bound to win in the end. The work needed skill, too, to judge the sort of blow suited to the size, the texture, the age, the habit of the branches, and there were continual queer little dis-coveries to enjoy, last season's birds' nests filled with broken twigs, an eccentric oak bush that kept its dead brown leaves when all the other trees had shed theirs, a luxuriant ivy sprawling round a rotten ash pole, relic of a grim tragedy in the past; a fresh, sappy smell oozed up from the jagged stumps; there was the prospect of a bonfire, too, and he had always liked bonfires. But what Everard liked best was the mere violence and sweat, the cut-and-slash of it, which seemed to answer some newly risen primitive need in him. He had worked like this for day after day without finding it drudgery. Standing there with his feet planted firmly down on the banks among the bushes that stiffly brushed his legs, he wondered whether such close, rough contact with the soil was making him more primitive, and smiled.

He picked up his flasher and began whetting it slowly on the rub, looking along the hedge; this rub-up ought to last him as far as that patch of purple dogwood stems. His eyes wandered across the hedge into the field beyond, sloping up from the stream like his own orchard. There was Farmer Kindred at plough, scoring one thin line after another in the withered stubble and slowly transforming its drabness into a chestnut even richer and more brilliant than the glistening flanks of his two Suffolk horses. Everard watched him stumbling along behind them in his furrow, bending warily over the plough-handles, balancing, guiding; it looked far harder work for him than for the horses, who, poised a little inwards towards each other (for one was on the stubble and the other down in the last-ploughed furrow), their sorrel necks rising and falling and their quarters swinging forward in the same patient rhythm, marched on with an untroubled stateliness which made them a veritable part of the landscape. A task even more violent and sweaty than his own, Everard thought, more primitive, fighting with hands and tools and feet against the soil itself; he gripped the handle of his flasher hard, envying the man.

The plough was back at the end of its journey, and Kindred, as he took more stubble into his compass, drew on up the headland to the spot where he intended to start his new furrow, stopping just level with Everard to give his team a breather. They had met before once or twice at *The Olive Leaf*, but Kindred, though not uncompanionable, was a shy man of few words, and they did not know each other well. He was square-shouldered, of middle height; his long face, ruddy and straight-nosed, was made even longer by a straggly fair beard, greying now – he was verging on sixty – but there was a quick, live gleam in his pale-blue eye. His ancient, ribbonless hat, his baggy coat and close-fitting corduroy breeches had been faded by sun and rain to a harmonious pattern of nondescript colour, which gave them almost a timeless aspect, as if they might have grown out of the soil on which he worked. He raised a finger to Everard, who returned the greeting.

'Was that you I seed,' he said, leaning against the

plough-handles and refilling his pipe, 'the other Sunday over by mine, along o' Henry Runacres?'

'Yes,' Everard replied.

'Have much sport?' he asked.

'Well,' grinned Everard, 'we got Jim Farrow, or a bit of him, not to mention a bit of vegetables.'

Kindred laughed; the story was common property now.

'You're making a wholly good job of that fence,' he said. 'I remember that was seven years ago when Henry last buckheaded that; I had a crop of peas here then. I may get a crop off my hidland now that's cut agin; that keep the sun off something terrible. You've cut that wholly tidy too.'

'I'm glad you think so,' said Everard, gratified at the compliment. 'It's pretty tough work, but it doesn't look so tough as your ploughing.'

Kindred paused to light his pipe.

'Oh, I don't know,' he said, after a few puffs. 'That ain't so bad as it fare to you. That's on a slope, you see, and the horses make you hurry, but that don't plough so bad. That'd be a real nice piece of land if only I could drain it. Come a wet time that's wonderful mushy. We have to plough it on the stetch, but there, I doubt you 'on't know what that mean as you ain't done no ploughing.'

'No, I haven't,' said Everard, 'though I know what the stetch-work is. But I was just thinking how I'd like to be able to; and that field of yours is a picture.'

'Yes,' said Kindred. 'I do like the look of a bit of fresh plough. I can't deny it. But do you step over the hedge and try a furrow to see how you like it.'

Everard hesitated. 'I shouldn't like to spoil the look of your field,' he said.

90

'Oh, that don't matter,' Kindred reassured him. ''Tain't as if that was on the road for folks to see; and you 'on't do all that harm.'

'All right then, I will,' said Everard, pushing his way through a thin spot in the hedge and leaping the ditch. 'But you'll have to tell me how to set about it.'

'I'll do that, all right,' said Kindred, who had faced his horses up the field again. 'Now get you hold of the handles. What you've got to do is watch the coulter, that there knife in front that cut into the weeds – you can't see the share, 'cause that's underground; and you've got to keep that coulter allus the same distance from the edge of your last furrow – you can see the line it make; so, when you want your coulter, and becourse, your share underneath, to go to the right, you bring down your left handle, and when you want it to go to the left, you bring down your right. Got that?'

'I think so,' said Everard, desperately trying to repeat the instructions in his own head.

'Well, now, to enter your share, lift up your handles just a bit, and tell 'em to goo on. No, no, don't touch the line. Dolly'll do all the guiding. She can't go wrong 'cause she's a-walking in my last furrow. Now then, up with them handles. Dolly! Short! Goo on!' He uttered these last commands in a curious complaining tone from the back of his throat, a little like the mooing of a cow.

There was a rattle of chain harness, the whipple-trees lifted, the horses strained. There was a tiny pause while the uptilted share burrowed its nose in the stubble, and then with a soft slither it plunged underground, as the horses dropped into their stride.

'Down with them handles!' cried Kindred.

Everard obeyed, and suddenly found himself pulled away after the horses, his feet in the soft yielding furrow striving desperately to keep up with his hands, which with equal desperation strove to hold the swaying handles level. His eye was fixed upon the coulter blade in front of him and the thin wriggling line that it traced in the brown earth; he had no time to look at anything else. Kindred's voice, admonishing the team, seemed to come out of the far distance. How that line wriggled, it would set away to the right, towards the edge of the next furrow; he could not stop it, it veered nearer and nearer.

'Hey!' cried Kindred, 'Look what you're doing! You'll be out of your furrow.'

Everard groped in his mind for the remedy; it was something to do with the handles, he must veer to the left. He put his weight on the left handle. The next moment the plough was out of the ground, jolting and tearing in the bottom of the adjacent furrow.

'Woa, woa!' shouted Kindred.

The horses stopped obediently.

'No, you should have pressed the other way,' he cried. 'Right handle take you left, left take you right.'

'Like a boat's rudder,' thought Everard. 'Sorry,' he said, 'I forgot.'

'Oh, don't you worry,' replied Kindred, laughing, 'that 'on't do no harm. Only that's the worst thing to put right, 'cause you've got to hup-back to where you came out of the furrow, and you've got to drag the plough yourself 'cause the horses can't push with chains. Come on now. Hup-back, hup-back!' he called to the horses.

They backed reluctantly and awkwardly as horses always do.

'Pull now, man,' said Kindred, 'back with her!'

Everard tugged at the handles with all his weight and

brought it jerk by jerk to the spot where he had broken his furrow.

'That's heavy,' he puffed. 'I'm glad I don't have to pull the plough.'

'No,' laughed Kindred, 'you don't want to leave your furrow too often, do you? Now, do you remember about them handles this time.'

The share was entered again, Kindred shouted to the horses and Everard was off again on what seemed to him like a steeplechase for the opposite hedge. He mastered the handles this time; it was wonderful how the coulter answered to them, and he made his furrow describe a good deal more curves than was needful, displaying his skill.

'That ain't a see-saw,' growled Kindred beside him. 'Watch the coulter.'

Everard curbed his enthusiasm and the furrow straightened.

They reached the headland and Kindred stopped the horses.

'Now you've got to turn,' he said. 'You shall do it yourself. No, leave the line alone. They answer better to word o' mouth, no end. "Woory" when you want 'em to go right, "come 'ere" for left, or "cuppy-we" if you like. Now then, press on your handles, pry on 'em. Now give 'em come 'ere.'

'Come 'ere!' shouted Everard. The words sounded thin and unfamiliar, unlike his own voice. The horses did not move.

'No, man,' laughed Kindred, 'let 'em hear it – like this.'

'Come 'ere!' he repeated in his sing-song, protesting, yet ringing voice. 'Dolly! Sho-ort! Cuppy-we!' They sounded like real commands.

The horses gathered themselves and shamblingly side-stepped. The chains slackened and dropped to the ground. Nothing happened until the horses were half-way round, and then, the chains tautening suddenly, the heavy iron plough swung round on its base with an obedience which witnessed to the stress of those shambling quarters.

'Now then,' said Kindred, 'let her tilt on her side – she slip better so; you're not a-ploughing here. Goo on, Dolly! Sho-ort!'

The plough jolted idly along the headland to the beginning of the next furrow, Kindred turned the horses and almost before Everard knew where he was, he had started them back across the field. But this time Everard had command of the plough, and his feet no longer seemed to lag. The sight of the fresh furrow growing perpetually underneath his feet filled him with a blithe sense of his own power. And truly, the plough itself was a wonderful instrument with its leash of simple forces cunningly combined; the straight coulter, piercing down vertically to meet the invisible horizontal path of the arrow-headed share cleaving along below ground, and behind, the curved breast of shining steel, following close in their track and perpetually turning the never-ending slab of writhing earth clean over on its back; and the smell of earth never rose so strong and heady from the spade, he was thinking, when Kindred's voice broke on his ear.

'Woa there! Where d'you think you're going? We don't plough the hidland up, not yet.'

'All right,' said Everard, smiling back at him. He was full of confidence in his own voice now. 'Come 'ere!' he cried. 'Dolly! Sho-ort!' mimicking his teacher to the life.

'Woa there!' shouted Kindred, and roared out laughing. 'Not this time, though you got it right well. We've got to go the other way now, we've gathered enough furrows; must split some now.' He put his tongue between his teeth and grinned.

'Lord! what's that?' said Everard, scratching his head.

'Well,' replied Kindred, stroking his straggly beard, 'gathering is heaping up furrows round a ridge and splitting is knocking 'em off round a furrow, but do you plough where I tell you; that there can rest a bit.'

'I should damn well think so,' laughed Everard. 'Woory, Dolly, woory!' It was a fine, rich imitation of Kindred's shout, which, for all that it was a command, always sounded like a warning.

'Well done,' said Kindred, as the horses came round. 'Couldn't have said it better myself. We'll make a horseman of you yet.'

The plough was off again, and up and down it journeyed over the field for the best part of half an hour, with Everard turning the horses himself and Kindred trudging alongside, occasionally offering a word of guidance. Twice more he came out of his furrow, once on a big buried stone and once through his own high spirits. At last they stopped by the orchard hedge to rest the smoking horses. Away from the plough-handles, Everard felt himself infinitely small and insignificant; his wrists quivered from relaxed tension and his knees moved uncertainly.

'Well,' said Kindred, as he relit his pipe. 'I 'on't say as that'd 'xactly win a ploughing match, but I must say you make an uncommon good hand at it – for a gentleman.'

Everard winced at the qualification, but he was pleased.

'A long time since I enjoyed anything so much,' he said. 'I'd like to do some more of it; though I don't expect I work fast enough for you.'

'Quite fast enough,' said Kindred, winking. 'My two mares'll see to that. Dolly's wonderful hasty, a young 'un, she is. And you can save my owd shoulders a bit.'

'Good,' said Everard. 'What about a drop of beer? I don't think the cask's empty yet.'

'That'd go down sweet,' Kindred agreed.

'Come on then,' said Everard, making for the gap in his hedge.

Out of respect for the kitchen bricks they drank at the back door, Mrs. Quainton bringing a jug and glasses from the larder. She nodded good morning to Kindred and left them alone.

'Good beer, this,' said the farmer, handing his empty glass to Everard. 'No, no more now. Do you come down to mine one of these days and I'll give you a drop of my own, we brew it ourselves. That's not so strong; but that taste of hops, real nutty that is. And you ought to see my sheep, Mr. Mulliver. I'd reg'lar like to show 'em to you; as fine a flock of black-face lambs as you'd see anywheres!'

'Well, I'm going back to Bury today,' said Everard, 'but I shall be back on Saturday. And now I think of it, I may be going out that way on Sunday morning,' he added, thinking of a fine head of winter broccoli in his forsaken Bury garden. 'Yes, I'll be along that way then, I expect.'

'Well, you'll find me about the buildings some-where,' replied Kindred. 'I must get back or my mares'll wonder where I am.'

'And I must finish my hedge,' said Everard, 'before I leave Lindmer.'

96

They went back to their tasks. After the excitement of ploughing, Everard seemed to have somewhat less zeal for his hedge-cutting and cast frequent regretful glances through the bushes at Kindred and his team, passing and re-passing on the slope. The work, however, came at length to an end; the last bough was down, and he now had a clear view along the valley as far as the bend behind which lay Kindred's farm.

Mrs. Quainton was laying the table when he went indoors.

'You do look happy,' she said when she saw him.

'Do I?' he said, laughing.

'Yes,' she replied, 'your face is all pink and shining, as if someone had left you some money.'

'Ah, I expect that's because I've been ploughing,' he said, not displeased at hearing how he looked.

'Ploughing?'

'Yes, I ploughed for half an hour up there with Farmer Kindred,' he said proudly.

'Well I never!' she exclaimed. 'What will you be doing next, Mr. Mulliver? You're becoming a regular farmer.'

'So it seems,' he laughed, rather liking the idea. 'I might do worse.' He went upstairs to change.

He did not see her again until after his cold lunch, when he had arranged for her to come and take the money he owed her; it hardly pleased him to think of it as wages. She was cheerful again and looked better, as if her burst of confidence on Christmas Day had relieved her of a burden, and, if anything, her manner seemed easier and more natural than before, perhaps from the feeling that now he understood her. But since that afternoon neither of them had returned to the subject, Everard purposely, to allow his own words to sink more into her mind, she for fear of tiring him with her own misfortunes.

He was quite ready to go, in coat and hat, and carrying his bag, when he opened the kitchen door. She was standing by the fireplace with a shovelful of coal in her hand. She turned round with a smile as he came in.

'I'm going, Mrs. Quainton,' he said, putting his bag down on a chair.

'Are you?' she replied. 'It'll be quite strange without you, Mr. Mulliver – after a whole week, eight days in fact. I shall feel quite lost without the work to do.'

'I shall soon be back to keep you busy,' he replied, smiling. 'Here's the money, Mrs. Quainton.' He handed her some notes. 'And, Mrs. Quainton,' he added earnestly, 'I should like you to keep it for yourself.'

'What do you mean?' she stammered wonderingly.

'Why, not give it to him,' said Everard, picking up his bag.

'But, Mr. Mulliver,' she began.

'Just you think it over, Mrs. Quainton,' he interrupted. 'I must run or I shall lose my bus.' He abruptly shook her hand and hurried out of the room.

IX

DURING the ensuing week Mulliver and Son's were busy taking stock and casting up monthly and quarterly accounts for delivery in the new year. Everard, who had returned unwillingly, was weary of it all to exasperation; but despite his efforts he was unable to escape from Bury until late on Saturday afternoon, and it was well after dusk when he reached his cottage. Mrs. Quainton was all smiles and unaffectedly glad to see him when she brought the tea in, but after exchanging a few words with him, she left him to himself, expecting him, as she said, to be hungry. When she came back to clear away, he was deep in his armchair, poring over the manual of agriculture, *Fream's Elements*, which he had purchased quite early in the week and brought down from Bury. He was so absorbed in the mysteries of splitting and gathering furrows that he did not even look up when she came in, and having collected the things on her tray, she tiptoed out without a word, closing the door with noiseless precision so as not to disturb him. Later on in the evening when she brought in the supper, he was bending over a piece of paper covered with intricate lines and arrows which represented the path of his imaginary plough-share. Mrs. Quainton glanced curiously at him once or twice, but was discreetly silent, and it was only when she had finished laying the table and quietly told him supper was ready, that he seemed to notice her at all. He looked up, almost with a start, thanked her and turned to his diagrams again. He was still occupied with his books and yet another sheet of diagrams when she came in again to clear, and she went out without even venturing to say goodnight to him. He went to bed quite late that night, after consuming several sheets of paper, still rather uncertain whether what he thought was splitting was not really gathering after all, and regretfully leaving untouched such further refinements as skim-coulters, drag-chains and hake-setting.

He lay later than usual next morning, but as soon as he was downstairs he returned to his book, and though he greeted Mrs. Quainton quite cheerily when she brought in his breakfast, she did not stay to talk to him, seeing the book in his hand. After the night's rest his brain was clearer, and a little while after breakfast he found that he had really unravelled the theory of splitting and gathering; then, picturing himself on a virgin stubble with a plough and a team of horses, he laughed, wondering if he would know which way to turn. But it was already ten o'clock, he noticed, and he closed his book with a snap, remembering that he had other matters on hand, quite as interesting and considerably less difficult. He picked up a carefully wrapped, bulky parcel from the corner of his sitting-room, put on his hat and went out, descending the village street and making along the valley floor.

Ruthie Gathercole was at the bottom of her garden when Everard opened the gate, and hearing the latch click, she turned round and watched him as he came towards her up the path with the parcel under his arm. She was leaning on a Dutch hoe, he noticed, and her dark-gold hair, twisted into loose, heavy plaits, was coiled low on her ears.

'Good morning, Miss Gathercole,' he said, doffing his hat.

'Good morning, Mr. Mulliver,' she replied, with a firm, unsmiling gaze.

'I expect you thought I should never be coming,' he went on, tugging at the cord of his parcel, 'but I've been waiting for it to grow to its full size. There, what do you think of that?'

He held out to her a giant head of broccoli, fully a foot in diameter, creamy-white and succulent. She took it from him and examined it critically.

'That is a beauty,' she said admiringly; and then, at last breaking into a smile, 'That's bigger than mine was.'

Everard laughed. 'You know,' he said.

'Well, I told you I'd tell you the truth,' she said, a little reprovingly. 'That's nearly twice as big; you must tell me what seed you use. But did you grow it yourself?' she added suspiciously.

'Oh yes,' said Everard, smiling. 'I've got some more left too. You can come and see them if you like.'

'I'll believe you,' she replied, softening again.

She turned the thing over and re-examined it. To Everard watching her, there seemed a hard expression on the single sweeping curve of her full mouth, an insolent light in her dark-grey eye; but in the plump, round white cheek and firmly sloping jaw were infinite power and life. She could be cruel, he thought. Looking up, she met his gaze a little defiantly.

'Who's gardener here?' he asked.

'I am,' she replied. 'I was just turning up a few weeds.'

'Instead of combing your hair?' he suggested slyly.

She blushed and turned her head away, to his

surprise, for she had not blushed to comb it in front of him.

'Do you like gardening?' he asked, changing the subject to spare her confusion.

'Ye-es,' she replied non-committally, 'better than some things.'

'What things?'

'Well, you see,' she replied, in sudden confidence, 'when I was sixteen, mother sent me to a sister of hers who keep a draper's shop in Bures, to help her sell the tapes and buttons. But I couldn't stand that, so I came back, and mother do most of the work in the house and I have to do something, so I grow all the vegetables. I do rather like it. I ought to have been a farmer's wife.'

'Well, why don't you become one?' said Everard, thinking how proud any farmer would be to have her as she stood there, leaning on her hoe and unconsciously quickening all the supple curves of her body, the sunlight glimmering in the petal-like flesh of her neck; a lovely, lush woman, but for a slight forbidding coldness.

'I've never met one I liked,' she replied, with a contemptuous pout which showed that she would certainly not be content with what she did not like. 'Have you got any celery?' she asked abruptly.

'Not down here,' he replied. 'I came in too late for buying young plants.'

'Well you'd better have a stick of mine,' she said, turning to a bank of neatly earthed-up celery.

'I've got some nice hearts here and I don't want to cheat you over that broccolo.'

'Thank you,' said Everard.

She picked up a fork and prised out a stick which she handed to him.

'What do you think of that?' she said.

'If it tastes as good as it looks—' he began.

'Well, it have had the frost on it,' she said, 'so that taste all right.'

'A fine heart,' he said, just parting the stalks and peering between. 'I'll have that for tea today. Thank you, Miss Gathercole.'

He looked up and found her scanning his features quite intently with that cold look of hers.

'You're welcome,' she replied.

'Are you always gardening?' he asked, feeling he ought to go, but unwilling to relinquish the conversation.

'Not always,' she replied, still gazing at him. 'I goo out driving with our old pony sometimes, and always of a Sunday afternoon, if that's fine, along the Boxford road.'

Her gaze was very intent and he wondered – if it was significant.

'Always to Boxford?' he said.

'Yes, always,' she replied slowly, looking away. 'I suppose that's a habit.' She turned suddenly and held out her hand to him. 'I must now goo indoors and help mother with the dinner. Farewe—goodbye, Mr. Mulliver.'

He took her hand; it was warm and a little hard and gripped firmly; he could feel the life flowing in it. Then she ran off up the path to the house, leaving him to follow at leisure.

Everard let himself out of her gate and strolled down the slope towards the Vale Farm, wondering what was the meaning of her strange hardness of manner and what lay at the back of it. It did not frighten him, embarrass him, in the least; if anything, it drew him, touching his curiosity, though it was evident that she did not assume it with that intent; a defensive mask, perhaps, to cover her uneasiness with strangers, through having lived much alone. And what a lovely body she had, instinct with how many more times the life that was in her hand; and he could still feel that in his own fingers, as if it had passed from her into him. He could well imagine her driving alone on the Boxford road, whether from innocence or guile she had told him so; but that was of no importance to him, thinking how sweet it would be to touch her neck, to hold all her body—

The wood-like note of a sheep-bell made him turn his head and look over a gate in the hedge of the cart-track along which he was walking. There was a small knot of hurdles at the far end of the turnip field and a man seated on one of them, hunched up and pensively regarding the sheep. Everard, recognizing Kindred, turned in over the gate, and having carefully stowed his stick of celery in the hedge, brushed his way along a water-furrow to the fold. Kindred did not hear him come up.

'Hullo!' he said, turning round to find Everard at his side. 'You came pretty quiet; made me jump.'

'So did your sheep-bell,' said Everard. 'If I hadn't heard it, I should have gone on to the farm.'

'My sheep-bell,' Kindred laughed. 'Yes, I've only got one on 'em, and by rights I don't need that, 'cause my sheep are allus folded, but, to tell the truth, I like the sound of it and I believe they do too; so I allus put the bell on the fattest teg. Then if another beat him, I put it on him. Nothing like encouraging on 'em.'

Everard leant over the hurdle and laughed while the tegs trotted up and inquisitively nosed his knees.

'Nice lot of tegs, aren't they?' said Kindred. 'As good as any round here.'

'Yes they are,' said Everard, wisely nodding; though his eye judged and approved them less for their mutton-bearing virtues than as part of a simple but singularly striking landscape. The turnips were now in full growth and the deep, blue-tinged green of the leaves, fluttering a little in the breeze, completely hid the soil, like a stretch of rippling sea-water. On every side blackness bounded the view, in the distance the looming black stain of the leafless copse, nearer at hand the gaunt black lines of the hedgerows. But the sun, hovering on the edge of a bank of dark rain-cloud, burnished the colours with light and played them off, one against another, so that even the colourless hurdle-staves and the dingy fleeces of the black-faced sheep stood out brilliant in their vivid green setting. Fat or lean they would have played their part there just as well.

'But is that the fattest of them?' he added, pointing to the bell-teg. 'That chap next to him looks bigger.'

'No, he ain't,' replied Kindred, 'not by five or six pound. Do you put your hand on their backs and see.'

Everard plunged the fingers of both hands into the wool of the two sheep below him.

'H'm,' he said, quite unable to tell the difference in fatness between them; but there was something in the rough, springy, greasy, animal feel of the wool that he liked. He opened and closed his fingers on the two handfuls that he held until the sheep backed shyly away from him, and then gave them a parting tap on their shiny black snouts.

'Yes, he's the pick of that bunch,' affirmed Kindred. 'I must set out a few more hurdles now for tomorrow's feed.'

He slid off his seat, and picking up half-a-dozen hurdles on the end of a pole and slinging them on to his shoulder, lumbered off to the other side of the fold.

'Oh, you might fetch the fold-drift along,' he called over his unladen shoulder.

'What's that?' asked Everard, quite uncomfortably ashamed of his ignorance.

'Oh, that there iron bar on the ground,' came the reply.

Everard picked it up, a grim, heavy tool with a solid, spear-shaped head surmounted by a round, cup-like disc. Then there followed a short lesson in fold-setting, taken by Everard rather than deliberately given by Kindred. Everard soon picked up the knack of plugging a deep hole for the post and a shallow nick for the hurdle foot. The fold-drift, just vertically dropped, bored through the yielding soil almost by its own weight, a satisfying tool that fitted the hand; the flat of the disc served to drive the post home without splitting; a thrust of the heel served to steady the hurdle. The new fold was soon up, and Everard, looking down upon this brief work of his hands, could not help seeing a certain beauty in the simplicity of its construction; one end of each hurdle strained to a post with a loop of string, the other end overlapping against the end of the next hurdle, in its turn strained to the next post, and so on all the way round the four several sides of the fold.

'Funny how you hold the fold-drift left-handed,' said Kindred, as they seated themselves on a hurdle again, lighting their pipes and knocking their feet together to shake off the clinging soil.

'Do I?' said Everard. 'I hadn't noticed.'

'I must get some more hay down here,' said Kindred.

'You want it with turnips, they're nearly all water, you know.'

They smoked reflectively for a few minutes, watching the sheep busily nibbling the roots and tugging at the hay in the wooden racks. There was nature at work before the eye, in the never-ending exchange of fertility, sheep gnawing fatness from the earth, earth sucking back fatness from the sheep.

'Sheep are a wonderful nuisance at times,' observed Kindred, stroking his moustache with his pipe-stem, 'specially in hot weather time, but I like to have 'em on the place. They do the land no end of good and I just like pottering about with 'em, they get to know you like. I'd have three times as many if ondly that wasn't so damp on this owd land.'

'Yes, I suppose so,' said Everard, wondering why dampness should be harmful to sheep, 'but can't you drain it?'

'Well,' said Kindred, 'that'd cost more money than I could afford, and if I could do it, what'd my landlord do but put my rent up after? I wish that was my own. Then I'd drain it by hook or crook. That's a queer owd farm, but I like it somehows. Me and my father afore me, we've farmed that this sixty year. Let's come and have a glass of beer. I've just tapped a new cask.'

They clambered down off the hurdle and sauntered slowly across the fields to the farm.

'That want the carpenter,' said Kindred, jerking his thumb at the rickety barn. 'Just pass the broom round your boots. My Emma's a tartar for mud.'

Emma Kindred, tall as her husband and built to match her height, was an imposing figure, made still more imposing by the bristling old-fashioned corsets which helped to support her amplitude. Her face was

107

smooth and round and comfortable, and her pale blue eyes twinkled kindly as she exchanged civilities with Everard and went off to draw the beer.

'Ah, Mr. Mulliver,' she said, coming back with the jug, 'when I seed you together crossing the midder, I said to myself, "Bob have been making that gentleman work and I reckon them two'll be wanting some beer."'

She looked several years older than her husband, and her harsher speech, already growing more and more uncommon in the district, was a survival from a still earlier generation.

'Funny,' said her husband, filling the glasses, 'but he hold a fold-drift left-handed, just like our William.'

'I didn't know you had a son,' said Everard.

'Nor we haven't,' said Mrs. Kindred a little sadly. 'He was killed in the War – about your age he'd be now and about the same build, ondly not so good-looking, becourse.'

'Yes, he do remind me of William a bit,' said Kindred. 'The way he handle horses too. He'll make as good a hand at plough one day, I reckon.'

'My beer can't stand up to this,' said Everard to check the flow of compliments, and gazed critically at the clear orange-brown liquor in his half-empty glass. 'Just like a crisp filbert.'

'That's just what I say,' said Kindred. 'That's a feather in our cap, Emma. Drink up, Mr. Mulliver, and have another glass.'

'Ah well, he must come and try some of my bullace-and-blackberry jam one day,' said his wife, 'and see if he like that. I doubt you've not tasted that before, Mr. Mulliver.'

'Oh yes,' said Everard. 'Mrs. Quainton made some out of my own bullace.'

'Well, did she pick the blackberries in September or October?' asked Mrs. Kindred.

'October, I think,' he replied.

She shook her head ominously. 'Do you be careful, Mr. Mulliver,' she said. 'At the end of September the devil breathe on all the blackberries and they're reg'lar p'ison to the innards after that. Do you be careful, now.'

'Well, I haven't suffered much so far,' said Everard, smiling. 'My digestion's in excellent order.'

'Ah, there's more ways than one of p'isoning the innards,' she admonished, with a severe countenance, not to be laughed out of her belief, which in truth she held quite sincerely. 'Do you look out.'

'Perhaps yours will serve as a cure,' said Everard, to make amends for his levity.

''Haps that will,' she replied, ''haps that 'on't. But you must come and have a cup of tea with us – some day when I've baked a cake. My goodness, there's my greens a–b'iling over!'

She rushed away to the kitchen stove.

'Time I went home,' said Everard, seizing the occasion. 'My dinner'll be waiting for me. I shall be along next Saturday. P'r'aps you'll have a bit of ploughing to do, Bob?'

'Oh yes, I reckon we can find you a bit,' said Kindred. 'Don't, there'll be some harrowing or rolling. Going down to *The Olive Leaf* tonight?'

'Well,' said Everard, 'I don't know. Perhaps. Good-bye, and thanks for the beer.'

'You're welcome. Farewell, Mr. Mulliver. See you tonight.'

A well–spent Sunday morning, Everard told himself, as he threaded his way along the stream back to the village, with the stick of celery under his arm, conning over in his mind the succession of minor experiences which had made him so contented. He had enjoyed every one of them, digging his fingers into the rank, live sheep's wool, gripping the smooth, shiny handle of the fold-drift, pecking holes, ramming home posts with it, digging his heels into the soft moist earth, and then just sitting on a hard, ridgy hurdle-bar, gazing and smoking meditatively. All these things, when he recalled them, seemed to exert a slight pull on him; he felt conscious of being closer to something – he could not tell what – that had somehow done him good; he wanted to repeat these experiences. That good light bitter beer, too, was a fitting conclusion to the morning, rounding off this fruitful sense of spiritual content with a soothing bodily satisfaction; and there was Mrs. Quainton's good dinner yet to come. And then, with childlike artfulness reserved to the last, there had been Ruthie Gathercole. It would be quite possible for him to take a walk to Boxford in the afternoon, though she might think him forward, and he had done no gardening that day: on the other hand, if he waited until next Sunday, she might think him backward. He would wait till after dinner to decide; she looked more beautiful with her hair loose over her shoulder.

He was so possessed with this last thought when he opened his front door and passed through the kitchen to his sitting-room, that he did not speak to Mrs. Quainton, who was standing at the stove warming plates, and hardly noticed her when she brought in the roast pork, which he proceeded to eat in the same state of abstraction. It was broken at last by quite a violent rattle on the window-pane. He looked up. The afternoon's problem was solved; it was raining hard.

He was taking up *Fream's Elements* from the table when Mrs. Quainton came in to clear.

'Oh, I shall be late for supper tonight, Mrs. Quainton,' he said, calling to mind *The Olive Leaf*, 'so don't wait for me.'

'Very good, Mr. Mulliver.' She opened her mouth to say something else, but perceiving that he was no longer looking at her, shut it again and flitted silently out of the room.

Everard opened up his book and began to read.

'Suffolk. These short-woolled, black-faced and horn-less sheep, which originated in the crossing of horned Norfolk ewes with improved Southdown rams, have been recognized as a pure breed since 1810. Points . . .'

X

'DO you know, Mr. Mulliver, it's nearly a fortnight and you've hardly spoken a word to me.'

Mrs. Quainton's voice was almost tearful and she looked at Everard reproachfully. Everard, who had been sawing wood in one of the outhouses, carefully deposited his armful of logs on the kitchen floor and, putting his hands on his hips, gazed contemplatively at her.

'Haven't I?' he stammered. 'Why no, I haven't said much.'

'I should think you hadn't,' she said severely. 'I almost thought you'd forgotten I existed at all.'

Everard scratched his chin.

'Well, it's like this,' he began rather lamely. 'You see, I did some work with Bob Kindred ploughing and setting out hurdles and I wanted to find out more about it, so I bought that book and I couldn't put it down. The fact is, Mrs. Quainton, I'm quite in love with farming.'

'Oh,' she replied rather tartly, 'but that didn't prevent you from spending all the evening at *The Olive Leaf* last Sunday.'

'Still,' protested Everard, 'Bob Kindred asked me to go, and we talked about farming most of the time.'

'You're always going there now, Mr. Mulliver,' she said reprovingly.

'Why, what's the harm of a glass of beer and a smoke and a chat?' he asked.

'Oh, I don't know,' she replied a little pettishly, 'you get into the habit and then you can't keep away. Besides, you're a gentleman, Mr. Mulliver.'

'Not down here, Mrs. Quainton,' said Everard. 'I reckon I earn my pint as well as any honest man here. But really, Mrs. Quainton, I behave myself. I don't come home drunk.'

'No – well.'

She was obviously not satisfied, and for a moment he was tempted to resent this uncalled-for rebuke. Then, remembering Steve Quainton, he softened; she might well moralize even upon so innocent a pastime as drinking at an inn. He laughed.

'No, Mrs. Quainton, I won't go to the bad, I promise you, and I'm sorry I didn't speak to you last week. I won't forget another time. Do you forgive me?'

'Yes, I forgive you.' The corner of her mouth lifted in her wry little smile, as if even now she were not quite sure whether to believe him or not. 'I've got something to tell you, Mr. Mulliver.'

'Yes, Mrs. Quainton?' He leant back against the kitchen table.

'You know you told me to keep that money you gave me last week?' she began.

'Yes,' said Everard.

'Well, he didn't ask me for it that week, I don't know why. P'r'aps he'd won at cards and was flush of money. Anyhow, on Monday night he did ask me.'

'And what did you say?' said Everard, gripping the edge of the table hard.

'I said I was going to keep it myself. "It doesn't cost you anything for me to work there, and you don't help," I said, "so I don't see why you should have it. I want some clothes; I'm tired of patching."'

113

'What did he do?' said Everard.

'He swore a good deal and spat on the floor till I was nearly sick, and I've been used to a great deal; but I wouldn't give way.'

'Good!' exclaimed Everard.

'"All right," he said, "I shan't give you any more housekeeping money, that'll learn you."'

Everard bit his lip.

'I hardly slept that night,' she continued. 'I didn't want to give way, and yet I couldn't think what to do; and then just before I did go to sleep – I heard four strike – I thought of something. I got up early next morning and made myself a cup of tea, and then I started to get ready for the washing – it had rained on Monday, you remember, so I hadn't washed then. Well, about an hour after he came down. "What, no fire?" he shouted, "and where's the breakfast?" "I haven't lighted the fire," I said, "and I'm not going to get the breakfast. We'd better save what's in the cupboard if I'm not to have any more housekeeping money." He called me no end of names, but I said nothing and he got his breakfast himself. I can tell you, I was shivering with fright the whole time, wondering what he was going to do. I didn't think I should have the courage to hold out; but I couldn't bear the thought of giving in.'

'Well done!' said Everard.

'Well, that evening,' she continued, 'he came home late and I went to bed early without getting the supper ready, with my heart in my mouth, as you can guess. I heard him drive home and put the trap away, open the door and clatter some plates and knives on the table, getting his supper. Then he came upstairs and into the bedroom. He walked over to the bed and bent over me with the candle. I pretended to be asleep, but my heart beat so loud, he must have heard it. He watched me for quite half a minute, then he went away and undressed and got into bed without saying anything. I hardly slept again that night for terror. Next morning I got up first again and went downstairs, and I was just wondering whether I should dare to refuse to get his breakfast when he came down into the kitchen half-dressed and slapped the housekeeping money for the week on the table and went upstairs again without a word; and there's not been a word since.'

'That's splendid, Mrs. Quainton,' said Everard. 'You see you really are brave, aren't you?' He was genuinely surprised at her courage.

'I'm so glad you think so,' she said, suddenly brightening up. Then her expression grew wistful. 'I did it to please you.' She coloured a little and then stammered, 'I mean, I don't know what I should have done if I hadn't been able to tell you about it; it's been hurting me all the week. It's so difficult to be brave unless you've got someone to be kind to you.'

Her half-intentional admission did not escape Everard, but he spoke as if he had not noticed it.

'Yes, I know,' he said sympathetically, 'and I'll help you all I can. Still, you've got the courage, Mrs. Quainton, and it shouldn't be a difficult task.'

'What task, Mr. Mulliver?' She opened her eyes wide, as if in surprise.

'Why, of rebelling further and further,' he answered, regarding her steadily, 'until you're quite free. Your husband's like one of those noisy, yapping dogs that slink off when you turn round on them.'

A fearful, half-desperate look shot into her eyes.

'Oh, don't speak of it, Mr. Mulliver,' she said. 'I

couldn't go through a night of terror like that again. And all the things he said to me – not that I haven't heard them all before, you know. It does seem a shame to be always treated like that and never have a moment of pleasure. I've never really lived at all.' She was unconsciously repeating Everard's own words, but she turned them to feed her own self-pity. 'When I think of it, I wonder how I bore it all, and yet somehow I've learnt to put up with it. Don't you think it's a shame?'

Her eyes were filling and Everard was afraid she was going to cry. He wanted to encourage, but that did not soothe her, she wanted sympathy; it was not to be wondered at after fifteen years of brooding alone on her griefs, and such griefs. He was painfully sorry for her; and yet he did not want to yield to her mood, but to wheedle her out of it.

'Of course it's a shame,' he said indignantly, 'and that's why you mustn't put up with it any longer, Mrs. Quainton. It's no use going over and over what you've suffered. It'll never change him. You must learn to hate instead.'

'Yes, I suppose so,' she replied, looking sadly up at him. 'Only, you must forgive me for bothering you with all my troubles. I've never had anyone to tell them to, and now I've begun, I can't stop.'

'You know I don't mind,' he said gently, 'but you mustn't let your troubles worry you. Think what you're going to do with the money. Go into Bury and get some new clothes.'

'Oh, Mr. Mulliver!' She put her finger on her lip. 'Do you think I could?'

'You could do anything you wanted to,' he replied, 'if you only dared. Besides, if you have any trouble with – him, just you call me.'

She shuddered. 'I couldn't do that, Mr. Mulliver.'

'Why not?'

'Why, he'd think all sorts of things and I don't know what he'd do. He's terribly strong.' She shook her head.

How she wavered, Everard thought, and opened his mouth to reason with her; but catching sight of the fearful look once more in her eyes, he restrained himself.

'Still, don't worry,' he said quietly. 'It'll come right soon.'

'Do you think so?' she asked incredulously.

'I'm sure.' He smiled at her and she returned his smile with a wistful but trusting look.

'Now, Mrs. Quainton,' said Everard, 'laugh, come along, out loud.'

They burst out laughing in each other's faces, and Everard returned to his wood-sawing.

For half an hour he worked savagely as if to keep pace with his thoughts: for although before Mrs. Quainton he had been calm enough, the conversation had thrown him into a curious state of excitement, in part due to the success of this first step in her liberation – far more than he had hoped for – and in part to her naive little confession that she had only been brave to please him. It was not unnatural perhaps, after so many years with no kindness to repay, and he had been kind to her; but that did not prevent him from taking it also as a compliment to himself. Perhaps, too, if she went on being brave to please him, she might learn to be brave for her own sake. Then the memory of her frightened eyes and her sudden wavering checked his exuberance. Clearly she needed slow and gentle urging; a premature flare-up with Steve Quainton might cow her for good and put her beyond all further persuading. But now, at least, he saw the nature of his path and began to wonder what the next step would be. Meantime, however, Steve Quainton still had access to her, he could still ring her dark eyes—

Everard swore out loud, and gritting his teeth, began sawing more furiously than ever to vent his loathing, as if each log that rolled from his sawing-stool were one of Steve Quainton's limbs, the sawdust spurting in showers from his saw.

'How hard you're working!' said Mrs. Quainton, appearing suddenly in the doorway. 'Do you know,' she said, coming inside the shed and smiling up at him, 'I feel so much better now after telling you all that – almost happy.'

All the strain had gone out of her face and her eyes were serenely bright. Everard patted her gently on the shoulder.

'I'm glad,' he said. 'Is tea ready?'

XI

IT was a misty mid-January afternoon when Everard started out for his first walk along the Boxford road. It was freezing hard, although little rime was to be seen on the grass-stalks, freezing with a dull, pitiless cold that sank into the flesh and numbed it. The mist hung like a colourless fleece, quenching all shape but the black outline of adjacent hedges; the road rang flat and meaningless to the foot like a counterfeit coin; all nature was lifeless and only the elm trees, their frozen twigs a maze of ghostly filigree, were beautiful. It was not a propitious afternoon for a walk, but Everard, having been twice thwarted by circumstance – in the form of rain and an invitation to tea at the Vale Farm – was only the more set on seizing the first opportunity that offered. There was something quite peculiar in the singleness and insistence of his desire to meet Ruthie Gathercole. He had not once questioned its prudence nor debated its genuineness; to nothing in his life was it comparable except the undeniable urge which had brought him to Lindmer; to feel it was to obey. The disappointments of the two previous Sundays had only goaded him further, and although he would have been more comfortable in front of his sitting-room fire, or more usefully occupied laying out his neglected parterre, he doggedly turned his face to the road.

The road was deserted – even the village street had been empty, except for a little boy at a gate who had stared and said hullo – and the fear crossed Everard that perhaps Ruthie Gathercole, too, would prefer an after-noon by the fire to a drive in such bleak, forbidding weather. If she came, at least they would have the road to themselves. A startled bird fled at his approach, as if it were ashamed to be seen on such a day, and the whir of its wings was an outrage to his ear, straining for the sound of hoofs. A mile further on he stopped to listen. There was a faint sound in the depths of the mist, at first like the muffled tap of a distant woodpecker, and then gradually resolving itself into the loose rhythm of a slow-trotting pony, followed by the rasp and rattle of iron-tyred cartwheels. He peered into the greyness but could see nothing: nor could she, if it were she, until she was almost on top of him, but the sudden recogni-tion would be less embarrassing than sighting each other at a distance. The sound of wheels and the stroke of hoofs merged into one confused clatter, and a high dogcart rolled out of the mist into view. Everard's heart beat hard. The driver lolling on the high seat was a woman, and he recognized her as Ruthie Gathercole more by her height and build than anything else, for he had never seen her in a hat before. At the sight of a pedestrian she drew off the crown of the road towards the hedgerow, and as she came level, Everard looked up and raised his hat.

'Good afternoon, Miss Gathercole,' he said.

She stared down hard at him as she passed, and recognized him with a start. She fumbled hesitantly with the reins for a moment, and then pulled up sharply a few yards ahead of him.

'Why, who'd have thought of seeing you here, Mr. Mulliver?'

'Or you?'

Neither deceived the other, but politeness was satisfied.

'Are you going to Boxford, Mr. Mulliver?' she asked gravely.

'I thought of going that way,' he replied with equal gravity.

'Can I give you a lift?' she said, symbolically shifting to the end of her high seat.

'Thank you, I'd be glad,' he answered, doing his best to keep the eagerness out of his voice, but succeeding ill.

He climbed up hastily into the trap and swayed down beside her as the pony ambled off. She did not trouble to urge it into a trot, and for some minutes they watched the rise and fall of its quarters, tongue-tied and abashed with their proximity. Then, as on the brink of blushing, Everard's cheeks began to tingle; he could feel her eyes upon his face, furtively scanning its details – the square chin, full lips and long, straight nose, the calm, high forehead over wide-set, still, dark-blue eyes. He went on desperately gazing at the pony's quarters, his heart thumping louder every second, and he would have blushed outright if she had not broken the silence. It was a relief to have an excuse for looking at her.

'What brought you out on an afternoon like this, Mr. Mulliver?'

He shrugged his shoulders.

'I just came out for a walk,' he said nonchalantly. 'And you?'

'I always come this way,' she replied.

'Did you come this way last Sunday?' It was an unnecessary question.

'Yes, and you went to Vale Farm,' she answered, as if to justify it.

'How did you know that?' he asked quickly.

'I saw you from our window after I came back,' she replied, idly tugging at the lash of her whip. 'We can see right down to the bottom of the valley. It was wet the Sunday before,' she added irrelevantly, but not without understanding.

'Yes, it was,' said Everard thoughtfully.

They were silent for a minute or two, during which Everard's eye travelled approvingly to a well-shapen ankle and a firmly rounded calf, revealed by the slipping of the black horse-rug from her knee. Her flight from the draper's shop in Bures had evidently not precluded a taste for silk stockings and short skirts. She, too, seemed to notice them, for she gathered up the end of the rug in her hand.

'Put this over your knees,' she said. 'It's cold.'

The rug was short, and Everard, to cover his own knees, had perforce to draw closer to hers; but she did not object.

'Do you like the Kindreds?' she asked rather perfunctorily.

'Yes, very much,' he replied. 'Mrs. Kindred's a good soul and she makes lovely cakes. Last Sunday she was talking about witchcraft; she said she knew an old woman who witched a little girl lousy and another who witched a scythe blunt.'

'My mother tell tales like that sometimes,' she said, smiling for the first time. Her dialect was softer and less pronounced than that of the Lindmer folk, as befitted the daughter of a yeoman farmer; but it was Suffolk speech.

'I like Bob Kindred too,' Everard added. 'He's a good fellow, and he's taught me to plough.'

'So I saw yesterday,' she said, with a half-scornful smile.

'You see a lot from your window,' said Everard.

'Well, I can't help it, can I?' she said, 'if you will goo and plough right in front of it.'

'No, I suppose not,' said Everard, laughing too.

'What did you think of my furrows? It was very hard going, but I ploughed half an acre.'

'Well, I couldn't tell your furrows from the rest,' she said.

'Now you're flattering me,' he protested.

'The other furrows were crooked,' she mocked.

They both laughed out loud and then looked away from each other, silent, until they reached a fork in the road with a grass-grown track leading off into the fields between high overhanging hedges.

'Let's goo down here,' she said, bringing the pony's head round. 'It's rather a nice old lane.' It was certainly not the road to Boxford.

'So it looks,' said Everard, not caring where she took him, so long as he could remain beside her.

'What make you goo ploughing with Farmer Kindred?' she asked, turning to him.

'Well, I like it,' he replied. 'Heavy work like that suits me somehow. I like being out in the air, and there's so much to show for it all when you've finished – just as you like gardening, perhaps.'

'Yes, yes,' she nodded, 'I think I understand; I do like gardening.'

'And then,' he went on, 'it's a real pleasure to go striding along behind those lovely Suffolk horses, guiding them and the plough too; it gives you such a wonderful sense of power over things.'

'Do you like showing your power over things?' she asked, a little critically.

'Sometimes,' he answered.

The wheels of the trap lurched on over the ruts, jolting them from side to side and constantly flinging their bodies together. Everard could feel the warmth of her soft, yielding thigh creep into his veins; her knees pressed tightly against his. For some minutes they drove on in silence, the girl gazing abstractedly at the pony's ears, Everard casually eyeing the hedges as they slowly took shape from out of the mist and then merged into dimness again. They were two long ranks of ancient hawthorns that could not have seen the knife for twenty years, arching down over great curved buttresses of briars and brambles; here and there a downy white tuft of old man's beard, a bough of yellow, frost-bitten crab-apples or a cluster of pale, rose-coloured spindle-berries stood out against the prevailing blackness as a meagre reminder of their summer luxuriance. What a place for blackberries, he thought, and those arching hawthorns, it seemed every moment as if their pendent branches must meet overhead.

The mist was settling ever thicker upon them as they rounded a little jutting shoulder in the lane.

'Look out!' cried Ruthie Gathercole suddenly, ducking her head and dragging on the reins.

Something hard and black shot into his face; he shut his eyes and felt something tear across his forehead; his hat fell off backwards. The pony stopped, and as soon as Everard opened his eyes he turned and saw Ruthie stretched out over the back of the seat with her hat off and her hair caught fast in a bristling blackthorn branch. She was still clutching the reins.

'All right,' he cried, 'keep still! I'll untangle you.'

He reached up over her head and weighing down the branch with one hand, began to unravel her thick plaits of hair from the thorns with the other. She lay

124

perfectly still, watching him through half-closed eyes. The branch was so thick with thorns that it took him several minutes to extricate it. At last, however, all seemed clear and he let the branch go, but as it sprang up with a swish, an overlooked twig snatched one of her plaits up with it and the whole mass came tumbling down. Everard looked down at her. She still lay there with half-shut eyes and lips parted, her bosom faintly heaving, a thick skein of her soft gold hair in his hand; her body hung limp against his shoulder. Everard's breath caught and he dropped his mouth to hers.

After a long, sweet kiss he raised his head and gazed down at her. All the mockery, the scorn, the hardness, the almost cruelty had gone out of her face; in the flushed, ever so slightly distorted features and languid, unseeing eyes the only expression was of vague, helpless ecstasy; the utter weakness of that look, touching in its unexpectedness, entranced him. He smiled and brushed her soft throat with his fingertips. She turned her head, opening her eyes wide, and stretching out an arm drew his head down again.

Half an hour later she was gathering her plaits together and blushing a little as Everard shyly watched her.

'Have you been showing your power over me?' she said huskily, with a sly, sidelong glance at him as she pressed the last pin home.

'Or you over me?' said Everard, taking hold of her wrist.

She pouted, then turned and kissed him softly on both cheeks.

'Why, you're all blood!' she exclaimed, pointing to the scratch above his eyebrow.

'That was the thorn,' he said. 'It doesn't hurt now,

but it's left a stain on your temple. Let me wipe it off.'
He took out his handkerchief.

'No, no,' she said, seizing his hand. 'I want to keep
that for myself.' She kissed his torn eyebrow.

'I'll get your hat,' said Everard, leaping down from
the shaft.

'You might turn the pony round while you're
down,' she said, taking the hat from him. Everard
obeyed. 'We shan't get to Boxford today, I think.' She
smiled as he mounted again.

'I never set out to go there,' Everard confessed
boldly.

'No, nor did I,' she whispered, shyer.

They drove back with Everard's arm tight round her
waist, exchanging a glance now and then, but saying
nothing. When they reached the Boxford road, she
pulled the pony up short, prudence having succeeded
the first careless rush of passion.

'I think you'd better walk home from here,' she,
said. 'Do you mind? I don't want anyone to know.'

'As you wish,' said Everard with a sigh, loth to leave
her warm side.

'Yes,' she said anxiously, 'we mustn't meet on the
road again. There's the copse behind our house – all to
ourselves, you see?' She gripped his hand.

'Tonight, then?' said Everard.

'No, not tonight, next—'

'Next Friday, then?'

'Yes, there's an empty cowshed at the far end – after
tea – soon.'

He nodded reluctantly. 'It's a long time.'

'I know that is,' she replied, 'but, but – I don't know
your name, dear.'

'Everard,' he said.

'Everard, Everard,' she repeated it, trying the sound on her lips. 'Goodbye, Everard,' she said, holding up her mouth.

'Goodbye, Ruthie.'

He clambered down; she shook the reins and was swallowed in the mist.

XII

EVERARD'S shrunken weeks in Bury had already lost most of the importance and reality they had ever possessed for him; they were just periods to be passed through, endured and got rid of, until the weekend came round and life began again. But no week had passed more slowly or seemed more unreal and unimportant than that which followed his drive with Ruthie Gathercole. With the best will in the world he would sit down to his correspondence or his coffee-blending, and straightway he was back in that narrow misty cartway or, anticipating, in the unknown but imaginable cowshed on the edge of the copse. The events of last Sunday were such as no inward re-enactment of them could render threadbare, and certain memories never failed of their sweet sting. Then, as he came to earth again and the soft thick plait in his hand turned to a coffee cup or an invoice, he would laugh at himself and thank his stars that his father, Albert Mulliver, had built up the business on so sure a foundation. Its organization was so complete and harmonious, its staff so long-established and trust-worthy, and its custom so assured, that it would survive far worse neglect than his, and at least he was not squandering its resources. To tell the truth, some of his activities were all but superfluous; for even had he entrusted the blending of his tea and coffee to the chief cashier, the coarse palates of most of his customers would hardly have known the difference. He little repented, therefore, of the time he wasted; but occasionally he could not help wondering at the delicious state of tenseness in which he found himself; nothing, nobody that he could remember had ever moved him so before.

In spite of their tediousness the days passed. Thursday night came, and he went to bed, happily excited because the next day would be Friday. Early after lunch he was back in Lindmer and spent all the afternoon at work, laying out the turf paths for his parterre. The garden had not had much of his attention since Christmas, and he worked hard on his paths, telling himself that he would soon need all his time with the vegetables for sowing and planting, and perhaps laying down an asparagus bed, such time, that is, as would remain over from his ploughing and fold-setting excursions on Vale Farm. He laughed, remembering that his prime duty and occupation in coming to Lindmer, as he then saw it, had been to create a garden. Still, whatever happened, his little parterre with its wiry grass paths, its rose bushes and beds of old-fashioned perennials, once done, could be left largely to itself. Roses, lavender, marjoram and thyme would bloom and smell sweet, his strip of massed marigolds, self-sowing and self-sown, would more than satisfy his appetite for colour; and all they asked was a little weeding now and again.

He smiled at his own wisdom. With body and mind thus bent together on the task, it was easier to store up for later enjoyment his thoughts of Ruthie, now that she was within easy reach, and the afternoon passed quickly enough. However, he knocked off early and went indoors to spruce himself up before tea.

'You sound cheerful, Mr. Mulliver,' Mrs. Quainton

laughed, as he passed through the kitchen, humming a tune.

'Well, so do you, Mrs. Quainton,' he replied, noticing a happy ring in her laugh.

'P'r'aps I am,' she replied, as he disappeared.

When he came downstairs, she had already brought in the tea, and he did not see her again until he was half-way through the meal, when she tapped at the door and opened.

'Oh, Mr. Mulliver!' she exclaimed, 'I'm so sorry. I thought you'd finished.'

'It doesn't matter, Mrs. Quainton,' he answered, though thinking she had not allowed him much time for the meal. 'Come in and sit down. I've nearly finished.'

She shut the door, by no means loth, and walked across to the fireplace, where she remained standing.

'Well,' she said, quite brimming over with smiles, 'what do you think of them?'

'What?' said Everard, lowering his teacup.

'Why, my new clothes,' she said.

'Why, of course,' he exclaimed. His mind had been so full of other things that he had not noticed them before; now he understood why she had been so impatient to clear the table. 'I thought there was something strange about you, but I couldn't make out what it was. I must come and look at you.'

He got up from his chair and joined her at the fireplace where she stood, still smiling, with her arms stiffened a little, self-consciously showing herself off. The new dress was in two pieces, jumper and skirt, of pale-grey knitted, silky stuff. She turned round under his eyes to show him the back with a little giggle, obviously much excited.

'That's really magnificent,' he said admiringly.

'Do you think so?' she asked eagerly.

'Really.'

'And look, I've got some grey silk stockings to match,' she added, holding back her skirt and pointing down at her feet, like a child proudly displaying its new toys, 'and I had to buy a new pair of black shoes.'

'You couldn't have chosen better,' he replied. She certainly had excellent taste. 'Where have you—'

'But, Mr. Mulliver,' she interrupted anxiously, still holding back her skirt and looking down at her legs, 'tell me, do you think the skirt is long enough?'

It was well below her knees, though several inches shorter than she had been accustomed to wear.

'Of course it is, Mrs. Quainton,' he replied. 'You've no cause to be ashamed of your legs, I can assure you.'

'Haven't I?' she queried, still examining them critically, as if incredulous, and then blushing with embarrassment. 'But, Mr. Mulliver,' she went on, looking up at him again in spite of her blushes, 'I want you to tell me whether the whole thing is too young for me or not. I was terribly nervous about buying it.'

'Why, I was just going to say, Mrs. Quainton,' he said enthusiastically, 'that it makes you look ten years younger.'

'You're flattering me, Mr. Mulliver,' she expostulated.

'No, I mean it,' said Everard. 'Those other clothes of yours added years to you. These suit you perfectly, and make you look as young as you are.'

She flushed again, this time with pleasure.

'I do want to believe you,' she faltered diffidently. 'I did like it so.'

'Indeed you can,' Everard assured her. 'I wonder if

131

you know how bright and happy you look. You should have bought them long ago. You're glad you kept that money, aren't you?'

'Yes, I am,' she admitted, 'and look how it matches the necklace you gave me at Christmas. I thought of that when I bought it.'

'Oh!' said Everard a little awkwardly; he had not expected his beads to play such an important part.

'I went on Wednesday,' she continued, 'by the Bury market bus. I was terribly frightened about going, but I remembered you said I could if I dared. And he wouldn't know, I thought, because he'd already gone out and I should be back before he was. So I dressed and went out into the street to wait for the bus, but when I saw it come over the top of the hill, my heart went pit-a-pat and I turned back to go indoors again. But the key stuck in the lock somehow and I couldn't get the door open; and I couldn't stay out there and make a fool of myself, so I took the bus, and everything was all right after that.'

'I told you so, didn't I?' laughed Everard, puzzled that her courage in big things should so fail her in little. 'Of course it was all right – once you had won over the money.'

'Still,' she demurred, 'you mustn't forget it's years since I've been so far by myself. But I enjoyed the ride and I looked at all the shops and I saw that dress in the window and I had to buy it, but I was so nervous about it, till you told me what you thought of it. Then I had something to eat and bought my shoes and stockings, and looked at more shops till it was time to catch the afternoon bus back.'

'Did you see my shop?' he asked.

'Yes, I passed it,' she replied, 'and I peeped in and

there you were, standing in the middle, looking very tired and angry, as if you wished all the people would leave you alone.'

'I expect I did,' replied Everard. 'I generally have to come down and look at things on a market day, but why didn't you come in and speak to me?'

'Oh, I didn't dare do that,' she said hastily. 'You might have turned me out. You wouldn't want to see me.'

'Of course I should,' he protested. 'It would have been such a change in that dreary place; and I might have given you the packet of China tea I forgot to bring down with me this afternoon.'

'I wish I had, then,' she replied, her eyes brightening with pleasure. 'I shall know another time.'

'I'm glad there is going to be another time,' said Everard. Her smile betrayed assent. 'Has he seen you in your new dress?' he added; he, too, had fallen into her way of alluding to her husband.

She shook her head.

'I haven't worn it before today,' she explained. 'I wanted you to be the first to see it. I have you to thank for it,' she added quickly.

'Thank you,' he said.

'He won't see it till Sunday now,' she went on. 'I'm going to take it off before he comes home. I don't suppose he'll say anything. It doesn't matter if he does,' she ended, in a little burst of defiance.

'That's the way to talk,' said Everard approvingly. 'I am so pleased. You must go on looking young like that.' He was genuinely impressed by the change in her appearance.

'Then I'm pleased too,' she said gratefully.

Everard looked up hastily at the clock.

133

'Good heavens!' he exclaimed, 'I must be off; I've got to go over to Vale Farm.'

'Oh, I hope I haven't kept you,' she cried in dismay.

'No, quite all right,' he said reassuringly. 'I've got time, but I must be off now. I might be late for supper, Mrs. Quainton.'

He hurried out into the street, pulling on his overcoat as he went, and at the bottom of the hill turned furtively, although it was already dark, into the path along the valley. Mrs. Quainton had kept him and although the fault was all his own for letting the time slip by so carelessly, he was really a little annoyed, for fear lest Ruthie should take his lateness at this first assignation amiss. She might not even wait for him, or that hardness of expression, half-critical, half-perverse, which last Sunday he had seen completely put to flight, might return to her features; she might scold him, or worse, taunt him in that cold way of hers, and although he knew how to parry it in words, at heart he dreaded it, having experienced her warmth. In his haste and anxiety he almost broke into a run. He crossed the track that led up from Vale Farm to Mrs. Gathercole's cottage, fearing to be seen by some chance visitor to the farm or even Kindred himself, and slipped up along the hedge of the turnip field to the side of the copse. Leaping the ditch, he plunged in among the trees and then halted, suddenly conscious of his own uncertainty concerning the whereabouts of the cowshed. The far end, she had said: if he pushed straight in he was almost bound to strike a path or, failing that, the other side of the copse, which he knew to be narrow. He plunged forward again, dry twigs cracking ominously under him at every few paces; she might think him a poacher for all the noise he was making. He smiled into the darkness as he parted his way between two enlaced hazel bushes and the boughs sprang together with a snap behind him; there was the path at last, hard and level. He looked this way and that in the darkness; his road must be to the right. There was a rustle of leaves behind him, a tall, dark form glided out of the bushes and next moment there was an arm under his arm, a warm hand clasping his hand and Ruthie gazing up into his eyes, though in the darkness neither could see the other clearly. She clung tight against his side for a moment without speaking.

'I'm late,' he mumbled at last, apologetically.

'Still, you're here now,' she replied. 'I heard you shuffling about in the leaves. Had you lost your way, dear?'

'I'm not sure,' he faltered. He was almost surprised at his own sense of relief that she was not angry with him. 'I was going to the right.'

'No, that's the wrong way,' she said in a teasing voice. 'Come you along with me. I won't lose you.'

She drew him gently down the path beside her without waiting for the kiss he was turning to give her, and unable to see her face, he felt a slight misgiving that perhaps she was angry after all. They trudged along over the damp fallen leaves, saying nothing, but holding very close together; there was a nip of frost in the air. The path made a sudden curve and came to an abrupt end between two gate-posts on the edge of a ploughed field. The dim outlines of a thatched roof towered above the hedge.

'There it is,' she said, loosing his arm and taking him by the hand. 'The entrance is round the other side, and it's rather muddy; so do you follow me.'

She led him by the hand round the side of the building, leaping from island to island in the mud.

135

'There you are!' she exclaimed, as they set foot on the firm, dry floor. 'I wonder if you'd have found it.'

Everard looked curiously around him; as far as he could see, the place was in good repair, the posts all standing and no holes in the thatch.

'But why don't they use it?' he asked.

'Well, so they did,' she replied, 'till a few years ago; and then Farmer Kindred ploughed the pasture up. That's why that's so clean, and so quiet too. They only use it for storing a few things, like that harrow by your foot. See those faggots over there?'

She pointed to a small dark stack in the corner which he could just distinguish through the darkness.

'They've been there a long time,' she said, 'and I hope they won't take them away.'

'Why?' said Everard, bewildered, and still holding on to her hand as his only guide in this strange place.

'Because we're going to sit up there, dear,' she replied. 'It's quite dry and so much warmer than down below; and I've already been up and spread the horse-rug on top. You know, mother think I've gone to Boxford to a dancing-class.' She laughed softly.

'How you do think of everything!' said Everard admiringly. 'You're wonderful.' He stroked her hand.

'Well, you see,' she replied, 'I've known the copse and the shed inside out ever since I was a child. Besides, if anybody do come into the shed, they won't notice us up there.'

'I suppose I mustn't strike a light up there,' he said all at once, putting his hand in his pocket.

'No, no,' she said apprehensively, 'you'd burn the place down.'

'Then I'll strike one down here,' he said, taking out a match.

'But you surely don't want to smoke now,' she expostulated.

'No, no,' he said, laughing. 'I only want to have a look at you.'

As he struck the match, a pocket of faint, fluttering light swelled out into the darkness between them and played upon her face. He could just see the flush on her cheeks and the gleam in her eyes as she stared back at him; her lips were parted, tremulously weak and soft; then the match flickered out. All his fears melted away.

'Are you satisfied it's me?' she said, with a pout that he could not see.

'Yes, it's you,' he replied, laughing.

'Come along then,' she said, walking over towards the wood-stack. 'I'll show you the way to climb up.'

She put her foot on a loose faggot, and catching hold of a ring in the wall hauled herself up into the manger; from there she clambered up on top of the stack, having already removed one of the faggots to form a step. Everard followed close upon her heels, but not close enough to help her, and she needed no help.

'There,' she said, as they knelt down on the horse-rug, the dry boughs crackling under them, 'don't you like it?'

He looked round at the dusty beams that hedged them and smelt the thin, strawy smell of the over-hanging thatch; the dry, enclosing warmth of it was unmistakable.

'It's lovely,' he said. 'So much cosier than that old lane, Ruthie.'

He laid his hands on her shoulders, she took his neck in her hands and they drew close together; but at first she only gave a burning cheek for him to kiss, as if that were all she could bear; then slowly she turned her cheek against his lips until they met her own, which were trembling beyond control; she gasped aloud as they kissed again.

Then her strength returned to her, and she held him at arm's length as they knelt facing each other in the darkness, caressing his face in her hands; Everard stroked her hair.

'We're like two animals,' she said with a little laugh.

'Are we?' he said.

'Yes,' she replied, 'haven't you seen two horses nose each other – to see if they're all there and still the same?'

She ran her fingers over his eyelids, down his cheeks and across his lips. 'You haven't altered, dear,' she added. 'Still the same face as last Sunday.'

'Are you glad?' he asked.

'Yes,' she answered faintly.

'Your hair is still the same too,' he whispered, burying his fingers in her plaits. 'Only I like it best down.'

'Do you?' she said. 'Wait a minute.'

She hastily pulled out some pins and with both hands scattered the whole sheaf loose around her shoulders. She bent her head towards Everard and he wreathed his face in her tresses. This was the simple wild creature, the hardness all a mask.

XIII

WINTER yields unwillingly to spring and March was niggardly with signs of the ascendant year. Early blackthorn flower and willow catkins hung delicate clouds of white and gold in the hedges; brave little coltsfoot stared wide-eyed and leafless out of the faded grass; blackbirds and thrushes sang of love among branches which were swelling with bud. But Everard was already impatient for the real spring and warmth in the sky as well as light, the hedges all green and the orchards down by the village white with blossom. Nevertheless, he had enjoyed this winter at Lindmer more than any he could remember. Out in the fields at plough he saw it in place with the rest of the year; the long respite from growth became natural and necessary; he was doing the work of the season and this striving with the earth and showing himself its master was in itself a deep, exhilarating satisfaction. His team came swinging down the slope, with the share rasping busily behind them; he turned at the headland, and while he paused to breathe the horses, bent down to alter the set of his hake, the part of the plough which takes the tug of the draught-chains and so helps the plough-handles to determine the path of the share. He slipped the pin along the rack another hole to the right, to counteract the lie of the land. These little niceties of adjustment gave him a feeling of importance; he knew the points of a good furrow now. He was about to set off again up the slope when Kindred, who was harrowing on the other side of the field, stopped his horses and came over to him.

'Time to jack up now, Mr. Mulliver,' he said. 'We'll go home and have a cup of tea now; we've done a good bout today.'

Everard nodded and Kindred looked critically up the field.

'You know, that's a wholly good bit of plough,' he said, turning to Everard again. 'I couldn't tell those furrows from my own and I've been ploughing close on fifty year. That's a marvel to me how you do it.'

'Well, it surprises me too,' replied Everard, leaning up against the plough-handles, 'when I think about it.'

'It fare to come natural to you, somehows,' added Kindred.

'Yes, I wonder,' Everard mused. 'You know, Bob, it may be because it's in my blood. My father was born in the country and his mother, I know, was a farmer's daughter, and when I was a youngster, I always wanted to farm, though I forgot all about it afterwards till I came to Lindmer.'

'Ah, I reckon that's the thing of it,' agreed Kindred, slowly filling his pipe, 'but that's an uncommon bit of luck for me. What you've done today's a real help. I shall be able to get this bit drilled next week. I wish you'd let me pay you for it.'

'I ought to pay you for the pleasure I get out of it,' Everard laughed, 'so we're quits, aren't we? Besides, you didn't charge for teaching me to plough.'

'I don't know so much,' grumbled Kindred. 'I pay the three men as work for me, and they don't work harder'n you – not so hard neither.'

'Still,' Everard argued, 'I'm always stopping down at Vale Farm for tea, you know.'

'Lor!' what's a cup o' tea?' exclaimed Kindred contemptuously. 'That ain't no more'n hospitality. We're right glad of a bit of company, and my old Emma have wholly took a fancy to you, Mr. Mulliver. You're like that there boy of hers.'

They smoked in silence for a while, Everard still leaning against the plough and watching the horses switch their flowing, sand-coloured tails, Kindred staring on the ground with his hands on his hips.

'I see,' said Everard, by way of setting up the conversation again, 'there's a flock of forty ewes going near Bildeston. There's an auction notice up outside *The Olive Leaf.*'

'Yes, I know,' said Kindred, looking up, 'that's old Harry Godbold. His wife have died, quite sudden like, and he can't bear to stay in the farm no more. I hear he'd sell 'em private like before the sale if he could – along o' their lambs, at five pound the couple.'

'What are they like?' asked Everard.

'Oh, wonderful good they'd be,' replied Kindred enthusiastically. 'He allus kept a good flock – though these last years he've sold off a good few – getting old like. I'd rare like them forty on my land. They do no end of good to the land, what with the manure and the trampling firm, and it come cheaper breeding your own lambs.'

'Why don't you make him an offer?' said Everard.

Kindred shook his head a little sadly.

'Things are too tight,' he said. 'That'd be close on two hundred quid, and I know he 'on't break 'em up. Now if that was only twenty—'

They both stood and thought for a minute.

'Yes, nice ewes,' Kindred murmured regretfully.

'Tell you what, Bob,' Everard broke out. 'How'd it

141

be if you and I went shares in that flock? – you say you could manage half the money. Then I could go shares in their keep and help you with 'em when I come down at weekends.'

Kindred's eyes brightened.

'I don't like risking your money, Mr. Mulliver,' he demurred.

'That's not risking,' said Everard. 'I could have a share in the profits, and I should like to do something right on the land. I should be really happy if I had some sheep of my own. Then you wouldn't feel I was giving you my labour for nothing.'

'No, no, that's so,' admitted Kindred, 'but I some-hows don't like to let you; that's too wholly kind of you. Them forty ewes – they're good enough to give us sixty lambs, I know.' His mind was already at work, contriving and planning.

'Of course,' said Everard, knowing that he would give in. 'Well, what about it?'

'Well, if you're set on it,' began Kindred haltingly, and a grin spread over his face.

'I am set,' said Everard, 'so that's finished.'

'Well, that'll be wholly fine,' said Kindred, half to himself. 'I've allus wanted a flock of ewes. You're a good 'un, sir, and no mistake.'

'Still, I reckon you're the only farmer in Lindmer Vale or anywhere else,' laughed Everard, 'who'd go shares with a chap like me.'

Kindred was looking away across the valley at the opposite slope, thoughtfully stroking his beard.

'I wonder,' he muttered, 'I wonder.'

'Wonder what?' Everard queried.

'I was thinking of that piece of summerland over there,' he explained. 'You see, we shall have to scheme

142

a bit to make feed for all them animals. Now that piece of summerland up there, that'd do right well for a bit of rape and turnips; only that'd be so wet for the ewes. That have got a tidy good slope, and you'd think the water'd run off. But that don't. Come a rainy season, the water lie about in puddles, and that's all swarmed with cattail however hard I try to clean it. That's heavy owd land and that want draining.'

'Why couldn't it be drained?' said Everard.

'Well, that's landlord's business,' said Kindred, – 'not that I'd mind putting in a drain or two myself. That wouldn't need money; only there's the pipes.'

'Are they dear?' asked Everard.

'Yes,' he answered slowly. 'Becourse, that could be bush-drained.'

'What's that?'

'Oh, you dig down two spits,' he replied, 'and then instead of putting down drain-pipes you put in a layer of bushes. Becourse, they rot after seven year or so; but while they last, they drain it. But then, that's a lot of labour.'

'Still,' Everard suggested, 'you could manage with-out that field till, say Christmas, and suppose you and I did it together, a bit at a time, when I come down at weekends; we'd get through it.'

'Yes,' agreed Kindred ruminatingly, 'we could. That wouldn't take such a terrible long time neither. I've allus got something else for my men to do, and somehow I've never been able to face that alone. But that's stiff owd work, a-digging with the spade.'

'Well, shall we do it?' said Everard.

'If you'd help,' said Kindred, smiling, 'I reckon we might. But mind, I didn't speak of it for that.'

'Well, that's settled,' said Everard. 'It looks as if

143

we've got our work cut out for the next few months.'

They both burst out laughing.

'I'm a-losing heat,' declared Kindred. 'Let's go and have a cup of tea. That's near five o'clock time.'

They unhitched the horses and trudged down with them to the farm.

Mrs. Kindred that afternoon was in a railing mood, which was her way of showing affection.

'What a time he do take a-prinking,' she said, pointing to Everard, who was washing at the kitchen sink. 'You'd wholly think he was going a-courting.'

'Well, I am,' replied Everard brazenly.

'No good telling me that,' she retorted. 'There's some grand lady a-waiting for you in Bury, I know. Becourse, you 'on't never bring her down here to see you at plough, nit nothen like that.'

'I think you're rather hard on me,' protested Everard. 'I've done your man a good day's work.'

'Ah, that man,' she cried, 'I know him; he'd get work out of a tom-cat, he would. You mind out what he do.'

'And you mind I don't best him,' said Everard. 'We've done a deal this afternoon.'

Bob Kindred, as they sat down to tea, related their projects to her, full of high spirits.

'Well there!' she exclaimed, 'if that isn't wholly fine! I wish you were foreman here, Mr. Mulliver. That's just what my Robert want. This last ten year have he been a-talking about draining that there field, but he've never had the heart to do it. Do you keep him up to it. You'll be a farmer yit, I can see.'

'I wonder,' said Everard.

'Well, do you eat a good tea anyhow, Mr. Mulliver,' she replied, looking critically at his glistening red cheeks. 'You don't fare as if you ate half enough. You must try some of this damson cheese.'

The men fell to heartily; ploughing sharpens the appetite.

'Why 'on't you stay to supper?' complained Mrs. Kindred, when, just before seven o'clock, Everard rose from his chair by the fireplace to go.

'Not tonight, thanks,' he replied. 'I must give an eye to my house in the village.'

'Well, another night then.' Mrs. Kindred wagged a finger at him. 'But let me give you a glass of beer afore you go.'

'No, thanks,' he said, edging to the door. 'It's too soon after tea.' A full hour had passed since the meal; but the beer would make his breath smell.

'All right,' cried Mrs. Kindred disapprovingly, as he opened the door, 'but mind you hurry home; that's going to freeze tonight.'

Everard did hurry, but not homewards. He took the track up the hill and then, leaving it for a field-path that was now familiar to him, struck across to the end of the copse. The church clock was just tinkling the hour through the frosty air when he found himself in front of the cowshed; he had gauged the time nicely.

Ruthie was waiting for him in the entrance, peering out into the night under her hand.

'See, I'm not late, Ruthie,' said Everard, smiling. 'Listen.'

'No, dear,' she said, 'but I was here ten minutes ago, and it's so cold.' She put her arms round him and kissed him softly on the cheek. 'Come along, Everard, it is so cold.'

She led him over to the wood-stack and let him help her up to the manger; she did not need his help, but she liked the strong, supporting thrust of his arms and he, too, liked the soft, weighty swing of her body against him, dependent on him. Up they climbed to their accustomed hollow, quite deep now with use; they folded the rug over them, warm and enveloping, and began to murmur to each other in the darkness. It was her habit to tell him all the little things that had filled her week, the vegetables she had planted in the garden, the drives she had had and the things she had seen, a little like a child giving an account of itself to its parent. Everard, in turn, would tell her how he had passed the day out with Kindred on Vale Farm or in his Lindmer garden – of Bury he never spoke and she never asked. Then, like two thirsty children, they sought and found each other's lips and kissed a whole hour away, sometimes with soft, quivering kisses of exquisite, half-frightened gentleness, sometimes with deep, hot, searching kisses that did not seem to know what they searched and never reached it. Or perhaps she would let loose all her hair over his face and tie it behind his head while he stroked her neck, the flower-like whiteness of which he could almost feel through his fingertips. So, night after night, for two months they had caressed each other, now ardent, now gentle, but asking no more of each other. Having once perceived her essential simplicity, Everard had taken her just as she came to him, without any thought of reading her mind, because his own needs were simple, and no one had ever so soothed and lulled his senses. He came to her, his body sated and relaxed with strenuous labour: Ruthie, by the quiet, caressing virtue of her presence, sated and relaxed his senses; he felt complete. Vaguely, at the back of him, he guessed that he could provoke her to more violent ardours; but loth to shatter the atmosphere of tranquillity and restfulness in which she enveloped him, he shrank from these thoughts and hid them deep away in his own mind. In her strong, unplayful tenderness there was something almost maternal; that was what he, because of his own thwarted, unloved childhood, hankered after.

But tonight Everard noticed a difference in her: her kisses were drier and more burning, her embraces closer and more straining; even the air about her seemed made tense. At last she lifted her hair from his face and he could feel her eyes looking down upon his through the darkness.

'Now, I'm going to send you away, Everard, my darling.' She spoke rather solemnly, dwelling upon the last two words in a way that startled him a little; they were neither of them lavish with their endearments. 'I'm going to send you away tonight and you mustn't come back till next week. Do you hear, Everard, do you hear?'

'Yes, Ruthie, I hear,' he whispered. Yet even to him her words sounded far more as if she were repeating them for her own good. 'But why, dear?' he asked, gripping both her hands tight in his.

She let go quite a desperate sigh.

'Because, because—' she began, and paused. 'Because I mustn't be out every night or my mother'll begin to wonder. Not that that matter much; but I'd rather she didn't know. And besides, you ought to spend more evenings in your house; people'll wonder about you too.'

'Then I shan't see you till Easter, Ruthie,' he complained. 'Can you be so hard to me?'

'Or to myself?' she added, almost bitterly. 'Yes, I can, Everard. You will do what I tell you, won't you?

I'm going to kiss you.' She brushed his lips with her own. 'Now let's get down,' she said.

'It's so cold,' he remonstrated.

'I know,' she said, 'and you've got to walk all the way home through it, poor Everard. But I've got something in the manger for you. There's a little spirit-stove and some tea in a tin saucepan that I stole out of the house. Aren't I wicked? Come along, my dear one.'

Unwillingly he clambered down from the stack and she followed him with the horse-rug. She put the saucepan over the stove and took a cup out of her coat pocket.

'Do you hold that,' she said, 'and give me a match.'

She took the box he handed her and struck a light, holding the match still before her face a moment, to allow the flame to gather. Everard gave a little cry of surprise.

'Why, what's the matter, Ruthie?' he said.

'Why?' she replied unconcernedly, as she bent down to light the stove.

'You look quite haggard,' he said, 'and your eyes are all ringed.'

She laughed, half to herself, still busy with the stove.

'I love you, Everard,' she said, with a calmness that seemed almost like resignation.

Everard remained silent. She loved him, and now it occurred to him that she very well might. But she had not asked him if he loved her, and he was instantly grateful to her. He could not have told her, he himself did not truly know, what was the quality of his feeling for her. That it was something natural was sure enough; the force which drew him to Ruthie was quite resistless, like the force which drew Ruthie to him, two dear wild creatures, that was all he knew – but was that love?

They watched the saucepan, hand in hand, their fingers twined together.

'There, that's hot enough,' she said, taking the saucepan off and filling the cup. 'Drink that up, my darling.'

'So warm,' he gasped between his sips.

'That'll warm you home,' she said.

She blew out the stove and watched him.

'A drop for you?' he said, holding out the cup.

'Yes, dear,' she answered, 'but give me the side you drank from, Everard.'

He twisted the cup round for her, and taking it, she drank from the spot where his lips had touched, just a sip. Then she suddenly let the cup drop on a faggot and threw her arms round his neck. Her mouth folded hot and clinging upon his; her body hung upon him close and heavy, so that he was at once aware of all that it was, round and yielding, soft and firm, throbbing, alive. With equal suddenness she sprang away from him, gathered up stove, saucepan and horse-rug, and walked away. At the gateway she turned and walked back to him; then, standing close to him, she kissed him ever so softly on each cheek.

'Goodnight, Everard darling,' she said. 'Come you back on Good Friday. Farewell.'

'Farewell, sweetheart,' Everard whispered.

He followed her slowly out of the shed: he knew now what was the matter with her.

XIV

EVERARD stood up straight for a moment to ease his back, and bent again to his steady, deliberate raking on the little black patch of ground beside the back door of his cottage, facing south and the most sheltered spot in the garden. In spite of his new distractions, the little parterre was now laid out and, so far as possible, planted; the vegetable garden was at least as neat and full as any other in the village, and with that he had regarded his duty to the garden as ended. But only the previous morning, as he stood gazing at the empty spaces between his clumps of sage, thyme and lavender, the inveterate gardener in him had felt a pang of remorse at his neglect, and with it an instant, over-powering temptation to sow all the annuals he had for-sworn as unnecessary. A few slender spikes of rampion would brighten up those blank spaces with their demure pale-mauve bells – rampion rhymed with campion and yet the poets had wasted it; some night-scented stocks, too, he must have for the summer evenings, and all the salad-herbs, the names of which had so frightened Mrs. Quainton; it would be worth while, too, to grow a little angelica of his own and teach her how to candy it, and then, perhaps, some sweet marjoram and, of course, some coriander.

Accordingly, that evening, after an early tea, he had taken out his rake to prepare as much as he could of the seed-bed while the light lasted. It had not been altogether easy to filch even this scanty hour for it, and he had had to be very firm with Bob Kindred. That same morning, determined to lose no time, they had driven over to Bildeston and struck a bargain with Harry Godbold for his ewes. The rest of the day had been spent in getting them over to Vale Farm and settling them into their new quarters. Then, when all their backs had been carefully prodded and their other fine points judiciously admired, Kindred was for carrying Everard off to the Vale Farm for tea; Emma would never forgive him if he came back alone; but Everard, remembering his seed-bed, had been firm.

But even now Everard's mind was not on his seed-bed, nor was he tasting in imagination the warm thrill of ownership he had experienced as he watched the newly purchased ewes, his ewes, timidly nosing the turnips in the strange fold. He was – not unnaturally – thinking of Ruthie Gathercole, just one simple, isolated thought, which ousted from his mind all the others which she might well have aroused in it. Last night, when he had felt the proud curve of her bosom crushed against him, he had wondered if that, too, would have the softness of her throat to touch, and he had not ceased to wonder ever since. It would not be difficult to find out. He leant upon his rake and shut his eyes.

'Hey, Mr. Mulliver!' came a hearty voice across the fence. 'You going to sleep already?'

Everard opened his eyes and looked round guiltily. It was Runacres, standing in the road with a small sack under his arm.

'Hullo, Henry,' he replied. 'I was just feeling a bit dizzy, that's all.'

'You've been working too hard, Mr. Mulliver,' said

151

Runacres reprovingly, 'that's what that is. Do you come here. I've got something for you.'

Everard walked over to the gate and Runacres handed the sack across to him, his voice dropping to a whisper.

'You didn't get no real sport,' he said, 'when you came a-ferreting with us that Sunday; so I thought you might like this for your Sunday's dinner.'

'No sport?' said Everard. 'What about Jim Farrow?'

'Still,' grinned Runacres, 'you replaced young Missie Gathercole's broccolo; do you take that and welcome.'

'You didn't get that with a ferret,' said Everard, smiling as he peeped down through the mouth of the bag at a fine plump hare.

'Maybe I didn't,' replied Runacres with a sly wink. 'But I know you 'on't go telling no policemen or gamekeepers.'

'Thanks, Henry,' said Everard, 'it'll suit me nicely for tomorrow. That's very kind of you.'

'Welcome, I'm sure,' said Runacres, dismissing the subject with a wave of his hand. 'We shall be starting quoit matches soon after Easter, and we want a few games now of an evening like, to get our hands in. I met Jim Farrow and Tom Cobbin up in the village, and they're coming along "What about a fourth?" Tom say. "I'll now go and ask Mr. Mulliver if he'd like a game," I say. You'll come along, 'on't you?'

'Well, I want to get this seed-bed finished,' Everard began.

'Why, that can wait, Mr. Mulliver,' said Runacres scornfully. 'You can rake that down before breakfast any morning. Besides, what with them sheep and ploughing and all that, I reckon you've been working too hard like, Mr. Mulliver. You mustn't go getting dizzy like that. All work and no play – you know.'

152

'Well, well, p'r'aps I will,' said Everard, lifting up his rake; debarred from Ruthie, he felt the need of company tonight. 'Just let me put these things away.'

A minute later Cobbin and Farrow joined them at the cottage gate, and all four men walked down to the quoit ground, which was in the corner of a small meadow behind the inn under two old willow-trees. Farrow and Runacres raised the two small wooden hatches which covered in their bed of soft clay the iron pins at which the quoits were pitched.

'Now, who's going to play agin who?' said Runacres.

'I don't want to play agin Mr. Mulliver,' said Tom Cobbin, scratching his scrubby chin. 'I don't forget how he beat me at darts and I had to stand drinks.'

'I must have a good partner,' said Everard, 'I've never played the game before.'

'Tom's all right,' said Jim Farrow, 'but don't you look at his eye when he throw. That's enough to frighten anybody. He look one way and throw another.'

'All right, I'll take you, Jim,' said Runacres. 'Jim's a devil with the quoit, Mr. Mulliver. Do you watch. We'll have to hurry up. That'll soon be dark.'

For a few minutes the throwing was somewhat erratic, the game being the first of the season. Then, as they began to get their hands in, the quoits came closer to the pins, and at last, more by luck than anything else, Everard scored the first ringer.

'There, didn't I tell you so?' cried Jim Farrow. 'I knowed he'd be a good 'un. Now you're going to join the club after that, aren't you, Mr. Mulliver? We have several good matches every year.'

'Well,' Everard demurred, thinking of the evenings that it would waste, 'I haven't much time to spare, you know.'

'Why yes, I reckon you can give us an hour or two at the quoits,' said Runacres. 'We hardly ever see you now. You haven't been in at *The Olive Leaf* these two months. We reg'lar miss you. Why, only the other night we were talking about it, weren't we, Jim?'

'Yes, that we were,' agreed Jim, 'and you say "Mr. Mulliver's allus down at Kindred's now." You mustn't cut yourself off from us, sir, now the fine, light nights are coming.'

They were coming, Everard reflected, and perhaps if he never joined them, they might suspect that there was something more than the Vale Farm to keep him away; and though he wanted all those fine, light nights with Ruthie, it might be well to give up some of them to have the rest undisturbed.

'Well, Jim, I'll do my best,' he said. 'Here's my shilling.'

'I'll enroll you tonight, Mr. Mulliver,' piped Jim, with as much importance as he could muster.

The game went on and the shadows began to fall; it was becoming difficult to see.

'Last throw now, Jim,' said Runacres, strolling up to the other end. 'We'll jack up arter this. Do you make it a ringer.'

'All right, Henry,' said Farrow, 'but do you put a finger down on the pin to guide me. I can't see that no more.'

'All right,' said Runacres, bending down and touching the pin. 'Do you put it there, Jim.'

The cobbler took very long and careful aim. There was a rumble of wheels from the road, and the other three all looked round, just in time to see Steve Quainton in his trap go splashing through the ford in the shadows. The man's presence, even at a distance, turned them sour at once.

'There go that surly bastard,' said Tom Cobbin.

'Last night,' growled Runacres, 'he came home drunk as a bloody owl, reeling all over his trap.'

There was a whir in the air and a heavy iron quoit came down on Runacres' finger with a thud. He leaped up with a roar, jamming the finger into his mouth.

'You clumsy little swine, Jim!' he shouted, as soon as he could find his tongue. 'What the hell did you want to throw like that for? I reckon you've brook my finger.'

'Well, you said "Put it there,"' protested Jim, 'and I thought you could look arter your own finger. And now you've gone and spoilt my ringer and lost us the game.'

'Blast the game!' said Runacres. 'What about my finger, you damnation fool?'

'That's not brook, is it, Henry?' asked Farrow in an awe-struck voice.

'No, but that bloody near is,' answered Runacres.

'Jim Farrow's a devil with the quoit,' said Tom Cobbin maliciously, 'and no mistake, ain't he, Henry?'

'He's a bloody fool too,' snarled Runacres.

'Now, lookye here, Henry,' protested Farrow, 'that wasn't me said that; that was that jim, Tom Cobbin.'

'If you ask me,' Everard broke in, 'it's Steve Quainton who's to blame. The sight of him put us all out of our stride, I reckon.'

'Ay, you're right there,' said Runacres, forgetting his grievance, 'that'd make any man throw crooked, that would.'

'But I tell you that was straight as a pole,' persisted Jim Farrow, who would not hear his skill disparaged at any cost. 'That was a fair ringer.'

'Well, my finger ache like hell,' grumbled Runacres.

'Yes, I reckon that's just like how my buttock felt,'

said Farrow, not without a suspicion of triumph in his voice, 'the day your ferret got his teeth into it.'

Runacres swore volubly.

'Come on, Henry,' cried Cobbin. 'You and Jim have got to stand us two a quart this time.'

They put the hatches down over the pins and trailed over to *The Olive Leaf*. The whole story of Runacres' finger had to be retailed for the benefit of Mr. Chinery, the landlord, and Runacres swore all his oaths again in a lower, more guttural key.

'That's all right, Henry,' said Mr. Chinery cheerfully. 'You'll just lose the nail, that's all.'

'H'm, and lost us the game too.' The protest issued so faintly from under Jim Farrow's trap-door of moustache that Runacres affected not to hear it. Peace descended upon the company once more.

'Did you ever hear that story about Tom,' said Runacres, by way of changing the subject, 'when he used to work for the miller down on the turnpike?'

'No,' said Everard, looking up suddenly. He was just calling to mind how dark the shadow had been beneath Mrs. Quainton's eyes that morning, but he had not paid much heed to it then, having so many other more agreeable matters for reflection; she had looked quite ill – and Steve Quainton had come home drunk last night. With an effort he brought himself back to the company. 'What's the story, Henry?' he said.

'Why,' said Runacres, 'he went there as a lad to pull the weeds off the mill-wheel.'

'No, that was to tie up the sacks,' Tom corrected.

'Ah yes, I forgot,' continued Runacres ironically, 'and old Gathercole – he was alive in those days – he take some beans down there to be ground. Well, he come along agin in the arternoon.'

'That was the evening,' said Tom Cobbin, stickling for accuracy.

'Well, the evening then,' said Runacres, accepting the correction, 'and Tom, he come up to old Gathercole quite innocent like and he say, "Oh, Mr. Gathercole, do you know, them beans o' yourn were so wholly hard, we had to put acorns with 'em, to make 'em grind." "Oh," old Gathercole say in his short way, "did they now? Well, boy, come you up to *The Olive Leaf* and have a drink." And he stood him a pint o' mild, and that was the first he'd ever been known to stand in his life. But Tom, he got the sack next morning.'

There was a general laugh in which Tom himself joined; he was secretly a little proud of the story.

'Ah,' said Mr. Chinery, 'but do you remember how he became a knacker's man?'

On any other night so reminiscent Everard would not have been able to tear himself away from the inn before closing-time; but ever since the game had finished, Mrs. Quainton's eyes seemed to hover in front of him and he could not listen to the conversation. He got up abruptly, mumbling something about letters to write, and made his way out despite the company's protests.

'You've not been here five minutes,' said Runacres.

'You haven't drank your beer, Mr. Mulliver,' called Chinery. But he went out, nevertheless.

Mrs. Quainton was in the kitchen, mending a hole that he had inadvertently burnt in the tablecloth with a cigarette-end; she greeted him perfunctorily. Everard stopped in front of her, and looked at her eyes; they were lustreless and despairing, and ringed with purple, sagging lines. She raised her head enquiringly under his gaze.

'I thought you didn't look well, Mrs. Quainton,' he said huskily.

'No, I thought you'd notice it,' she said dully. 'I expect you know why,' she added, looking at him meaningly.

He nodded. 'I heard he was drunk too,' he said.

'Yes.' She shuddered.

'My God!' He bit his lip and shuddered too, in his pity half-suffering her hurt. 'This must stop,' he said savagely.

She looked on the floor and fidgeted with her needle.

'Do you know, Mr. Mulliver,' she faltered, 'I'm afraid of something else too. Suppose I had another baby.' She looked up at him boldly now. 'Wouldn't that be terrible? Of course, I do my best always and I've been very lucky, but ever since my little boy died, it's been a continual dread to me. I can't bear the thought of it. I loved my first, in a way, but a second, I'm sure I should hate it. His child, ugh!' She shook her head in disgust. 'One's quite enough to live in misery.'

'Indeed it is,' Everard burst out; then, checking himself, continued in a quieter tone. 'You know, there's only one thing to do, Mrs. Quainton.'

'What's that?' she said, looking doubtfully at him.

'Separate rooms,' said Everard. 'You've got another bed, haven't you?'

She shook her head decisively. 'I couldn't, I couldn't, Mr. Mulliver. He'd kill me, I know, he'd kill me. He's never been denied in his life. There are some things I can't do.'

'Better be killed, then, than half-killed,' he rejoined.

'Yes, you're right,' she replied tragically, settling down to her blank despair again.

'Still, Mrs. Quainton,' he said, 'he wouldn't kill you; he's not got the courage – remember about the money. Suppose you just told him what you were going to do, and left your window open, handy, so as to call me. I'd slip in if he gave any trouble. He'd think twice then.'

She shook her head again. 'I couldn't have you coming to any harm, Mr. Mulliver, for my sake. And even if you didn't, I couldn't bear it. You don't have to live with him. It's best just to submit and pray to go blind and numb and senseless; and then one day you die and there's the end.'

'Oh, it hurts me to hear you talk like that!' he cried.

She looked up at him for a moment, a little startled by his vehemence, and then sighed.

'No, no, Mr. Mulliver,' she said, 'I shall get over it. I've learnt to put up with these things and I must go on putting up with them. It's not so often now as it used to be. Hark!'

A muffled shout came across the garden from the house next door.

'That's the man,' she said, biting her lip. 'He wants his supper.' Her resentment overcame her. 'The beast, the pig!' she exclaimed. 'It isn't fair, is it, Mr. Mulliver, at my age?'

'It's an outrage, it's a crime,' he protested, eager to inflame her resentment.

'Your supper's all laid now,' she said, 'I'd better go and keep him quiet.'

'Yes, don't let me keep you,' said Everard mechanically.

She put her finger on her lip.

'Wouldn't it be awful, Mr. Mulliver,' she said, with a terror-stricken look on her pale face, 'if I had another baby? I believe it would be a pig.'

'It's unthinkable,' said Everard.

She blushed suddenly, and hid her face.

'The things I say to you!' she cried, and dashed out of the house.

Everard went into the parlour and threw himself huddled into an armchair. How could he give her courage?

XV

EVERARD, cautiously skirting the hedge, rounded the last corner of the copse and halted in surprise as the empty cowshed came into view; it was the first time he had seen it at close quarters by daylight. There was nothing strange about the shed itself; it was all that he would have expected a cowshed to be, with mossy thatch and massive joists above a dilapidated manger and the drab wood-stack that he had so often scaled. What really startled him was that it should be daylight at all in this spot which he had only known in the darkness. Then, forgetting that he was also half an hour early for his assignation, he reminded himself that the nights were getting lighter, as Jim Farrow had pointed out less than a week ago; and that itself was only one among the many signs, all round him to see, that spring had really and truly come to Lindmer since he last left it. The sharp little apple-green leaves piercing their sheaths on the hawthorn and the abounding chorus of bird-song within the copse told him the same; but, above all, the air, softly, caressingly warm, and, besides the scents which floated into it from the earth, laden with a pure, living sweetness of its own − the air was full of the spring. These things Everard now took in for the first time that day, although he might well have observed them earlier, in the morning descending the village street after the Good Friday service, or in the afternoon as he sat beside Bob Kindred on a hurdle and

161

gazed at their forty black-faced ewes with their lambs beside them. But although Everard's body was in the midst of spring, his mind was far away, dwelling with Ruthie Gathercole and the particular engrossing speculation which her last embrace had aroused in him; all his actions had been mechanical, in the nature of a device for passing the intolerable time, he had seen without seeing and heard without hearing.

He turned, and looking again at the wood-stack, missed the warm horse-rug with which Ruthie had always come well beforehand to spread it; it looked cold and unkind in the daylight. He had come far too early, but he could not help it; nor perhaps could Ruthie, who at this same moment had stolen up to his side, without the horse-rug. Neither surprised at the other's earliness, they both stared shyly, almost abashed at the sight of each other's faces, bare in the light, untempered by dimness. They did not, as at other times, draw together in a greedy embrace, but still stood there, awkward and tongue-tied.

With an effort Everard groped for his voice.

'How long it is since we last met!' he stammered at last.

'Yes,' she replied, 'seven whole days.'

The seven longest days of his life they had seemed, and of hers too; Good Friday was like a release from purgatory, but they dared not speak of these things.

'And so much happened,' he said – to themselves and all things.

'Why yes,' she answered, echoing his thought, 'spring have come.'

'See how light it is already,' said Everard, looking forlornly at the wood-stack.

'Yes, let's go for a walk,' she said impulsively. 'We

162

can't go up there yet; and there won't be anyone in the wood now.'

'Good,' said Everard gratefully; she had voiced the thoughts that he had been afraid to utter, himself dreading that cold, naked stack of wood.

They left the shed side by side and walked slowly to the edge of the copse, where both of them, seized with a sudden clumsiness, tripped on a fallen bough, so that they lurched together, wrist to wrist. They laughed a little self-consciously and then, as if prompted by their touching fingers, they linked hands and swung them idly to and fro as they entered the copse, looking away from each other.

'Look at those primroses,' said Everard at last, to break the silence which lay upon them like a crushing, stifling cloud, and thinking how limp and moist she must find his hand; Ruthie was thinking the same of her own.

'Yes, aren't they lovely?' she replied, snatching eagerly at a handle for conversation. 'Everything's coming out, isn't it?'

'Yes,' said Everard. 'I've got some pear blossom already in my orchard.'

'And there's blackthorn out in our hedge,' she added, 'and I've been sowing seeds, all sorts of them.'

'So have I,' said Everard, 'this morning before church.'

'That's wonderful what a difference spring make,' she went on, taking up the thread again. 'Our old cob stand up straight and trot like a two-year-old; the sun warm you right through and I can't stay indoors, not even when the dusk is coming on.'

'Neither can I,' said Everard, quite truthfully.

They walked on down the path, still idly swinging

hands and racking their brains for further matter to maintain at all costs this earnest discourse on the spring. Whenever silence fell, it became tense and made them ashamed, as if their thoughts had become naked.

'Why, look!' she cried, pulling him over to a willow clump, 'the palm's all out. I must smell.'

She plucked a sprig and inhaled the cloying sweetness of the woolly yellow blooms.

'Now you've made your nose all yellow,' he teased.

'Well, I'll do the same for you,' she giggled, mischievously dashing the sprig in his face and dusting his nose for him. 'Now we're a pair, aren't we?'

She threw the sprig away and they both laughed out loud, glad of the relief, but straightway after they both looked away.

'Before we know where we are,' Everard began, 'the may'll be out.'

'Hark!' she exclaimed, stopping short at the sound of a brisk, clear-throated warble in the bushes. 'That's a thrush.' They listened for a moment to his simple, jolly notes. 'Now what's he doing, singing so loud just before dark?' she asked curiously.

'Saying goodnight,' suggested Everard.

'Who to?'

'Another thrush, I suppose.'

They walked slowly on and turned up another path, in the middle of which appeared a little russet-coloured streak, jerking erratically hither and thither among the leaves.

'Look! what's that?' cried Ruthie, hastening her step.

The streak stopped dead as they came near, and suddenly turned into a russet-coloured, spiny ball; it was only a scared hedgehog. Ruthie bent down over it, still holding Everard's hand.

164

'Look at the dear,' she said, cautiously drawing her finger over his spines. 'Oh, how he tickle!'

Everard, still holding her hand and gazing down at her bowed shoulders, saw the whiteness of her neck and the bold side-curve of her breast; her whole body seemed in bud, like the hedges, with exuberant life. A languid tremor ran through him and, stooping quickly, he kissed her softly on the nape of the neck. A hundred times before and more he had kissed her, but her cheeks went fiery-red and she straightened herself, darting a swift, sidelong glance at him so that her moist, glistening eye flashed momentarily on his own like a streak of light. But she did not speak and her fingers, still clasped in his, gave no sign as she stepped over the fast-curled hedgehog and sauntered on. Everard, following at her side, himself blushed, for no reason that he knew. An amorous cock-pheasant screeched at their side and then flapped noisily away.

'All the creatures seem out tonight,' said Ruthie, starting at the clatter, her voice faint and hoarse. 'I wonder why?'

Everard left the query unanswered, and unrelieved, tormenting silence descended on them. They had repeated all the common tokens of spring like a lesson and now neither could think of any more to talk of, though the silence galled them and they trembled at each other's presence. To Everard the evening freshness of the spring air seemed choking and he wanted to scream. Instead, he fetched a tremendous sigh; as if in answer, Ruthie did the same.

The path had brought them now to the further brink of the copse, issuing in a field of pasture between two hedge-banks. Dusk was creeping on and they paused in the opening, peering into the shadows. All at once

Ruthie gripped his fingers tightly and, as if just released from the spell of their shyness, turned to him with eyes bright and eager.

'Do you smell them?' she asked. 'The violets?'

Everard snuffed the air several times and shook his head.

'No,' he said, 'I can't smell them. Your nose is sharper than mine.'

'No, I can't smell them now,' she replied. 'But that's just like violets; scent here one minute, gone the next. But I didn't mistake it. No, I wasn't wrong. Look, I can see one, two, three, and they're white too.'

She pointed to the slope of the bank where a few tiny mauve and white specks glimmered darkly in the grass-stalks.

'I must pick some,' she cried, letting go his hand and dropping down on her knees.

She searched among the grass until she had made herself quite a little posy of white and pale-mauve violets, and having offered them to Everard to smell as he stood watching her, she sat down on the bank to fix them under the brooch that gathered the neck of her white silk blouse. The stalks were bulky and she crushed them tight against her to clasp the brooch. All at once, with a little cry of pain, she flung them down.

'Oh, there's a nettle in those stalks,' she pouted. 'It have stung me.'

'I'll get you a dock,' said Everard. 'Where there's a nettle, there's always a dock.'

After a minute's groping on the bank he found what he wanted and came back to her. She was rubbing herself ruefully.

'A little tiny young one it was,' she said, 'and ever so green. They always sting the most.'

166

'Here's the dock,' said Everard. She looked slowly up at him, wide-eyed. 'Shall I do it?' he faltered timidly.

She nodded and he dropped on his knees beside her.

'No, not there,' she corrected, as he applied the dock to her neck. 'Lower down, lower still.' She took his hand and guided it down to the parting of her breasts. 'that's the spot.'

Everard began gently to rub with the dock leaf, his fingers trembling, and Ruthie closed her eyes. Perforce, with the motion, his knuckles brushed the little curved slope of her breasts and his head reeled. He saw a red flush steal into her cheek, and stayed his hand.

'Is that better?' he gasped.

'Yes,' she replied faintly, without opening her eyes. 'Goo on.'

He began again, soothingly, until he saw her breath catch, and his own caught too. She was only a simple country girl, enamoured of his town manners, and he was taking advantage of – a nettle-sting. These last sophisticated scruples of his old life and breeding checked him and changed him. His hand stilled, and he made to lift it. Ruthie opened her eyes, dilated, liquid and alight; her lips parted.

'No, no,' she gasped, seizing his hand in her own. With one rude stroke she tore open her blouse, she strained his hand against her full white breast, and then closed her eyes.

'Everard,' she murmured, 'my love.'

Night had fallen and they lay together on the bank in peace, their minds no more at stretch, their shyness departed, their tongues loosened.

'What are you thinking, darling Everard?' she whispered.

167

He hesitated.

'That all of you, Ruthie sweetheart,' he said at last, 'is soft like your throat – like violets.'

She answered him with a kiss.

'And what were you thinking, Ruthie?' he asked in his turn.

Her lips twitched and broke into a smile.

'I was thinking,' she said slowly, 'of a prime head of broccolo that someone blew to smithereens.' She looked at him gravely. 'Suppose he had missed it?'

He took her in his arms.

XVI

THE early morning sun, trickling smoothly down between the chimneypots and mounting smoke-wreaths of Lindmer, lit upon a trimly-raked little patch of ground and discovered two long streaks of succulent green. Everard's seeds were beginning to sprout and he gazed down upon them benevolently. Purslane and marigold, he had planted them last Sunday, along with half-a-dozen other rows, but, rank-fibred things, they were always up first. As for yesterday's, Good Friday's, sowings, they might not show for a fortnight if the drought went on. He hoisted his water-can and, swaying it from side to side, gently sprayed his bare, wind-hardened drills. There had once been springs when wet nights balanced the fine, warm days for months on end, until the whole earth was rank with growth: but they seemed so long ago that perhaps they never really existed, belonging to that fabulous golden age of which every farmer and every gardener dreams at times. He looked cautiously up at a fleet of harmless little clouds scudding across the sky overhead: whatever happened, it must not rain tonight; the dry spring was indeed a godsend. And so his thoughts streamed back where they had been hovering ever since he awoke that morning, to Ruthie and the scent of the violets which she resembled; thoughts which, below the surface delights of passion and tenderness, seemed now to float, as it were, upon an undercurrent of deep contentment.

That was what the previous evening with its fulfilment of natural desires had done for him; it all seemed of a piece with his present existence, rounding it off, obliterating all trace of those momentary misgivings, which had no place in it, and carrying him along into the universal stream of life.

The back door opened and Mrs. Quainton came out with a bundle of wet tea-cloths. She passed him without speaking and began to hang them out. Everard observed her out of the corner of his eye. He had hardly noticed her presence these last two days, so full was his mind of other things, but this morning there was something strange in her face; her cheeks were paler than usual, her mouth tight-set and severe. Her silence made such a pointed contrast to her usual cheerfulness that Everard could not help reading it as a sign of offence. Instantly a guilty suspicion arose in him that she was in some way aware of what had happened last night and was now intimating her disapproval; still, that was hardly probable. He had not come back until well after ten o'clock and as he had absently forgotten to tell her beforehand that he would be late, the supper was cold; perhaps she was angry with him for that. He determined to find out.

'You look very grim this morning, Mrs. Quainton,' he said, turning round to her and laughing.

'I've good reason to,' she replied, without smiling.

'What's that?' he enquired.

'Wait a minute,' she said, stretching up to peg out the last tea-cloth. She walked over to the door. 'Come in,' she said, 'and I'll tell you. I've been wanting to all the morning, only you were busy.'

'I wasn't,' said Everard, following her with the water-can.

'Still, you looked it,' she replied, carefully shutting the door behind them. 'I didn't want to disturb you.'

She looked at him solemnly.

'Well?' he said with a smile, desperately wondering what his crime was; could she, could anyone know about Ruthie, or did his features proclaim it?

She leant her arms on the back of a chair and looked steadily across the table at him.

'Last night,' she said slowly, 'I slept away from – him.'

Everard's own little emotion of personal relief was swept away in a wave of excited amazement.

'How did you do it?' His voice trembled.

'Well,' she replied calmly, 'I fitted up the spare bedroom during the day and carried all my things there. Then I waited for him to come back. He was quite early – just before nine o'clock – and we had supper. My heart was in my mouth all the time, I can tell you, and I could hardly eat anything or even lift a cup, my hand trembled so. Well, about half-past nine, when we'd finished and he'd lighted his pipe, I dragged myself together and got up. I got a candle from the window and lit it, and then went back to the table. For a minute or two I couldn't speak, and even now I don't know how I did it, but somehow the words came. "I'm going to bed," I said. He grunted, his usual way. I made another effort. "You're sleeping alone tonight," I said. "What's that?" he cried. "It's all right," I said. "You'll find everything you want there. It's only that I'm going to sleep in the spare room." Then he spat and swore at me. "You're not," he said, showing his teeth.

'I was shaking like a leaf, but somehow his spitting and swearing put heart into me. I felt I wasn't going to give in. "I am," I said, looking him in the eyes, just as

171

I'm looking at you. He jumped up so suddenly from his chair that he knocked it over backwards. "You 'on't," he said, "you – you bitch, I'll learn you." I looked all round me: I couldn't run away and he was coming towards me, calling me bitch. There was a piece of cold pork on a dish in front of me and I felt I couldn't give in now; so I snatched up the carving knife and pointed it at him. I'm afraid I bared my teeth too. "You dare!" I said.

'He stopped and spat on the floor. Then he laughed. "You'd be afraid to use it," he said. "There are some things I hate worse than death," I said, – I've never felt calmer than I did then – "so I shan't be afraid of using it on you." "Put it down," he said. "If you'll take it away, I will," I said. "Come along."

'I went forward a step towards him, and you should have seen him back away to the door; I could see he was afraid of me.

'"All right," he said, "I 'on't hurt you." "No, you won't," I answered, "and now I'm going to bed and I'm going to take this with me." And I walked out of the room with the knife under my arm.

'I went upstairs to my bedroom and locked the door. I undressed and got into bed and then I waited. About half an hour later I heard him come clumping upstairs. There's a narrow passage, you know, between the big bedroom and the spare room. He came up to my door and stopped outside for a minute, listening. I lay there, holding my breath. Then he began kicking the door and making a terrible hullabaloo, calling me dreadful, filthy names and threatening what he'd do when he got at me. I let him go on for a bit and then I got out of bed and went over to the door.

'"Stephen," I said. He stopped kicking. "Open the

door," he shouted. "I'm going to open the door now," I said, "and I'm coming out and I've got the knife with me."

'I unlocked the door and opened it. There was no sign of him in the passage. I took the candle and went to his door; but when I tried the handle, it was locked. I could hear him swearing to himself inside. I tapped on the door with the point of the knife.

'"Are you going to leave me alone?" I said. He waited a minute and then growled, "Yes." "For good?" I said. He didn't answer and I tapped again on the door with the knife. "For good?" I repeated. "Yes," he growled, and then I heard him start to swear again.

'I went away and locked myself in. You can guess what a night I spent. I was afraid to go to sleep properly because I thought he might come and break the door down − he's terribly strong, you know − and then I thought he might kill me. But I felt I couldn't ever suffer him again, and I lay all night with the knife at my side, and whenever I dozed off, the feel of it woke me up. Well, in the morning I got up early and dressed, and went downstairs to see after the breakfast. The carving knife I put away in the cupboard. He came down at his usual time and ate his breakfast, but never a word did he say, though I thought he looked more hateful than he ever had before. I began to wish I'd not put the knife away. Then, when he'd finished, he began to make out he was hard done by and be sentimental. "To think," he said, "that you left me alone last night after all these years, sixteen years!" I think he'd have cried, if he could have. "It's sixteen years too many," I said, and what do you think, Mr. Mulliver, I laughed. I don't know what made me do it, but I did.

'At that he got up and went out, swearing and

173

cursing under his breath, but I stood firm and watched him out, and after that I somehow felt I shouldn't ever need the knife again. But when he'd gone, I felt as if I should collapse.'

She ceased and looked up at him with sad, tired eyes. Everard stood for a moment unable to speak.

'Why didn't you tell me you were going to do this?' he burst out.

'Why, you see, Mr. Mulliver,' she explained, 'I knew you'd be in the house because you didn't say you'd be out late, and I left the kitchen and bedroom windows open so that I could have called you, though it wasn't necessary. But I didn't tell you about it beforehand because I didn't know whether I should have the courage to go on, until the moment came, that's why.'

Everard noticed a moist cloud flit across her dark eyes, dimming them, and her mouth puckered, but she stiffened herself. Then, indeed, he understood the meaning of her tight-set lips and severe manner that morning. They were the expression of all the terror she had endured and all the courage she had summoned up during the past twelve hours, with such intensity that she was still unable to relax. He went round the table and gently pushed her into the big wooden elbow-chair.

'Mrs. Quainton,' he said quietly, 'you want to cry, I know. Don't trouble about me.'

She gave him one little glance, half-grateful, half-curious, and then, dropping her face on her hand, burst out sobbing as if her heart would break. Everard took her other hand and held it tight, watching her gravely. For fully five minutes her shoulders heaved and shook with deep, painful sobs, till it hurt him to see her. Then suddenly the gust ceased and she raised her tear-stained face to his.

'There now,' said Everard, smiling and squeezing her hand, 'you feel better now, don't you?'

She smiled weakly back at him, but her eyes were bright through her tears.

'You are kind to me,' she murmured, as Everard gave her his own handkerchief to wipe her eyes. 'Tell me, Mr. Mulliver,' she said, when she had composed herself a little, 'do you think I've done right or do you think I'm a terrible woman to go handling knives like that?'

Everard's eyes grew moist in their turn.

'Why, Mrs. Quainton,' he stammered, 'I think you're quite magnificent; I can't tell you how I admire you. I only wish I could have been there to help you.'

'Oh, as for that,' she said, 'I knew you'd have come if I'd called, but there was no need.'

Everard felt a twinge of conscience at the thought that while she was fighting her battles he was away in the copse, dallying with Ruthie – even though he could not be blamed for his ignorance.

'Still, I see you don't really need my help,' he said, relinquishing her hand. 'You're brave enough for both of us; and I think you've shown that he's a coward. He's afraid of you, isn't he?'

'I think he is,' she replied. 'I'm so glad you're pleased,' she added, smiling warmly at him. 'That's everything to me.'

'And now you'll have a little peace,' said Everard. 'It's well worth it, isn't it?'

'Yes,' she nodded, 'and, you know, it's all through you. If you hadn't encouraged me, I'd never have thought of it.'

'You can certainly count on me for that,' said

Everard, always eager to foster the spirit of rebellion in her, 'and for more than that.'

But she sighed heavily, and seeing that she was feeling the strain, he did not press her.

'You're tired,' he said.

'Yes,' she replied, 'but that cry has done me good. I wonder how you knew I wanted it.'

'You must go and rest,' said Everard, 'and look here, Mrs. Quainton, you're not to get me any dinner today. I can stop and have a bite with the Kindreds. I'm going up to look at the sheep in a moment.'

She got up from the chair and peered at herself in a little mirror over the sink.

'Oh, what a fright I look!' she exclaimed. 'How could I let you see me like that?'

She ran out of the room in a flurry. Everard laughed as he watched her disappear; she was very feminine in spite of all. Then, looking at the clock, he hurried out after her; Farmer Kindred would be expecting him up with the sheep, and when they had done with them, they might open up the drain they were contemplating on the summerland. But as he walked up the valley to the farm, he had no room in his mind for these tasks. The unconscious irony with which Mrs. Quainton and he had chosen one and the same evening for their entirely contrary purposes did not absolve him from feeling some remorse; if all had not gone well, if he had failed her sure confidence in his presence – he shuddered for her: at least he would be early this evening. But she, in the same night, had suddenly doubled her stature. That knife – it was not courage that she needed, but simply a little persuasion to make her use the abundance she had. Already she had money of her own, she was going into Bury and buying herself nice clothes, and now, at least, she would sleep in peace; before the summer was out, he could see himself persuading her, gently and imperceptibly, to complete freedom, an event which even in prospect to contemplate was a profound and unalloyed satisfaction. It would be a whole and four-square piece of work, the refashioning, as it were, of a human life, and a valuable life at that. But the more his esteem for her grew, the greater became the outrage of her subjection to such a husband as Steve Quainton, the mere sickening thought of whom brought oaths to his lips; then, having delivered his opinion of the man forcibly enough, he looked up, and in an instant all his loathing and indignation vanished at the sight of the delectable greening copse where he was to meet Ruthie again at the end of the day.

XVII

EVERARD lifted his eyes from the trench, smoothed the crook out of his back, and leaning on his spade looked down across the valley. The tops of the tall, slim willows by the stream still looked like delicate, many-fingered hands, upstretched to the sky, but the young leaves were already sprouting and they would soon be waving languid, silvery plumes in the breeze as he had seen them when he first came to Lindmer last July. The copse on the opposite slope was sprinkling more and more of its blackness with every shade from yellow to fresh apple-green; a little while ago and it had been wholly black, further back in autumn-time it had flaunted purple, gold and copper, and before that it had merged all its differences to the distant eye in the evenness of full leaf, which in a month or two it would reach again. Below it the turnip field had long lost all its sea-green leaves, eaten and trampled to drabness by the tegs; a swift ploughing had awakened it to the gleaming brown of new, damp furrows; harrow and roller had dulled the shine, making a level tilth of it; and now at the end of April it was greener than grass with a springing crop of barley. Almost under his eyes peeping cowslips and spry jack-in-the-hedge bloomed on a ditch-bank which last summer had been a wall of swaying willow herb and hemp agrimony and would be again this summer too. It pleased him thus to pass the landscape in review, reading its signs and predicting its future; he had known it now close on a year, and his growing intimacy with its details, in change and permanence, had endeared it to him; there was always a fresh picture to look at and he himself was part of the picture.

He looked down at the narrow trench in which he was standing, dug deep because the land was wet – and indeed, the water was already oozing up around his feet. A little way behind Bob Kindred was at work with the draining-spade, a heavy iron tool with a step for the foot and a narrow blade like an exclamation mark, cutting out the slit at the bottom of Everard's trench, into which a layer of hedge trimmings would be stuffed to keep the drain open and guide the water down the slope. A useful piece of work it would be. Next winter the field would grow a good crop of turnips which those ewes of theirs would be able to eat without sinking up to their knees in mud; the ewes would tread the soil firm and enrich it with their excrement, so that the following summer it would bear a good crop of barley; the barley-straw would come back, perhaps, to shelter the ewes at lambing in the winter (though Bob Kindred might have told him that barley-straw, as litter, always breeds vermin), and the grain would be ground to feed the pigs; the muck from the pigstyes would go to fertilize some field across the valley and grow a crop of mangold to fatten the lambs which the ewes had borne; they in their turn would enrich another field; it was a cycle without end and he, too, had his place in it.

He bent again to the trench and noted the dry, brown top-soil passing gradually into the pale, harsh second spit; his own legs displayed the same transition, being powdered with the one at the knee and smeared with the other at the ankle, but he did not heed it. He lifted his spade and drove it in. Three sharp downward

179

cuts with the blade reversed to disengage the clod, then a searching stroke from the shoulder beneath it and two smaller thrusts to drive that home; a few pebbles rasped against the iron. Now a downward push with all the body on the handle, to lift the blade; the earth clung stubbornly to its roots, the water squelched; then with a final gurgle the clod yielded itself to the stress. Forearms lifted it, elbows shot it forward and landed it on the side of the trench, on top of the soil that for more than six months past had been on top of it. The tangy smell of clay and water, flavoured with iron, filled Everard's nostrils, and with something of a gusto he went on to the next stroke. All those muscular stresses, thrusting, prising, lifting, swinging, in each little tussle with the soil, seemed to double the life in his body, while the sense he had of always winning the tussle exhilarated his mind. The harder the clay bit, the more he enjoyed conquering it. Not every day of the week perhaps, but just now he could not have enough of such lusty work, for the past week had made all life outside of Lindmer uglier than ever. There were representatives of a trust in Bury, buying up the grocers' shops; they hoped one day to control the whole provision trade of the Eastern Counties. Everard, in his turn, had been approached and a fair offer made him. But all his instincts, inherited from Albert Mulliver who had built up the business with them, were against this project, although it was to his own advantage. He and his staff knew all their customers as persons with personal wants, to be considered accordingly; they prided themselves on the excellence of their common goods, the rareness and variety of the dainties which they called up from all parts of the earth for the discerning palate, and above all, on the blending of their tea and coffee. These things were the qualities

180

of the trade, just the things which would perish under the blank, impersonal, standardized and standardizing drive of the big trust-owned store. One by one all the good old things in Bury were being done away; but its old-fashioned county grocery should remain, so long, at least, as he could maintain it. Even though it meant a fight for existence, the business was well entrenched; he refused the offer. The previous night he had left Bury sick and worried, but now this morning how insignificant the whole matter, food and figures, customers and financiers alike, how insignificant it appeared beside this landscape, this strip of trench to be dug! So insignificant that it dropped out of his mind altogether.

Kindred laid aside his draining-spade and began to fill his pipe.

'That fare a real pity,' he said, 'that seven year from now all these bushes'll be rotten and our work as good as if that hadn't never been done. Still, we can't afford drain-pipes. They're wholly too dear.'

'Ah well, Bob,' said Everard, turning round and laughing, 'we shall have made so much out of our ewes by that time, we shall be able to afford the pipes then. Forty ewes – that's sixty lambs this winter, half of them ewe-lambs, eh? increase our flock by thirty – that makes seventy ewes; next year over a hundred lambs, eh?'

'Here, steady on,' laughed Kindred. 'That sound all right, but that's counting your lambs afore they're got – which put me in mind, Mr. Everard, we must be looking out for a ram some time. I want a good 'un. Hullo, who's that down there?' he exclaimed, shading his eyes with his hand and looking down the slope.

Everard turned and looked in the same direction. A man, a stranger, was standing by the hedge, waving his arm as if he wished them to come to him.

'If you want us,' shouted Kindred, 'come you over here. That 'on't hurt the land. We ain't a-going to traipse over there just for you.'

The man hesitated at first, and then, stepping gingerly, began to make his way across the rough ploughland. As he came nearer, Everard observed that he was young and rather smartly dressed, in bowler hat, light spring overcoat and neatly spatted town shoes; he carried gloves and an umbrella. His feet stumbled on the hard clods and sank in the loose earth, so that he lurched from side to side; his shoes were losing all their polish and he looked very hot and uncomfortable. Everard, understanding exactly what he was suffering, felt quite sorry for him.

'Well, what do you want?' said Kindred, as he came up.

'Could you tell me,' panted the young man, 'where to find Mr. Mulliver?'

'There he is,' said Kindred, jerking his thumb at Everard.

The young man looked at Everard's muddy corduroy breeches and collarless flannel shirt with rolled-up sleeves, and frowned.

'It wasn't a farmer I was looking for,' he said, with some annoyance. 'Mr. Mulliver is a gentleman, in business in Bury.'

'Well, here's a gentleman, if ever there was one,' growled Kindred, 'and his name's Mulliver, so what more do you want?'

Everard stepped up out of the trench and folded his brown arms. He felt very big and powerful in front of the young man; he could look over his head.

'Do you mean Mr. Everard Mulliver of Mulliver and Son's?' he said.

'Yes,' said the young man eagerly.

'Well, what is it?' said Everard.

'But are you Mr. Mulliver?' asked the young man suspiciously.

'Of course I am,' replied Everard, laughing, 'though I don't look it. How can I prove it? Ah, look at the name on my handkerchief. I didn't steal that, by the way.'

It was a very good handkerchief of hem-stitched linen, far too good for a common farmer. The young man was convinced and at once became deferential.

'I'm very sorry, sir,' he stammered, 'but you see, I didn't expect—'

'I quite understand,' said Everard, cutting him short. 'What do you want me for?'

'Well, Mr. Mulliver,' he replied, 'I'm secretary of the trust that was negotiating with you last week, and I should like to speak to you privately.'

Everard with a sigh of vexation drew him aside a little, out of Kindred's hearing. This was a preposterous affair; it pursued him out of the week into the weekend, out of Bury into Lindmer, from the profane to the inviolable.

The young man stared uncomprehendingly at Everard's bare neck and sweaty forehead, cleared his throat and flicked a piece of earth from his pointed toe; he would have known what to do if he had been head of Mulliver and Son's. Everard looked from his own square toes to the young man's light spring overcoat and spats and pale, weak face, and silently gave thanks that he was not as he.

'I was sent by the trust,' the young man went on, 'to convey you a message. I couldn't find you in Bury and I was directed here. I came out in a car and they sent me up here from the village.'

He produced a sealed envelope which Everard took and opened. The trust was evidently thinking twice before beginning the struggle with Mulliver and Son's. Would he be willing to amalgamate with their combine and accept a directorship on their board? The following terms were suggested – merely as a base for discussion; an early reply would oblige.

Once again Everard looked from his own muddy feet to the young man's pasty cheeks and expressionless blue eyes, under the trim, hard bowler hat. He was not thinking about the trust.

'I have pen and paper,' said the young man, fumbling in his pockets, 'if you wish to write an answer.'

'No need to write my answer,' said Everard slowly. 'You can remember it.'

'Yes, Mr. Mulliver?' said the other obediently.

'Please tell them, "No,"' said Everard. 'that's all; or rather, "No, thank you."'

'Is that to be taken as final?' queried the young man breathlessly, endeavouring to conceal his surprise.

'Quite final,' said Everard, regarding him calmly and knocking a fleck of mud off his knuckle.

The young man, realizing that his presence was no longer desired, grew suddenly embarrassed, fidgeted with his umbrella, and adjusted his tie.

'Very well, I'll go now,' he said. 'Good morning, Mr. Mulliver.'

'Good morning.'

Everard watched him lurch and stagger across the clods to the hedge, his elbows cocked to balance him, a pathetically undignified, incongruous figure. Once on firm ground by the hedge, his gait became more confident, even jaunty; he adjusted the set of his hat and swung his umbrella. Everard still gazed after him with a

184

smile, till he disappeared into the next field; then he turned and walked slowly back to the trench.

'Well there!' exclaimed Kindred indignantly, 'to think that miserable little bantam wouldn't believe you were Mr. Mulliver! 'Struth! and he take you for a common farmer.'

'I'm not so sure that I don't look it,' said Everard, smiling, 'and I'm rather glad if I do,' he added pensively.

'Anyone could see you're a gentleman,' said Kindred, as Everard stepped down in front of him and took up his spade again, 'leastways, with your hat off.'

'Then I'll keep it on in future,' Everard laughed.

'And the niminy-piminy way he walk,' pursued Kindred, still harping on the young man, 'in his fine town clothes!'

'Poor chap,' protested Everard, 'he couldn't help it. He wasn't made for walking in ploughed fields.'

He still felt sorry for the young man, so manifestly out of his element, and still rather gratified at being taken for a farmer. How he had changed in the past few months! Everard Mulliver, farmer, Lindmer, sounded well; then, as he fell to his digging again, he wondered if the change was more than skin-deep.

'Hullo!' cried Kindred suddenly, pausing to look up, 'here come Henry.'

Everard, too, looked up and saw Henry Runacres crossing over to them from the hedge, a gun and spade under his arm and a large sackcloth bag slung tight with string over his shoulder.

' 'Morning, Bob, 'morning, Mr. Mulliver,' he said, as he came up. 'What's that young dandy in the boughler hat doing, that I met down by the stream? Been to call on you, Robert?'

'Come to see Mr. Mulliver,' Bob grunted, relighting his pipe.

'Oh,' commented Runacres, 'I thought he might be a-poaching, 'haps.'

'Do you put on your spats and hard hat when you go poaching?' said Everard, laughing.

'Now, haven't I told you, Mr. Mulliver,' the old man expostulated, 'I never poach? Becourse, I don't allus shoot straight and I sometimes hit a hare when I aimed at a rabbit; but that wouldn't be right then to leave that to rot, would it?'

They all laughed.

'What have you come for, Henry?' asked Kindred. 'To watch a bit of real work? We're busy enough.'

'I'm going down to your meadows to look for moles,' said Runacres, 'though their pelts don't fetch much now; afore Christmas you get a shilling for 'em. Still, I've got to make a living. But why I came here, I've got some messages for you, Mr. Mulliver. First of all, Jim Farrow want to know if you'll play in the quoit match against Hartnest this arternoon. I said I knowed you would, but I thought I'd just ax you first.'

'But,' Everard objected, 'I'm not good enough, and this drain—'

'I ain't a-going to do no more on this drain this arternoon,' said Kindred. 'Do you go and play, Mr. Mulliver.'

'Well, that's all right,' said Runacres. 'Then, Jim Farrow, he want to know if you want hobnails on that pair of boots he've mended for you?'

'Of course I do,' said Everard.

'Ah, he told me he'd put 'em in,' said Runacres, 'but he wanted to make sure. And Nesley Honeyball say he'd be wholly obliged if you'd let him have a score of those young lettuce plants for the rector's garden. The rector like a bit of rabbit's food along of his tea, he do.'

'All right,' said Everard, 'he shall have 'em. Anything else, Henry?'

'Now let me see,' said Runacres, pushing back his cap and scratching his head. 'That's like when I used to do the shopping for my owd woman, what's dead and gone now these thirteen year. Ah yes, I remember. Ah yes, yes, Jack Tooke's cat have just had kittens, and he want to keep one for you. I told him I thought you wanted one; I seed a great big rat come out of a hole at the bottom of your wood-shed the other day and you're sure to have several meece in the house – Mr. Chinery next door's swarmed with 'em and I knowed you didn't keep a cat.'

'Yes, I ought to have a cat,' Everard nodded reflectively, 'so long as Mrs. Quainton doesn't mind.'

'Oh, she 'on't mind,' Runacres reassured him, 'she's that fond of animals. That's a little beauty Jack's a-keeping for you – all black that is, with yaller eyes like its mother, or leastways, that will have, 'cause they're blue now.'

'All right,' said Everard, 'I'll have it.'

'Good,' said Runacres, rubbing his hands with satisfaction. 'That's the fourth I've got rid of today for Jack. You see, that cat have had five kittens and Tom Cobbin – he's allus ready for a bet; when he die, I reckon he'll lay the parson evens they meet in the hot place or summat – well, Tom Cobbin, he lay Jack Tooke a quart he wouldn't get rid o' them five kittens without a-killing on 'em, and I've been doing a bit of business for Jack. Jack hisself palmed one off on the district nurse and she couldn't well refuse 'cause he'd mended her bike for her for nothing. Then I made the vicar's wife take one – to save it from a cruel death, I say to her, and owd Mrs. Cobbin, while Tom was out at work – she's owd and a bit soft, easy to get round her, and then Mrs. Chinery, 'cause the bet help their trade, I say, and now Mr. Mulliver. I reckon Jack and I'll have that quart out of Tom Cobbin tonight.' He shook his head knowingly and burst out laughing.

'Poor Tom,' said Everard, 'he's always standing you quarts, Henry. I call that false pretences too.'

'Now, do you take a drop of drink along o' me, Mr. Mulliver,' said Runacres, drawing out a bottle from his bag, 'and then I know you'll take that kitten. It ain't Tom's beer we want; he'll get that back from us. But he must be beat.'

He pulled out the cork, and wiping the mouth of the bottle on his sleeve handed it to Everard, who took a swig and thanked him. Kindred followed, and then Runacres himself, who after his swig held the bottle up and looked at it contemptuously.

'Why look,' he said, 'that's half gone now. Full or empty, that's what a bottle should be. Drink up, Mr. Mulliver.'

Everard drank again, and having passed on the bottle, complacently watched the two throats jerk until it was empty; Runacres would not have asked that young man to drink with him.

'There now, my lood'll be lighter,' said Runacres contentedly, as he stuffed the bottle into his bag. 'That's the stuff for us chaps as work. I must now be going. Farewell, Bob, farewell, Mr. Mulliver.'

He trudged away across the furrows and the other two set to work again.

'You know, I don't like leaving this drain this

afternoon,' said Everard, between strokes of his spade. 'We shan't finish this one today.'

'That don't signify, Mr. Mulliver,' said Kindred. 'They want you down there at the quoit match, they like you – they wouldn't ax you else; so I reckon you ought to go. Besides, I'm going to put a man on this field next week so as to hurry it up. It's Saturday, too, and I've done enough for the week.'

'Well, I suppose I shall have to go now,' said Everard, still half-grumbling.

'Becourse you will,' said Kindred, who was looking up at a big black cloud that had just crept in above their heads and blotted out the sun. 'Fare to me, we shan't be able to work on this anyhow. We're in for a shower and that'll be too dirty here. My! That cloud's wholly low,' he added, stepping out of the trench and picking up his coat. 'I reckon we'd better find some shelter.'

Everard, too, jumped out and they both set off at a run; but they were too late. The storm burst suddenly, right over their heads, and before they had reached the hedge, they were in the middle of a thunderous down-pour. There was so little leafage in the hedge that it was useless to crouch there, and doomed now to a soaking whatever happened, they picked up their tools and made straight down the bare hillside for the farm-buildings. When they reached the yard, the water was running down their necks from under their caps and oozing out of their boots.

'Come you along in,' said Kindred, when they had stowed the tools. 'We must dry you off in front of the fire.'

'I'd better go straight home and change,' said Everard.

'Not you,' retorted Kindred. 'We'll find you some

189

clothes to wear. Besides, that's near dinner-time and you're going to stop and have a bite with us.'

There was no gainsaying him; Everard laughed and followed him in.

'Why, Lor' bless me, Robert!' cried Mrs. Kindred, as soon as she caught sight of their bedraggled forms, 'have you been a-persecuting of Mr. Mulliver agin? He's near drownded he is, the pore lamb.'

'Lamb indeed!' echoed Robert, 'that's what she used to say to me when we went a-courting, Mr. Mulliver. Do you get him some dry clothes, Emma. He's wholly wet.'

'And run you out and get some more wood for the fire, Robert,' she rejoined, 'and don't stand there scattering water all over my kitchen floor. Oh, Lor'! what a man I did marry!'

Kindred stumped out of the kitchen, leaving a large pool of water behind him where he had been standing.

'Come you over to the fire, Mr. Mulliver,' said Mrs. Kindred, now grown quite motherly. 'I'll run up and get you some clothes while you dry your face on this towel. And do you mind not to get in the draught.'

She bustled away upstairs, while Everard stood in front of the fire, steaming and dripping and mopping his hair with the towel. Two or three minutes later she came down again with a bundle of clothes in her arms which she laid down on a chair with laborious gentleness.

'See here now, Mr. Mulliver,' she said, 'I'll put the screen round you so as you can change in the warm.'

She trotted down to the other end of the room and staggered back with a large canvas screen stuck with scraps, which she set up in front of the fire.

'Lookye here, Mr. Mulliver,' she panted, 'that was

no use giving you none of father's clothes; you're too big for 'em. So I've brought you down my pore boy's last best suit. He was killed in the War, you know, and he was just about your size, Mr. Mulliver. I've kept 'em locked up in his drawer ever since he died and nobody have never touched 'em. But they'll just about fit you, Mr. Mulliver, and I know William'd have liked you to wear 'em. So I hope you 'on't mind like. He was such a nice boy—' she hesitated and then smiled – 'and anyhow, Mr. Mulliver, you're one of us like now.'

She slipped away behind the screen, adding as she disappeared, 'I'm now getting the dinner up, Mr. Mulliver.'

For a moment or two Everard stood gazing at the bundle of tough green Derby tweed, stiff as cardboard, which had been young William Kindred's best suit, touched by his old mother's kindness. Then a strange, warm feeling of elation stole over him; it was as if the question he had asked himself about Everard Mulliver, farmer, earlier that morning, had been answered.

XVIII

MORE than half the month of May had gone and the whole valley was green when Everard and Kindred covered up the last drain on their hillside field. They had worked feverishly on until late in the evening to finish the job before Sunday came; the twilight was already deepening and a white mist rising from the brook to sharpen the cloying scent of hawthorn blossom that floated on the air, as they plodded back to the homestead with their spades on their shoulders.

'Well, that's a good job done, Bob,' said Everard contentedly, as he lit his pipe.

'That is, Everard,' replied Kindred, lighting his own pipe.

It was only during the past month as they jogged elbows in their trenches that Kindred had come to use Everard's Christian name, rather shyly and haltingly at first, as if he found it strange to his tongue, but now quite easily and naturally, and Mrs. Kindred had followed his example; it was a great satisfaction to Everard, who prized every step in their intimacy.

'Yes,' he continued after a pause, 'we'll get that ploughed up agin next week, and then that'll soon be fit for a sowing of turnips. That'll do our ewes wholly well, come winter-time. I'm right glad you put me in the mind to do it.'

They turned into a cartshed just outside the farmyard and began to clean their spades with pieces of stick.

Kindred, having finished his, stood up against a cart-wheel and gripped Everard by the arm.

'See here, Everard,' he said quietly, 'I ain't a-going to ask you in to ours tonight 'cause I guess you'll be wanting to go off up the drift.'

Everard looked round sharply at him. Kindred smiled.

'Don't you worry, Everard,' he said. 'I know all about that now – but I 'on't tell nobody, not even Emma. Ondly last Sunday and last night, too, I seed you up on the edge of the copse, a-walking arm–in–arm with Ruthie, and I thought I'd tell you 'cause 'haps you don't want nobody to know.'

'Thanks, Bob,' muttered Everard. 'I didn't know anyone could see us from down below.'

'Well, they can,' said Kindred, 'so do you be careful. Some folks, when they're a-courting, don't mind if everybody know their business, but I'm like you; when I courted Emma, we kept it close till a fortnight before the marriage.'

'Good, Bob,' said Everard gratefully, 'I'll remember.'

'Ah, you're a sly one, Everard,' said Kindred, know-ingly wagging his finger. 'I wondered why you were allus in such a hurry to get away from here o' nights. But she's a wholly handsome, upstanding gal, she is, and no mistake. She's about the same build as my owd woman was, and very near as pretty.' Everard grinned sheepishly. 'Get you along,' said Kindred, clapping him on the shoulder, 'and make the most of your young time. That's just the weather for courting. Farewell, boy.'

'Farewell, Bob,' said Everard, laughing.

He slouched off up the track with his hands in his pockets, humming a tune to cover his excitement, partly at being found out, but far more at Kindred's approval; it seemed perfectly natural to the old man that he should be going to meet Ruthie – courting his girl and making the most of his young time like any other young countryman, like Kindred himself in his young days, full in the true rustic tradition. Besides, even though Kindred was mistaken about Emma's good looks, he thought Ruthie handsome. Everard's cheek warmed as he caught sight of her tall, supple form in front of the cowshed. Her face gleamed white in the moonlight when she turned at his approach, reminding him of the waxy, wide-eyed hawthorn blossom; she, too, was in full flower.

'How late you are, Everard,' she said. 'I've been waiting ever so long.'

'I had to stay to finish a drain,' he explained, taking her hands in his.

She looked at him wistfully and then kissed him.

'There's such a heavy dew tonight, darling,' she said, 'the ground'll be wholly wet. Let's goo up on the wood-stack. That'll be just like old times.'

She folded his arm round her waist and led him into the shed. In the old way he helped her on to the manger and climbed up on to the stack beside her. She stroked his body gently with both hands.

'I must see if it's really you,' she whispered, laughing, 'like the horses in the field, just as we used to do.'

'I'm still the same,' said Everard, stroking her hair, 'and so are you.'

'I'm not so sure,' she said with sudden querulousness. 'Why, look at this great smear of mud on your breeches. That's a nice state to come to meet me in.'

'Well, I was working till nearly a quarter of an hour ago,' he pleaded.

'Yes, but you always used to be early,' she rejoined, 'and you used to be so particular about your clothes when you came to meet me. I don't believe you care whether you come or not. You're just used to me now and it don't matter.'

'But I do care, Ruthie,' Everard protested. Yet it was quite true, what she said: since he had bought the ewes and begun the draining, he had ceased to trouble about his appearance and he was often late; he knew he would always find her there.

'I don't believe you do,' she faltered, shaking her head slowly.

'I do, darling,' said Everard, 'and after tonight I'll always go home and change first.'

'Oh no, no, darling,' she cried, melting suddenly, 'I didn't mean that. I like you best as you are.'

She stroked the harsh clayey patch on his knees and laid her head against his shoulder so that he could feel her hot breath on his chest through his shirt.

'Oh, Everard dear,' she went on, 'you don't know how I love you; but of course you couldn't know. And I don't love you now like I did at first. Then, you know, Everard, I thought you were so wonderful, so strange and above me. You lived such a different life, you were so quiet and you had a funny way of speaking as if your thoughts were far, far away above my head, and I was half-frightened of you, though I had to love you. Then, after that night when I picked the violets – do you remember, Everard?' Her voice shook and she clutched his knee tightly. 'I forgot all that then and I loved you because I felt you're the same as me, somehow. The way you wanted me and the way you took me in your arms – they're so big and strong – and I wanted you the same way; so you no longer fared

195

above me, but just like me. That's why I love your clothes all muddy like this and the smell of you when you come in from the fields. I feel you can't be so different then; and you do come to me even if you are late – Everard darling.'

She laid her cheek against his, as if tired by her outburst. Everard clasped her in silence, inarticulate before this passionate declaration, all his blood throbbing hotly in answer; yet something behind kept his mind taut and disquieted, a lurking dread of what she would say next. He knew well enough what was on her mind, but he could not help her. She spoke again.

'And I wonder what you think of me, Everard,' she murmured. 'But there, I expect there's some other woman, some fine lady in Bury you're in love with.'

'There's no one else, sweetheart,' said Everard reassuringly; that at least he could assert with complete truthfulness.

'Really?'

'Really and truly, sweetheart.'

She kissed him on the temple.

'Still,' she went on almost desperately, 'I'm not going to ask you what you think of me, I know you want me and you come to me and I want you. That's all I care to know.'

Everard kissed her brow; he felt relieved. Ruthie drew back from him and began to uncoil her hair.

'Take off your coat, Everard,' she whispered, 'I want to feel your bare arms around my neck.'

Everard obeyed. The desire in her was almost a thing that could be felt – like the hawthorn scent in the air; it enveloped him and swept him away with it. Ruthie turned and drew his head down on her cool breast; her hair fell over them both.

Half an hour later Everard lay quiet and relaxed, with Ruthie's head languid on the crook of his arm, her eyes closed, her warm side rising and falling against him. Little by little his mind seemed to steal back, as from a void, and take shape in thought, thought that destroyed his peace. Once more Ruthie had not asked him if he loved her, and once more he was thankful that she had not asked him, because he could not truthfully have answered yes. He certainly was in love with no one else; but that he did not love Ruthie had suddenly become startlingly clear to him, revealed to him, as it were, by her own impulsive words, and the knowledge troubled him. He might well be relieved that she had not pressed her question, but what, after all, was the bond which held him to Ruthie? He desired her as she desired him; yet there was something besides desire in her that he could not find in himself. Search and sift as he would, he could find nothing more and again he felt troubled. Mere desire, seen bare and unadorned, a trivial, selfish thing; and Ruthie, a simple, generous country girl – perhaps he ought to give her up. The thought of it was quite intolerable; it would be no less intolerable to her. Everything showed that the force which drew them together was something inevitable and natural; neither of them had willed it, neither had resisted, they had obeyed something that was irresistible, animal perhaps, but natural and irresistible; it was best to resign oneself to the irresistible. This last reflection consoled him; and after all, Kindred had told him to make the most of his young time. He was young, Ruthie was young, it was spring and one desire answered another. Of course it was natural; they were making the most of their young time. He was quite convinced now, and all misgiving faded from his mind.

Ruthie raised her head, and bending over his face, kissed him. Her lips were moist and warm and Everard's thoughts, yielding before his senses, floated dreamily back into the void from which they had transiently emerged.

XIX

A FITFUL gust of wind swayed the branches of a bowed old spice-apple and sent a cloud of pink-and-white blossom shivering down, cutting short Everard's yawn with a mouthful of petals. He spluttered them out and sat up straight against the tree-trunk by which he had been lying, blinking and rubbing his eyes. He was unquestionably sleepy, which was unusual with him at that hour of the morning, even on Sundays. But that particular Sunday morning, in the middle of a leisurely chat with Bob Kindred among their joint flock of ewes, a strong desire had come over him to be silent and alone, to lie down in the grass and bask like a cat in the sun; and so, with yet a full hour to go before dinner (instead of, as commonly, half an hour late), he had promptly left Bob Kindred to go and drowse in his own orchard. It was most soothingly pleasant to lie there in the scent of his own apple blossom, lazily watching the withered cowslip heads jostle the sturdy spikes of the purple orchids that were now pushing up out of the grass to take their place in the world of bloom; it was pleasant to be surrounded by the works of his own hands, the vegetable garden in front that he had dug and planted, the trees above that he had pruned, the hedge on three sides of him that he had buckheaded, and beyond that the field of spring corn that he had helped to plough; it was pleasant to be tired, cleanly, bodily tired after yesterday's hard long bout of digging in the fields. In half an hour it would be time for dinner, after which he and Kindred would make their accustomed leisurely perambulation of the valley fields, ending up at the farmhouse for tea; the evening would come and with evening Ruthie – a well-spent day. Ruthie – he was glad Kindred knew about her; there would be no difficulty now in slipping away from the farm when he wanted, of an evening; and it somehow seemed right and natural that Kindred should know. Ruthie – how she had stirred him last night and troubled him too! But the trouble was quite allayed now; it even seemed strange that he should have been troubled at all; it was as natural that he should be going to the copse tonight to meet her as being tired today after yesterday's digging. Dreamily he conjured up her goodly image, but it quickly fled, no longer able to hold his mind as in the first days of their intimacy. Ruthie was right; he had become used to her. She had become almost a habit, but a habit not to be discarded; he would see the real woman tonight.

The garden gate creaked and Mrs. Quainton entered with a dish in her hand. Catching sight of Everard in the orchard she smiled at him as she let herself in by the back door. She was wearing a new light cotton frock and light silk stockings, and she looked very fresh and summery. Everard smiled back approvingly, congratulating himself; for in part, at least, he was responsible for the change in her, and ever since Easter, when she had begun to sleep apart from her husband, it had become more marked. There was a new blitheness in her demeanour, her step was light and she sang about the house as if, so far as was possible in such circumstances, she were really happy. She evidently throve on freedom, even partial freedom. How much happier, how much more complete a woman she would be if her freedom were complete? And the time to advance to it could not be so distant now. Her husband seemed to have been cowed by her resolution in their last clash of wills, and had not dared to molest her since; he was silent and seldom in the house or at *The Olive Leaf*. Indeed, Everard had almost ceased to think of him as a person; he was just a material obstacle to be surmounted in due course. It ought not to be difficult now, but she must not be hurried. Let her enjoy her present state a little longer and perhaps she herself might suggest the next step. That would certainly be worth waiting for, and he sighed with anticipated satisfaction.

There was another change in her, too, which he remembered as he saw her dark head flit across the back window of the kitchen. That cast of youthfulness, which before he had only surprised on her face in occasional moments of pleasure, seemed now to have become quite permanent. A warm sparkle had come into her eye, her lips had gained in colour, her cheeks had filled out, softening the angular effect of her high cheek-bones and long, firmly drawn nose, and her skin, though still naturally pale, had become fine and luminous. There was nothing any longer of the tragic character about her, and altogether, now he thought of it, she was rather a good-looking woman, a very pleasant person to have in the house, as he had discovered long ago, much more like a sister than a housekeeper; that was her relation to him. Ruthie was his sweetheart, which Mrs. Quainton, good-looking though she was, could never be. He did not stop to think why; it seemed self-evident. His feelings to her were brotherly and he wished she were his sister; Laura was a nice name. Indeed, ever since Ruthie had become his mistress, he seemed to have had far more time to reflect on Mrs. Quainton than before. He smiled at the idea, without seeing that it was yet another proof that a mistress can become a habit.

The garden gate creaked again, and Everard, looking up, saw two men enter, followed at a few paces' distance by a third. They paused to knock at the back door, but sighting Everard, who had risen to his feet, they at once made their way down the garden path towards him. The two in front were Henry Runacres and Jack Tooke, the latter carrying a basket; the straggler was Tom Cobbin, as usual unshaven, and more red-faced than ever. They all looked very solemn, and Everard wondered if it was a deputation of protest from the quoit club, because he had declined to play in yesterday's match in order to help Kindred with the last of the draining.

' 'Morning, Mr. Mulliver,' said Jack Tooke, as he and Runacres came to a halt in front of Everard; Tom Cobbin, keeping his distance, halted too. 'I've now come to give you that kitten I promised you. I'd have let you have that before, but I wanted to keep 'em on a bit for the sake of the mother like. Do, she get the milk fever wonderful bad, and that's the truth.'

'Thanks, Jack,' said Everard, as the blacksmith began to undo his basket from which there ascended a thin stream of agonized wailing. 'But what have you brought Tom Cobbin for?'

'Well, you see,' said the blacksmith, with a grin, 'he wouldn't pay for that quart till we'd delivered all the kittens, although we'd placed 'em all getting on for a month ago.'

'So I've followed 'em round,' said Tom, stepping forward, 'to see fair play. I ain't a-going to pay up till I

202

see 'em all delivered, and I've got a word to say to you about that there kitten, Mr. Mulliver.'

'Now, look here, Mr. Mulliver,' protested Runacres, 'you promised me you'd have that and a promise is a promise.'

Everard laughed. 'Well, let's hear what Tom's got to say,' he said.

'Well, it's like this here,' began Tom, solemnly holding up his forefinger and squinting violently at it. 'That there is a she-cat and I tell you what that mean. Whenever she's in season, you'll have all the tom-cats in the village round your doorstep, kicking up such a scream and such a stink as you never seed in your life, and then twice a year that'll throw a litter and you'll be swarmed out with kittens.'

'Yes, Tom,' rejoined Tooke, 'we know all that, but Mr. Mulliver ain't a-going to be such a fool as you, to bet he'll get rid of all his kittens without killing on 'em, and besides when she's in season, he can shet her up in his shod. 'Sides you want a she-cat where there's rats and meece; they hunt all the sharper if they've got kittens.'

'But Mr. Mulliver ain't got any meece,' said Tom.

'I tell you he have,' said Runacres. 'I sold him the place, so I ought to know.'

'Well, I warn you, Mr. Mulliver,' continued Tom, 'its mother's a wholly terrible poacher. I know that 'cause Henry gave her to Jack as a kitten and Henry's old cat was a poacher too. That'll allus be bringing rabbits home and then that'll get shot.'

'Now he's telling you untruths,' expostulated Jack Tooke. 'Her mother's a wholly quiet cat and that's only round harvest-time she do bring home a rabbit or two.'

'Besides,' put in Runacres feelingly, 'what harm if

she do now and agin? It'd ondly be on Bob Kindred's land she'd poach, and he 'on't shoot her if he know she belong to Mr. Mulliver.'

'Becourse,' said Jack Tooke, drawing out the squealing kitten and handing it to Everard.

'Well, I tell you,' cried Tom Cobbin desperately, at the end of his resources, 'I knowed a man as was scratched by a young kitten and he got blood-poisoning and he had to have three fingers cut off, and he allus had to drink left-handed after that.'

They all burst out laughing at him.

'A pity that wasn't you,' guffawed Tooke. 'You might have drunk a little less then, Tom. Now, Mr. Mulliver, a promise is a promise.'

Everard was stroking the kitten, which clung to his coat, mewing plaintively.

'Why, what a lovely coat she's got!' he exclaimed, 'just like a Persian; all black and a white star on her forehead.'

'Yes, her father was a Persian,' said Runacres mendaciously. 'We chose her special for you, Mr. Mulliver; all the rest took after their mother.'

'Sorry, Tom,' said Everard, 'I really can't let her go; she's so pretty.'

'There you are, Tom!' Jack Tooke turned to Tom Cobbin. 'Didn't I say Mr. Mulliver was having it?'

'Ah, they've beat me once agin, Mr. Mulliver,' said Tom, sadly shaking his head.

'Well, what did you want to lay us that quart for?' said Jack.

''Cause you think I'm a fool,' retorted Tom, and I want to show you I'm not.'

'All right, Tom,' said Everard, gripping his shoulder; he felt sorry for him. 'You'll do it one day.'

'Yes, I will,' said Tom, firing up. 'I'll put it acrost 'em.'

'Now, what about a glass of beer?' said Everard.

'Thank you kindly,' said Runacres, 'but we've got to go and leave one more kitten on Mrs. Chinery and then it's Tom Cobbin that's going to stand the drinks; so if you want a free drink, come you along of us.'

'Well, my dinner'll soon be ready,' said Everard, 'so I'll say no, thank you.'

'Well, come along, Tom,' said Jack Tooke, putting his basket under his arm. 'I want to taste that quart o' yourn. 'Morning, Mr. Mulliver.'

Everard watched them trail away down the path, Tom Cobbin scratching his head disconsolately; he always lost, but he was always ready to lose again.

Everard stroked the kitten, which was trying to find its way inside his waistcoat; it was a pretty little animal.

'I wonder what Mrs. Quainton'll say to you,' he said, addressing it. 'She'll have to look after you when I'm away. We'd better go in and make friends with her.'

Mrs. Quainton was setting plates to warm when he entered the kitchen.

'What do you think of my new kitten?' he said.

She stood up and looked at it quizzically.

'It is pretty,' she said, smiling. 'I suppose now I shall have to look after it for you.'

'Yes,' replied Everard apologetically. 'I suppose I ought to have asked you first, but I forgot. Still, we do want something to keep the mice down.'

'But there aren't any mice, Mr. Mulliver,' she said in surprise. 'I let my cat in several times during the week and there aren't any left now.'

'Why, Henry Runacres said the place was swarming

with them,' replied Everard, 'but I thought I hadn't seen any.'

'Ah, he wanted to palm it off on you,' she said, laughing. 'But it is a pretty little thing. What are you going to call it?'

'I hadn't thought,' said Everard, looking thoughtfully down at it. 'What a dark coat it's got – about the same colour as your hair, Mrs. Quainton.' He smiled, recalling one of his thoughts earlier in the morning. 'Suppose we call it after you,' he added, looking up, 'shall we, Laura?'

A strange, hurt look crossed her eyes and then she closed them, as if involuntarily. Her lips paled completely and she tottered backwards. Everard dropped the kitten on the table among the dishes and seized her arms to prevent her from falling. Her hands gripped his wrists, grasping and ungrasping them. A moment after, she opened her eyes and the colour came back to her lips.

'I'm so sorry, Mrs. Quainton,' said Everard, as he released her arms, 'I was only joking.'

'Of course, I know you were,' she gasped, summoning up a wan smile. 'It's I who ought to be sorry. You must think I'm a ridiculous woman. I don't suppose you quite understand what it's been like in my home, but you see nobody's called me Laura since my mother died. He never calls me anything. He just says "here!" or "you!"'

'I see,' said Everard, quite reassured.

'And when I heard my name from you,' she continued, 'after all those years, it was such a shock, I lost all control of myself. I do that sometimes; I am so silly.'

'No, you're not,' said Everard. 'I quite understand; it must have been a shock.'

206

'Still,' she said, smiling quite naturally now, 'it was a very pleasant shock. I rather liked hearing it again; it's rather a nice name, I think.'

'So do I,' said Everard.

She turned her head away and looked at the floor; her mouth twitched shyly.

'I wish,' she faltered, 'I wish you'd always use it.'

'Do you?' said Everard, half-amused and half-taken aback, but concealing both. 'Well, of course I will; it is a very nice name, far too good for a kitten, Laura.' It fell very pleasantly from his lips; he was quite pleased she had asked him to use it.

'Yes, you know,' she said, looking up with a joyful smile, 'it sounds so much more friendly; and we know each other quite well, don't we? – even though I am your housekeeper,' she added a little roguishly.

'Of course we do,' said Everard, 'and I actually never do think of you as my housekeeper, but just as – well, Mrs. Quainton, or rather, Laura, and that is much nicer – and shorter. But you'll have to do the same for me.'

'I should like to,' she said a little timidly, 'Everard – that's right, isn't it?'

'Yes,' he said, 'you'll soon get used to it.'

'Of course I shall,' she smiled. 'A Christian name's so much warmer on the tongue – like homemade wine; and it went to my head, Everard.'

They both burst out laughing.

'What a silly housekeeper you've got!' she said, when they had recovered. 'Now go in and sit down and I'll get the dinner up – Everard.'

Still laughing, he obeyed, and as he turned to close the parlour door he saw that she had caught up the kitten from the kitchen table and was covering it with kisses. It was well that she had so taken to it, he thought; it was a pretty kitten, and he would have to find it a new name now. But he was not sorry; for when the day came, Laura would be far easier to persuade than Mrs. Quainton.

XX

MAY passed into June and in every part of Lindmer Vale Everard watched the slow ripening of spring into summer; in the hedgerows, where hawthorn and crab-apple had yielded to dog-rose, buckthorn and early honeysuckle, where chaffinches, sobered by family cares, had ceased to chase each other, pink-pinking, from bush to bush and already the yellowhammer was beginning to complain of the lack of cheese to his bread; down in the water-meadows, where the proud purple orchids had in their turn withered like the cowslips and a host of yellow rattle and white moon-daisies waved exultant over them among tall grass-heads, swollen for bloom; up in the copse, too, where an ever denser leafage sheltered Ruthie and him from ever lighter evenings, with only the monotonous churr of the nightjar to serenade them in place of the departed nightingale. There was no lack of work at this season, and during that part of the week when he lived – for in Bury he seemed to move among unrealities in a suspended, trance-like state – he was early and late at Kindred's side, taking his part in whatever task was on hand and steadily increasing his knowledge of the arts of husbandry, more by practice and observation than by any direct instruction from his master. Already they had drilled the mangold together, chopped it out and cleaned it of weeds with hand-hoe and horse-hoe, they had rib-rolled the spring barley against wireworm; and

every Sunday morning it was not until they had diligently searched their ewes for maggot and staked out a
fresh fold, that they allowed themselves the luxury of a
quiet smoke among the hurdles. All these coarse activities were to Everard a source of profound pleasure,
which he accepted joyfully without enquiring for a
reason, simply conscious that life was very good. His
whole body, cleansed by sun and air and eased by constant sweating and the play of muscles, seemed full of a
strange virtue that was always eager for fresh exertions
without ever flagging; he slept deeply and his appetite
was enormous. Then, when evening came and work
was over, unless the village claimed him for the inn or
the quoit club, where, being a good hand with a quoit,
he was much in demand, there was always Ruthie in
the copse, and her, too, he accepted in that same joyful,
unquestioning spirit, which she seemed now to share;
for though her ardour was still undiminished, she no
longer troubled his peace with embarrassing doubts and
avowals. Their relations, like all the rest of his life, had
become in their very naturalness part of the landscape, a
landscape in which he roamed at large like a wild
animal in its native forest.

However, although Everard felt himself to be tireless,
there were of necessity times when he was really tired,
and Kindred, who from long experience had a quick
eye for such things, would at once find some shift for
resting him by a change of work, or if that failed, would
refuse downright to let him exhaust himself any further.
On these occasions Everard, however reluctant, always
obeyed. Thus it happened one Saturday late in June, at
the end of a long morning which they had spent in the
young green wheat, pulling up the docks before they
seeded, under a sky like brass. As they paused in the

hedge by the heap of docks piled for burning, to pick up their coats before separating to their dinners, Kindred gripped his bare arm.

'Lookye here, my boy,' he said, 'there's enough for today. I've got to take a couple of horses down to the smith's this arternoon.'

'Well, I'll get on with the docking till you come back,' interposed Everard quickly.

'No, you 'on't, my lad,' said Kindred firmly. 'That's hard work on a day like this with the sun a-beating on your neck, and them roots are wholly deep; that wring your loins to pull 'em. 'Sides, you near split yourself last night shifting them pig-troughs.'

'Still, Bob,' Everard grumbled, 'it's a pity to leave all those docks still standing.'

'They 'on't hurt a day or two,' said Kindred, still gripping his arm. 'I ain't a-going to let you overdo it, Everard, and that's the truth. We shall be starting haysel next week, all being well, and you'll want all your strength for that.'

'Oh well, I suppose I shall have to do as I'm told,' said Everard, with a rueful smile. 'You're a hard master, Bob.'

''Haps I am,' said Kindred, letting go Everard's arm and slipping on his coat. 'Now if I was you, I should have a good forty winks on a chair in the garden after dinner. There ain't any quoit matches today. Then, when you've done tea, you can have a bit of quoit prac-tice to give you an appetite for supper and I'll meet you in *The Olive Leaf* for a glass just about eight o'clock time. How do that suit you?'

'All right, Bob,' said Everard, 'p'r'aps I will.'

That was how Everard came to be taking his ease in the afternoon, stretched out full-length on an old wicker chair in the middle of his little grassy parterre, which had responded generously to the scanty attention he had given it. On one side, waist-high clumps of lavender and an ancient cabbage-rose, inherited from Runacres, hedged him from the sun, mingling their perfumes above his head; on the other, pale-mauve rampion spikes and sulphur hollyhocks swayed, fanning him, over a dark-blue hyssop border; further below, where on the verge of the kitchen garden the grass paths ended, a solid strip of lustily blooming marigolds made a defiant boundary of flaming colour. The whole air pulsed drowsily with the hum of bees, sucking greedily at his thyme, sage and marjoram. A delicious calm stole over him, imprisoning his senses and inviting sleep; he was glad that he was not docking wheat that afternoon.

'Good arternoon, Mr. Mulliver.' A deep booming voice floated round the side of the house from the road, startling him back to wakefulness. He sat up in his chair and saw Nesley Honeyball standing by the fence and looking at him. 'Taking it easy, I see, Mr. Mulliver,' he continued, unaware that Everard, who rose and went to him, had been on the brink of sleep.

'Yes,' said Everard, 'I'm taking an afternoon off farming, Mr. Honeyball.'

'Well, that can well spare it,' he replied, rasping a finger on his bristly moustache, 'but I don't know how you can lay there and do nothing like that.'

'Well, to tell the truth, I was a bit tired,' said Everard, stopping a yawn and smiling. 'I haven't been idle these last days.'

'Ah yes, we all get a bit tired, we know,' replied Honeyball sententiously, ''specially when we don't want to work. But you know, Mr. Mulliver, your

212

garden do want a bit of prinking up and no mistake. I ain't talking about the flowers and all that; they fare all right enough. But them vegetables, they do want the hoe in 'em bad. I wonder when you last hew 'em.'

'I hardly remember,' said Everard, laughing: this was not the first time Nesley Honeyball had reproached him about his vegetables. 'I have neglected it, I know; but there seems so much else to do.'

'Ah, we all know that, Mr. Mulliver,' said Honeyball, 'but that's a pity to let a good garden down like that arter the way you started with it. Why, last Febuary that was wholly clean and trim, as good as any in the village, and now look at it; you 'on't have any potatoes neither, if you don't soon earth 'em up. I ought to know what's what, being as I've kept the rectory garden these twenty year, as the saying is.' In Honeyball's mouth the commonest expression became proverbial.

'You're quite right,' Everard admitted. 'It does want doing; I shall have to get to work on it.'

'Now, why don't you put a hand to it this arternoon, Mr. Mulliver,' said Honeyball earnestly, ''stead of lazing all your time away on that there chair? I don't like to see a young man idle, nor yet a good garden going to rack and ruin for want of a hand's turn, as the saying is.'

'Well, perhaps I will,' said Everard with a sigh, quite forgetting all Kindred's good advice. 'It'll have to be done some time and I might as well do it now.'

'That's right,' said Honeyball, 'do you use your time and don't mind me a-telling of you; but I've been young and lazy myself. I must now go and plant out some celery. Farewell, Mr. Mulliver.'

'Farewell.'

Everard looked after his short, squat figure as he went straddling down the hill, and laughed. Old Nesley was no killjoy; he was an assiduous quoit player, and no man in Lindmer could toss down a glass of beer at one gulp more neatly; but whenever gardening was in question, he became a stern, uncompromising moralist, and, as always, he was quite right about the kitchen garden. Indeed, Everard felt thoroughly ashamed when he looked at it, and having now lost, with the sudden waking, all inclination for further sleep, he determined to set things to rights; nothing should delay him. He was just turning into the toolshed to get a hoe when his elbow caught in a rose-bush and he turned to extricate himself. It was another of the cabbage-roses that to his delight he had found in the garden when he purchased it. It was loaded with great pink blossoms, full-blown and shapeless. He smelt one and breathed a deep breath of satisfaction at its inexpressible sweetness; what excellent conserve it would make! He looked round him. The four old cabbage-roses were covered with bloom, and the new stocks he had planted in the autumn were making a fair show; there ought to be enough for a little pot. He went into the shed and a moment after came out again with a basket and a pair of garden scissors in his hand, the hoe forgotten.

For close on half an hour he moved about his garden from one bush to another, leisurely rifling them of all except the tenderest buds and stopping between whiles to dip his nose in the petals of some more than usually luscious bloom. The cabbage-roses, of course, yielded most, but the odd handfuls from the younger bushes were not to be scorned. A few Provence roses would add sweetness to the conserve, damask would deepen its colour. Sweetbriar alone was barren, and musk and moss were not sweet enough to the taste, but he plucked and bruised their leaves to smell as he passed. It was only when there no longer remained a bud which he had the heart to touch, that he ceased his snipping and shook the roses down into his basket; it was nearly full. At that moment a door across the hedge banged open, there was a scurry of hastening feet along a gravel path and he saw his own little black kitten worm its way through the roots of the hedge, staring up at him with scared, saucer-like eyes. It tit-tupped across the garden into the orchard and scampered up a tree where it began to play with its own tail. A moment after, Laura Quainton's head appeared above the hedge.

'Have you seen the kitten, Everard?' she cried, all out of breath. 'Ah, there she is! Do go and get her for me. I don't want her to get lost.'

Everard put down his basket, and running into the orchard, grabbed the kitten just before it had climbed out of reach among the branches. He brought it back to Laura, tickling its ears and laughing.

'Thank you,' she said, as she took it from him. 'I'm so afraid she'll stray and get killed by a dog or something, and she's always getting out. I'd just left the door an inch ajar and out she went and I couldn't catch her. You naughty little thing!'

'Still, she'll have to go out into the wide world some day,' replied Everard, still laughing.

'Yes, I suppose so,' she said; then, catching sight of his basket, 'Why, Everard, what have you been doing, picking all the roses? What a shame!'

'That's all right,' said Everard, 'those are only the full-blown ones; there's plenty of buds left.'

'But what's it for?' she asked. 'Are you going to a funeral?'

'No,' said Everard solemnly, 'I'm going to make some rose conserve.'

'Whatever's that?' she asked wonderingly.

'If you'll come and help me, you shall see,' he replied, smiling. 'I'd already thought of asking you – that is, if you're not busy.'

'Yes, I'll come,' she said, her face brightening. 'I'll be in in a minute. I think I'd better bring the kitten with me to keep her out of mischief.'

She disappeared and Everard went into the house with his basket, glad that she was going to help him; he had only made the conserve once before, a long time ago, and she would be able to clear up certain obscurities in the recipe. He poured the roses out on the kitchen table and was beginning to pluck the petals off when she came in with the kitten.

'Now what's this you're going to make?' she said, as she put the kitten on the floor and shut the door. 'I'm all agog to hear.'

'Well,' said Everard, laughing up at her, 'as I've told you before, you folks who live in Lindmer are just the people who ought to know all about these things; your great-great-great-grandmothers did, but you've forgotten all about them.'

'Well,' she pouted, 'suppose you teach me.'

'It's only a sort of jam,' said Everard, 'made of roses.'

'What a shame!' she cried, 'spoiling all those lovely flowers just to eat them! And I can't imagine what they taste like.'

'Ah, you wait till you taste, Laura,' said Everard with a mysterious air, 'or are you going to refuse to help me out of sympathy for the roses?'

She smiled ironically at him. 'Yes, I'll help you; tell me what to do.'

'Well, first of all,' he said, 'you've got to pull the leaves apart and then snip off the white heels at the

216

bottom because they're not good to eat and don't taste of anything; and perhaps we could have a bowl to put them in?'

Laura got up and went to the china-cupboard.

'How about a pudding basin?' she said.

'Not nearly big enough,' he replied, 'we shall fill three of them.'

She came back with the great two-gallon earthenware jar in which she kept the bread.

'Is that large enough?' she said, laughing.

'It may do to go on with,' he replied. 'Now mind you don't drop any grubs, ladybirds or earwigs in, won't you, Laura? They spoil the taste.'

'All right, Mr. Mulliver,' she rejoined archly – the now unaccustomed name was quite jarring to his ears – 'you're master here.'

The plucking of the leaves and the snipping of the heels kept them occupied for fully half an hour, and there was very little time to talk. Every now and then she looked up and said with mock-humility, 'Am I doing it right, Mr. Mulliver?' to which he replied, with a corresponding mock-gravity, 'Yes, Mrs. Quainton.'

'You haven't filled my jar,' she remarked maliciously, when they had finished.

'No,' said Everard cautiously, 'they're very deceptive when you take the seed-head off. How much would you say they weigh?'

'Oh, I couldn't say,' she replied, 'and I daren't guess – if you won't. Suppose we weigh them.'

'H'm, about two pounds, I should say,' murmured Everard, as she went to fetch the kitchen scales from the cupboard.

She put the scales on the table and shot the mottled

pile of rose leaves, pink, white, gold and crimson, on to a sheet of paper which promptly curled over them in the deep metal scoop.

'How refreshing they smell,' she said, pulling back the paper and sniffing them, 'poor dears!'

'A nice housewife you are,' teased Everard. 'You've forgotten the weights.'

'Well, if you'd offered to carry them,' she returned tartly, 'I shouldn't have forgotten them. No, don't you go, Everard, you'll never find them!'

Together they rummaged in the bottom of the cupboard and carried back the weights between them.

'Now, whatever did you want to bring the four-pound weight for?' she laughed. 'I know you haven't got all that.'

'Don't you be so sure,' he replied wisely. 'I'll swear there's two pounds, anyhow.'

She put on a pound weight, but the scoop did not move.

'What did I tell you?' said Everard.

She tantalizingly added a half-pound weight; still the scoop was motionless.

'Of course it's two pounds,' cried Everard victoriously, 'only you won't believe it.'

She replaced the pound and half-pound by a two-pound weight which made the scoop quiver, but it needed two more ounces before it rose.

'There!' he cried triumphantly.

Laura with a puzzled look parted the curled ends of paper in the scoop and looked down into it. Her lips twitched.

'Is it jam or meat-paste you're making, Everard?' she said drily. 'Look here.'

Curled up in a little hollow among the rose leaves lay

the kitten, fast asleep. It had slipped in behind their backs while they were getting the weights.

'You little devil!' said Everard, picking it up and hugging it. The weights went down with a bang.

Laura tittered. 'I think a pound weight'll serve,' she said wickedly, 'after all.' It served exactly. 'Now who was right?' she said, smiling.

'I yield, Laura,' replied Everard gallantly. 'I must go now and have a look at the recipe.'

He went into the sitting-room, and pulling *The Closet of Sir Kenelm Digby* down from the shelves, hastily turned up a passage beginning, 'Dr. Glisson makes his conserve of red roses thus.' He scanned it rapidly, nodding to himself as he recognized the directions; then, leaving it open on the table, he went back to the kitchen.

'We've got to boil the rose leaves,' he said, 'a pint and a half of water to the pound.'

'How long?' she asked.

'Till they're tender,' he replied, 'half an hour, that is. May I use one of your saucepans? They won't stain it.'

'I suppose I shall have to let you,' she said with a sigh.

'I hope you don't mind my making a mess of the kitchen like this,' he said, doubtful suddenly whether the sigh were pretended or not.

She burst out laughing at him.

'Of course I don't, Everard,' she said. 'I'm only too glad to let you have your own way, bless you. Only I don't know what you think you're going to turn out of that saucepan with rose leaves and water; but boys always do like playing with saucepans.'

'You wait,' said Everard, 'and find me a half-pint measure.'

They poured the water over the leaves and set it to

219

boil on the little oil-stove that Everard had installed for summer use. Laura fetched some needlework and sat down to sew while Everard stood over the pot, stirring diligently and scarcely taking his eyes off it. As he was silent, she did not speak, but occasionally she glanced up at his bent back and smiled. Little by little the rose leaves paled as the essence distilled from them, flushing the water deeper and deeper, until at the end of half an hour it was quite crimson.

'Now, look at that colour,' he said, turning round with the saucepan in his hand. 'It was worth picking all those roses just to produce that. Smell it. It's like wine.'

She put down her sewing and sniffed it – suspiciously.

'It doesn't smell like roses, does it?' she said sceptically.

'Ah well, it isn't finished yet,' said Everard, who had taken out the leaves, strained them and put them aside. 'I must go and look at my recipe again.'

'Aren't you going to put any sugar in?' she called after him. 'You can't make jam without sugar.'

'I'm just going to find out the quantity,' he called back.

'Ah,' she teased, when he returned, 'I don't believe you'd have put any sugar in if I hadn't told you. You and your old book!'

'Very well, madam,' he replied, 'I won't take offence. We set it to boil again and put in four pounds of sugar, one by one as they dissolve, and then go on boiling till it just doesn't reach candy height. Will you weigh me four pounds of sugar?'

They both stood over the saucepan this time, Everard stirring, Laura sifting in the sugar, pound by pound. A rose-like smell floated in the air which Everard sniffed appreciatively; Laura smiled and said nothing.

'By the way, Laura,' he said all at once, 'what is candy height?'

'Ah, you can't do without me, can you?' she mocked.

'Oh, I know quite well what happens when it candies,' said Everard, 'but this must just not candy.'

'Ah well, you haven't made jam,' she replied, 'else you'd know by the feel. Give me that spoon.' She dropped her teasing and became the serious housewife for a moment. 'It's getting heavy; look, it's sticking to the spoon; did you hear that crackle? Off with it! Lucky you asked me; you were only just in time.'

Everard whisked the saucepan off the stove, tipped the pale rose leaves back into the liquor from which they had been strained, and stirred them together.

'I thought you were going to throw that mess away,' she said sarcastically.

Everard feigned not to hear.

'Some little pots, quick, Laura!' he cried.

'I've got some little meat-paste jars,' she said. 'They came from your shop. They'll be just the thing; and you were going to put the kitten in, weren't you?'

Everard said nothing, but smiled a knowing smile as he poured the conserve out into the little stone jars she ranged on the table.

'Just like a man,' she scolded, as he spilt a drop and wiped it up with a finger which he licked greedily, smacking his lips. 'Well, what next?' she said, smiling.

'It's all over,' he said, putting down the saucepan. 'Just leave 'em out in the sun till the top candies, and then tie 'em up.'

'Oh, I see,' she replied, 'and now I suppose I can get the tea ready. It's ever so late.'

'Poor Laura!' he said, laughing. 'But look here, I've

221

turned your kitchen upside down, so I'll invite you to tea and I'll get it ready for a change.'

'Oh, that doesn't matter,' she protested. 'It's no trouble.'

But he would not listen to her.

'You go in and sit down while I see to it,' he said. 'Go along with you.'

He motioned her into the sitting-room and she laughingly obeyed. Two minutes later she heard a shout from the kitchen. 'Where's the tablecloth?'

'You can't do without me,' she repeated, as she helped him to find it.

'Back you go!' he insisted. 'That's all I want.'

The kettle began to sing and Everard came in with a large tray which he proceeded to unload on the table.

'Are we going to have dry bread?' she said, as he put down the loaf.

'Why no,' he replied, 'but I'm not cutting bread-and-butter; you can eat so much more butter if you don't.'

She shook her head over him, and as soon as he was gone, began cutting bread-and-butter; tea was not tea to her without it. A few minutes later he was back again with the teapot and a little jar of warm conserve.

'Why, it's not cool yet!' she exclaimed.

'Still, you've got to taste it,' he replied. 'I'm giving you sugar and milk.'

He tilted the teapot and a steamy jet of pure water descended into the cup. Laura threw herself back in her chair and rocked with laughter.

'Oh yes, of course,' he stammered with an embarrassed smile, 'that was only to warm the teapot.'

'You can't take me in, Everard,' she gasped, wiping her eyes, as he went out into the kitchen again. 'You don't fill the pot right up to warm it.'

'Why, you've cut bread-and-butter,' he said, as he came back with the teapot.

'I should think so too,' she retorted, smiling.

'Now suppose you try a little of that conserve,' he said quietly, feeling almost self-conscious. 'You only want a little.'

With a humorous air she helped herself, made a sandwich and suspiciously took a little bite, Everard closely watching her. A sudden change came over her face as a remarkable combination of different sensations impinged upon her palate. She stared at Everard, thunderstruck.

'I didn't know it was like this,' she said, taking another bite. 'It seems to taste different every mouthful. It's quite rough now.'

'But it's warm,' he said.

'Yes, and tart now.'

'But sweet as well.'

'And now it tastes of nothing but roses,' she said. 'It's wonderful, Everard.'

'That's what all the scoffers say,' he replied sardonically, 'once they've tasted it. My mother did too, but she didn't ask any questions afterwards. You were the same with my salads, weren't you? Have some more, Laura.'

'I will,' she said eagerly, 'to give you credit for it. I won't scoff again.'

He thanked her with a smile, and for a few minutes they were silent, being both of them hungry.

'Well now,' said Everard, leaning back in his arm-chair, as she was finishing her fifth rose-conserve sandwich, 'how do you think I managed the tea after all?'

'Oh well,' she replied condescendingly, 'it wasn't so bad for a man. But not cutting the bread-and-butter, and forgetting to warm the pot and put the tea in – you want a woman to look after you, you know.'

'Perhaps I do,' Everard admitted, 'and I must say, you do it very well, Laura, better than anyone else ever has.'

'Do I?' she said faintly. Her whole face lit up and her eyes positively danced. How she responded to a compliment, he thought; that was what she needed to give her confidence in herself, she did not know her own worth.

'Have some more conserve,' he said, as she swallowed the last mouthful of her sandwich.

She shook her head.

'No, really I can't,' she said. 'I've had an enormous tea today. I can't think why.'

'You've been laughing so much,' he said railingly.

'Have I?' she replied. 'I suppose I have.'

'Why, you're always laughing now,' he said.

'You're in great high spirits, I think. I expect you know why you are,' he added significantly, in a lower tone.

She looked at him thoughtfully and nodded.

'I can see it in your face,' pursued Everard. 'Every day you seem to look younger. Laughter makes good looks.'

She flushed up to the eyes and turned her head away, then turned it back and looked at him wistfully.

'You mustn't flatter me,' she faltered.

'I'm not flattering you, Laura,' he replied earnestly. 'I mean it.'

Her eyes shone. He had meant it, and he had said it purposely, hoping thus to draw her on to the consequences of her own admission and broach once more the subject of divorce. It was a good opportunity, but he hesitated. She seemed so happy just then, and he felt loth to disturb her happiness with such grave matters; better perhaps to wait a little and let that compliment sink in.

Everard was more tired than he knew; a sudden languor, further induced by the vapours of the hot kitchen and the hearty meal he had eaten, surged over him and overwhelmed his consciousness; without a struggle his head dropped and his eyes closed. Laura, taken by surprise, peered at him incredulously; he was indubitably asleep. Straightway rising to her feet, she tiptoed out of the room, and then, had he been awake he would have seen all the youth in her face turn to bitter, disappointed age – as if his involuntary act had taken all the savour out of his compliment for her: he meant it, but it meant nothing to him.

XXI

THE first moonbeam was just quivering in the silver mesh of a birch-top in the copse when Everard dropped down on the hedge-bank, clasping his ankles and pillowing his head upon his knees. He was alone and would remain alone, because Ruthie had gone with Mrs. Gathercole to Bures on a visit to her aunt, and would not return until the following morning. But tonight he did not miss her. It had been a memorable day; it was also his birthday, although he had completely forgotten it.

As Kindred had predicted a week ago, haysel was now in full swing and, tomorrow being Sunday, all the tasks on the farm had been most carefully apportioned so as to make the most of the fine weather while it lasted. Everard, too, had his part to play in the day's economy, and early in the morning he set out for the sheep-pens by himself with a half-filled sack over his shoulder, in high spirits and secretly a little proud that such serious account should be taken of his labour. The ewes were so accustomed to him now that they recognized him from a distance and trotted up to the hurdles to meet him; and when he stepped into the fold, he had some difficulty in forcing his way to the troughs through the crowd of eager black muzzles pressing round his knees and sniffing at his sack. However, a few handfuls of crumbled linseed cake from it in the bottom of the trough soon diverted their attention and he was able to empty the remainder of its contents in comfort. For a minute or two he stood watching them as they nibbled, flank tightly wedged against flank. There was always one ewe that failed to find a place at the trough and wandered about, hungrily nosing the quarters of the others. He made an opening for her, and when she, too, had settled down, contented, to her nibbling, he felt her back with his fingers in the best professional manner; she had not suffered much for being always last. He felt a few more backs and then, picking up the fold-drift from under a trough, he began to stake out a fresh fold in the lucerne. It was a job he had often done and he worked almost like clockwork now; a few pecks, a few taps with the fold-drift, a thrust with the foot and so on to the next hurdle. Still, the ground between the lucerne roots was stone-hard with drought and sun, and he was sweating freely by the time the last hurdle was in position. He leant up against it and paused to mop his face and light his pipe, gazing the while with satisfaction at the new fold.

It was all his work; he had made each hole, driven in each post and clinched each hurdle. The ewes would not go hungry now, and so much of the life of the farm he had carried on for another day, a heartening thought. They had already finished their linseed cake and were peering longingly at the green new strip of lucerne that he had just penned off for them, and impatiently bleating their disapproval of his delay. He smiled, and striding over to the partition between the two folds slid back a hurdle. There was a swift scurrying patter of little hoofs as they all rushed into the gap, where all but the foremost remained firmly blocked until he drew back another hurdle and they all went plunging forward into the sweet, fresh lucerne, snuffing, tearing and munching it with as keen a relish as if they had never tasted so wonderful a delicacy before in their lives. Everard, having put back the hurdles, still stood a moment to watch them; they were so happy now, they had forgotten all about him.

There on the hillside the air was still crisp and clear, but the sun was mounting over the valley and the larks soaring to meet it. He mopped his face again; there was no time to waste, and he would have to sweat a good deal more before the day was out. He slung his sack over his shoulder and set off down the hill.

Arrived in the farmyard, he made straight for the stable, and Dolly, the big chestnut mare, whinnied as he opened the door. She had been in harness all the week, pulling the mower or carting the hay, and this morning all the other horses except Short, her team-fellow, whom Kindred had taken with him, had been turned out to grass. She turned her head round, wondering if her turn had come now too. Everard patted her shining flank and fondled the smooth skin beneath her underlip while he poured a handful of oats into the manger.

'There, have another bite, Dolly,' he coaxed. 'You'll need it before tonight.'

He took down a ponderous, much-patched horse-collar, unbuckled the headstall and slipped the collar over her neck.

'That's right, old dear,' he said, as she resumed her crunching, and clapped the wooden saddle with its jingling network of chain-harness on to her back. He buckled the belly-band, put her flowing tail through the crupper and set the breeching straight on her quarters.

'Come along, my gal,' he said, as he stood by the

manger and stroked her neck, waiting for her to finish. 'You're drawing it out on purpose.'

He had a great affection for that old thatched stable with its dusty black beams and worn mangers, its familiar furnishings of chain-harness and horse-collars, lanterns, pitchforks, straw skips and bottles of drench; a clumsily scratched legend on the bar of the hay-rack recorded snow on September 19th, 1849; the air smelt of hay and the sharp taint of horses. Generation after generation of horsemen must have baited their horses there at daybreak before their own breakfast, and again at sunset before their own supper, with oats that the same horses had helped to sow, reap and garner. Its whole existence had been bound up with the life of the farm, its good times and its bad times.

Dolly, having crunched her last mouthful of oats, cut short his meditations by turning round and nuzzling his hand for more, but all she got was the stale iron bit in her mouth and the bridle over her ears. Five minutes later she was pulling him along the valley in a jolting farm-waggon to his next destination.

Kindred was waiting for him on the little clover-ley beside the iron horse-rake, the clover all neatly piled across the field before him in long brown rows.

'A good bit of work,' he said, as Everard pulled up the waggon before him and sprang to the ground. 'I've just now finished raking. Now we can turn to and carry it.'

'Where's the rick to be?' said Everard.

Kindred pointed across the hedge to a little tarred and thatched bullock-shed in the abutting pasture; they were right down in the bottom of the valley.

'Over there by the ne'thouse,' he replied. 'That'll make a nice little owd rick. You see, late autumn-time it often happen I buy a few head of young things – driv over from Wales in bunches, they are, calved in Ireland afore that – and I fatten 'em up on that there grass; but a mote of stover – like this clover make, that do 'em good now and agin, wintertime. That's why I thought me and you together could do this job all to ourselves. My other three blokes are over in the water-midder, a-mowing.'

He unhitched his own mare from the horse-rake and tied her up to the hedge with a heap of stover under her nose.

'Come along,' he said, climbing into the waggon and handing Everard a fork. 'You pitch, I lood.'

Already at odd jobs in the rickyard Everard had got into the way of handling a fork, and he had no difficulty in keeping Kindred's hands full as they slowly crept along the first line of stover. There seemed no limit to the weight he could hoist on the end of his fork; the more his arms stretched, the more they wanted to stretch. His zeal growing, he took larger and larger pitches until at last he transfixed so mighty a truss that he could not lift it above his shoulder into upright; that was always the hardest part of pitching, the hoisting after was child's play. Determined not to yield, he brought the handle down flat against his foot, and clutching just under the prongs, he hauled it up to his shoulder by main force; then, staggering but trium-phant, he poised it above his head and shot it aloft at Kindred's feet. But Kindred had no praise for him. He crossed his arms on his fork and looked down censoriously.

'Now don't you let me catch you doing that agin,' he said reprovingly. 'That's wholly silly, that is. You'll strain your guts or something, and them bloody great trusses don't ondly hamper me.' He laughed. 'In the old days when a man grounded his fork, we used to make him stand a quart of beer.'

Everard laughed, but he felt abashed, as if he were not, after all, half the farmer he had felt himself to be.

Kindred was right. The quiet, steady lift was far more suited to the long day's toil in the sun and the middling-sized pitch was of far more use to the loader. He went to work again with less violence and the pile on the waggon rose ever higher. But Kindred always asked for more; there seemed no end to what he could stow away up there. Suddenly at last he called down for 'one more pitch to top her up,' and having disposed of it, slid down off the load with the haft of Everard's fork, stuck in the side of the load, to steady him.

They led the waggon over to the neathouse where Kindred had already prepared a little rick-bottom of bean-straw and hedge-brushings, and here Everard mounted the waggon to unload while Kindred stayed below to make the rick. At first Everard found himself continually treading on the pitch of stover that he wanted to lift, and during the first unloading, in his efforts to keep Kindred constantly supplied, he became quite flustered and breathless. He was very anxious to please, but Kindred seemed too much engrossed with his rick-making to notice him or even to talk. Then, to his relief, he found himself on the hard boards of the waggon again, among the scattered clover-heads. Once more they filled the waggon and once more Everard began to unload. It was worse than ever this time and Everard was in despair. However hard he heaved and tore, nothing but ridiculous little wisps seemed to come up on the prongs of his fork. There was more about haying to learn than he had ever imagined; he wondered what Kindred must think of him, there at work on the rick, strangely silent. Then, half-way through the load, quite unexpectedly, the knack came to him. He knew where to tread, where to plunge his fork, as if by instinct, and thrust the stover down to Kindred in great rolls now, with half his former effort. It ceased to be a labour and his spirits rose.

'H'm,' said Kindred, as they led the empty waggon back into the field for another load, 'you've caught the hang of that now, haven't you? I somehow thought you would.'

He grinned and was silent again. Everard flushed with pleasure, but did not reply. He, too, now found himself gradually taken in the grip of the same tense, preoccupied silence, the sun beat down upon his bare neck and arms, the sweat streamed from his cheeks and all he seemed to see was stover, stover on the field, stover on the load, stover on the rick; but his muscles moved almost without his willing it, without fatigue, as if they could go on for ever; he had worked himself in, he no longer wanted to speak.

So the morning slipped away, and it was with something of astonishment that Everard first caught sight of Mrs. Kindred standing in the hedge with the dinner-basket; it was twelve o'clock. They sat down quietly together in the shade of an elm-tree, still in their shirt-sleeves, while Mrs. Kindred served out the food and set the heaped plates between their knees.

'Tired, Everard?' she asked, pouring him out a glass of beer.

He smiled and shook his head.

'Don't you let him work you too hard.' She pointed at her husband – her perennial warning. 'He'll work you to the bone, he will.'

'Everard's shaping well,' said Kindred. 'He know how to use a fork; we'll larn him to lood this arternoon.'

The praise made Everard's ears tingle.

'Aren't you having anything, Mrs. Kindred?' he said, sipping his bitter beer.

'No, Everard,' she said, 'I'm now gooing back for my bit; must feed my men first. I wholly hope you find that duck and green peas to your liking; and there's a gooseberry fool in that there basket. Robert, do you see Everard make a good dinner. I must now be gooing back. And don't forget that basket,' she added, as she stumped away.

'This is good beer,' said Everard, gazing into his glass.

'Ay, a good bit of malt,' agreed Kindred. 'That was our own barley too. I got it malted special and then brewed the beer. That's allus best what you've growed yourself.'

'Like this,' said Everard, following Kindred's example, and picking up his duck's leg to gnaw it in his fingers.

'Yes,' said Kindred with a laugh, 'that and the peas and the taters and the goosegogs and the milk, why, all our dinner come off the farm, now I think of it.'

Everard laughed and then became thoughtful; it was the best meal he had ever tasted. They lit their pipes and Everard lay back in the grass, puffing tranquilly and gazing into the hedge. The whole air was dizzy with heat; a poplar above him, in the faintest of breezes, beckoned; a score of dog-roses bared their yellow hearts to the sun; a grasshopper rasped at his feet, a bee boomed past his head, a yellowhammer uttered its monotonous, plaintive cry; the spicy scent of stover and the cloying breath of meadowsweet floated together into his nostrils; he felt all their life pass into him, becoming his, and closed his eyes.

'Time's up!' exclaimed Kindred, pulling himself to his feet. 'Wake up, Everard!'

Everard staggered up, rubbed the drowsiness out of his eyes, worked his arms a few times and felt his strength come back to him. They walked over to the waggon, with Dolly still between its shafts, placidly chewing over a heap of new stover, and put Short in her place to give her a spell.

'Ah, she like that,' said Kindred, tugging at her reluctant head. 'Common hay's only bread-and-butter, but stover's cake to them.'

Everard smiled and said nothing; he still felt rather humble.

'Get you up in the waggon, Everard,' shouted Kindred, 'and do you do just what I tell you; we'll larn you to lood.'

Everard climbed up and the waggon jolted away across the field, Kindred leading. It stopped and Everard felt alone and very helpless.

'Fill up your bottom first,' said Kindred, shooting a large pitch over Everard's feet, 'and tread that well down.'

The stover seemed to drop naturally from his fork in the place where it was wanted; Everard hardly needed to touch it.

'Now fill the front rack,' cried Kindred, deftly placing a pitch on the forward corner. 'A bit more over the edge; that 'on't fall.'

Dumbly Everard obeyed, till the front rack was covered.

'Now your sides,' cried Kindred. 'Let that hang well over. Its own weight keep it from falling.'

So they went on, till both the sides and the rear rack as well were filled on a level with the middle, Kindred placing almost every pitch.

'Now fill your middle again.'

Everard caught the idea. The stover in the body of the waggon overlapped the inner edge of the stover on the sides and racks, and held it fast; and so on, layer after layer, till there was no longer middle nor sides, but only one vast, level oblong, bounded by space. That was how the unwieldy pile reared itself in equilibrium on the fragile base that it far overhung in every direction.

Everard was high up now and Kindred could no longer see to place the stover; it came up in heaps at Everard's feet and he had to hurry to dispose of it before more arrived, his eye roving the load in search of inequalities to level, at times up to his knees in stover and lurching from side to side at the mercy of the jolting waggon.

'Not too far out in that corner,' cried Kindred, with a warning tap of his fork. 'Do, you'll have the whole show over. Pull it in.'

Everard obeyed. The load mounted.

'Fill up the hole you're standing in,' commanded Kindred, sending up a last pitch, 'and down you come.'

'Another time, you can stay up there,' he said, 'to unlood at the rick, but I wanted you to see your lood from below.'

Everard looked shamefacedly at the pile that rose above him. It was not the compact square block he had proudly imagined under him, but a tall mound, with curving sides and a peaked top.

Kindred laughed. 'That ain't so bad,' he said, 'for first time, but that want to hang over more. Don't you be afraid; I'll tell you when you're falling.'

The afternoon wore on and Everard acquired a surer balance on top of his load; he began to feel like a captain on the bridge, commanding his ship; he had time to scheme now, between one pitch and the next. His arms and legs were black with clover dust, his muscles felt like board; but he need never stop. Then all at once he was emptying the last load and Kindred was topping up the little circular rick. The field was cleared, the rick was done, the waggon bare.

'Well, there's a nice bit for my youngsters,' said Kindred, surveying the rick from the ground. 'They ought to thank us next winter, I reckon, and that's the truth.'

'They ought,' said Everard, and smiled; the thought of their gratitude pleased him; he had helped to feed them, after all.

'Now then, Everard,' said Kindred, 'I'm going along to the mowers to tell the cowman to go home for milking and I'll take his scythe. Do you take the horses back and let the cows into the yard on your way. Don't you forget.'

'Trust me,' said Everard, 'and then I'll fetch you your tea.'

They parted and Everard rumbled back along the valley behind the two mares, comfortably sprawled in the waggon beside the empty dinner-basket and idly watching the pieces of broken clover-leaf sift through the cracks between the boards. On the way to the stable he stopped to open a paddock gate and let the throng-ing cows shamble out into the farmyard to wait for the lightening of their swollen udders. Then, after the waggon had been left in the rickyard, the horses had to be taken to the stable, unharnessed and given a small bait before the cowman came and turned them out to grass with the other horses. The cows were still resign-edly waiting for him in the yard when Everard left the stable and went into the farmhouse kitchen. Mrs.

Kindred, who was churning butter, stopped the handle and looked up.

'Ah, you want the tea,' she said. 'You must wait a minute; butter's coming. The kettle's b'iling.'

'Let me have it,' said Everard, taking the handle from her. 'Then you can make the tea and Bob won't have to wait for it.'

Mrs. Kindred, all red and blowzy with exertion, wiped her forehead as she relinquished the churn.

'That make me sweat,' she sighed, 'this weather.'

The cream sucked and gurgled rhythmically in the churn as Everard plied the handle. Then all of a sudden the rhythm changed, broken by a dull thudding against the sides of the churn; the butter had come.

'Well done, Everard,' said Mrs. Kindred, who was pouring tea into a glass bottle. 'You've made enough butter there to last us a fortnight, I doubt. that's a good colour too; feed's just right. Now come you and sit down and hev a cup of tea.'

'Not I,' said Everard, laughing. 'I'll have mine out in the field with Bob.'

'Now do you set down,' she pressed him, 'and hev your tea proper like a gentleman.'

But Everard wanted to be out in the air and she could not stop him. Five minutes later he was on his way to the water-meadow with the tea-basket on his arm. All the other hay on the farm had been cut with the horse-drawn mower, but this, the only water-meadow on the farm, broken as it was by the ridges and irrigation channels which enabled it to be flooded at intervals all the year through, had perforce to be mown with the scythe. The other two mowers were already sitting in the hedge, with two little children who had brought them their tea playing beside them. Kindred,

237

who was still bent over his scythe in the grass, came over and joined them as soon as Everard shouted to him.

'Ah,' he gasped, when he had wetted his gullet with a draught of tea, 'that do a man good after mowing. That's real work, that is, and that's my idea of what mowing should be. These here machine-mowers sorterly bruise and tear the grass, but a scythe, that real cut it. And there's lovely grass in this midder.'

'Yes,' said Everard, taking a bite out of a thick jam sandwich, 'but you wouldn't get haysel done half so soon that way.'

'That's wholly true,' replied Kindred, with a sigh, 'though I can't help wishing for the old times every now and then. There ain't many now as can use a scythe proper on grass, not to cut that as that should be cut. And yet, I can remember in my father's time when we mowed every mote by hand and I was lord of the mowers. When I stopped for a rub, all the others stopped for a rub, and when I started agin, they started, and they had to keep up with me. And how they used to talk when mother sent down half-a-gallon of beer!'

His eyes became vacant, and he went on eating in silence, as if still reliving in thought his old mowing days.

'Now, Everard,' he said, when they had finished tea and pushed the cups into the basket, 'we'll do a bit of mowing together. I've strung up an old scythe for you.'

They walked over to the spot where he had been working, and he put the scythe in Everard's hands.

'Now, listen here,' he began, 'I want to tell you something. If you want to cut a bit of stick easy, you don't cut that straight like a bit of meat, but on the slip, don't you? Well, that's the same with grass. Your scythe's sharped and set a bit up'ards, so that all you've got to do is to swing it and that do the cutting on the slip by its own weight.'

Everard nodded; there was little for him to say today.

'Now, come on,' Kindred continued. 'Get your legs well apart, right foot forrard, and let the scythe hang natural. Your hands don't do no work; they're just sorterly a pivot; you mow with your back. Now then, put your point in the grass and swing.'

Everard obeyed and swung the scythe as he had seen Kindred do. The blade rasped and some stalks fell; then half-way it stopped and refused to go further.

'Becourse you stopped,' said Kindred. 'You didn't put all your weight behind it. And as the grass gather on the blade, becourse, that's heavy. Try agin.'

Everard swung again, bending his back and putting all his body into the swing. The scythe cut its way further this time, but only to bury its point with a sickening grate beneath the turf.

'Oh dear, you mustn't do that,' cried Kindred. 'That'll spoil your edge and buckle your scythe. Now you know why that was – you didn't keep your heel down. You must; don't, you'll dig your point in, or anyways, you'll leave the grass standing in ridges at the beginning of your swath, and in the owd days your master wouldn't have paid your wages till you'd cut 'em all down. Now do you watch me.'

He picked up his scythe and bent over the grass. Immediately scythe and man seemed to become one being. With slow, creeping steps the straddled legs advanced, keeping measured time with the swinging shoulders and sweeping blade. One faint hiss against the steel and a whole swath lay prostrate. Everard watched him in admiration and despair, too, of matching such effortless skill.

'There now,' said Kindred, stopping, 'I'm going to leave you to yourself. You'll have to make your own mistakes and I'd only hinder you. Do you take that little swath and I'll come and give you a rub later on.'

He went back to his own swath and left Everard alone with the scythe in his hands. The next half-hour was a torture to him, partly of discomfiture at his blunders and the sorry figure that he was cutting in Kindred's eyes, partly of sheer bodily discord, because his own legs and shoulders were not yet properly attuned in their movements and every pull or thrust clashed with another. The scythe hung, an intolerable weight upon his wrists, and his loins ached. The blade either missed the grass or tore it up by the roots, the point stuck time after time in the turf and had to be bent back into the straight by force; the path he left behind him was full of little unmown ridges and tussocks; and finally he cut his thumb out of sheer carelessness, whetting his blade.

'Don't you worry,' said Kindred, who came along now and then to mow down the ridges he left behind him. 'Keep your heel low. That'll come – to a chap like you.'

But Everard doubted if it ever would.

Sounds hushed and the lustre went out of the sky as the soberness of evening crept over it. Everard still struggled with his swath. Then, whether it was that his muscles had resolved their strife of their own accord or had caught the rhythm from Kindred's bent back, he suddenly discovered that he was mowing. Body and scythe were advancing, both inspired by the same momentum. The lush grasses met the blade crisply and

240

fell with only a sigh. Vaguely he could distinguish them – cocksfoot, timothy, Italian rye-grass, with here and there a pale bloom of spotted orchid or red spire of sorrel; his feet reeked with the rank smell of spilt juice. Sweat poured down from his forehead, but the dull ache had dropped from his loins like a husk. He saw nothing now but his wet blade and the falling grasses; rapt by the spell of his own motion, he lost all awareness of self; he was part of the earth on which he stood and must go on mowing until the world's end.

Dusk was beginning to fall and the other two mowers had already shouldered their scythes and started homewards. Kindred, having reached the end of the field, turned round and watched Everard coming up along the last strip of standing grass with a smile of approval. Nothing baulked his progress now, and although here and there behind him an accusing tuft of grass still appeared to show that he had not always kept the heel of his scythe down, Kindred, for fear of discouraging him, did not move to cut them off. Everard pulled up beside him as the last stalks fell, a little blankly; there was nothing left to do now.

'I'm that sorry,' said Kindred, as they stood side by side, leaning on their scythes, 'I'm that sorry I haven't got another water-midder, 'cause I'd wholly like you a-mowing along o' me. You've picked that up all right.'

Everard nodded gratefully, and wiped the sweat off his brow with the back of his hand.

'I expect you're tired,' said Kindred.

'I suppose I am a bit,' replied Everard. He certainly was, and yet he had never felt more strength in him than at that moment.

'Well, I'm going off home now,' said Kindred,

241

taking Everard's scythe from him. 'I'll carry that for you. You'll now be wanting to get up to the copse, I doubt.'

He grinned knowingly. Everard flushed and then smiled; the old man was most thoughtful.

'Thanks, Bob,' he said, 'I think I will go now. See you in the sheep tomorrow. Farewell, Bob.'

Ruthie would not be there, he knew, but nevertheless he felt a desire to go there, a desire to be alone, away from roof and walls. He was tired, but something deep and powerful pulsed in his blood; the rhythm of the mowing was still in his body.

Slowly he made his way up the hill by the shadowy hedges, soft willowherb and hemp agrimony rustling against his thighs, spear-headed teazles and ghostly umbels of hogweed nodding in his face. The throb in his blood grew fainter as he plodded up, but it still was there, diffusing itself now in a profound contentment. So he came to the copse, and just as the moon was rising, cast himself down upon the same bank where three months before Ruthie and he had lain together among the violets. Only now there were no violets; white splashes of guelder-rose, pale wreaths of sleeping honeysuckle loomed in the hedge, white-belled con-volvulus peered like faces among them; herb Robert, chervil and knapweed tumbled in the grass. All their scents were fading into the dewy scent of the night itself.

Everard sat there gazing at the ghost-moths flitting in the half-cropped pasture before him, vanishing like phantom white candle flames as they alighted on the grass-heads. A great white owl floated down from the branches of a hollow elm trunk and glided noiselessly thrice across the pasture, stately and mysterious. A young hedgehog trotted out from the hedge, routing in the grass and grunting vigorously. Out in search of food, he thought, as all living creatures, man among them, must. He, too, throughout the day had been busy with food, for man and beast. He had helped to churn butter for the Kindreds, he had fed the ewes and baited the horses, he had carted stover for young steers yet scarcely born, he had mown hay to feed the horses which ploughed the land that grew corn to feed him. Looking back upon his memorable day he perceived that this was what had made it so memorable; this was the secret of his new happiness and his affection for Lindmer Vale; even the food he had eaten in the fields that day had tasted sweeter for being grown on the soil where he had worked. From the earth man came, all his days she fed him and at length he returned to her; she held within her the springs of life, and the closer man was to her, fulfilling her immemorial purposes, the more fully, the more truly he seemed to be alive. Everard looked down at his sun-burnt, clover-blackened arms, earth-colour, he smelt the musky, sweaty smell of his own moist shirt. It seemed right that these things should be so; they were all part of the simple, primitive, earthy setting to which man had been born and to which he himself wished to belong. His ancestors had belonged to it and he was irresistibly drawn back to it because his roots were there. Earthy he was and closer to earth he wanted to be, for though she was an adversary to be wrestled with, enslaving man to the struggle, she was also a smiling and bountiful yielder of fruits in season, whom man called mother. He wanted to hold her in his hands, to be part of her; he loved her. He turned over and buried his face in the grass.

XXII

EVERARD removed his empty plate to the other side of the table, and picking up a postcard that was propped against the salt-cellar, inspected it with amused curiosity. It had come the previous night, forwarded from his house at Bury, but he had been too much abstracted to take any notice of it when he eventually came in from the fields to his waiting supper. It was not important. On one side was a coloured picture of the Norman tower at Bury; on the other in a formless scrawl Mrs. Graynorr wished him Many Happy Returns of the Day. Kind of her to remember him, but it was like a voice crying out of the past, she seemed so distant to him, more distant than ever since yesterday's unforgettable experiences and the new exaltation of self-knowledge. The excitement of it all had died down, but it had left behind a comforting inner warmth that blended pleasantly with an agreeable tiredness of body. Yet it was less than a year since Mrs. Graynorr had been inviting him to tennis parties. He was still laughing quietly to himself over this thought when the door opened and Laura entered with a large dish in her hands, surmounted by a proportionately large dish-cover, which she set down in front of him with a half-mysterious, half-triumphant air.

'The pudding,' she said with a smile, and picking up his dirty plate, she left the room without another word.

Everard lifted the cover and peered at the pudding. It

was quite a common pudding with a crisp, brown crust, baked in a tin. He cut himself a slice and examined it. The inside was a deep yellow, of a soft, compact texture that pointed to suet and breadcrumbs; there was something familiar, too, in the flavour of the steam which floated up in his face. He dissected a morsel with his fork and discovered several tiny fragments of shrivelled orange stuff that looked as if they had found their way in by mistake. He recognized them at once and dropped his fork on the plate in surprise; it was a marigold pudding. Nor had she stinted the marigolds. The flavour came full on his tongue, dainty, yet aromatic, better than any spice; it was done to a turn. He attacked it with a zest, wondering where she could have got the recipe; perhaps she had come across it, dusting his books. The pudding began to disappear. The sound of wheels in the street made him look up from his plate, just in time to catch a passing glimpse of Steve Quainton setting off for his Sunday afternoon jaunt, wherever that might be – he was seldom in the village, which was all to the good. His flat cheeks looked sallower and his bleary eyes more bloodshot than ever. Everard clenched his teeth at the sight of him.

'You swine!' he muttered. 'You don't think I'm going to get her out of your hands, do you?'

He turned back to the pudding, which continued to disappear till there remained only a thin, fragile slice which he had deliberately restrained himself from devouring with the rest; perhaps Laura would like to taste.

A few minutes later the door opened and she entered with an expectant look in her face.

'Thank you very much, Laura,' he said, as soon as he saw her. 'It was extremely nice.'

245

'And many happy returns of the day to you,' she replied, her eyes sparkling. 'I made it for your birthday, though I'm afraid it's a day late.'

'But how did you know it was my birthday?' he asked.

'Well, I couldn't help seeing it on your postcard,' she said, colouring a little. 'I hope you won't think me inquisitive, but it was written so large, I couldn't help seeing it. So I made you the pudding and I'm glad you liked it.'

'Where did you find the recipe?' he asked.

'Why, you told me yourself on Christmas Day,' she said. 'You seemed to know it off by heart and I've remembered it ever since.'

'Why, of course, I remember,' said Everard, 'and you turned up your nose at it. It looks as if I've made a convert, doesn't it.'

'Ah, but I haven't tasted this yet,' she laughed. 'It isn't rose conserve, you know.'

'Well, see, I've carefully kept you a bit to taste,' he replied.

'Not much, eh?' she interposed maliciously.

'That's because it was so delicious. Now you sit down and eat it and tell me the truth about it. There's a fork.'

She broke the pudding with her fork and sniffed it suspiciously.

'Come along,' said Everard, laughing, 'don't be afraid of it. You can't say you're older than I am. We're both thirty-four now.'

'So we are,' she replied, looking thoughtful, and toying with her fork.

'I saw him go by just now,' said Everard, after a minute, with apparent irrelevance – he had been thinking of the twenty-four years between Laura and her husband. 'He looked more sour-tempered than ever.'

Laura put down her fork and her face became grave.

'Yes, he is today,' she replied. 'We had a sort of row this morning or, not that quite – he did all the talking.'

'What was that?' said Everard, who was glad of a chance to reopen the subject.

'Well, in some ways,' she continued, 'it's been going on for some time, but it's so nasty, I haven't liked to tell you.' She paused.

'What?' Everard prompted her.

'Well, you see—' she hesitated a moment and then, taking courage, hurried on, 'since we had separate rooms, every now and then, and especially the last week or two, in the hot weather, he's been saying most horrible things to me, quite disgusting things – not often, you know, but enough to be unpleasant. And then this morning he called me into his bedroom when I was downstairs and – well, I came out again at once.' She shuddered with loathing. 'Then after breakfast he started a long palaver about it. He said he didn't know what he paid me housekeeping money for and he was going out to find someone else, and a lot besides. Well, that wasn't news to me, so I took no notice of it and went on with my work. That's why he looked so bad-tempered. It's not nice having a man in the house like that.'

'I should think it isn't,' said Everard warmly. 'Poor Laura!'

'Still, I suppose he's made like that.' She shrugged her shoulders.

'Whether he is or not,' said Everard, 'you oughtn't to be in that house with him.'

247

'What am I to do?' she replied wearily.

Everard looked at her solemnly for a moment; the time had come, he thought. 'You ought to get rid of him,' he said.

'Get rid of him? How get rid of him?' she queried.

'Of course you know how, Laura,' he said gently. 'You ought to get a divorce.'

She shook her head desperately. 'Impossible,' she said.

'Now listen, Laura,' he went on earnestly. 'You're much freer now than you used to be, aren't you? I mean, at Christmas time you'd never have thought of sleeping in separate rooms, would you?'

'No, that's true,' she admitted.

'And you're ever so much happier, aren't you? The change in you is wonderful; I shouldn't have believed it possible six months ago. And you know it's all because you've cut yourself off from him. Well, supposing you were completely cut off from him and didn't have to live in the same house or even see him, and had nobody to think of but yourself – think how happy you could be.'

'Ah, that sounds all right,' she said, clasping her hands on her knees and gazing wistfully at her feet, 'but I'm afraid, Everard.' She looked up.

'Afraid?' he exclaimed, smiling at her. 'Why, how many times have you shown your courage? He can't stop you.'

'It's not him I'm afraid of,' she replied, shaking her head. 'I'm afraid of myself. Think – I've never been out in the world. I don't know what it is. Everybody's ready to prey on a woman all alone, and how should I live? I've got no money, no friends.'

'You've got one friend,' replied Everard quietly,

'who'd help you his utmost; and there are plenty of ways of earning a living for a strong, clever woman like you. And even if you don't know the world, you'd soon get used to it. It's not all rogues, and once you made a start you'd find it easy enough.'

'Of course, I know you'd help me, Everard,' she said, with a deprecating gesture. 'You're so kind to me, and please don't think me ungrateful; but what, what would life be for me all alone, and everybody looking down on me because I was divorced? They always used to say it's wrong.'

How she wriggled, he thought, never admitting when he answered her objections, and always finding a new one.

'It's much more wrong to go on living with a pig like him,' he replied, 'and people don't look down on you for it. Things have changed a lot in the past few years. You know,' he smiled, 'as I told you once before, Laura, you must forget the parson's daughter and remember you're a woman. Besides, there's a new divorce law now. You wouldn't have to prove cruelty, though you easily could.'

'Yes,' she replied dully, 'but they'd only say "Why didn't you get a divorce before?"'

'But there's plenty of evidence up-to-date,' said Everard. 'Look what he said to you this morning.'

'It wouldn't be so easy,' she said, 'he's more careful now, I know. No,' she folded her arms with a decisive air, 'it's no use talking about it, Everard. It's too late to change. I was born to suffer, it's my destiny, and I shall go on suffering; it's no good resisting your destiny. I've put up with it so far and I suppose I can go on a bit longer. Life doesn't go on for ever.'

Everard felt quite angry to hear her talk in this

despairing vein; he determined to be downright with her.

'Why, Laura,' he said severely, 'it's unworthy of you to talk like that. Of course you weren't born to suffer; and it only wants a little effort to end your suffering and make yourself happy. You're young and strong and capable, and life's full of good things. It's a waste of a good life – not only for yourself, but for other people. And after you've gone so far already, to draw back, just for nothing, it's a shame, it's a shame, it's – cowardly.'

'Oh, Everard,' she cried, beginning to whimper, 'don't be so cruel. You know I'm not a coward. You don't understand. I'm a woman, and a woman has to think of a hundred things a man never thinks of; it's not easy for a woman. But if you're cruel to me, Everard, I don't know what I shall do.'

She broke down completely and Everard, seeing that severity, however well-meant, was useless, went over and laid a hand on her shoulder.

'All right, Laura,' he said, 'I didn't mean to hurt you, you know I didn't; but I do want to help you.'

'Yes, yes, Everard,' she gasped, getting up from her chair and pressing his hand, 'I know you wouldn't hurt me. I'm a weak creature. I must get the tray and clear now.'

She picked up the plate of marigold pudding and carried it out of the room untasted.

Everard walked out into the garden and flung himself down in the old wicker chair. He felt worried about Laura. It was true that he had little that was new to say; his arguments had been almost identical with those he had used at Christmas. But what was there else to say? Time and a taste of freedom itself, he had thought, might convince her. But even these had failed. She still brought up the old arguments against him, arguments that were no arguments at all, and when they were refuted, she took refuge in the weakness of her sex and that maddening, unreasonable fatalism from which nothing could dislodge her; reproof only reduced her to tears and he could not bear to see her cry. He chafed at the folly of it. She was unafraid and yet afraid, as if something he could not detect were holding her back; or was she just a woman? It seemed no answer. At least, he reflected, she was, in a way, fond of him and perhaps that yet might help. Certainly he could not be happy until he had persuaded her.

He sank back in his chair and closed his eyes, still wrestling with his problem. But as he lay there, it gradually but surely faded from his mind, as if yielding to a superior force, and the image of Ruthie, whom he had not seen these two days, floated up to take its place, growing momently more and more distinct. A deep, booming voice that he instantly recognized, came echoing across the fence.

'Say, Mr. Mulliver, if you don't net them black-currants of yourn, the birds 'on't leave a single berry, as the saying is.'

'Blast you, Nesley, they can have the lot,' muttered Everard, turning over and feigning sleep.

He was longing for Ruthie as he had never longed for her before.

XXIII

LATER on that Sunday, while the bells of Lindmer were still tolling the people to church, Everard stealthily entered the copse at its further extremity, having fetched a wide compass to make sure that he was unobserved, and plunged straight through the hazel undergrowth. He was almost on the edge of the copse again when he stopped, at a spot where the ground shelved away and formed a little dell. Once upon a time men had dug there for brick earth, but now it was all overgrown and in the middle of it lay a sizable pond, so completely enclosed by steep mounds of bramble that it seemed inaccessible. At one point, however, the ring was broken by a thick cluster of sallows which also screened the pond from view, but when Everard parted their branches, they yielded with surprising ease and disclosed a tiny strip of bright greensward, sloping down to the water's edge, by the roots of a great, over-hanging willow tree. Here, ever since Kindred's warning, he and Ruthie had been accustomed to meet and here they had spent most of their time together, never venturing out to wander in the copse or neighbouring fields until dusk had fallen. Everard slid down on to the grass amid the warm odours of crushed catmint, his back against the willow trunk, and took out his watch. He was full early, but although Ruthie had never yet failed him, a sudden doubt crossed his mind that perhaps she might not come. He clenched his hands feverishly; it was terrible to contemplate. There was a faint whistle back in the copse and he thrust his head forward, listening tensely till it came again. It was a blackbird calling in the treetops, and he relaxed once more. A sharp rustle at his side made him turn his head with a violent start; it was only a moorhen pushing her way through the dry stalks to her nest in last year's bulrushes, where she was just hatching her second brood. She was quite a friend of theirs and took no notice of them in her comings and goings. Everard, unable to rest any longer, leaped to his feet and nervously plucked a twig from the willow. Then, when all was still and he least expected it, the sallow branches parted and Ruthie stepped softly out on to the grass. He took her in his arms and held her close.

'Why, Everard!' she exclaimed, drawing back from him, 'you're all trembling.'

'Am I?' he said with a nervous little laugh. 'Oh, I expect that's the mowing I did last night. How long you've been coming!'

'I haven't really,' she replied, with an amused smile. 'You're early, that's what it is. Didn't you think I was coming? Poor Everard!' She patted his cheek. 'Let's sit down. You mustn't tremble like that. Do you know, dear,' she continued, as they sat down against the willow trunk, 'I've only just got back from Bures. Mother stayed and stayed, and I was terribly frightened I shouldn't be in time.'

Everard stroked her hand. Now he was beside her, he felt more composed.

'It's such a long time since I last saw you,' he said.

'Why, that was only Friday night, Everard,' she laughed, 'hardly two days.'

'It's seemed like a week,' he said, shaking his head, 'at least, all the afternoon it has.'

'So it did to me,' she added more softly, looking away. 'Oh, and my aunt is such a crusty old thing and mean. She've got a lovely cherry tree in her garden, full of lovely sweet early cherries, and she didn't offer us one.'

'Ah, that reminds me,' said Everard, putting his hand in his pocket. 'I've got something for you.'

He pulled out a small paper package, unwrapped it with clumsy fingers and drew out a tiny white stone pot with a white parchment cover.

'What's that?' she asked, taking it from him.

'Rose conserve,' he replied, watching her expectantly.

'Whatever's that?' she asked, with a puzzled frown.

'I thought you wouldn't know,' he said. 'It's just a jam made from roses. You taste it. I made it myself.'

'What, all yourself?' she teased.

'Well, Mrs. Quainton helped me a bit,' he admitted, 'but I did most of it.'

'What did she do?' she persisted.

'Oh, she just stood by,' he answered, 'to see I made no mistakes and didn't boil the pot dry.'

'How long did it take you?' It was like a cross-examination.

'A good long afternoon, your worship.'

'Are you in love with Mrs. Quainton?' she asked, turning on him sharply.

'Of course I'm not,' he protested. 'I like her, she's a very good housekeeper and looks after me very nicely. That's all.'

'She've been buying such a lot of new clothes lately,' said Ruthie musingly. 'She's wholly smart now, and she look so much brighter than she did, as if she was happy.'

254

'Yes, that's quite true,' replied Everard enthusiastically, glad to find that he was not alone in perceiving the difference.

'You're sure you're not in love with her?' she queried again, eyeing him warily.

'Quite sure, Ruthie,' he said, laughing at her doubts. 'Should I come here else?'

'I don't know.' She pouted incredulously, and then broke into an affectionate smile. 'Yes, I'll believe you, dear,' she said, pressing his wrist. 'But when am I to taste this jam?'

Everard undid the cover and slipped it off.

'I'm afraid I forgot to bring a spoon,' he said apologetically. 'You'll have to use your finger.'

'Shall I?' She bit her lip and smiled mockingly at him. 'I think you'd better do it for me. I might spill it.'

'What, with mine?' he said. She nodded, her eyes twinkling.

'All right.'

He dipped his forefinger in the conserve and held it out to her, red and sticky. She clasped his palm in her two hands, regarding the finger suspiciously for a moment with her head on one side, and then put it between her lips. Everard almost winced at their softness.

'Oh, how wonderful that taste!' she cried, lifting her head. 'Now what do that taste like?'

'Like a kiss?' suggested Everard, and then, for no apparent reason, blushed.

'Why, so that do!' she exclaimed, and in her turn blushed, dropping her eyes and fondling his hand which she still held in her own. For a whole minute they were silent.

'What great rough fingers you've got!' she said at last,

looking up at him roguishly, 'all brown and full of cracks and just like leather.'

'That's the work I did yesterday,' said Everard, 'pitching and mowing.'

She suddenly burst out laughing, as if tickled by a new idea.

'Isn't it funny, Everard?' she said. 'When you come down first, on a Friday night, your hands are all smooth and fine and white like a gentleman's, and then on Sunday night, just before you go away, they're brown and hard like a farmer's.'

'Which do you like best, Ruthie?' he said; his voice trembled.

'Oh these, these!' she instantly replied. 'These dear old brown, hard fingers. I love them.' She hugged them to her cheek and kissed them tenderly.

Everard felt a moment's sweet faintness as he watched her bent over his hand. Her hair was not thicker nor more gold, her throat not more exquisitely soft and petal-like, nor her breasts more nobly poised and moulded than when he had seen her last. Yet she seemed to him infinitely more beautiful – for bringing back to him his thoughts of last evening and confirming, as it were, their truth.

'But of course, you like the others best,' she said, looking up at him and smiling a little wistfully.

Everard shook his head and tried to smile too, but his lips would not frame themselves to his will. He could not help being solemn tonight.

'I like what you like,' he said in a low voice.

Her eyes lit up, but she laughed incredulously.

'But that do fare strange,' she pursued, 'and you a gentleman. I wonder why you really do it.'

Everard gazed at her thoughtfully and as if for answer

he laid his head down gently in her lap.

'My poor Everard,' she whispered, running her fingers through his hair and stroking his cheek, 'you're tired, you mustn't work so hard. I well know how scything wear you out. Go you to sleep in my lap, my love.'

But all her soothing, far from lulling him to sleep, only awakened him to keener sensibility. Even as he lay there, last night's pulsing ecstasy returned upon him in even fuller measure, and his eyes were opened wider still; for Ruthie now had swum into the vision, taking her place in his newly realized universe of simple, primitive and earthy things, more beautiful, more inspiring than all. Her warm body slowly rose and fell against his cheek; her deep, round breasts hung over him; he could feel the abundant life beating strongly within her, imparting its own virtue to him. She, too, was close to earth, herself a dear symbol of its fruitfulness and bounty, answering his simple need with her own, giving all he asked and asking nothing more in return than he could give, linking them both to the roots of things, so that the sap of the world flowed in them and moved them to its own eternal ends. Then something primal and all-compelling, a new, hot passion, far surpassing in intensity that first intense desire which had drawn them together, welled up from, it seemed, some unknown depth in him and streamed into all his veins as if it were the blood of his body, flooding all his consciousness, of thought and feeling. A tremor shook him and he involuntarily tossed his head upon her lap.

'What's the matter, dear?' said Ruthie, who was still caressing his face. 'How hot your cheek is!'

All at once he raised his head and with firm,

half-fierce gentleness gathered her in his arms, kissing her again and again with close, fiery kisses on her brow, her cheeks, her lips and the white swell of her throat.

'Oh, my love,' he gasped, gazing at her with exultant eyes, 'my love, my darling, my sweetheart, my jewel, my flower, my lamb, my delight! I love you.'

The words poured from his lips as if his tongue had but just discovered its liberty of speech.

Ruthie for a moment gazed back at him wonderingly, bewildered by his sudden transport; then, as its meaning was borne home upon her, her arms curled tight around his neck, her pupils dilated and her eyes glowed with a bright light. He felt her whole presence quicken and enfold him, sweeping him away.

'Oh, my beautiful, my precious, my lovely!' she cried. 'Tell me, tell me again.'

'I love you, Ruthie,' he whispered.

'Since the day I first met you have I waited for that,' she murmured, and closed her eyes.

The moorhen croaked, calling its mate, but they did not hear her.

XXIV

THE following Friday afternoon, not long after *The Olive Leaf* had closed its doors, Everard was already at the foot of the church steps, looking down upon Lindmer as it had been on the day when he first saw it; the year had come full-circle. The languid, feathery willows fluttered in the valley-bottom, along the now shrunken stream, rank-bordered with purple loosestrife, meadowsweet and comfrey; they seemed to beckon him; higher up on the valley-side the cornstalks, turning for ripeness, surged, now green, now yellow, against their placid, heaped-up hedges, as if they, too, like the willows, beckoned him; even the village street, asleep, gable, thatch and chimney, in the winking summer haze, seemed to smile in its sleep at him, from among the misty green orchards, huddling with young fruit. Everard read its welcome with infinite gratitude as he strode down the hill, leaving Bury and the odious week behind him forgotten. It had been more odious than usual. The trust had been making further overtures, which he had rejected, further threats, which he had ignored, and both sides were now preparing for the fight which was soon to begin. It was necessary – he must do his duty by the business – but it all seemed degraded and insignificant, it tired and disgusted him. However, neither his cares nor his exertions should cheat him of his weekend at Lindmer; indeed, he had arrived there half a day earlier than his wont on purpose to escape them.

259

When he turned in at his garden gate, his eye was suddenly struck by a black stain on the fringe of the orchard where his bush-fruit was, and he strolled down the garden to investigate it. The black stain, he discovered, was a large square of fishing net that had been thrown over his two rows of blackcurrant bushes, completely enveloping them. He examined it curiously. Two rows of stakes had been driven in to support the netting, and it was carefully pegged down on the ground. Whoever had done it knew well what he was about. He strolled up the garden, mystified, and looking up, observed Laura in her oldest working frock, her hair a little untidy, hurrying down to meet him.

'Oh, I've got a message for you, Everard,' she said, when they had greeted each other, 'from Mr. Kindred. He looked in just after dinner and told me he was going in to Sudbury to see his landlord and wouldn't be back till late; so it's no use your going over to the farm tonight.'

'Thank you, I see,' said Everard, 'but what's all this mean, Laura?'

He turned round and pointed to the currant bushes.

She laughed.

'Oh, it happened this way,' she replied. 'Last Monday evening, just as I was going in to shut the windows for the night – I like to keep the rooms aired during the day when you're away – who should be at the gate but Mr. Honeyball and Tom Cobbin, carrying that great sheet of netting between them. Well, Mr. Honeyball said he couldn't bear to see the birds eating your blackcurrants like that and he was going to net them himself; else there wouldn't be a berry left—'

'As the saying is,' interjected Everard, laughing.

'Yes, that's right,' she answered, laughing too.

So I said I knew you wouldn't mind, and they came and did it. They were more than half an hour over it and they took such a lot of trouble.'

'Ah, I remember,' said Everard, 'last Sunday afternoon, while I was lying out in the garden, he stopped by the fence and said it ought to be done, but I was tired and pretended to be asleep. Old Nesley's very strict about my gardening, you know.'

'Yes,' she added with a sly smile, 'he said the weeds in your vegetables and even in your precious herbs were something shameful.'

Everard laughed. 'Did he? Well, I suppose he's right. But it's terribly good of old Nesley to come and net those currants for me, and that must be his own net too. He must have taken it to heart, mustn't he? I expect the starlings would have had 'em all if he hadn't done it. They're most of 'em ripe now, already.'

'Yes, they are,' she agreed.

Everard thought a moment. 'I know,' he said. 'I'll pick old Nesley a quart, just for his kindness. I've got nothing in particular to do this afternoon, and then I'll get to work on some of those weeds.'

'That would be a good idea,' said Laura, 'and while you're about it, you might pick another pint or two, so that I can make you a blackcurrant pie for tomorrow's dinner.'

'All right,' he nodded.

'I must be off,' she said. 'I've got a lot of work to do, I'm cleaning clothes. You're very early today.' She looked down at her old frock. 'That's why I'm so dirty.'

She smiled again and ran off up the garden path to her own house.

Everard, having taken off his coat, rolled up his

sleeves and provided himself with a basket to hold the currants and a box to sit on, went down again to the currant bushes, and unhitching a corner of the netting from its peg crept underneath. He crawled on all fours to the largest bush, placed his box so that he could lean his back against a stake, and set himself leisurely to pick.

Although his seat was somewhat hard and he had to bow his head a little to avoid the netting, it was a quiet, agreeable task, well suited to that hot July afternoon, and while his hands worked almost mechanically, stripping off the little black bunches, his mind, too, found occupation in reflecting upon the new and wholly delightful experience of being truly in love. It was a thing to be accepted joyfully and unquestioningly, without analysis; yet even so, certain things stood out clear to him. The larger and more vital passion in which all his former desires had merged, was acquiring new and spiritual qualities. He had discovered a new bond between himself and Ruthie, not so much a conscious, spiritual sympathy as a sort of inner, pre-existent harmony of being which he felt to be inherent in the scheme of things. It had transformed everything for him. Ruthie was no longer merely the winsome country girl who had first charmed and soothed him; she now had her part in the earthly plan, at his side, and that was why they loved each other; that was how affection had been grafted on to desire, all the stronger for being so simple in its source, all the more delectable as the just and natural, if belated, response to Ruthie's own long-cherished, unconcealed affection for him. He was unfeignedly happy, and just because he believed his happiness to be part of the scheme of things, he wanted everyone around him to be happy too; it helped to justify his belief. And happy most of his neighbours in the valley seemed, in their respective ways, the Kindreds with their farming, old Runacres, Tooke and Farrow with their quoits and ferreting, Tom Cobbin with his tippling and his perennially unsuccessful bets; even his own currant-picking to repay Nesley Honeyball's kindness, fell into place in the pattern. Laura, too, was happy, happier, at least; she smiled and sang.

Then, as he shifted his seat to another bush, and looked up through the meshes of the net, he caught sight of a green whipcord coat hanging out to dry on the clothes-line across the hedge, and a sudden sourness filtered into the sweet of his contentment. She could not be happy, however much she pretended, with the wearer of that coat in the house, serving him, sitting at table with him and listening to his lecherous talk, even if, now, worse was spared her. There was a flaw in the scheme of things after all, which somehow dimmed the lustre of his own happiness; and the memory of his failure to remedy that flaw only deepened the gloom. He had been so near success; she had followed him to the brink, but she would go no further – the pity and the unreasonableness of it! A cloud of melancholy settled upon him, blotting out all the joy that had preceded it; perhaps it was an obsession, but Laura's happiness seemed far more important to his own than he had ever imagined.

At that moment the net before him quivered, and glancing up, he saw Laura herself standing beside him with a white china bowl in her hand. She had changed into a flowered pink cotton frock and patent leather shoes, and had tidied her hair.

'May I come in, please?' she said. 'I want to top-

263

and-tail some of the currants for the pie tomorrow. I've brought a bowl.'

'Yes, come along,' said Everard.

He lifted the free corner of the net while she crawled under with her bowl and a little three-legged milking-stool that she had brought with her from the wood-shed. She seated herself over against his basket and taking out a handful of currants, began to top-and-tail them. Everard resumed his picking.

'You've soon finished your work,' he said, remarking her spruceness; it was only a short while since she had left him.

'Oh, I let that go,' she said, laughing. 'I was only cleaning clothes for him – he always makes them in a frightful mess; but he can wait. And I like to get the topping-and-tailing done well beforehand. It's so tiresome having to do it in the morning, just before you make the pie.'

'Oh, I'd have done that for you,' said Everard. 'You know I'm always ready for jobs like that.'

'P'r'aps you'd like me to go, then?' she replied archly.

'No, no, please don't go,' said Everard, with a smile. 'It's nice to have you here.'

He meant what he said, but his smile was forced; he suspected her gaiety today, feeling that it was a sham.

'Oh well, if you're sure,' she laughed playfully, finger on lip, 'I will stay. It's such a beautiful afternoon; it's a shame to spend it indoors, bending over those nasty old clothes.'

'By the way,' said Everard gravely, pausing with his finger on a currant stalk, 'how is he behaving now?'

'Oh, just the same as ever.' She shrugged her shoulders. 'He still says the same beastly things to me, but I don't take any notice of them. What's the use? But don't let's talk of that now. I want to forget all about him now, on an afternoon like this.'

Her lips parted in a bright, open smile; but Everard did not return it, thinking of the bitterness which it must conceal, with how admirable a mask. Yet she went on gaily chattering, as if there were no bitterness in her thoughts at all. He bent to his picking again.

'I'm so glad I'm not so tall as you, Everard, or else my hair would get all caught up in the net.' She looked round her and laughed. 'Why, we're just like two birds in a cage, aren't we, Everard?'

Everard was silent and did not take his eyes from the bush. Laura frowned.

'What's the matter, Everard?' she said, with concern in her voice. 'You won't look at me or speak. Have I offended you or do you want me to go away?'

'I'm sorry, Laura,' he said, looking up at her. 'I didn't mean to be rude. Of course I don't want you to go away.'

'Well, what's the matter?' she said more gently, the brightness returning to her face.

'I was thinking,' he said hesitantly, 'how true what you said is of you – only you could get out of the cage if you tried.'

'Oh dear!' Her face clouded again. 'I wish you wouldn't worry about me. It's not worth it. I'm trying to forget it and live for the moment.'

Everard shook his head.

'I can't help it, Laura,' he said sadly. 'I can't help worrying about you. It makes me most unhappy – most unhappy,' he repeated, partly from conviction, partly – from design.

'Does it, Everard?' she said, looking wistfully at him.

'Yes, I'm afraid it does,' he replied slowly. 'And I

suppose I shall remain so while things are as they are.' It was the truth.

'Oh!' she gasped faintly, gazing at him with eyes full of anxiety and compassion. 'I don't like to make you unhappy.' Her lips moved faster. 'I wouldn't for worlds. I'll do anything you tell me!' The last words came out with a rush. Everard stared at her, scarcely able to believe his ears in amazement.

'Do you really mean,' he stammered, 'that you'll leave—'

'Yes, yes,' she said recklessly, 'of course I will, to please you.'

'Do you really mean that?' he repeated.

'Why, yes, Everard,' she answered with a strange, gentle laugh. 'Don't you believe me?'

For answer he took her hand in his and gripped it solemnly.

'There!' she exclaimed frivolously, 'you've covered my fingers with currant juice!'

Everard fetched a deep sigh, as if an enormous, stifling weight had been lifted from his heart; it was so unexpected.

'What was that for, Everard?' she asked, still playful.

'Just gladness,' he replied, smiling now. 'That means so much to me.'

'Ah, but what will become of me?' she said in a low voice; her playfulness had changed to an air of profound dejection; she looked hollow-eyed and scared. It was Everard's turn to reassure her.

'Wait, Laura,' he said deprecatingly. 'You mustn't worry either. You'll be all right – that is, if you aren't afraid of earning your own living.'

She gave him a questioning look.

'I mean, I mean—' he hesitated a little when it came

to the point of revealing his new idea, 'it so happens that – in the shop – we want another cashier. It's not much, I know, but it'll be a start and you'd do splendidly for us.'

She stared at him a moment with open mouth and round eyes and then suddenly clapped her hands.

'Why didn't you tell me before, Everard?' she said.

'Well,' he replied, 'for one thing, the vacancy has only recently appeared and then, I wanted you to make the decision of your own will. I didn't want you to think it was only because I wanted a cashier.'

'Of course I shouldn't think any such thing,' she remonstrated. 'You know I shouldn't, Everard. But how wonderful! I should be near you after all; it wouldn't be half so difficult.' She blushed all at once and looked down at her bowl. 'How excited I'm getting!' she murmured, raising her eyes again and smiling.

'Not half so excited as I am,' said Everard. The scheme of things had not betrayed him after all; it worked sagely to its appointed ends and he had been disloyal ever to doubt it. 'Yes, I shall be there to help you,' he added, 'and see you're treated properly.'

'Oh, and I'll work ever so hard for you!' she cried enthusiastically. 'Won't it be lovely to be away from him, never to see him or think of him, and do what I like?'

Everard smiled; she was almost repeating his own words of less than a week ago. A deep, glad warmth kindled in his heart; this was happiness indeed. It was now Laura's hand that clasped his juice-stained fingers.

'You are so kind to me,' she gasped, quite beside herself with joy. 'I don't know how I shall ever repay you. I'll work so hard for you, you won't be able to do without me!'

Then, as if suddenly ashamed of her own impulsiveness, she dropped his hand and picked up a bunch of currants.

'I wonder what the time is,' she said casually.

'Half past four,' replied Everard, pulling out his watch.

'Good gracious!' she cried, 'I must go and get tea ready. And look how much topping-and-tailing I've done! Scarcely twenty currants.'

She held up the bowl to show him and they both laughed.

'No matter,' said Everard. 'I've only picked enough for Nesley Honeyball; so we're quits. I'll pick some more for you later on. But I want to get out of here; my neck's aching. Let's go and have tea together, to celebrate this afternoon – like the rose conserve.'

'That'll be lovely,' she replied, smiling and gathering up her bowl and three-legged stool. Everard lifted the net so that she could crawl out. 'I've really let you out of the cage now,' he said, as he crawled out himself.

'I could cry for joy, Everard.' She glanced gratefully at him and hurried away up the path.

Everard followed more slowly with the basket of currants in his hand, and as he reached the scullery door, he noticed Runacres passing in the street with a couple of rabbits slung on his stick. Everard hailed him and he stopped by the gate.

'Are you going home, Henry?' he asked.

Runacres nodded.

'Well, would you mind leaving this basket of currants at Nesley Honeyball's on your way?'

'Sartinly,' said Runacres, reaching for the basket.

'That's for his kindness,' Everard explained, 'in lending me his net and coming to put it on himself. I shouldn't have had a currant left if he hadn't done it.'

Runacres grinned.

'Do you know, Mr. Mulliver,' he said, 'what he really did that for? It's like this here. Our big quoit match with Nayland come off next Saturday and Jim Farrow, he say he want you to play for us. We must win, 'cause that match may decide whether we get the League cup. But we know you're allus a-running off to Vale Farm on Saturday arternoons and all, and we wondered how to make sure of you. So Nesley Honeyball, he say, "I'll go and net his currants for him and then he'll have to play; don't, I'll charge him half-a-crown for the loan of the net."'

Everard laughed out loud.

'The sly old dog!' he exclaimed. 'But don't you think these currants are worth half-a-crown, Henry?'

'No, but you will play for us,' said Runacres in alarm, ' 'on't you, Mr. Mulliver?'

Everard quizzed him a moment and then clapped him on the shoulder with a laugh.

'Yes, of course I will,' he said reassuringly. 'It's an honour for me to be chosen. So Nesley'll lose his half-crown.'

'Ah,' replied Runacres sententiously, 'that's wholly worth more'n half-a-crown to us if you'll play, that that is. Well, I must now be getting along to my tea. Farewell, Mr. Mulliver.'

'Farewell.'

Everard walked slowly back to his door, smiling to himself. Half-a-crown? Of course he would play for them; that net had been worth its weight in gold to him.

XXV

THE following morning, soon after breakfast, Everard set out briskly along the valley for the farm. He was in love with the world that day; even the sun above seemed to shine more brightly and every thought that came into his head turned to gold. He still glowed with the memory of last evening in the copse when Ruthie and he had once again avowed their loves; after a week's absence the avowal sounded sweeter than ever, their embraces were twice as ardent and full of new meaning. It was delicious to be in love, and he light-heartedly basked in the present enjoyment of it without a thought for the future. Laura, too, was bubbling over with high spirits. Never before had he seen such youth and radiance in her face; and there was no danger now of its being a mask. Next week he must set in motion the machinery which was to compass her freedom; a lawyer must be consulted, evidence hunted up, a lodging found for Laura herself. She would make a good cashier he thought, sensible and methodical; he would teach her himself and make things easy for her. On every hand the wheat fields were yellowing, already even yellower than yesterday they seemed. Soon they would be red and harvest would be upon them, harvest and his summer holidays, which he had planned for harvest; he could not afford to miss a day of that. It was an exciting prospect. Three whole weeks of Lindmer, cutting, shocking, pitching, stacking corn, three whole weeks, with Ruthie's embrace each night awaiting him in the copse; it was not long now. Why, soon enough he would be on the stubbles again, at plough in the soft September light and winy September air, as the cycle of tillage revolved again to its beginning – how rich the bright new furrows smelt!

The farm reached, he found Kindred in the rickyard, engaged in pulling a long iron rod out of the side of a new hayrick. He looked concerned and greeted Everard curtly.

'Rick's heating,' he growled. 'We carried that too soon; that stink like a brewery yard.'

He pulled the rod clear and critically felt the end in his palm. The tip carried a sort of blunt barb which had pulled away a wisp of hay from the middle of the rick.

'That's mighty hot,' he said, shaking his head. 'That's heating proper. And that mote of hay, I 'on't say that's black, but that's wholly dark. Becourse, a little heating don't do no harm, but that might fire. I reckon I'll have to tell Bill, the cowman, to cut a square hole right through it. That may save it; don't, we'll have to knock it all down. Oh dear, oh dear!'

He gazed despairingly at the rick, which was visibly steaming and exhaled a rich, malty odour.

'Well, well!' He turned away. 'I'll go and tell Bill.'

'What are we going to do this morning?' said Everard, as he followed him to the neathouse.

'Well,' replied Kindred, without looking up, 'I did think of going up to do a bit of thistling in the spring beans, but I feel too tired for that, I do.'

Everard was surprised; Kindred had never complained of being tired before, certainly not at that time in the morning, and he spoke as if he were talking to himself.

'There's a bit of doddy up on one of my clover leys,' he continued. 'That isn't much, but I want that clover for seed, come September, so we'll burn that doddy out. I've got a load of straw in the tumbril all ready.'

After the cowman had received his instructions for holing the rick, the two men plodded away behind the tumbril to the clover ley. Kindred was very silent and walked with his eyes on the ground, hardly noticing his companion. Everard was frankly puzzled. Kindred was generally so cheerful and a heated rick was a small thing to cause such a change in his demeanour. But, respecting his silence, Everard, too, said nothing. They took the tumbril across the newly sprouting clover to a white patch that stood out quite boldly in one corner.

'There!' exclaimed Kindred bitterly, as he stopped the tumbril. 'Look at the damned stuff!'

Everard bent down and examined the clover-stalks. They were thickly wreathed with whorls of fine, fleshy, yellowish fibre, that seemed to have its roots in the stalks themselves; it was sticky to the touch and here and there pretty little clusters of pink flowers, smelling sickly sweet, peeped out of it.

'Where did that come from?' said Everard, looking up.

'Why, from the bloke as sold me the seed,' growled Kindred. 'That was dirty seed though there wasn't much rubbish in it; do, I'd have seen that at once. That's doddy, that is, dodder, some call it. That live on the clover till that strangle it, and when you cut the clover that make such a mat, that's like lifting a carpet. That spoil your stover and heat the rick 'cause that's full of juice.'

'What's to be done?' said Everard.

'Why, burn it,' replied Kindred angrily, 'and the

clover with it, 'cause I want my sample of clover seed to be clean; and then, not grow clover in this field for another twelve year, till the doddy seed in the ground's dead. There's a rum 'un for you! I'll have something to say to that bloody swindler who sold me the seed when I see him. Lucky that wasn't much.'

Still swearing to himself, he took up a fork and began to toss down straw from the tumbril, Everard helping him. Between them they completely covered the infected part with it, and a generous margin beyond, to catch any strayed seedlings. Then, having piled on a layer of hedge brushings to give body to the fire, they set the whole alight and stood back to watch the blaze and encourage its laggard portions. It was soon over and they went forward with their forks again, raking through the ashes to see that all was burnt.

'Look at that!' muttered Kindred, who had remained morose and silent since his last outburst. 'All that good stuff wasted 'cause that bloke couldn't take the trouble to clean his seed!'

He tossed his fork into the empty tumbril, and a jay, startled by the clatter, flapped up, noisily screaming, from a neighbouring field, to find refuge in a convenient thicket.

'Them bloody jays!' exclaimed Kindred. 'I'll warrant there's a heap more in them peas. Do you see.'

He walked over to the hedge and cupping his hand round his mouth for a trumpet, uttered the plaintive sing-song call of the bird-scarer.

'Ee-yarico! Ee-yarico!'

Instantly half-a-dozen more jays started up with the same ear-splitting scream of fright and rage and disappeared into the thicket.

'Huh!' grunted Kindred. 'What's the good? They'll

be back again as soon as we've gone. A fine mess they'll make of my peas. This farm have wholly gone to hell, I reckon.'

He stared balefully at the thicket where the jays were still screaming. Everard could hold out no longer; trifles like that did not upset Bob Kindred.

'Look here, Bob,' he said coaxingly. 'What is the matter?'

Kindred looked up at him without answering.

'There is something the matter, isn't there?' Everard added.

'Well yes, there is,' admitted Kindred, staring helplessly at him. 'It's like this here, Everard. I went in to Sudbury yesterday to see my landlord 'cause he sent for me. He don't know nothing about farming – he keep a big hotel there – but it fare he've heared about that bit of draining we did up on the hill there, though that ain't ondly bush-draining and no good after seven year. "I hear you've been improving of your land," he say. Well, I told him that wasn't ondly a bit of bush-draining we'd done in our spare time. "Yes, but you've got forty ewes on your land now," he say. "Stand to reason that have improved." "But half of them belong to Mr. Mulliver," I say, "and not to me." "No matter," he say, "that land have improved; do, it wouldn't take them ewes. I must raise your rent; or leastways," he say, "I must appeal to arbitration to get that raised."'

'But we made the improvements,' expostulated Everard, 'not the landlord.'

'Becourse we have,' replied Kindred, 'but that don't signify to them bloody landlords. The improvement's there and the land's worth more, they say, and the arbitration blokes listen to 'em.'

'What did you say?' asked Everard.

'Why, I told him I couldn't pay it and he say, "I don't suppose you want to buy it?" and I say I ondly wish I had the money. "Well then," he say, "I expect I shall have to give you notice to quit. I've had an offer made for that there farm and if I can't get a better rent for it nor what you're paying, I shall sell it." That's what he say. I reckon he's tired of it and he want to get rid of it as best he can if he can't get a better rent.'

'Who's the chap who wants to buy?' asked Everard.

'I don't know who that is,' replied Kindred, 'but it fare he want to farm that for hisself, and my landlord say he might give me compensation to clear out this Michaelmas 'stead of next.'

'Good God!' exclaimed Everard; there would be no stubbles, then, for him to plough in the autumn. 'Would you take it?' he asked anxiously.

'Well, what else can I do?' replied Kindred despairingly, 'if I've got to clear out? I can't help myself. You see, I don't think he really want to sell if he could get the higher rent – 'haps he'd never have thought about that if we hadn't done that bit of draining – but the land ain't worth the money he want and my back ain't broad enough to pay that, so what is there to do? And if we can get a bit more money by going early, we'd best take it. Ah, if only I'd bought the farm during the War, when times were good!'

'Are there any other farms going in the district?' enquired Everard, with fear in his heart; it was as if someone were wrenching his farm, his soil, from his grasp.

'No, no.' Kindred shook his head. 'And if there was one, I shouldn't have the heart to take it, not now. That's not easy, starting again at my age. No, me and my old woman'll have to take a cotterage somewheres and go and live on what little bit of money we shall get out of our valeration, and hope that'll last till we can get the old age pension.'

'Do you mean that?' cried Everard, aghast; he felt his own roots being torn bodily up.

'I wholly do,' replied Kindred sadly. 'That's mortal hard, Everard. Me and my father together, we've farmed Vale Farm nigh sixty year between us. That ain't a rich farm like, but that was enough to keep us going. And then, to think of the work we put into it! Why, you get to know every inch of a place and it kind of know you. I was born and bred in this here valley and I'm somehow fond of it. That'll be hard to leave it.'

A tear trickled down the old man's nose and another followed it, but he hastily dashed them away. Everard's eyes, too, felt moist; the grief was his no less, it was his valley. He gazed blankly at Kindred, who had now recovered himself.

'I expect you wholly wondered, Everard,' he went on, 'why I was all that short and awk'ard this morning. I couldn't help that and somehows I didn't want to tell you. You'd fared so happy here with the ploughing and the haymaking and all that; I didn't want to spoil that for you. And all those ewes you bought, too, and the digging you did for that drain! That's a shame, that is, and that's the truth.'

'Let me help,' Everard burst out.

Kindred shook his head. 'That'd be waste of your money, Everard. That there bloke is a pigheaded fool as don't know nothen about farming; the rent he want, you couldn't make ends meet with it. I wouldn't rob you of your money, Everard.'

He shook his head again and went to the horse's head.

'I'm now going down to the sheep,' he said over his shoulder. 'They must have their bit, whatever happen to us. But don't you bother to come, Everard. I can manage that. Do you come down and have a cup of tea along of us this arternoon. 'Haps I'll be better then. We must keep going, I doubt.'

He went off with the tumbril rumbling behind him, and left Everard standing alone in the clover, looking after him. It was plain that the old man wanted to be alone and Everard did not press his company upon him; indeed, he, too, was conscious of a sudden desire to be alone. He walked over to the hedge and threw himself down in the grass at the edge of the ditch, gazing over on the outstretched valley where pale corn and cattle-flecked pasture, sombre copse and ploughland, all now met in a dim blend of soft shape and colour, spell-bound in the noonday hush, the brown roofs of Lindmer nestling shyly in the background. Yet here was another misfortune come to poison his happiness, to sweep away a friend and sever his new-found contact with that familiar soil. Or – strangely it did not seem to weigh upon him – was it a heaven-sent opportunity?

Deliberately he checked the current of his thought and carried himself back across his past year, recalling how he had first come to Lindmer and how by its own quiet beauty it had compelled him first to become its benefactor (now a long-forgotten role) and then to take up his abode with it. Thus it was that he had met those good souls at the inn and on the quoit ground who had admitted him to the warmth of their fellowship as no men before; thus, too, that he had come to know Laura's unhappy story and pledge himself to a work which promised to be the best, most forthright achieve-ment of his life; and in the meanwhile with his own

277

hands he had built and planted a garden, which had led him out to a wider garden, where Ruthie and Kindred had taught him the secrets of his own heart. These were the ties with which Lindmer had steadily woven itself into the very thread of his being, and now, as he looked back over them, they took on an almost fatal aspect. He smiled at the memory of the Bury businessman who had proposed to spend his weekends there. Lindmer seemed no longer content with his weekends; it had provided him with the larger half of life, indeed the whole of real life, and now it was asserting its own rights. He saw with a calm, untroubled clearness of vision, as if a glimpse had been vouchsafed him of the pattern of existence, that he could no longer deny those rights. Why continue to waste himself in bolstering up a distasteful business, bound in the long run to succumb to the trust which was even now playing into his hands? Why deny himself in all its fulness that life which the deepest, truest part of him coveted, when it was freely offered him? It was indeed his destiny, and, far from bowing his head before it, he embraced it joyfully. He was going to buy the Vale Farm and farm it himself, with Kindred his partner and Ruthie his wife.

He looked ahead, too, and saw Kindred gradually sink, die and fade from the picture, leaving him to carry on the tradition, master of his flocks and herds, tilling his acres in the valley – the farmer he, too, grew old and Ruthie beside him, her dark-gold hair greying, her buxom figure spreading and her red cheeks pouched, a tall, upstanding old woman of Emma Kindred's mould – the farmer's wife. And after them their children too. He was content; the pattern was complete.

XXVI

IT was market day at Sudbury and the square, covered with the usual rows of market stalls, swarmed with the usual miscellaneous market crowd of buyers, sellers and idlers. There were the young farmers who moved with the times and affected flimsy low shoes and gay-coloured, waisty town clothes, making eyes at giggling silk-stockinged, short-skirted wenches, in from the country for a day's frolic. There was also the solid cohort of the older generation against whom the tide of changing manners, accelerated by the War, broke in vain; they had not abandoned their old square-cut coats of Derby tweed, their tall single collars and made-up stocks, their heavy square-toed boots and buskins stiff as board, nor would they, until they themselves had passed away. In and out of the public-house bars they streamed, along with their attendant train of pig-nosed butchers and besotted-looking drovers, keen-eyed corn-dealers, horse-doctors and travellers in agricultural implements and artificial manures, making good deals and bad deals and chattering of other deals, past, present and to come, of the next probable bankruptcy and who had stolen his neighbour's wife. Flashy cheapjacks harangued clusters of incredulous, thrifty housewives, persuading them by sheer weight of endless patter into buying lengths of stuff, ugly china ornaments and patent medicines which they did not want; smaller dealers, with all their stock-in-trade on their shoulders, moved about in the throng, hawking rabbit-nets, baskets and children's toys; a brawny lout was selling fresh-caught fish by Dutch auction from the tail-board of a motor-van. And as if all this human hum and activity were not enough, there was an ex-servicemen's band in one corner of the square, blaring out the latest explosive fox-trot imported from America, while in the opposing corner two romantic, careworn figures, father and daughter perhaps, clad in faded tartan kilts and strutting pretentiously up and down before an admiring group, answered with the melancholy skirl of bagpipes; and at the rare moments when these two parties were both taking a rest, fainter strains, of a very different order, floated up from the church at the head of the square, where the Thursday organ recital was in progress.

Everard elbowed his way through the press into the smoke-room of a large commercial hotel and struggled through the maze of outstretched legs and jostling shoulders to a vacant seat in the corner, from which he proceeded to catch the eye of a harassed, but still flippantly responsive barmaid and order a mug of beer. Neither the hubbub of clacking tongues, nor the thick, smoke-clogged atmosphere caused him any qualms; they were a good-natured, easy-going crowd, all of them in their various ways enjoying their market day far more than they ever enjoyed Sunday, and Everard's heart warmed to them, for, after all, he was one of them now.

He took out his watch and looked at it impatiently. What a time Kindred took haggling with his landlord! Everard himself, in his anxiety to make the farm his own, would have accepted without demur the first price asked; but Kindred was determined to drive a bargain and insisted on Everard's keeping well in the background, so as to give the man no colour for holding to his price. However, this was the last of the negotiations; today the price was to be finally named and the cheque for the deposit signed. Things had moved indeed since last Saturday, when he had first roused Kindred's spirits from the ashes of dejection; even now he could not forget that afternoon.

They were both sitting in their accustomed places at the tea-table when he had entered the kitchen, Bob Kindred staring vacantly at the hearth with a cold pipe between his teeth, Mrs. Kindred ruefully mopping her eyes with a handkerchief. Everard walked over to the table, trying to keep the jauntiness out of his stride.

'I say, Bob,' he said. 'I'm thinking of taking up farming.'

Kindred looked up at him.

'Surely you haven't come to mock us, Everard,' he said reproachfully.

'No, but I mean it,' replied Everard, smiling.

'Well, take my advice and don't,' growled Kindred, looking back at the hearth.

'Well,' continued Everard, 'if I do, will you be my partner?'

'What do you mean?' said Kindred suspiciously.

'I mean,' replied Everard, 'that if you will, I'll buy Vale Farm.'

'What's that?' cried Mrs. Kindred, turning suddenly round from the table where she was pouring out tea.

'I'll buy Vale Farm,' repeated Everard.

Kindred jumped to his feet and seized Everard's hand, his lips struggling, but unable to utter a word.

'By God, I will!' he stammered at last. Then the tension collapsed and he burst out laughing. 'Why, look at Emma,' he gasped, 'she's a-washing of the tablecloth in tea!'

Mrs. Kindred hastily righted the teapot, which, in her amazement at Everard's words, she had continued to empty until the whole table was flooded.

'Do you keep your tongue to yourself, Robert,' she said sharply. 'I've got better things nor that to think of.'

She put the teapot down, and going up to Everard, she gave him a smacking kiss on either cheek.

'I could never have put up with another kitchen,' she declared five minutes later, when she had put a clean cloth on the table. 'Now let's have tea.'

It was a wonderful meal.

A busy week had ensued. While Kindred was engaged in beating down his landlord at Sudbury, Everard in Bury had been negotiating with the trust and except for a few details the matter was as good as settled. To their great satisfaction he had accepted a directorship, but he was still to retain a ruling voice in the control of his old business – he had insisted on that in order to keep the cashier's post open for Laura, who would soon be needing it. Her case was simple enough, the lawyers said; all they needed was some definite recent evidence; the next step was to procure it.

He sighed contentedly; it was a good week's work, though it still lacked its crown – for he had not yet put the question to Ruthie. This, the easiest and pleasantest of his tasks, he had deliberately postponed until all his other plans were assured – for Friday night, as he first had hoped, but now there was to be a board meeting on Saturday morning, and he would have to wait until after the great quoit match with Nayland in which he had promised to play; which reminded him that he must write and tell Ruthie – and Laura too – that he would be a day later than usual. He sighed again, this time with vexation. But it was better thus; his mind, freed from all other obligations and set at rest, could give itself up wholly to the enjoyment of that supreme moment. And, he wondered, should the question be, 'Ruthie, will you marry me?' or, 'Ruthie, will you be my wife?'

He had not yet found an answer to the problem when a heavy hand, descending suddenly upon his shoulder, brought him back to the present with a start.

'There's a good bit of business done, Everard!' exclaimed Kindred. 'I've beat that blasted owd hunks down from twenty to eighteen pound an acre. That's all that owd land is worth and that'll save us hundreds of pounds.'

'Well done, Bob,' said Everard, squeezing his palm. 'You'll have to do all our marketing, I can see. Here, miss,' – he made a sign to the barmaid – 'another pint of beer, please.'

'I say, Everard,' said Kindred in a low voice, as he sat down beside him, 'I shan't never be able to thank you—'

'No, I won't have it, Bob,' interposed Everard. 'It's the other way round.'

'No, that ain't,' persisted Kindred, not to be denied his gratitude. 'But for you, me and my missis'd have went away and lived in poverty; but now I shall die in the house where I was born. You don't know what that mean to me. That's more than kind, that is.'

'And what about you?' rejoined Everard. 'You've taught me your trade all for nothing and taken me into your house – a stranger.'

'Ah, but you wholly belonged there by rights,' said Kindred. 'You were made to be a farmer, Everard, and no mistake. You're a real gentleman, I say.'

'Now be quiet, Bob,' said Everard, handing him the mug which the barmaid had just brought. 'Let's drink to our partnership.'

'Here's the best to it,' said Kindred, and they both gulped.

Everard's nose was still in his pot when Kindred tugged sharply at his sleeve.

'Look there,' he said, pointing to a pair of square shoulders at the far end of the room, 'that's Steve Quainton!'

'So it is!' exclaimed Everard.

He was standing with his back to them, entirely engrossed in conversation with a pasty-faced, middle-aged woman, dressed in a bedraggled blue serge costume. Gold teeth flashed whenever she opened her sticky red lips, and there was no mistaking the leer in her eye.

'I know that fairy well,' said Kindred in a low voice. 'She've been round here of a market day this last six year.'

'Listen, Bob,' Everard whispered, moving close to his ear. 'Say Mrs. Quainton wanted to be quit of him; that'd be good evidence, eh?' Kindred nodded. 'Would you stand with me as witness, supposing she did?'

Kindred bit his moustache reflectively and nodded again.

'I will if you will, Everard,' he said, 'but there ain't no harm in that. That ain't evidence.'

'No,' Everard whispered back, 'but we'll watch 'em. Drink up your beer, Bob, and be ready to follow 'em out when they go.'

Kindred nodded and raised his mug.

'Can't waste this,' he said with a grin.

The conversation between Steve Quainton and the

pasty-faced woman lasted a few minutes longer; it was neither mirthful nor animated, and when finally the woman drained her glass of port and moved to the door, he dismissed her with only the faintest, chilliest of smiles.

'A pretty pair they make!' muttered Kindred in Everard's ear. 'Ah, do you see, he's a-going to foller her now, the damned owd hog!'

Steve Quainton, with a furtive glance round the room, too hurried to take in the two men watching him in the distant corner, swallowed the dregs of his whisky and went out. As soon as the door closed, Everard, with Kindred behind, darted out after him, so as not to lose sight of him in the crowd, and they were just in time to see him round the corner of an alleyway leading off the square. They followed at once and peeped cautiously down. Kindred was right – the woman, who had about a minute's start, was some twenty yards ahead, looking over her shoulder to make sure that her man was there. Then, with a swift jerk of the chin to him, she set off at a rapid pace, keeping her distance and every now and then looking back to see if he was still behind.

Everard and Kindred strolled after them with clumsily assumed unconcern, at a longer interval, for fear of being observed. But Steve Quainton's eyes were glued to the woman's heels and he did not once look back during the long roundabout dance she led them, although several times they nearly lost sight of him; they were not used to shadowing people. Through alleys and conduits and courtyards the three men followed her until at last, ten minutes later, she fetched up before a door in a mean street on the outskirts of the town. She turned round, stared significantly up the street and then disappeared. Steve Quainton walked steadily on to the door, which had been left ajar, and disappeared too. It was just what they expected. Everard stopped.

'It's the house by the lamp-post,' he said. 'We can count the numbers from here. Look – twenty-two, four, six, eight, it's thirty, that's the number. We'll make enquiries about that. My God, what a pair!' he added with a grimace.

'And he haven't seed us neither,' said Kindred jubilantly.

'No,' said Everard, who was noting the number on an old envelope. 'We'll go and pay that deposit now, Bob, and then we'll have another drink. I reckon we've earned it.'

'That's the truth,' laughed Kindred, as they walked away.

Their backs were scarcely turned when an upper window level with the lamp-post flew open and Steve Quainton's grizzled head peered out to watch them down the street with a baleful, fish-like stare; the woman had seen them.

XXVII

ON Saturday afternoon, as the church clock was striking four, Everard, having but three hours ago signed away the independence of Mulliver and Son's and become director of a trust, but only remembering that he was – though the documents were not yet signed – virtual proprietor of Vale Farm, Lindmer, blithely pushed open his cottage gate; he had properly struck root in the valley and this was his home now. The first thing in the garden to catch his eye was the figure of Laura in a pink cotton frock and pink sun-bonnet, crouched over a basket among the herbs, gathering a salad, perhaps. He walked over to her and peeped in her basket; there were no herbs in it.

'Hullo!' he said, as she sat back on her heels, perceiving him. 'What are you doing, Laura? You look very busy.'

'I'm weeding your neglected garden, Mr. Mulliver,' she said with a smile, pushing a stray lock of hair under her bonnet with the back of her hand. 'Mr. Honeyball stopped at the gate yesterday—'

Everard threw back his head and laughed.

'Yes, you may well laugh,' she went on. 'He said he was quite ashamed of you, it looked so dreadful. So I thought I'd pull up a few of the weeds for you.'

'Thank you, Laura,' said Everard, laughing, 'but poor Nesley, how he does take on about my garden!'

'Well, look at the state it's in,' she replied, holding

out her hands despairingly. 'Did you ever see such a thing? That yarrow growing up in the middle of the thyme and bellbind twining round the lavender and stinking mayweed everywhere; it's a disgrace.'

'Yes, you're quite right,' he admitted impenitently. 'It is. I never seem to have time for it.'

'Ah, that's what comes of all this farming and slaving for other folks,' she said with a sidelong smile. 'Charity begins at home, I say.'

Everard chuckled enigmatically. What would she say if she knew that he would soon be a real farmer? But he would wait till all was settled before he told her.

'Still, you know,' he protested, 'on two afternoons I quite virtuously set out to clear those weeds, but both times I ended up in something altogether different. Let's see, the first time it was rose conserve, and the second it was picking currants, wasn't it?'

'Ah,' she said, casting down her eyes, 'that was my fault you got no further than the currants that day.'

'Well, I'm very glad it was, Laura,' he said. 'What we did was far more important than weeding the garden. But you oughtn't to go dirtying yourself to make up for my sins, Laura.'

'Why not?' she replied. 'After you've done so much for me, I must do something for you. I expect you really want me to go in and get tea ready.'

'No, I don't,' said Everard. 'I'll stay and help you. I shan't want my tea today. I had lunch late and I'm not hungry. And the quoit match begins at five o'clock; so I mustn't risk spoiling our chances by a full stomach. It's the big match of the season.'

'How important you're getting!' she observed railingly. 'Nesley Honeyball told me yesterday they were sure to win because you were playing. But you will behave yourself, won't you? They often get very rowdy after that Nayland match.'

'Oh yes, I'll behave myself,' said Everard, smiling; he had the best of reasons for behaving himself that evening. She put her hands on her hips and looked him up and down with an amused, critical air.

'So you're the hope of the village,' she said, laughing outright. 'How I should love to see you play!'

'Well,' said Everard, 'there won't be much to see, – not from me anyhow; but why don't you come down and watch? We don't charge for admittance, and several of the members' wives do come.'

Her face grew serious again and she shook her head. 'No, no,' she said hurriedly, 'not yet – I mean it wouldn't do in my position.' Her cheeks went crimson and she began weeding furiously to cover her confusion.

'I'll go and get a hoe,' said Everard, turning away discreetly as if he had not noticed; how curiously her old timidities cropped out!

Half-way to the woodshed, which was also the toolshed, he espied Jim Farrow coming along the path towards him, with an empty bottle tucked under his arm.

'Hullo, Jim,' he said, '*The Olive Leaf*'s closed, isn't it?'

'No, it ain't that I want,' replied the shoemaker, 'but I'd be wholly glad if you'd oblige me with a drop of oil. We've fair run out down at ours, and I want that bad.'

'Of course, Jim,' said Everard, leading the way to the woodshed.

'Now I'll tell you what that's for,' said Jim, in a confidential whisper, as they entered the shed. 'There's a wasps' nest in the hedge down by the quoit ground. I twigged that this morning by the stones round it – that's a rum 'un how kids will stone a wasps' nest – and being seckertary of the club' – he squared his narrow shoulders importantly – 'fare to me I ought to see to that; them wasps might get troublesome during the match. So if I can jam a bottle of paraffin down the hole, that'll send 'em all to kingdom come, leastways, if the hole ain't too long and crooked – 'cause sometimes that'll suck up all the paraffin afore it get to the nest. Still, the bottle'll cork 'em up tight till the match is over. Wouldn't do if anybody got stung.'

'There you are, Jim,' said Everard, handing him the bottle which he had just filled from the oil-drum. 'Do you think we're going to win this afternoon?'

'Well, I can't wholly say,' said Jim Farrow, with a serious air. 'They're an uncommon hot lot, they are. Still, we've got you and Henry and Jack Tooke and Nesley and myself. I ain't altogether comfortable about Tom Cobbin. 'Times he's wonderful good, and that's why we're a-playing of him; but 'times, you know, with a lot of folk about, he get narvous like and then his crooked eye get hold on him and he throw terrible wild. Still, we've got a good chance, I reckon, s'long as we don't happen with no accidents. Now you 'on't be late, will you, Mr. Mulliver, 'cause we're a-counting on you.'

'Now, how could I, Jim,' said Everard, laughing, 'with that great net of Nesley's on the currants to remind me? Besides, I should stand to lose half-a-crown.'

'Well, don't you forget,' said Jim, stepping out on to the path. 'Five o'clock sharp. And I say, Mr. Mulliver' – he turned back, excitedly lifting up his moustache – 'you 'on't go running off too soon after the match, will you, to go and see after Bob Kindred's sheep and all that. 'Cause we allus have a wonderful good evening arter the Nayland match. A quoit match make you wholly thirsty, somehows, and Jack Tooke, he sing like a lark when he've got a few pints on board. Why, I've been known to sing myself,' he added with a bashful little smile.

'All right, Jim,' said Everard encouragingly. 'I'll stay as long as I can.' But he knew exactly how long that would be.

'Well, so long, Mr. Mulliver,' said Jim, going off down the path with his bottle, 'and thanks for that drop of oil.'

Everard hastened back with the Dutch hoe to the parterre, where Laura was still busy grubbing up weeds with her fingers.

'Here I am at last,' said Everard. 'Perhaps I shall be able to get to work this time.'

She laughed gaily, all her confusion now gone, and they worked together in silence for a few minutes, she tearing out the longer weeds with her fingers, while Everard hoed up after her. The sun was hot and he paused for a moment to wipe his forehead.

'By the way,' he said casually, 'you got my postcard yesterday, I suppose? I hope you didn't expect me last night.'

'Oh yes,' she replied; 'that was all right; it came in the morning. In fact, I had a bit of trouble over it. I was going to tell you.'

'Oh?' said Everard, settling himself more comfortably on his hoe to listen.

'Yes,' she continued, 'the postman knocked at the door while I was getting the breakfast ready, and he – my husband – went to the door. "One for Mrs. Quainton," I heard the postman say, but he took it and began reading it. Well, I didn't see why he should, so I went over to him and snatched it out of his hand. "It's mine," I said, "and I'm not going to have you read it, even if it is only a postcard!"'

'What did he say?' said Everard.

'He only laughed and then he said with a sneer, "All right, young woman. I'll bring you to heel yet." But I took no more notice of him and he said nothing more.'

'Well done!' said Everard. 'It was a good thing there was nothing important on it, – because I have got some news for you. We'll soon have you away from him now; in fact, I don't like the idea of your being in the house with him any longer.'

'No, I should be glad to get away,' she sighed, a little wearily.

'Well, I'll find some rooms for you as soon as I go back,' said Everard. 'I didn't have a moment to spare this week to look for them. But I've already got to work for you.'

'Yes?' She looked up gratefully.

'I've seen a lawyer and he says it'll be all right if we can get definite evidence, and I've got the evidence already.'

She opened her eyes wide.

'Yes,' Everard went on, 'Bob Kindred and I saw him with a woman at Sudbury market on Thursday – an awful-looking hag she was too – and we followed them right up to the house. I've got the address in my pocket and Bob says the woman's quite well known.'

'Ah, I remember,' she said thoughtfully. 'He'd had a lot of liquor when he came home on Thursday night and he went straight to bed without any supper. But didn't he see you?'

'No,' said Everard, 'that's the best of it. I think you

ought to get away next week. There oughtn't to be any difficulty about him now. Our present cashier isn't leaving for another fortnight; so you can get nicely settled down in your rooms before you start work.'

She clapped her hands in sudden enthusiasm.

'How lovely!' she cried. 'I shall have to be packing my things soon.'

A loud snort from a horse in the street made them both look sharply round. There was a high dogcart drawn up against the hedge with the driver still in the seat, staring grimly across at them; it was Steve Quainton. He must have approached very quietly, for they had not noticed the sound of wheels. Laura gave a little gasp of surprise.

'Look there!' she said.

Steve Quainton, seeing himself observed, waved his arm to her.

'I want you!' he shouted.

She walked calmly over to him, and after exchanging a few words across the hedge with him, went off into her own house. Steve Quainton did not move from his seat, but continued to stare grimly at Everard, who had resumed his hoeing, still, however, watching the man out of the corner of his eye.

'You ugly blackguard!' he muttered to himself. 'We'll soon settle your hash now.'

A minute or two later Laura came out again with a small package which she handed up to her husband, and after a few more curt words had passed between them, he wheeled his trap round and drove off.

'Well, what did he want?' asked Everard, as Laura came down the garden and joined him again.

'Why, he wanted me to get him some pig-rings,' she replied with a look of concern. 'He said he couldn't

293

find them this morning and went away without them. So I fetched them for him.'

'Is that all?' said Everard.

'Oh, he said there were plenty of weeds in our garden,' she added. 'So I said, "Well, why don't you do a turn in it?" Then he drove away.' She frowned and shook her head dubiously. 'It's strange. He never comes home in the day like that as a rule. And he must have known where those rings were; I found them in their regular drawer. I think it was just an excuse for coming home.'

'But why should he want to?' said Everard.

'I don't know,' she replied vaguely. 'To see what I was doing, I suppose.'

She put her finger on her lip in consternation.

'I wonder if he—' But she stopped short of putting what she wondered into words and only turned her head away, blushing quite violently, as if at her own thoughts. Everard looked at her curiously; her blushes came very freely today; she must be getting excited at the prospect of her approaching freedom.

'Don't be afraid of him now,' he said soothingly. 'We're going to bring him to heel. He won't hurt you.'

She turned to him again, but her face was still troubled.

'Ah yes,' she said slowly, 'I know, but he might hurt you, perhaps.'

'Oh, don't worry about me, Laura,' he said, laughing lightheartedly. 'I can look after myself.'

'Can you?' She looked at him wistfully, pondering something.

'Hey, Mr. Mulliver!' came a shout from the garden gate. 'Match begin in five minutes!'

294

It was Runacres, in his Sunday suit, with a pink rose in his buttonhole.

'There, Laura!' said Everard, throwing down his hoe, 'a fine lot of weeding I've done.'

'Never you mind,' she said, laughing. 'Off you go now, and see you win the match.'

'Goodbye, Laura.' He turned, smiling, up the garden path. 'Coming, Henry!' he shouted.

Laura watched him until he disappeared through the garden gate, and then fell furiously to her weeding again, as if her life depended on it.

XXVIII

AT Lindmer the match with Nayland had always been regarded as one of the most important events of the quoit season, if only because Nayland with its twelve hundred inhabitants ranked as a small town, whereas Lindmer was no more than a village with a third of its population. But this year a special importance attached to the contest. Both teams seemed to have outdistanced all their other rivals in the local League, both had so far scored the same number of points and consequently today's result might well give the winning team a decisive lead in the final struggle for the League cup. When Everard and Runacres arrived, the little quoit ground was already buzzing with an expectant crowd, consisting mainly of elderly folk, for the younger generation had recently lost all taste for the long-established sport of the district and those who were not courting preferred to spend their Saturday evening at the nearest cinema-theatre. The Nayland team of six men, along with their scorer and half-a-dozen supporters, had already arrived in the old black Ford van which now took the place of the local carrier's cart, and were standing alone in one corner of the field around an old wooden seat, laughing and cracking jokes among themselves with a careless, insolent demeanour; Lindmer was only a village after all and must be kept in its place. Runacres, who was captaining Lindmer, went over and conferred with their captain, a stalwart baker, and they paired their men off against one another.

'That's a wholly hot day,' said Runacres in his politest manner, as Nesley Honeyball and the first Nayland man, each with a pair of quoits, moved off to the foot-boards to open the match. 'Still, the pub'll be open in an hour's time.'

'Ah yes,' replied the baker with a supercilious smile, as if he had no doubt of the issue. 'I reckon there'll just be time to have a drink afore we go.'

Runacres, thoroughly nettled, rejoined his own men.

'The cocksure swine!' he muttered to Everard. 'They think they'll beat us afore the first hour's up. If they're as good as that, we'll keep 'em at it till nine o'clock.'

'Why can't they be familiar like,' complained Jim Farrow, 'like good sportsmen? We'll larn 'em, we will. Do you wait till I get a quoit in my hands, I'll show 'em.'

'What ever's the matter with Nesley?' exclaimed Runacres, as Nesley's first quoit descended, flat side up. 'He've throwed a lady and no mistake.'

His opponent ringed the pin fairly, which, as Nesley with his second quoit could not equal it, scored him two points right away. The two men walked over to the pin, picked up their quoits and began to throw to the other end. This time both Nesley's quoits went outside the three-foot circle round the pin and could not score a point.

'What have come over Nesley?' whispered Jack Tooke in dismay. 'I reckon those cheeky swine are making him narvous.'

That was exactly what was happening. The Nayland men were undoubtedly a good team, but somehow

297

their impudent self-confidence, far more than their skill, had flustered the usually imperturbable Nesley; he was quite red in the face. A few minutes later, however, his natural steadiness of hand and eye reasserted itself and the game began to go more evenly. But the Nayland man had got ahead, and when he reached the twenty-one up which concluded the game, Lindmer were five points behind.

'Now then, Jack,' whispered Runacres, as the black-smith took the quoits, 'do you play up and for God's sake keep calm.'

But where Nesley had failed, it was difficult for Jack Tooke to do better or even as well. He began to throw with a desperate look in his eyes, already a beaten man; and though he threw no wides or ladies, at the end of the second bout Lindmer were twelve points behind. The Nayland men, still clustered round their seat, were jubilant and kept up a constant fire of audible, disparaging comment on their opponents' play. Runacres was in despair and took counsel anxiously with his men. Onlookers, disgusted with the depressing spectacle, were already trickling away from the ground, impatient for the inn to open its doors. But how was the rot to be stopped?

Tom Cobbin, after the example set by his two predecessors, received the quoits from Jack Tooke with such trembling hands that he let one fall and badly bruised his toe. He had not troubled to spruce himself up for the match; his cheeks were as unshaven and his clothes as patched and ragged as ever. He advanced to the foot-boards with one eye on the pin and the other pivoting towards the Nayland men, who began to titter. Then, as he took aim with the quoit, his eyes still gazing in different directions, they could contain themselves no longer and burst into a loud guffaw.

'That man ought to be stopped!' shouted one.

'Do you mind you don't hit us!' cried another.

Tom's hand trembled more and more and he promptly threw a lady. The game that ensued was pitiful to watch. Poor Tom could not reach anywhere near the pin, and every minute he grew redder and hotter and more flustered, not knowing where to turn his head; but whichever way he turned it, one eye always seemed to light on those jeering Nayland men.

'Didn't I tell you?' exclaimed Jim Farrow. 'His eye have got a hold of him. Listen to them bastards.'

'Hey! put a collar on it!' cried one of the Nayland men.

'Try throwing back'ards!' suggested another.

Tom's throwing grew successively wilder and the laughter of his mockers louder. The Lindmer men frowned and bit their lips with vexation. Tom had only scored two points to his opponent's twenty, and now came the throw which must surely finish the game. Tom stepped forward with white, set lips and took a careful aim; perhaps if he got a ringer, he might contrive to hold out a little longer and score a few more points. He threw, but this throw was the wildest of all. The quoit loosed off at a tangent from his arm, sailed over the heads of the Nayland men and fell in the hedge with a crash that ended in a tinkle of broken glass, as if it had hit an empty bottle. A great shout of derision arose from the Nayland men, and one of them, walking over to the hedge, stooped down with outstretched arm to retrieve the quoit. All at once, with a loud yell, he leaped in the air and fled from the spot, madly shaking his fist. His companions watched him in blank amazement, but before they could guess what the matter was, they were all dancing frantically up and down and clawing the air with their hands, in desperate combat with an invisible enemy, which, however, soon became visible as an ever-thickening cloud of wasps. It was now apparent what had happened. Tom Cobbins' quoit had smashed the bottle of paraffin which Jim Farrow had stuck in the entrance-hole of the wasps' nest, and released the wasps, doubly exasperated by the confinement and the stench of the paraffin, which did not appear to have harmed them; the hole must have been crooked as Jim Farrow had feared. It was the turn of the Lindmer men now to be amused, and another great shout arose as they all dissolved in uncontrollable laughter; they held their sides.

'Oh my!' exclaimed Jack Tooke breathlessly. 'Look at them bloody fools! That's as good as a circus, that is. Look out, boys, they're coming this way now!'

Both teams fled and in a trice the wasps were left in possession of the field. Out in the street the Nayland men ruefully swabbed their stings with blue-bag from the inn while the Lindmer men stood round and watched their swelling faces, still helpless with laughter. When all had recovered their breath somewhat, the Nayland captain went up to Runacres and seized him angrily by the lapel of his jacket.

'Lookye here!' he cried, blinking fiercely with a rapidly disappearing eye, 'that ain't the way to treat visitors, that ain't. I shall stop the match and report to the League Committee.'

'Well,' replied Runacres coolly, 'if you do that, you'll lose the match. If you hadn't sat there a-making mock of poor Tom's infarmity, he wouldn't never have throwed that wide so's to hit that there bottle. He didn't know that was there. Now that o' yourn ain't the way for a visiting team to behave, fare to me. If you report that to the League, we shall have something to say too, I doubt.'

'Oh!' growled the other sullenly, somewhat taken aback. 'Oh well, I suppose we shall have to play it out. But that's a damned dirty trick, fare to me.'

'Well, we 'on't quarrel about that,' said Runacres diplomatically. 'Come you along back. I reckon the ground'll be clear of 'em now.'

Nayland still had a formidable lead of thirty-one points, but their three remaining players had suffered grievously from the wasps; one of them had two rapidly swelling cheeks, another's wrist bulged with a great red lump and on the captain's face only one eye was now visible, quite apart from more unobtrusive, but not less painful punctures in other parts of his body. Morally they had suffered even more; their self-confidence had suddenly shattered, they looked ridiculous and felt it. Several small boys from the village began to titter as the unhappy team made its way back to its stand on the quoit ground, but Runacres sternly silenced them; Lindmer was going to show Nayland the way to behave.

Everard now took up the quoits for Lindmer and found himself paired with the opposing captain. The stalwart baker did his best, but he could no longer see the target and the first few throws showed what the issue would be; nothing he could do was right. Everard, on the contrary, encouraged by his discomfiture, discovered that he could do nothing wrong; the quoits dropped wherever he placed them, with a felicity that seemed to echo the inner harmony of contentment that now filled him. Life could not be better, he felt, as he landed his quoit plumb on the pin for two good points;

301

and after that proceeded to score one ringer after another without a break, till the crowd cheered him and the Nayland captain limped mournfully away to his men.

'Six ringers, by God!' exclaimed Runacres, slapping Everard on the back. 'Pretty, pretty play, Mr. Mulliver! We'll beat 'em yet. Come on, Jim.'

'Don't you worry,' said Jim Farrow, with a convulsive fluttering of the hairy trap-door over his mouth. 'Do you give me the quoits, Mr. Mulliver. I'll show 'em, I will. I'm a devil with a quoit, you know, Mr. Mulliver, though I don't look it.'

Jim took the quoits and the trap-door closed tightly over his mouth, as if it were never to open again; his little beady eyes became burning points of light and his brow knit in a tense, concentrated frown. Such diabolical energy was more than the wretched man with the bulging wrist could hope to stem and he was disposed of more rapidly even than his captain, with scarcely a point scored. Lindmer was now already leading by four points, and it was obvious that Runacres would make short work of the man with the swollen cheeks.

The game was as good as won, and Nayland did not wait for further humiliation. Jim Farrow's last quoit had hardly fallen when they rose to their feet as one man and shuffled across the field, silently and painfully, with their tails between their legs. The Lindmer men stolidly watched them pass without a word or smile. Runacres was well satisfied.

'I say, Mr. Mulliver,' whispered Tom Cobbin, timidly sidling up to Everard as the Ford van started off in the street, 'do Henry and Jack and Nesley and the rest think me a terrible jim?'

'Of course they don't, Tom,' replied Everard reassuringly. 'You've served us well today.'

Tom's stubbly cheeks creased into a smile.

'Here, boys!' cried Everard, addressing the rest of the team. 'Three cheers for Tom Cobbin! He helped us to win the match. Hip-hip—'

The whole field cheered to the echo.

'And now,' cried Runacres, 'three cheers for Mr. Mulliver and his six ringers! Hip-hip—'

The cheers were even heartier, and before they knew where they were, Everard and Tom found themselves hoisted on to half-a-dozen pairs of powerful shoulders and carried in procession to the bar-parlour of *The Olive Leaf.*

'Now then, Mr. Mulliver,' said Nesley Honeyball, when the tumult had subsided somewhat, 'you're a-going to have a pint along o' me after that, and Tom Cobbin too. That was thirsty work, as the saying is. Three pints, Albert!'

'Now listen here, all you chaps,' announced Runacres in a solemn voice. 'I tell you I'll never take on another bet with Tom Cobbin, not if he go down on his bended knees and ax me, I 'on't. He did us a real good turn today and no mistake.'

'Ah, that he did,' added Jack Tooke, 'and sarve 'em right, the bleeders; that'll larn 'em a bit of sportsmanship. I 'on't never take you on agin, Tom Cobbin.'

'Nor I 'on't bet agin neither,' added Tom resolutely, 'from this day on.'

'Come on, Mr. Mulliver, drink up,' commanded Runacres. 'You've got to have one along o' me. No, I 'on't take no. I'm your captain, ain't I? And you too, Tom. Three pints, Mr. Chinery.'

'And I'm your seckertary,' put in Jim Farrow, holding up his moustache to make himself better heard in the hubbub, 'and you've got to have one along o' me, too. I'm a devil with a quoit, I am,' he added with a hiccough.

'Well, I reckon I've paid for the loan of your net, Nesley,' said Everard, laughing, as he drained his second mug, which Jim Farrow promptly handed to Mr. Chinery to replenish.

'Oh that!' exclaimed Nesley contemptuously. 'You can keep that, Mr. Mulliver, that ain't worth three ha'pence, as the saying is. But don't you forget to put that on earlier next year.'

'Now, Mr. Mulliver,' cried Tom Cobbin, whose nose was already flaming more brightly from the beer to which he had been treated, 'I bet you can't floor that pint without taking your lips from the pot.'

'Hark at him!' mocked Jack Tooke. 'He just now say he'd never make another bet.'

'Well, here goes!' shouted Everard recklessly, himself warming with the general excitement.

He tipped his pot back and drained it in one draught.

'Well done!' shouted Tom. 'I didn't say what I'd lay you, but I'll stand you another.'

'Gentlemen,' began Runacres rather throatily, rising unsteadily to his feet, 'silence, order, gentlemen! Gentlemen, we have won that there match with Nayland and that fare as if we shall win the cup too. So I call on Mr. Jack Tooke, shoeing-smith, farrier and general engineer, to give us a song.'

There was a burst of applause; then the buzz died down and the blacksmith rose to his feet, thunderously clearing his throat. Everard, with his fourth pint in his hand, was facing round to get a better view of him when something dark through the back window of the bar-parlour caught his eye; it was the outline of the copse. He looked up at the clock; it said a quarter to eight. He put down his beer untasted.

'Must go and relieve nature, Henry,' he whispered with a smile, and slipped out of the room into the sweet evening air. He did not return to the inn that night.

XXIX

THE sounds of day had ceased, but the sounds of
night had not yet begun and all was very still in
Lindmer Vale. A soft, golden light still hovered from
the setting sun and beneath its mellowing glow the
motionless cornfields nestled closer earthwards in
reposeful obscurity; meadowsweet and willowherb no
longer flaunted their separate colours, but merged in
one dimly sculptured mass, with the buckthorn and
maple above them; the slender willows, shining silver in
this as in every light, alone whispered faintly in their
topmost branches. To Everard, threading his way with
light step beneath them, it seemed as if the stage had
been expressly set for the closing scene of his incom-
parable evening. His heart was still warm with the
goodwill of his neighbours and gay with their laughter,
his blood danced with the exhilaration of the liquor he
had drunk and the six ringers he had scored; and now
every moment brought him nearer to Ruthie and his
journey's end; the whole earth was beautiful, the whole
earth was his. Delightedly he sniffed the hedge scents
and smiled on the dim red forms of the quiet cattle
couched in the grass, for being somehow part of his
happiness. It was well that he had drunk those three
pints of beer; he would not be tongue-tied now
before Ruthie; the words would come of their own
accord.

The path now skirted the stream itself and he bent

down for an instant to pluck a handful of forget-me-nots; Ruthie might like them – tonight. He stood up straight again and at once recoiled. Steve Quainton was standing at his side, the cold, malevolent stare of his watery eyes colder and more malevolent than usual.

'Well?' said Everard sharply, as soon as he had recovered from his surprise.

'I seed you leave the pub,' replied Steve in a leaden voice, 'and I've only now caught you up.'

'Oh, have you?' said Everard suspiciously, wondering what the man could want with him at this time of day.

'I've got something to talk to you about,' continued Steve Quainton.

'Well, you'll have to hurry up with it,' said Everard shortly. 'I haven't any time to spare.'

'Oh, but I ain't in no hurry,' retorted the other with a sneer, planting himself firmly in Everard's path.

Everard regarded him angrily, sizing up the details of his dense, square frame, the deep chest and short, bull-like neck, the great, wide shoulders and stocky arms that might well have hauled a bull from its stall; he would not be easy to shift.

'It's like this here,' Steve Quainton went on. 'Last Thursday I see you and Bob Kindred a-spying on me at Sudbury market; yesterday my wife have a postcard from you and 'on't let me see it; this arternoon I come home and I find her a-weeding in your bloody garden along o' you.'

'Ah!' Everard gazed at him with a steady eye. It was an unexpected encounter, though he might have foreseen some such thing; but it caused him no misgiving. Three pints of beer had made him indifferent to risks that in cold blood he would have weighed more carefully.

Steve Quainton wetted his straight, thin lips and went on again.

'And ever since she went to do for you, she've been that bloody pernickety, that's more'n a man can stand, and I 'on't stand that no longer. At first I thought that was the extra money, but now I know that's you have been a-meddling with her.' He moved a step nearer Everard with his hands on his hips and a threatening light kindled in his cold eyes. 'I want to know the reason why.'

Everard stood his ground and met his gaze without flinching, but the hot blood raced up to his cheeks and he had to make a great effort to speak calmly.

'You might well ask, Steve Quainton,' he replied, 'if you'd been a decent husband.'

Steve Quainton dropped his chin a moment to spit copiously between his feet.

'What's that?' he cried, raising his head and baring his yellow teeth. 'Do you be careful what you're a-saying. That don't matter what I do or what I don't do. That's my wife and you'll leave her alone, you swine; don't, I'll bloody well show you.'

Everard's brow darkened and he clenched his teeth.

'I'll see you to hell first,' he said.

'Hey? We'll soon see about that, you sod.'

Steve Quainton's lips set tight again, the light in his eyes became fire and he made a rush forward. Everard, who had been waiting for this, skipped lightly aside and put up his fists; he was no boxer, but he knew how to hold his hands. Steve Quainton was no boxer either, for he came at him with his fists clenched in front of his belly and when Everard aimed a left-hand blow at his jaw, he made a fierce grab at his wrist. Everard dashed clear just in time and backed warily away. This was no match according to Marquis of Queensberry rules; the man was fighting for his wife, his wife's body, his goods; all weapons were fair and no quarter would be given; they were savages. Everard moistened his lips and an obscure joy stirred in his vitals; he would meet the man at his own game, he hated him and gloried in his hate.

For a few minutes they circled cautiously round each other, looking for an opening; then all at once Everard's foot caught in a molehill, he reeled backwards and Steve Quainton darted in. Everard struck wildly, but before he could recover his balance, his arm was in the other's grip. There was a rapid scuffle, Everard felt himself flung violently in a circle and next moment Steve Quainton had his arm under his own shoulder, pinning it against his body and cruelly forcing the forearm back from the elbow; his grip was like iron and Everard was powerless.

'Now!' hissed Steve Quainton, baring his teeth, 'what about it, eh? Don't you move; do, I'll break your bloody arm.' He gave the arm another twinge, but Everard glared at him defiantly.

'Steve Quainton, you sod,' he said, with slow, biting emphasis, 'if you break my arm, I shan't stop till I've bloody well killed you.'

That beer had made him reckless, and vaguely, at the bottom of his heart, he knew it and was glad; but he knew, too, that if Steve Quainton broke his arm, he would no longer care what happened to him so long as he glutted his fury; he would be at the disadvantage then, but as haysel had shown, he was not a weakling and he, too, knew a trick or two – the kick in the fork, perhaps? – anyhow, Steve Quainton should pay, even if he himself died for it. All this flashed through his mind with grim clearness in the same second as he flung out his challenge.

For answer, Steve Quainton's lips curled back in a sour grin – there was something cold and fish-like even in his rage – and he bore yet harder on the captive arm, till Everard ground his teeth with the sick pain. The gentle rustling of the willows overhead seemed a veritable roar in his ears; he raised his eyes towards them – and caught sight of a long, smooth red ear. With a sudden desperate, ferocious impulse he lunged his head forward and caught the lobe in his teeth; the flesh was warm and soft and yielding; he bit madly. Steve Quainton, taken off his guard, screamed with the unexpected pain and then he made a fatal mistake. He let go Everard's arm and struck him on the forehead, wrenching his own head back. Everard feebly fended off the blow, but he still held on with his teeth, until all at once he staggered backwards and nearly fell. Something had given; it was Steve Quainton's ear. They both stood facing each other, legs straddled apart, shoulders bent, a small gout of blood on Everard's lips, and a heavy trickle gathering on Steve Quainton's jaw. Everard slowly moved his lips – at the moment the hot acrid tang of the blood did not displease him – and spat out something solid at his opponent's feet. Steve Quainton remained staring stupidly at him a moment longer, then his eyelids fluttered and closed, his cheeks went white, he tottered and fell forward with a thud on his face.

Everard drew himself up to his full height and uttered a hoarse laugh, more of relief than exultation; he was quite sobered, and how soothing the rustling of the willows sounded – now! He walked over to the stream, and having rapidly rinsed his mouth of blood, took back his cupped hands full of water and dashed it in the prostrate man's face. Steve Quainton grunted, his lips twitched and his eyes slowly opened. Everard made a pad of his handkerchief and put it to his ear, which was still bleeding.

'Hold that,' he commanded.

Steve Quainton painfully raised himself to a sitting posture and obeyed, glancing furtively up at Everard and then away again, as if he could not face his eyes, to stare vacuously at the red stains on his own coat-sleeve.

'Now then, Steve Quainton,' said Everard, determined to push his advantage to the utmost, 'we know who's the better man, don't we?'

The other gave one quick, timid glance up and nodded weakly, a wretched spectacle as he sat there, with his face white and drawn, crouched upon himself like a dog after a thrashing.

'Now you see what you'll get,' continued Everard, in a harsh, merciless voice. 'Are we going to have any more trouble from you?'

Steve Quainton shook his head without looking up.

'Swear it,' cried Everard.

'I swear,' he muttered.

'You'd better be off home now,' added Everard, 'and tie up that ear.'

With some difficulty Steve Quainton pulled himself to his feet, and having stood for a moment to make sure that his legs would hold him, stumbled unsteadily away along the path without a look behind him. Everard watched him until he disappeared in the lengthening shadows, and then, picking up his forget-me-nots, set off in the opposite direction. He was trembling all over now, but less from easing of strain than from this new joy that was tingling in his veins. Though he now

311

showed no signs of the battle, he had fought his man for a woman and beaten him, with nothing but a man's weapons; the very earth of his primitive being had been laid bare and it was satisfied. And now he was on the way to his own woman. The rustling of the willows was music to his ears.

Ruthie was sitting huddled in the grass when he parted the sallow branches by the pond.

'Oh Everard,' she said reproachfully, as he dropped down beside her in the mint-scented air, how long you've made me wait!'

'I've done my best, sweetheart,' he consoled. 'We won the match and then they wouldn't let me go.'

'Ah, you've been drinking, I know,' she scolded. 'You'd forgotten all about me, up here alone in the copse.'

'All right,' he said, to tease her, 'I won't kiss you tonight, then, and you won't notice it.'

'No, no, no!' She put her arms round his neck and kissed him again and again on the lips. 'What do I care for that,' she said, 'or how long I wait, so long as you come at last? I can't help loving you, Everard.'

'Look, Ruthie,' he said, 'I've brought you some forget-me-nots.'

She looked down at them a little wistfully and shook her head.

'You'll forget me one day, all the same,' she murmured ruefully. 'I can't go and weed your garden while you're playing quoits. Yes,' she added, with a sidelong, teasing smile, 'I saw her, Everard; I had to go down into the village this evening for a loaf.'

Everard put his arms gently round her, and the living warmth and staunchness of her body against him seemed like a final revealing token of the necessity and meetness of the thing he was going to say; a thrill ran through him.

'Why do you tremble, dear?' said Ruthie, startled out of her own sad forebodings and gazing at him solicitously.

'Ruthie, darling,' said Everard, without answering her question, 'how would you like to go back to a farm to live?'

She thought for a moment before she said doubtfully, 'I really don't know, Everard. Why?'

'Because you once said you ought to have been a farmer's wife – the second time I saw you.'

'Did I?' She looked up and smiled. 'I'm not so sure that I do now.'

'Why?' he persisted gently.

She pouted and looked away. 'I don't know – since I met you – that depend on the farmer, don't you think?'

'But, Ruthie' – Everard's voice shook – 'if the farm were Vale Farm and I were the farmer?'

She stared at him in wonder for a moment; then, as his meaning dawned on her, her lips parted in a tremulous smile and a new light crept into her eyes. She suddenly dropped her head and hid her face in his coat. He could feel her hot breath on his chest; her whole body trembled against him and very quietly she began to sob.

'Ruthie,' he whispered at last, stroking her hair, 'you haven't said yes.'

She raised her head and held him by the shoulders away from her, gazing at him. Her eyes were wet, yet they still glowed with that soft, tender light.

'Oh Everard,' she began – her voice was broken

and husky, but it sounded beautiful to him beyond measure – 'Oh Everard, my precious, my lovely, my own love – yes!'

She drew him to her again and joined her lips to his. She closed her eyes: time seemed to stop.

XXX

EVERARD was looking out of the parlour window at the antics of his kitten which was stalking a cabbage butterfly around the water butt, and so his back was turned when Laura Quainton came quietly in with the breakfast tray. She set it down on the table and tapped impatiently on the floor with her foot.

'You're too proud to speak to me now,' she said, with playful severity, 'aren't you, Mr. Mulliver?'

'Hullo, Laura!' he said, turning round and thinking of several things to be proud of, 'why should I be?'

'Why, after those six ringers—' she began, with a smile.

'Oh, that!' he interrupted.

'Yes, that!' she repeated, with an emphatic nod. 'Everybody in the village is talking about it; so you needn't pretend you know nothing about it.'

'Well, till you spoke of it,' he replied, 'I had forgotten all about it; so you can't accuse me of being puffed up.' Time had moved since then, indeed.

'I'm so glad you won your match,' she said, dropping her railing manner and then promptly resuming it. 'I share the honour, you see. Well, have you looked at the garden?'

'No, I haven't,' said Everard. 'I didn't get home till after dark.'

She shook her finger at him reprovingly.

'Didn't I tell you what it was like after the Nayland

match? Who knows what you were doing?'

'Who indeed?' echoed Everard. 'But what about the garden?'

'Oh, nothing,' she said, with a sniff of affected indifference.

He looked out of the window and saw that all the beds in the parterre were clear of weeds.

'Thank you, Laura,' he said. 'That was nice of you. It must have taken a terrible time.'

'And you came home too late to see it,' she teased. All at once she became serious. 'Do you know, Everard, he came home late too, or at least, I didn't see him, because I'd gone to bed early. But what do you think, when he came downstairs this morning he'd got a big white bandage round his head and a lot of strapping on his ear. I asked him what was the matter, but he wouldn't answer, and he went out soon after without a word. I've never seen him look so down.'

'I don't think he'll trouble you any more,' said Everard significantly.

'What do you mean?' She looked up sharply.

'Well, I'm responsible for his ear,' he answered apologetically.

'What do you mean?' She knitted her brows in an expression of mingled bewilderment and alarm.

'Well, you see,' Everard explained, 'he followed me last night after the match and stopped me along by the gull; he wanted to know why I was meddling with you, as he put it. So we fought it out and – I beat him, I shan't tell you how. But you can be pretty certain he won't bother us any more now. So there's good news for you; couldn't have been better, could it?'

Her mouth and eyes had opened wide in astonishment while he spoke, as if she could scarcely credit what she heard; then her lips wavered into a smile and her eyes lit up.

'Oh, Everard!' she gasped, clutching her hand against her breast. 'Do you mean, do you mean that you let him fight you and you beat him for – for me?'

'Yes, Laura,' said Everard, smiling. 'I did it for you.'

'He's terribly strong,' she murmured.

'He is,' admitted Everard, slowly nodding.

'How brave you are!' she exclaimed, stepping up close to him. Her mouth drooped and quivered and a tear stole out from between her lashes. All at once she seized his hand and pressed it against her cheek.

'Oh, dear Everard,' she whispered brokenly, 'he didn't hurt you then, the brute, he didn't hurt you, thank God.'

She looked up at him and there was in her smile that same tender, caressing light which last night had shone from Ruthie's eyes. Instinctively he saw that it only needed a quiver of his eyelid, the merest propulsion of his finger on her burning cheek, and her arms would be around him. Instead, he glanced uneasily across the room, at the opposite window and she straightway drew back from him.

'Oh goodness gracious!' she exclaimed. 'What would the neighbours think if they saw me? You must forgive me, Everard, but I was so thankful to see you safe and sound, and so proud too.'

Everard smiled, masking the sudden grave disquiet that had sprung up in his heart.

'You can begin to pack your bag now, Laura,' he said.

'How lovely, but' – her answering smile turned to a little pout of concern – 'what will become of the cottage when I'm gone?'

317

'Oh, that'll be all right,' he replied gaily. 'I'm coming to live here for good.'

'But you'll still want a housekeeper,' she laughingly protested.

Everard welcomed the opening; sooner or later she would have to be told; it was better now. 'I shall have one,' he said.

'Who?' she demanded.

Everard hesitated an instant and then plunged. 'I'm thinking of taking a wife,' he said.

She started violently back from him with a look of wonder, half-terrified, yet half-expectant, in her eyes.

'But who?' she gasped, colouring and dropping her eyes to the floor.

Once more Everard hesitated and once more plunged. 'Ruthie Gathercole,' he said.

She staggered and dropped like a dead weight into a chair that was standing beside her, threw back her head and uttered a shrill hysterical laugh. But instantly she clenched her hands and sat up straight, the old habit of control still strong in her.

'Laura, Laura!' cried Everard, who had rushed over to her side and was watching her anxiously.

She looked at him, but her eyes were lifeless and her blanched lips seemed twisted with strange new lines of age.

'Don't worry, Everard,' she said with a horrible forced smile. 'I shall be all right.'

'But listen, Laura,' he said with breathless earnestness. 'Don't be afraid. I shan't leave you in the lurch. I'll see your affair through and you safely settled before we marry.'

'You needn't trouble, Everard,' she said calmly, shaking her head, 'I'm going back to my husband.'

All the strength drained out of him in a stream and he tottered back against the table for support. She watched him almost critically.

'But why?' he gasped at last.

'Because, Everard,' she said slowly and quietly, 'because I love you. Didn't you know?'

He cast down his eyes, almost shamefacedly.

'I knew you were fond of me, Laura,' he said, 'but never like this.'

'Don't be sad, Everard,' she said gently. 'It's my fault, not yours.'

'But why go back to your husband?' he asked.

The mask of restraint fell from her.

'Why!' she cried passionately, 'because I love you and because I've never loved anyone else in my life. Oh, didn't you see, Everard, my darling? Right from the first, it was; not just because you were kind to me, but because you were – you, because I had to love you.' She drew in a deep breath and went on tumultuously, wrenching her clasped fingers. 'But I knew it was hopeless, yet I didn't want to let you go away from me. I know you wondered and wondered why I wouldn't consent about the divorce. Well, now you know. It was because I couldn't bear the thought of leaving you. You were always telling me how young and handsome I was becoming, weren't you? Well, it was you who made me like that; you talked to me and smiled at me and you let me come in and be with you and do things for you; you let me love you and love makes you young and fair, they say. And then at last – silly woman – I began to let myself believe you were beginning to care for me – just ever so little. Those beads you gave me, the things you said about being young and brave, and about my clothes – I bought them all for you – and

319

calling me Laura – how I loved that! – and then you asked me to get the divorce to please you and you were so pleased, I could have cried; and then you said I should still be near you. Of course, you were only being kind to me, but I thought that perhaps one day you really might come to care for me properly; it might be a long time, but it would be worth waiting for. I ought to have known better – I do now.' She shook her head despairingly.

'But, Laura!' Everard burst out, 'that's no reason for going back to him!'

'Ah, you don't think so,' she replied bitterly, 'because you don't know how much I love you. I'd never loved in my life before, I'd always been a slave and it was wonderful to love. Now that's all broken. What should I do if I were free now, what do I care what becomes of me, now I know that you can't love me? What does it matter what happens to me? I shall be dead to it – it's not new. Better be useful to someone, even a brute, while I still have to live, – it won't be long now.'

'But, Laura—' Everard stammered, but could go no further. The whole universe seemed to be crashing in pieces around him; his mouth was dry and foul, his blood ran cold with the vileness and unreason of it all.

'I was doomed to it,' she continued, half-savagely, as if driving herself on to lacerate her own heart. 'I seemed to see this coming, and yet I couldn't stop it. The only time in my life – how beautiful it was, but how much better if I'd never loved you at all! Life's hard.'

'That's no reason for wilfully wrecking it,' cried Everard, finding his voice again, 'with your eyes wide open. Remember you promised me.'

'Ah, things are different now,' she said, shaking her head.

'Then, Laura,' he cried, half-beside himself with anguish, 'I beseech you, I implore you to unsay those words. You said you loved me.'

'But do you love me?' she retorted quickly. 'No, Everard, you once told me to forget the parson's daughter and remember I was a woman. I am a woman; it's only too true; and you think like a man, you don't know what goes on in a woman's heart.'

'But it's all wrong!' he groaned, maddened by her seeming perversity.

'How do you know?' she answered, with a piercing glance.

'Oh, Laura, please, please,' he begged, 'wait a little, till we're both calmer.'

She shook her head again.

'It's no use,' she said. 'It's just my fate, that's all.'

'That abominable word!' he cried in exasperation. 'It's cruel, it's horrible, unholy, it's a sin!'

'I think you might spare me that,' she murmured with a dry, choking sob. 'You, at least, will be happy.'

'How can I be happy, Laura,' he answered gently now, 'while I know that you are not? You don't know what my friendship means.'

He bent over her as if to take her hands, but she pushed him rudely away.

'What is your friendship to me?' She tossed her head and then ran on impetuously in a low, trembling voice. 'Oh, forgive me, Everard darling, I don't know what I'm saying. I'm hurting you and I love you, you've been so good. Yes, you'll be happy if she loves you as I do; but I could have borne it better if it had been a lady in Bury.' She caught her breath. 'To be set aside for a baggage like her!'

Everard bit his lip in a sudden flare of rage at the

taunt; for an instant he almost hated her.

'Don't you dare say a word against Ruthie!' he half-shouted. 'She's as good a woman as you and I love her.'

Laura rose to her feet and her lips flickered into a sardonic smile.

'You ought to be happy with her, then,' she said coldly, and fled through the open door.

Everard, dazed and overwhelmed, sank into a chair and buried his face in his hands.

XXXI

THE church bell ceased its tolling, and at the sudden void of soundlessness that it left behind, Everard wearily raised his head from the green bank where he lay outstretched. The hour of his assignation with Ruthie was approaching, but, for the first time since he had known her, he felt reluctant to keep it, not for any want of loving her – he loved her only too surely now; but on such a day as this even love itself seemed a paltry thing. Thus his mind stirred from the kindly torpor of exhaustion into which at last it had sunk, self-devoured, and began again the giddy round of thought which all day long had tormented him.

He, too, had fled the house that morning, leaving his breakfast untasted, and as if unable to bear the burden of existence alone, had pushed straight out along the valley to the field where Kindred was already staking out a fresh piece of lucerne for the ewes.

'Here, give me that,' he said abruptly, taking the fold-drift out of Kindred's hands and setting to work with it.

'All right,' laughed Kindred, pulling out his pipe. 'I'll set and smoke for a bit while you work; that just suit an owd man like me.'

Everard pecked a hole and began to drive a pole home in it, but with such savage, ill-aimed blows that he split it in two.

'Hey!' cried Kindred, 'you don't want to work at that rate on a hot day like this!'

'I want to keep warm,' replied Everard, with an ironical laugh. He went to work again more carefully, but he did not slacken his pace.

'I hear you did wonders last night at the quoit match,' said Kindred, settling down against a hurdle and puffing amicably. 'Six ringers! that's wholly fine. I reckon them chaps'll be as glad as me and Emma when you come to live here for good.'

'I'm going back to my husband, I'm going back to my husband!' Laura's voice smote like a hammer in Everard's brain; he must drown it. He worked harder than ever.

'Go on talking, Bob!' he shouted. 'I'm listening.'

'Did you tell Mrs. Quainton that about Steve?' hazarded Kindred, watching him curiously.

Everard was about to knock in another pole, but at Kindred's question his hand slipped and the fold-drift came down with a crash on the hurdle he had just set up, shivering the top bar to splinters.

'What is the matter with you this morning, Everard?' cried Kindred, walking over to his side. 'I don't want all our hurdles smashed.'

'Sorry, Bob,' said Everard, pausing for a moment to breathe. 'My hand's not very steady today.'

'Well, give that to me,' said Kindred, stretching out his hands for the fold-drift.

Everard pushed him away. 'No, leave me alone,' he said. 'I want to do it. I'll be careful now.' That voice must be silenced somehow. 'Go on talking, Bob.'

'He fare real crazed,' muttered Kindred to himself, and began to chatter about the coming harvest and what they would do with the farm next autumn when it was their own. Everard worked on frantically, returning now and then an absent answer to Kindred's remarks, though he took no account of what they said; how he wished the man would stop talking, but he could not bear him to be quiet.

'Well, I reckon you've put that up in record time,' said Kindred with a laugh, as Everard drove in the last hurdle.

'You said there was a gatepost wanted sinking over there,' said Everard, throwing the fold-drift down, 'didn't you, Bob?'

'Yes, but we ain't a-going to do that this morning,' protested Kindred. 'That's Sunday. Do you set down and have a smoke.'

'No, I want to do it,' replied Everard, staring wildly at the broken gatepost in the hedge that was to be replaced. 'I must do something. I did no work yesterday, you see.'

'But we ain't got no spade,' said Kindred. 'Do you keep quiet for a bit. I shall think you're wholly crazed.'

'I'm all right, Bob,' said Everard, laughing. 'I'll go and get one. You stay here and smoke and poke the ewes' ribs.'

It was no use trying to stop him. He hurried off to the farmyard, and twenty minutes later he was back again with a spade and began hacking furiously round the butt of the broken gatepost. Kindred, his protests unavailing, resigned himself to watch and for a while continued to talk, but eventually, as Everard no longer uttered a word, he, too, was silent. The sun mounted higher and higher, but Everard still dug on, his face streaming with sweat, never pausing to rest. He had silenced the voice, but he could not still the tumult of incoherent, racing thought that had taken its place. At last Kindred took him firmly by the shoulders and stopped him by main force.

'Don't you be such a bloody fool, Everard,' he said. 'You've made yourself wholly pale and you've got great rings round your eyes – on a hot day like this too! Besides, that's now dinner-time and you know you're a–coming to dinner along of us.'

Everard smiled and gave in; he was thankful not to be having dinner in his own house; he could not have faced Laura then.

Mrs. Kindred was in high spirits; she babbled away about the lawyer business in Sudbury and last night's quoit match, while her husband chaffed Everard about the morning's labours.

'Couldn't stop him,' he chuckled. 'Fare to me he had a drop too much last night after the match.'

Everard answered mechanically, scarcely hearing them; the food made him sick; his head ached and he inadvertently passed his hand across his forehead.

Kindred glanced significantly at his wife.

'What's the matter, Everard?' she said.

'Oh, nothing much,' he replied casually. 'I got a touch of the sun yesterday, I expect, weeding the garden – or p'r'aps this morning.'

'Ah, very like you hev,' said Mrs. Kindred severely. 'I'm a–going to make you lie down on that there sofa directly arter dinner. That's rest you want. Why ever did you let him sweat himself to pieces like that this morning, Robert?'

'He would do it,' said her husband, shaking his head despairingly.

'No, thanks, Mrs. Kindred,' said Everard, getting up from his chair. 'I shall be better at home. I'll go now.'

'You're a real naughty boy, Everard,' she scolded, 'real pernickety, you are. But if you will go home, mind you do lie down at once and stay there all the arternoon.'

'All right, Mrs. Kindred,' said Everard, forcing a smile as he pushed his chair beneath the table, 'I'll be good.'

He opened the door and went out, but as soon as he was out of sight of the farmhouse, he strayed off up the hillside and threw himself down in the grass at the edge of one of the cornfields.

How his head ached! It seemed as if there were a hard, jagged crystal boring into his brain and around it his thoughts lapped like waves around a rock, striving vainly to dissolve it. If only he could go to Laura and say, 'Come, Laura, I love you!' but he knew that that was a mockery. Friendship, affection, devotion even, he could offer her; she merited them. But love, that was for Ruthie, for Ruthie's hair and eyes and throat and bosom, for all her lush youth – he shuddered at the cruel clearness of the truth, but it was true. Yet what, after all, had happened? – he strove to be frank with himself – why should he torture himself for a woman he did not love, when there was so much else that claimed him? He had done his best for her, he had laboured to spare her pain, to make it all easy for her, had failed her in nothing; and now she had requited him by – falling in love with him. And because he did not love her in return, she was going back to her husband. But why? Why was that the only alternative, why must she have all or nothing? Was it to revenge herself on him or to find some ghastly, perverted satisfaction in desperate self-immolation? Or was it just the ungrateful, unreasoning cowardice of – a silly woman? Surely she was not worth so much concern; he could well forget her.

He sat up, clasping his knees, and shook his head. It was beyond his power to forget her; for rage as he would against it, he perceived that behind all her madness lay a thread of subtle, diabolical logic. The poor, thwarted life had built itself up anew around the wraith of his imagined love, like a tender climbing plant that clings to a stronger stem for support; but the support had failed, she had been hurled to the ground and all her strength scattered – in truth, it had been his and not hers – she was a woman. Yet – and this it was that heightened the tragedy, making it impossible of acceptance, endurance – there was a flaw in the logic. Broken and weak she was, but only in so far as she believed she was. There was no obstacle in her path now, human or material; her husband was crushed, there was evidence for her divorce, the means of livelihood awaited her; she had only to will herself to a new and – if not that to which she had vainly aspired – a better life. But for him to perceive the flaw was not enough; it was she who must see it, and how make her turn an impartial gaze upon the depths of her own heart? It lay outside his reach and he writhed at his impotence. If she perished, then something in him perished too, that she had made her own; the forces of unreason and evil would triumph, the whole world was wrong and all his own joys were built upon the sand.

His head throbbed sickly, but he strove again with his thought. What grains of hope were there? She could not be so weak and witless, the Laura he had so admired for her quiet sense and courage; at least, she could not act at once; it was unthinkable. That wild passion of grief must cool and surely she would open her mind to his coaxing; if of herself she would not repent, yet to please him, she might realize the ugliness and horror of the course she planned – she loved him. He, too, would be calmer; then quietly, with sweet earnestness, they would reason it out together and she must see the truth. It must be soon, however – tonight, tomorrow, perhaps – if only she would listen to him; or would she talk of fate? The tide of despair washed over him again and he cast himself back upon the grass, straining his heart against the earth, as if seeking answer or comfort from it. But he received neither. The ripening wheat-ears swayed, the scarlet poppies bloomed among them, the yellowhammer called; but all such human woe lay beyond the heartbeat of earth.

Tea-time came and he walked back to the village, sometimes almost breaking into a trot in his feverish anxiety to reach her and throw himself at her feet in passionate entreaty, and again at times hanging back in cowardly, shamefaced, almost guilty terror; yet he could conceive of nothing that he was guilty of – except of being himself, of trying to befriend another, of unwittingly inspiring love. He turned the handle of the kitchen door with trembling fingers. The kettle was simmering gently on the oil-stove, his tea was ready-laid in the parlour, everything was in order, elaborately so; but she was not there, she was avoiding him; and the sneaking relief that for a moment he had experienced at not finding her was overwhelmed in a new rush of despair. Mechanically he made himself tea and nibbled at a little food without appetite.

There was the chair where she had collapsed this morning and uttered that horrible shrill laugh and those horrible ironical words; she hated him now. Or was she perhaps, even at this moment, mustering her courage to return and let him plead with her again? – the table would have to be cleared – he must not fail her for want of a little patience. He conquered a desperate impulse to flee the house again and set himself to wait for her, restlessly pacing the room or lying back in an armchair, uneasily watching the windows and starting at every footfall or creaking hinge in the street. An hour passed, and then to distract himself he cleared the table and piled the things on a tray in the kitchen; thus, when she did come, there would be no barrier of irrelevant action between them. Another hour passed, but she did not come and he could bear the house no longer. Once more he strayed out into the valley, hardly heeding where his feet took him, until he fetched up against that grassy bank on the copse-edge, twice dear to him; but now it was only another spot on which to fling himself and string and unstring the worn chain of hectic thoughts which never yielded a new hope; till at last his tired brain would revolve no more and he fell into a troubled doze. The church bell, ceasing, wakened him. Love had all today to answer for; it seemed a paltry thing. Yet he must go to Ruthie and pretend to share her joy – he loved her but still he wavered.

At length he plunged into the copse and brushed hastily through to the pond; he was already nearly half an hour late. But Ruthie did not reproach him when he parted the sallows and dropped down at her side. How beautiful she looked, sitting there against the willow trunk! Her cheeks seemed more lustrous and her eyes more liquid even than yesterday; she thrived on love and what could he do but love her?

'Aren't you going to kiss me, Everard?' she said, after he had gazed at her, silent, for a space, her brow clouding a little.

'Of course, Ruthie dear,' he said, with a tremor of compunction in his voice; he had quite forgotten.

He hastened to make up for his omission, but her lips

seemed an alien thing, immeasurably distant from him, as if his own lips were not meant for kissing and had never kissed before. She, too, was conscious of a strangeness in him.

'Why, Everard dear,' she said, 'whatever is the matter? Your face is so pale and your eyes all hollow.'

'I'm tired, dear, that's all,' said Everard, trying hard to mimic his natural self; Ruthie must not know the truth. 'The quoit match, perhaps. Don't worry.'

'I don't like to see you like that,' she replied anxiously, with a dissatisfied pout. 'You know, I've got to look after you now. I'm the farmer's wife.'

She smiled and stroked his cheek and with an effort he smiled back at her; but he wished she would not remind him of these things now.

'Tell me, Everard,' she went on gaily, 'can I tell mother now about you and me? She will be so glad to hear.'

'No, no, not yet,' he replied sharply, but softening immediately. 'I mean, let's wait a little first.' It would be terrible to have all the village dinning the news into his ears and Laura's.

'Yes, but you know,' she demurred, 'mother's always asking me now where I'm going o' nights and I can't always make excuses.'

'But, Ruthie,' he pleaded, 'can't you wait just a little while — until it's all arranged about the farm and we're ready to settle down? Then we can get married at once and people won't have such a chance to gossip about us. It won't be long, darling.' He must gain some respite at all costs.

'Oh well, all right,' she consented, with rather a bad grace. 'Only I do so want to tell mother; I've deceived her for so long.' She cast a quick suspicious glance at

331

him. 'You're not sorry for what you said last night, are you, Everard? There's not somebody somewhere else you like better – in Lindmer?'

'No, no, Ruthie,' he cried in alarm, warming to her suddenly and holding her close, 'don't doubt me. Of course I'm not sorry; I love you, sweetheart. I'm only tired and not well; don't take any notice of that. You trust me, don't you?'

She heaved a sigh of relief. 'Of course, I trust you, my poor boy. It's naughty of me to talk like that when you're so tired. You must let me take care of you, my precious.' She drew his head down upon her breast and stroked his cheek again. 'There, there,' she soothed, 'go you to sleep, my dear one.'

The warmth of her bosom enwrapped him, radiating infinite peace and strength, which passed into him and melted the cruel, hard crystal in his brain; the tenseness eased and lifted from him. Like a tired child to its mother, he nestled closer until his head sank down upon her lap, safe from the world, content with love. He almost slept.

A long time he lay thus while she caressed him tenderly, maternally, and the dusk was gathering when he opened his eyes again and smiled up at her. She bent down and kissed his forehead.

'Better, darling?' she whispered.

'Ever so much,' he answered cheerfully.

'Such a lot of things I want to ask you,' she said.

'Ask away, sweetheart.'

'Shall we go and live with the Kindreds,' she said, 'when you've bought Vale Farm and we're married? Or will they go and live somewhere else?'

'No, I couldn't ask them to leave,' he replied, looking pensively up at her soft round chin. 'I'm buying the farm so that they can stay on, you see. They may ask us to go and live there with them when they know. But I think we should be best alone together for a little while, don't you?'

She nodded. 'All to ourselves.'

'And you see,' he went on, 'I've got the cottage all ready to go into. Will it be big enough for you, Ruthie?'

'Of course it will, dear,' she replied. 'We don't want much, do we, just two of us? That look ever so nice since you've had it. I should love to know what it's like inside; I've got to keep it in order some day. Isn't it funny, Everard, how well I know you and yet I've never been inside your house, nor you in mine?'

'No, that's true,' he confessed. 'You don't know how I live, do you?'

'Yes, a man all alone,' she laughed, 'I wonder how he do live. I should like to see your house, Everard dear. Couldn't you take me to see it?'

'Yes, I will, Ruthie,' he said – 'when your mother knows.'

'Ah, but when will that be?' she exclaimed, a little petulantly. 'To think that Mrs. Quainton know it all from top to bottom and I've never been there. I believe you're afraid to let her see me.' She gazed down at him, half-critical, half-cajoling, aimlessly toying with a lock of his hair.

'All right, I know what I'll do,' he said, raising his head from her lap. If only she would keep from harping on Laura! He was anxious to please her too – she had done so much for him this evening. 'You shall see it tonight.'

'But how?' she faltered, somewhat reluctant, now it came to the point.

'Like this,' he said. 'It's getting dark now; we can go along the gull and then strike off up to the back of my orchard – there's a gap in the hedge. Then we'll go in by the back door and nobody'll see us.'

'Oh, how lovely!' she cried. 'Now I shall see where we're going to sit and eat and sleep and where I shall hang my clothes. You are clever, Everard.' She took his cheeks in her two hands and kissed him.

With his arm around her shoulders and hers around his waist, he led her through the dim hazel thickets, down past the still, pale lakes of full-eared corn to the valley bottom. Everything was dark and peaceful and he felt he could wander on forever thus beneath the tired hiss of the flickering willows, buoyed up by her gracious presence, forgetting the world – and Laura. Their path ended and they crept through the gap in Everard's hedge.

'How sweet your garden do smell!' she whispered, pausing on the brink of the orchard to sniff the air.

'Yes, that's the night-scented stock,' he whispered back, and felt a warm flush of pleasure mount in his cheek; to what good purpose he had planted that – to welcome her!

'How early the Quaintons go to bed!' she exclaimed, pointing up at a lighted window in the house next door.

Everard's eyes followed her finger. The blind was not yet lowered and almost the whole room was visible. Laura entered the room – he could not take his eyes away – she did not close the door. A man followed with a great white bandage round his head; he came up behind her and put his arm round her neck. Everard clutched Ruthie's fingers convulsively and staggered back against an apple tree.

'Oh God!' he gasped. 'Look at that!'

The blind descended with a screech and Everard closed his eyes. Ruthie stood back and glared at him with parted lips.

'Ah!' she drew a long, trembling breath, 'I thought as much. It's her you love.' She drew another breath. 'That's why you didn't kiss me, that's why you didn't want mother to know, nor me to come and see your house. I hate you! I'll never speak to you again!'

Everard opened his eyes; his last defences were stripped; her love was jealousy.

'For God's sake go!' he muttered weakly.

With one vengeful look she ran from him. Everard put his arm round the apple tree and vomited.

XXXII

EVERARD sat among the lavender in the sunken arbour of his garden at Bury with his Cowper lying open upon his knee. It was more than a fortnight now since that last terrible Sunday at Lindmer, but still the vision of a white face and an encircling arm rose up continually before his mind to sicken him. All the tan had gone out of his cheeks, he looked weak and ill. Glancing idly down at the book, his eye fell upon a familiar title – 'The Pleasures of Retirement', and with an exclamation of disgust he tossed the book into a flower-bed, where it fell with a thud. In a week's time he would be abroad, he was not quite sure where; he had never – the War excepted – been abroad before.

A maid with rustling black skirts minced across the grass on high heels.

'A gentleman to see you, sir.'

Everard rose from his chair. It was Bob Kindred, attired in his dark-grey Sunday suit and best brown buskins. His manner was downcast and subdued.

'I've took the liberty of coming to see you, Everard,' he said, self-consciously fumbling his hat and stick, 'without an invitation.'

'Come and sit down, Bob,' said Everard, gently pushing him into his own wicker chair and squatting down on the grass in front of him. 'I can't tell you how glad I am to see you.'

He was truly glad, being tired of himself and his own

336

thoughts, but nevertheless, his heart sank; he had been dreading such a visit.

'This is a wholly fine garden you've got,' said Kindred politely, waving his arm at the lavender clumps, 'and a real grand house.'

'Yes,' replied Everard bitterly, 'but it's not like Lindmer.'

'No,' admitted Kindred, 'that ain't.'

They both averted their eyes and stared at the turf; there was an awkward silence. Everard well knew that Kindred had not come to discuss his garden. At length, however, the old man braced himself for the real business of his visit.

'We got your letters, Everard,' he said, looking up, 'and becourse, we don't want to go interfering with your affairs; them are things we don't understand. We're wholly glad to stay your tenants, and we can think ourselves lucky. But there was just one thing I wanted to tell you.' He hesitated.

'Go on, Bob,' said Everard, admiring the old man's tactfulness.

'Well,' continued Kindred, nervously stroking his beard, 'I don't know the reason of your leaving us, becourse, nor I don't want to know neither, but I sorterly wondered if that had anything to do with Mrs. Quainton, seeing as the cotterage was all shet up and a To Let notice in the window all of a sudden like. 'Haps, I say to myself, he've told her about what we seed at Sudbury the other day, and she've took it nasty like, so's he don't like to stop there no longer.'

Everard was about to interpose, but the old man silenced him with a finger.

'So I say to Emma yesterday night, "I'll go tomorrow morning, I will, and tell him if he like to come to ours and live along of us at Vale Farm, he'll be wholly welcome." And, as Emma say, you can have just as much of the house to yourself as you like; we 'on't trouble you. Becourse, I reckon you allus knowed you could,' he added despondently, as if confessing to the flimsiness of this excuse for his visit; he had really come to plead. 'But we wholly can't bear the thought of your going away from us and that's the truth.'

Everard shook his head. What would Vale Farm be with Ruthie over the way and yet without her? and was there any spot in the whole of Lindmer where the continuing wretchedness of Laura would not destroy his peace of mind? The pattern of life down there in the valley was irrevocably broken, because she had formed part of it; he could never be her neighbour again.

'I'm sorry, Bob,' he said slowly. 'You're more than kind. But I'm going abroad in a week's time.'

'Oh Everard, must you?' the old man mumbled. 'We wholly counted on having you with us for good, and all the village is that cut up, you don't know. Why, pore owd Henry Runacres—'

'It's impossible, Bob.' Everard cut him short with an effort; the words seemed so bald and heartless. He sighed; life would be lonely in a foreign country. Kindred sighed too; then, after a pause, he played his last and most important card.

'Why, only yesterday,' he said deliberately, 'I met Ruthie Gathercole up by the copse.'

'Ruthie?' Everard looked up with a start; then, covering himself with a forced air of unconcern, 'What about her?' he said.

'Well,' Kindred went on, watching Everard closely, 'she had such a long face as you'd never believe; and she say to me, "Where have Everard gone?" And I told her

I didn't know, but you weren't a-coming back. "How I'd like to see him again!" she say – just that and no more – and she turn away, looking sadder'n any gal I ever seed.'

Everard stared hard at the lavender clumps. So she had forgiven him, her jealousy had passed; how white her throat was – all his veins were a-tingle and his head went dizzily round, he could not stop it.

'If I was you,' said Kindred, still steadily watching him, 'I should make that up.'

Everard blinked dazedly at him; his grief for Laura seemed strangely shrunk, he had done his best for her, after all; there were still other things in Lindmer.

'Ruthie's a wholly nice gal,' Kindred went on perseveringly, 'and all that lovely hair too.'

'Yes, she is,' Everard faltered, and involuntarily he looked at Kindred and smiled.

'Well now, boy,' said the old man, and there was a faint note of command in his voice, 'if you like, I'll now go along home and tell her you're a-coming down tomorrow to see her. I should if I was you.'

Everard nervously brushed his cheek with quivering fingers and looked from side to side of him with lowered eyes, like an over-shy boy; somehow he could not bring himself to face the old man's keen, expectant gaze. At last, however, he timidly raised his eyes for a moment and, blushing furiously, nodded. Kindred leaped to his feet and put on his hat.

'Where are you off to?' exclaimed Everard suddenly, throwing his embarrassment aside.

'I'm now running off to find her,' replied Kindred jauntily, 'afore you change your mind.'

Everard rose and took his arm.

'I'll go with you,' he said.

339

THE END

Other Titles from Old Pond Publishing

Chaffinch's H W FREEMAN
H W Freeman's moving novel depicts the life of farm worker Joss Elvin and his struggle to raise a family on 19 acres of Suffolk farmland. Paperback.

Joseph and His Brethren H W FREEMAN
The saga of Benjamin Geaiter and his sons fighting to keep possession of their farm through misfortunes in late 19th century Suffolk. Paperback.

Farmer's Boy MICHAEL HAWKER
A detailed and truthful account of farm work in N. Devon in the 1940s and 1950s. Paperback.

Early to Rise HUGH BARRETT
A classic of rural literature, this is a truthful account of a young man working as a farm pupil in Suffolk in the 1930s. Paperback.

A Good Living HUGH BARRETT
Following on from *Early to Rise*, Hugh takes us back to the assortment of farms with which he was involved from 1937 to 1949. Paperback.

In a Long Day DAVID KINDRED AND ROGER SMITH
Two hundred captioned photographs of farm work and village life in Suffolk 1925–33. Paperback.

A Land Girl's War JOAN SNELLING
Work as a tractor driver on a Norfolk fruit farm and wartime romance vividly recalled. Paperback.

Land Girls at the Old Rectory IRENE GRIMWOOD
Light-hearted, boisterous memories of land girls in Suffolk 1942–46. Paperback.

Thatcher's Harvest R & J FOSTER & PAUL CONGDON
A delightful contemporary record of growing, bindering and threshing long-stemmed wheat and thatching a Suffolk cottage. Video.

Free complete catalogue:

Old Pond Publishing
Dencora Business Centre, 36 White House Road, Ipswich IP1 5LT, United Kingdom
Phone: 01473 238200   Fax: 01473 238201
Website: www.oldpond.com
Email: enquiries@oldpond.com

H. W. Freeman

The son of a schoolmaster, Harold Webber 'Jack' Freeman was born in Ilford, Essex in 1899. He won a scholarship from the City of London school to Christ Church college, Oxford where he read classics, narrowly missing a double first class degree. His studies were interrupted by service with the Somerset Light Infantry in France at the close of the First World War.

Following Oxford and a period of teaching, Freeman settled into a life of European travel and writing. In 1928 Chatto & Windus published *Joseph and his Brethren*, the third novel that Freeman wrote, but the first to be published. His next novel was *Down in the Valley*.

Freeman had four more novels published during the 1930s, followed by *Chaffinch's* in 1941. This was just after he was married to Elisabeth 'Betty' Bödecker, a German costume designer for the theatre who had worked in Berlin, Paris and London. They settled at the village of Offton, seven miles west of Ipswich in Suffolk where Freeman's parents had bought a sixteenth-century house and a couple of acres of ground.

After the war, Freeman had two novels and a travel book published. He and Betty remained at Offton, enthusiastically growing vegetables and fruit and continuing their annual travels in Europe. They died within three months of each other in 1994.

Acknowledgements

Down in the Valley was first published in 1930 by Chatto & Windus in the United Kingdom and by Holt in the United States. This is the first paperback reprint. The publishers are grateful to Astrid Massey and Harry Massey and their fellow beneficiaries of the Freeman estate for permission to publish this edition.

Printed in Great Britain
by Amazon

66853644R00161